19
PURCHASE
STREET

ALSO BY GERALD A. BROWNE

GREEN ICE
SLIDE
HAZARD
11 HARROWHOUSE
IT'S ALL ZOO

19 PURCHASE STREET

A NOVEL BY

Gerald A. Browne

ARBOR HOUSE
New York

Library of Congress Catalogue Card Number: 82–72051

ISBN: 0–87795–413–5

Manufactured in the United States of America by The Haddon Craftsmen

10 9 8 7 6 5 4 3 2 1

For my spirit guide, Merle Lynn

With personal gratitude to Zelda Manacher, Mary Merritt, Norman Weisberg, Tony Leeds, Jimmy P., Linda Burnham and Eugene and Eva Graf

CHAPTER
ONE

THIS delivery.

He had made it twice every week since the weather had allowed. Thirty-two times counting this time, so, by now, at practically any point along the way he knew how much farther he had to go.

A hand-painted municipal sign hung over the edge of the road said *Town of Harrison 1696* in Colonial-style lettering, and up ahead coming into sight was the final intersection where Anderson Hill crossed Purchase Street. In his mind that marked three-quarters of a mile exactly to Number 19.

He was tempted to pedal faster, to get there and have it done with again. But hurry would be out of character, he knew. Better that he keep on at the typical indolent pace.

If needed, he had proof for the name Tyrone Wilson and could give a White Plains address.

Grocery deliverer. Nothing more than that from the looks of him. He wore a gray work-out jersey with its sleeves ripped off at the armhole seams. A white handkerchief tied for a sweatband around his head. High-top sneakers with most of their canvas sections cut out, exposing his bare feet. Trousers bound by twine in place of bicycle clips.

Also, in keeping, a two hundred dollar portable cassette player was up on his left shoulder. Matte black, serious-looking stereo with numerous indicators and switches. The volume of it was turned all the way up so he couldn't hear anything but Donna Summer. His left hand kept

7

her balanced close to his ear while his other hand steered.

It wasn't truly a bicycle he was riding. It had three wheels, two in front. A shop at Yonkers made and serviced delivery bikes of this sort for Gristede's, Grand Union and other grocery markets. Between its two front wheels a specially constructed frame provided support for a welded metal compartment about two feet by three feet and thirty inches deep. To contain the groceries. It had a hinged lid held closed by a hasp and a padlock. Ordinarily, for such a purpose an inexpensive lightweight padlock would have been sufficient, just enough to keep anyone from getting easily into it whenever the bike was left unattended. However, the compartment on this bike of Tyrone Wilson's was protected by an unpickable American HT-15 padlock with case-hardened shackle and body.

By now he had reached the intersection, was stopped alone there with second thoughts about having obeyed the traffic light. A minor thing, but it would have been more natural if he'd gone on through the red. To cover himself he placed his feet up on the handlebars and brought the cassette player down to rest on his thighs. He popped Donna Summer out and was turning her over when a car pulled up close beside him. Too close considering the width of the road there.

Wilson pretended not to notice.

The car's window lowered.

Wilson's hand went up in under his jersey, ostensibly to scratch his chest. At the same time he glanced at the car, took it all in. Brown Buick. One person. Man in a gray suit. Thin-haired man wearing rimless eyeglasses. Average looking, as, of course, he would be.

Wilson slowly rolled his head back, looked up at the traffic light. Long goddamn light.

"How do I get to Old Lake Street?" the man asked.

Wilson's immediate thought was to not answer, act as though he hadn't heard, turn up Donna Summer. He didn't know any Old Lake Street, although as a delivery boy he should. He relaxed his eyelids, took all the quickness from his eyes before turning his head to the man, right at him. He hardly moved his tongue or lips so as to have his words come out appropriately sluggish. Said Old Lake was two lights down that way and three blocks over, and the man believed him.

The light had already changed.

The Buick pulled away.

Wilson brought his hand out from beneath his jersey, put Donna Summer back upon his shoulder and began pedaling again, going north on Purchase Street, bound for Number 19.

8

It was the last of July, and so hot the asphalt had gone gummy. Even along those stretches where the branches of maples vaulted and shaded the way. The houses, especially those set back from the street, seemed to be cowering. Insects were moved to transmit what sounded like a sizzle, as though underscoring the temperature.

A similar sibilance was in Mary Beth Pullman's ears, even though she was entirely enclosed in her Chrysler sedan. Headed down the drive of Old Oaks Country Club.

For some reason the steering wheel felt thick in her hands and the windshield glass appeared somewhat fogged. Mary Beth gave the blame to the two gin and tonics she'd had on top of lunch. She wouldn't have indulged if Alice Woodson's husband hadn't sat and talked. Nor would she have eaten such a heavy meal, chicken a la king in a pastry shell and all that, if she hadn't worked up to it—played twenty-seven holes, taking advantage of there being practically no one on the course because of the heat.

Mary Beth often played in the cold or the rain for that same reason: not to have anyone snickering at the way her swing was more of a chop at the ball because her shoulders and upper arms were so fat. She weighed at least sixty over. If she lost forty she'd be just average heavy and, then, if she were four inches taller and larger boned she'd be able to carry it off. But as she was . . . No matter, she believed she enjoyed golf, would not give it up as long as she was able to tee up a ball. Several times she had sunk incredible putts.

She power-steered the Chrysler down the easy grade and around the turn that ran between the permanent caddies' living quarters and the sixteenth fairway. Normally, there were two or three off-duty caddies relaxing on the steps but evidently today was too hot for them. Also, Mary Beth noticed, the sixteenth was deserted. That made her feel superior. She'd played the long uphill sixteenth twice that day and had broken ladies' par both times. Her only regret was she'd worn a skirt instead of culottes, had thought a skirt would be cooler. All that walking and perspiring. The insides of her thighs were chafed raw from rubbing together.

The country club drive became a straightaway that ran between two dozen high-trunked trees, spaced evenly apart like an honor guard, leading to a pair of identical imposing gatehouses. Beyond lay Purchase Street.

At that moment it occurred to Mary Beth that something was wrong. With her. Then she realized what it was.

She had no special knowledge of anatomy, knew practically nothing

9

about the intricacies of her physical system. Yet, in that fraction of time, either in complaint or warning or explanation, her brain transmitted what was happening to it.

What was happening was that the occipital artery had dialated. Two centimeters above where it passed across the internal carotid artery. When Mary Beth was finishing her second after-lunch gin and tonic, holding an ice cube in her mouth and ejecting it back into the empty glass, a tiny bubble had formed on the arterial wall. The layer of muscle tissue there was less than half normal thickness in the first place, and the heat of the day, the twenty-seven holes and the food and alcohol had caused her bloodstream to put a strain on that weak spot.

The linings of the artery were not intended to take such pressure. Nor could it be expected that the outer connective tissue would withstand it, although those muscle fibers did try to hold, bulged until they were nearly unmeasurably thin.

Now, they ruptured.

Blood escaped from its course.

The hemorrhage was massive. At once it invaded the surrounding areas, congested the cerebellum, crammed the tenth cranial nerve.

Mary Beth's head snapped back as though she'd been uppercutted. Her cheeks puffed and her face became intense red, going to purple. Breaths like short snores came from her. Her eyes went wide, the black pupils dilated to the circumference of the irises.

Her legs stiffened, locked at the knees. Her right food jammed down the accelerator pedal.

TYRONE Wilson on the grocery delivery bike had no chance. No time to get out of the way even if he'd seen it coming. The Chrysler was like a three thousand pound metal bull charging at seventy-some miles an hour out of the gateway of Old Oaks. Caught Wilson and the bike flush, smashed against Wilson's left side. Tore all the left leg from him and heaved the rest of him up and thirty feet off to one side of Purchase Street. He landed on the back of his neck. Had it been the only sound at that moment, the fracture would have been clearly heard.

The Chrysler continued across Purchase at full speed, shot off the shoulder and over the ditch and slammed into the embankment. Front end up, rear wheels spinning, it bucked and tried to climb the slope. Its tires ate at the grass and topsoil, dug until its underparts were jammed in.

The first officials to arrive at the scene were two state troopers. They saw immediately that Wilson was dead, searched him for identification, found it in his damp worn wallet. Also beneath his gray jersey they found a .32 caliber revolver in a shoulder holster harnessed next to his bare skin. It didn't surprise them. Wilson was a black.

One of the troopers hurried to the Chrysler and found no life in Mary Beth. With the car nosed up so steeply she was practically horizontal, her pelvis pressed up hard against the steering wheel. The car's engine was still racing. The trooper turned it off.

By the time the Harrison town police arrived the troopers had the collision accurately interpreted. No tire marks. The mangled delivery bike. The final position of the Chrysler. An accidental death caused by a natural death was the conclusion.

It didn't cause much of a traffic tie-up, and surely there would have been more spectators if it hadn't been for the heat. Among the few who hung around were three boys of ten. They stood off to the side near as anyone to Wilson's contorted one-legged corpse. They didn't try to conceal their fascination. It was their first exposure to genuine death. Blood looked different, they thought, more oily, on black skin. Each of the boys privately expected to see a wispy, transparent likeness rise from Wilson and probably float straight up. They remained silent until a trooper covered the body.

Another siren.

An ambulance. On its way at unavailing high speed, taking futile chances. When it arrived Mary Beth was removed. It wasn't a matter of just opening the car door and lifting her out. The deadweight bulk of her was rigidly wedged against the steering wheel. The steering wheel had to be cut away, her grip pried from it before she could be transferred onto a stretcher. She was strapped on and covered entirely with a fresh sheet.

Yellow chalk was used to outline the position of Wilson, his severed leg and the delivery bike. Then Wilson and the leg were put into a bloodproof body bag and the bike was moved to the side of the road.

When the ambulance went off with the dead, nothing that remained was interesting enough to hold the spectators. Traffic began to pass at nearly normal speed. The state troopers left, and so did all but two of the local police.

Officers Lyle and McCatty.

They were to wait for the wrecker. They were also to make up the report.

McCatty, who was in his forties, had a stripe. He'd been on the Harrison force for five years, which was not enough seniority to take him out of range of any deep cutback. Lyle was new and much younger, had in less than a year's duty and, if all went as he hoped, no more than a year to go. He never let anyone, not even McCatty, know what he really wanted and had been saving for was a ski and tennis equipment shop.

Lyle took measurements and diagrammed the accident in the proper space on a report sheet. McCatty, meanwhile, nosed around the Chrysler. He knew they had taken Mary Beth's purse along with her. As though she'd need it. He tried the glove compartment, removed the key from the ignition to get into it. There was nothing in there worth having, and the only thing in the trunk was a wool blanket that appeared good but when McCatty held it up, he saw it had several moth holes. He tossed it back in and shut the trunk lid hard. Seemed there'd be no dividends this time.

The delivery bike.

It was so badly smashed it looked like a John Chamberlain sculpting at the Whitney. That would have been his wife's thought, not his. The frame of it was split, nearly folded in two, and all three of its wheels were bent lopsided oval. However, its metal compartment was intact. That thirty-inch-deep carrying box was dented and more scarred than before but its seams had held.

McCatty examined the compartment and its formidable padlock. He got a steel T-bar from the patrol car.

He worked on the hasp, jammed the T-bar in along the edge where the hasp was attached and got under enough to pry. He applied steady pressure with all his might. Finally the hasp snapped away.

McCatty opened the lid and saw the compartment contained two cardboard cartons of groceries. There wasn't a customer's name or an address on them. The cartons were so well packed only a few of the items on the very top had been knocked about by the collision. McCatty noticed the stamped price sticker on a small package of wild rice that said $4.95 and a jar of Tiptree peach preserves imported from England for $3.80. Anyway, not just Wonder bread and Ivory Snow. He transferred the cartons to the back seat of the patrol car. No one would ever know or ask. Besides, the bike could just as well have been returning from a delivery rather than making one.

The wrecker arrived.

The Chrysler was pulled to the road and hoisted into position. The delivery bike was thrown like a piece of junk onto the bed of the truck where it was secured to the hoist.

That part of it done, McCatty and Lyle drove off in the patrol car. It wasn't much out of their way to stop and leave one carton of groceries at McCatty's, the other at Lyle's. When they got to headquarters they went right to work on the official paperwork. McCatty disliked typing and Lyle wasn't good at it, an unsure, pecking typist who misspelled, X'd out too much and often omitted details important enough to get hell for later. With Lyle at the keys the report would take at least an hour.

They were ten minutes into it when McCatty's wife Connie called. She'd just gotten home. McCatty told her he was off duty but had the report to do. She wanted him home now, insisted. That wasn't like her, McCatty thought. Ordinarily she just lived with his hours. Also, there seemed to be something else to her tone, as though just below her words was something exciting that she couldn't come straight out with. It occurred to McCatty that it might be some sexual thing, a little specialty she'd decided to open up to and was impatient about. They'd enjoyed some of that not too long ago, and, he thought, this had the same ring to it. She kept insisting.

McCatty pulled the unfinished report from the typewriter and signed it in advance.

When he arrived home, the back door was locked. Connie had to let him in. She was in her stocking feet and her dark and gray hair looked as though her hands had been running through it. Her lipstick was nearly chewed away. Not a sexy sight. McCatty was disappointed enough to get grouchy.

The kitchen shades were drawn for some reason, so a light was on over the island counter. It shined down on the carton of groceries McCatty had placed there earlier.

Connie asked if the groceries were theirs.

Yes.

From where?

He told her.

She had unpacked and packed the carton a half dozen times since she'd come home. Now she had him do it.

Even before he had everything out and on the counter he realized the false bottom. Not elaborate, merely a piece of similar brown cardboard cut to size and dropped in. He removed it.

Hundred dollar bills.

Bound by wide rubber bands into packets, about two inches thick.

Twenty such packets layered the entire bottom of the carton.

Connie had hardly touched the money, only enough to prove her eyes weren't lying.

McCatty didn't react to it. He removed one of the packets, sort of weighed it in his hand and riffled through it.

Connie asked how much.

A million was his estimate.

"It's ours," Connie said

McCatty put the packet of hundreds back into place in the carton.
"It's ours," Connie repeated emphatically.

McCatty looked away as though to get her out of mind. After a long, thoughtful moment, he covered the money with the piece of cardboard and began repacking the groceries neatly.

"What are you going to do?"

McCatty didn't reply. He picked up the carton and went out to the car. Connie followed. She called him an asshole, a straight stupid cop asshole and she made a couple of tries for the carton.

He drove away with it, left Connie standing there yelling.

It wasn't far to Lyle's place. McCatty figured he had time, Lyle would still be at headquarters making out the report. There was no one else to be concerned about because Lyle lived alone.

McCatty broke in. Wrapped his fist in a rag and put it through a pane of Lyle's back door. The other carton of groceries was just inside. McCatty nearly stumbled over it. Rather than unpack it, he ran his hand flat down the inner side of the carton, felt it too had a false bottom. In under that layer of cardboard he fingered the unmistakable texture of paper that was money. He took the carton with him, placed it in the rear seat next to the first.

For a long while he just drove anywhere with the two million dollars. Killing time until night. Then he was on Purchase Street. Twice he went by the place, checking it out. He slowed to let two cars pass. When there were no cars coming in either direction he pulled into the drive of Number 19 and stopped before its huge outer gate.

He placed the two cartons in the shrubs to the left of the gate, where, from the gatehouse, they'd surely be noticed and taken in.

CHAPTER
TWO

NORMA Gainer was also in Harrison on that last of July.

She came down the drive of Number 19 and the heavy iron gates anticipated her, opened automatically one after another. Norma took it as a minor but important demonstration of acceptance that usually she could leave the place without even having to hesitate at the gates. It wasn't known, of course, that she was affected by such reassurances.

This time the man on gate duty signaled her to a stop. He informed her there was an accident down the way on Purchase Street.

"Bad?" Norma asked.

"From what I hear."

Norma didn't realize, of course, that she was circumstantially linked to the accident, that she and one of the victims, the dead grocery boy, had so much in common. Norma had never met another carrier. At least not that she knew of. And as far as the way Number 19 worked such things, she'd taken her brother Drew's advice and stifled her curiosity long ago.

She continued on out through the gates to Purchase Street, turned right. After a quarter mile she got onto Route 684 and its wide lanes that were like an undeniable chute to the Hutchinson River Parkway city bound. She had the top down on the Fiat 2000 Spyder, creating her own breeze. Strands of her hair, like tiny whips, snapped her cheeks and forehead.

There was hardly any traffic, however she kept to the far right lane with the speedometer at fifty-five, exactly the posted limit. Westchester County police patrolled in unmarked cars and used radar guns. Norma didn't want to get stopped. The piece of luggage was right there on the seat beside her.

She wouldn't think about it, passed the time with trying to put out of her mind all else except what she considered her blessings. Before long, there was the George Washington Bridge, its blue lines softened by unclear air, and in less than a quarter hour Norma turned onto East Forty-ninth Street, parked in the garage across from the United Nations Plaza. She took the suitcase up to her apartment in that building.

All the apartments that faced south had unobstructed downstream views of the East River. The United Nations building was practically in their front yard. Naturally, they were choice, most expensive. Norma's apartment had north and east exposures, nearly no skyline and only an oblique, somewhat restricted view of the river. Still it was in the four hundred thousand class. Being on the twenty-seventh floor gave it premium, that much out of range of the city's true surface.

Five rooms. Done mainly with furniture and accessories she'd found in Europe. Almost every trip over she had something sent back. Such as the calling card tray on the table in the foyer. A bronze of a girl in *dishabillé*, her arms extended to support an oversized scallop shell. Norma had come upon it five trips ago in Paris at the *Marche aux Puces*. She'd paid the very first asking price for it because she liked it so much, and after the transaction the stallkeeper, in a rare moment of candor, had told her she should have bargained. The foyer table itself she'd found in Amsterdam at an unlikely out-of-the-way shop that bought piece by piece from elderly people in its neighborhood. Norma believed that table with its graceful tapered legs and marquetry top had been most reluctantly exchanged by someone for mere subsistence.

In such manner she enjoyed personal connections to those things around her. It helped take some of the edge off living alone.

Now in her kitchen she poured a Perrier over ice, added a bit of Rose's lime juice and watched the swirl of the lime until she stirred it away with a long sterling silver spoon that could also be sipped through. She drew some into her mouth on her way to the bedroom.

There she sat in the chair she most often sat in, settled and let out a breath that was inadvertently a sigh. Everything here was in place, she thought, even every magazine. It would be exciting if someone, a certain someone, would suddenly appear and cause disarray. Wasn't it strange when she was with that person she could even let her clothes drop off just anywhere and not be bothered by it?

Her thought went to tomorrow and then the day after tomorrow, her birthday. Thursday she'd be thirty-eight, which on the chronological see-saw between thirty-five and forty was an altogether different balance. Norma, thirty-eight. It seemed the older she got the more she felt the name Norma suited her, as though time was on a convergent course with a predestined image. Futile to hope the two would never merge, she thought.

To her rescue came the desire to be elsewhere. At first anywhere else and then a particular place, because at that moment she needed to be kissed. Not just the light pressing of lips but rather her mouth crowded by another tongue in it, an identical part stroking, becoming resolute and extended within her to its limit, wanting to surpass that, stretching inward until the little ligaments beneath the tongue ached, stabbing as though furious at the impossibility of filling her, and taking persistent licks at the tiny sideways crotches of her lips, left and right.

Norma's eyes had closed involuntarily. She opened them but required movement to come almost all the way out of it. She took up a hand mirror from the side table, a silver art nouveau one etched with dragonflies and lily spears. Not intending serious self-appraisal. She glanced at her reflection only long enough to verify it.

She was a handsome woman, strikingly close to beautiful. Her features were definite and pleasingly related, although her mouth had a way of normally being a little too set and at times when the situation warranted her eyes could be so steady it seemed they might never blink. The pupils of her eyes were an extraordinary green, with black outlining circumferences. Her hair was dark brown, healthy, heavy hair that was naturally straight. She often wore it pulled back taut without a part, playing right into the impression of composure.

The drink in her hand felt colder than it should have. Rivulets of condensation ran down to her fingers. Using the back of the newest issue of *Geo* magazine for a coaster, she placed the glass on the table and took up the phone. All day it had been on her mind to call Drew but she hadn't wanted to call from Number 19. She suspected every phone conversation to or from there was somehow recorded, and although anything said to Drew would be personal, who knew what might be made of it. Her own phone was swept weekly by the Number 19 people. A requirement rather than a favor.

She dialed Drew's number.

After four rings his service answered. Norma knew that didn't necessarily mean Drew wasn't home. She left word she'd called, no other message.

Might as well pack.

She got two bags from the spare bedroom closet. An overnighter and another of medium size. Both matched the larger bag, the thirty-incher she'd brought down from Harrison. The thirty-incher looked as though it had endured equal travel. Norma wondered how they achieved that. Actually it got only half the wear, because two years ago when she'd bought this set of luggage she'd done as instructed, as she knew to do from times previous: bought an extra bag in the thirty-inch size. That allowed alternately one bag to be left at Number 19 and made ready while its counterpart was away being carried.

Norma wasn't the least indecisive about what to pack, nor did she strew things about. It seemed as though she was merely filling the bags, giving them proper weight and believable content, the way she removed things several at a time from drawers and didn't sort through. In twenty minutes she was done. She zipped, buckled and locked both bags and placed them in the foyer along with the thirty-incher. There was only one visible difference other than size. The thirty-incher had a red and white, rather than a brown, leather identification tag attached to its handle.

She tried Drew's number again.

His service was still answering and he hadn't called in for messages. She decided to trust her intuition. Quickly she changed into what she'd wear on the flight. She left the luggage in the foyer, went out and took a taxi uptown to Second Avenue and Fifty-ninth Street.

There was the Roosevelt Island tramway, all orange and blue and advertising itself thirty feet above street level. A tram car was about to depart. Nevertheless, Norma, on impulse, took the time to go into one of the small shops in the mall at the base of the tram station, a place that sold only candy. She bought all the Necco wafers the store had, five packs, three chocolate, two assorted. Because recently Drew had remarked that while Godivas and Teuschers were fine, they weren't any better to his taste than Neccos had been twenty-some years ago.

Norma ran up the steps. In contradiction to the usual city behavior, the tram's departure was delayed especially for her, the time it took her to purchase her ticket and get aboard. Her heart was pounding from rushing. She thanked the other eight passengers and the tram operator and then they were underway, suspended from a cable, proceeding above the city, going against the taxi yellow grain of the avenues: Second, First, York. And FDR Drive, the traffic headed home in both directions, the various car colors attractive from that high vantage. Actually, everything appeared cleaner from up there, the city's deterioration not nearly so apparent. The East River was almost as calm as a creek and closer alongside on the right the Queensboro Bridge was, as usual, being painted, splotched with orange.

From the tram on the way over Norma could also make out Drew's apartment. His was the highest at the south end of the Roosevelt Island complex. She knew it by heart. Whenever she happened to be going up or down FDR Drive she would glance across the river to it. At night his lights on, even the bathroom light, was their signal that he was home. Then she could rest easier. Other times she believed she could sense when he was there.

As today. His door wasn't bolted inside. She let herself in with her key.

He was where she had pictured he would be. Seated alone at the corner windows. Possibly he had noticed her walking over from the tram, although from what she understood he seldom looked down in that direction. Usually he paid attention to the river and whatever happened to be on it, or the Lilliputian animation among the highrises across the way, which were otherwise as dimensionless as a postcard.

Norma went directly to him, saved her hello until it was accompanied by her hand lightly on his bare shoulder. She also said her name for him. Only she called him Drew, short and familiar for Andrew, which she knew he disliked. To most people he was Gainer.

He offered his face up for her kiss. There was love for her in his smile. He said: "I thought I was supposed to pick you up."

"You were," she said matter of fact, not wanting to break it to him right off.

He was wearing a pair of blue lightweight cotton shorts and white athletic socks, knee-high socks that were pushed down to his ankles. His legs were extended across the lap of another chair, shins layered with gauze compresses. On the floor nearby was a clear glass bowl containing an amber liquid.

"Okay by you if we leave later, say around seven or eight? Otherwise we're liable to hit some tie-ups on account of vapor locks."

She didn't object.

"Leslie called, just a few minutes ago, from Oak Bluffs."

"You should take *all* your calls."

He got that and agreed with a slight nod. The trouble was his phone numbers were spoiled again. He had two separate lines, with two different numbers, both unlisted. Each time he had the numbers changed it was a relief to be that abruptly out of touch with the people he'd given the number to at the spur of a promising moment. When last the numbers were changed he'd vowed to be more discreet, conscientious about it, only Norma and Leslie and a few business connections would know what to dial. But now, just four months later, he couldn't pick up for someone he wanted to speak to because more often it would be someone he'd rather avoid. Anyway, next week when he got back from Martha's Vineyard he'd have both numbers changed and unlisted again.

"When did Leslie go up?" Norma asked.

"Early yesterday morning. Had herself flown. She wants us to bring some Zabar's raisin pumpernickel and a pound of birthroot."

"That's a pretty sizable order."

"She said there are a couple of holes in the screen porch that the mosquitoes are finding. She wants to use birthroot on her bites."

It would be truly Leslie, Norma thought, not to use anything for her mosquito bites until Drew got there with that carnal-sounding herb. Until then, she'd just scratch and bear it.

Norma's attention went to the room. She hadn't been there in three weeks. There in the corner were the *Realities,* six years of them next to an equally high stack of *Daily Racing Forms.* A forsaken shoe, a silver spike-heeled sandal, was almost out of sight beneath the couch. Three starfish from an Aruba trip were stuck like a personal constellation on one of the windowpanes. On the low table on the face of an edition of a Nabokov novel was a .32 caliber automatic. Next to a perfect dandelion pod preserved forever in a semi-sphere of clear plastic. Next to the telephones with adaptors attached by simple suction to their earpieces and wires running from them to a pair of Sony M-101 micro cassette recorders. On an alcove wall a numbered and signed Jasper Johns print was hung opposite a framed collection of counterfeit U.S. paper money.

There were enormous pine cones in a natural basket near a leg of the authentic eighteenth-century armoire. The double doors of the armoire were open to reveal a twenty-four inch Trinitron and a Betamax. On the shelves above, video tapes, bootlegged Truffauts and Loseys and Kubricks along with others, such as *Misty Beethoven* and *Inside Marilyn Chambers.* Representing not so much the quality of him but rather his scope, Norma knew.

"Your plants seem to love it here," she said. He had quite a few hanging and standing around.

"Because I ignore them."

She doubted that.

"They're trying to get my attention by looking good," he said.

Norma picked a withered leaf from an otherwise flourishing Ficus tree. She'd given up on Ficus. They always appeared so healthful and irresistible at the florists but became terminal as soon as she got them home.

"That's the one I swear at," Gainer claimed.

Norma felt up in under the tendrils of an obese Swedish ivy. Its soil was damp, cared-for.

Gainer removed the compresses from his shins, saturated them again by dipping them into the bowl of amber liquid. His legs were severely bruised, gashed open in places.

Norma had to look away from them.

His legs were hurt from being kicked while playing soccer. They were always hurt to some extent because he never gave them time to heal, played at least twice a week.

Soccer was his game.

He'd chosen it long ago before there were teams such as the Cosmos. When he was ten he'd gone alone on the subway to various remote city fields that usually didn't even have any bleachers to watch German New Yorkers against Polish New Yorkers or whoever. A weekend league of amateurs that occasionally got its scores noted in the smallest type in the *Daily News*. A few of the older players had once been with well-known European teams. Fred Holtz was one of those Gainer especially remembered. A block of a man with badly scarred knees who, during a warmup, had shown the boy, Gainer, how to bring down and control the ball with his chest. That same afternoon Holtz had scored two goals, the second from twenty yards out to win the match. And, afterward, on the sideline, while wiping at the perspiration that was dripping even from his blond and gray hair, he had acknowledged Gainer again with his eyes. Shared some of that important moment, was the way Gainer took it and kept it.

These days, eighteen years later, Gainer frequently went over to Randall's Island and got into a pick-up game. However, where he enjoyed playing most was in the Bronx on a field with practically all the grass run off it. The guys he played with there were Hispanics who had become used to being unemployed.

The compresses were again in place on his outstretched shins. He took notice of a blue and white private helicopter as it set down across the river on the huge red X of the Sixtieth Street Heliport. Almost immediately it lifted off and side-swooped eastward. Taking a heavy-weight type to his estate on the North Shore or even more likely sent in from out there in moneyland to import some high-priced company, Gainer thought. Offhand he asked Norma, "How's Phil?"

"Who?" As though the name was meaningless.

"That Phil from Michigan."

"What's that you're putting on your legs?"

"Peach pit tea."

"What good does it do?"

"For one thing it appeases Leslie."

Norma sat in the fat armchair diagonally across from him. She smoothed her hair back with both hands.

Gainer recognized it as her look before a fib.

She told him: "I haven't heard from that Phil."

"Why, do you think?"

A shrug.

More than likely, Gainer thought, Phil had become discouraged after having made too many unreturned phone calls or heard too many transparent excuses. For a while earlier in the year Norma had spent some good times with the man, seemed to be reacting happily to him. Then she returned from one of her regular trips to Zurich. Changed. From then on she starved the relationship.

"Phil was strange," she said ambiguously, though insinuating something a little sinister.

When recently Gainer had suggested introducing her to someone, she'd said lightly but pointedly that she'd prefer to do her own casting. Nevertheless, Gainer now told her: "At Clarke's the other day I met someone you might find interesting."

Norma was away in other thought.

"Seemed a nice guy, in his forties, full partner in a law firm."

After a moment she came back, asked: "What color tie was he wearing?"

"I didn't notice. Why?"

Norma decided. "It was blue, a dark, sincere blue. Is he married?"

"Was."

"How many times?"

"Once, I believe he said." Twice was more believable, Gainer now thought.

"Better he should be a lawyer at lunch without a tie . . ."

She had a point.

". . . and married," she added.

"Why married?"

"Drew, honey, if there's to be a divorce at least I should have the pleasure of being the cause of it." She couldn't keep a straight face.

Neither could Gainer.

She remembered the Neccos, dug into her bag and got them, tossed a roll to Gainer.

He was pleased, and, as usual, exaggerated his surprise for her. With one of the candy wafers in his mouth, melting, he remarked, "It's like tasting memories."

Norma thought perhaps the mood of the moment might help soften what she had to tell him: "I can't go up to the Vineyard."

"Why not?"

"I have to make a carry."

He lowered his head and rubbed at his brows roughly with the heel of his hand, as though to prevent having to look at something that wouldn't go away.

"There was no way out of it," Norma said.

"You've only been back a week—"

"Two actually." It seemed even longer to Norma.

"I thought their rule was at least a month between carries."

"I reminded them of that but it didn't matter. They seem to be in a bind of some sort."

Gainer stood abruptly. The wet compresses on his shins were disregarded as they fell to the floor. His stride across the room seemed purposeful, although all he did was get that day's racing form from the hall table, organize its pages and place it on the top of the stack in the corner. "They don't get into binds," he said.

"Darrow implied as much. He said he wanted me, particularly me, to make this carry. Someone he could surely depend on, he said."

Gainer pictured such words coming from Darrow, and Norma soaking them up, falling for the flattery. "Darrow phoned you?"

"I drove up there."

"Did you have to?"

"Probably not, but it was a nice day to get out of the city for a while."

No use reminding her again that she should keep her contact with Number 19 as remote as possible. Usually the carry was brought to her by an intermediary, not always the same man but always someone nameless and neutral-looking who brought the full suitcase and took away the empty. Gainer believed it was safer for Norma not to get closer to Number 19 than that, but she took it as merely his way of viewing things through his street-cautious nature. Hadn't her years of affiliation with Number 19 proved that? She'd always been treated well by Darrow and the others, in little ways made to feel that she truly was a trusted favorite. She wished Gainer would be more tolerant of them. That would make the situation more comfortable for her. As things were, the illegal side of it was always being stressed.

Norma retrieved the compresses, dropped them into the bowl that she set aside where it wouldn't get kicked over. "Hine was there today," she said. "On his best prep school behavior, as usual. I can't help but feel a bit sorry for Hine, the way Darrow talks right through him."

23

Going on about them as though they were ordinary people, Gainer thought.

"Hine asked about you," she said.

Gainer had been to Number 19 a few times with Norma, on certain social occasions when she hadn't wanted to go alone. He'd gone against his better judgment but reasoned that seeing who and what were there might lessen his concern.

It didn't.

No matter how pleasant the place appeared or how polite and upright everyone acted, Gainer knew all it would take was a scratch to reveal mob.

He had also accompanied Norma on several of her carries to Zurich. For the fun of it, was the way Norma persuaded him. To experience what she was up against was more his reason for going along. He knew, of course, what that certain piece of luggage of hers contained and it amazed him how nerveless she was about it. It never seemed to cause the uneasiness it deserved nor received any evident special care. It just got conveyed and heaved and lugged to its destination along with the rest.

Now, in a tone she knew he would not doubt, she told him: "I'm sorry Drew."

He shrugged and tried to smile it off but his disappointment was too thick. For weeks he'd been aiming his time to this coming Thursday —her birthday—the celebration he'd organized with Leslie's help, the special wines, thoughtful presents, little personal touches. He wanted this birthday of Norma's to tell her a lot for him. Now he couldn't even reach Leslie to tell her not to bother with any of it. There wasn't a phone at the cottage.

"It was just bad timing," Norma said.

Gainer returned to her, to his chair by the window. The mood was changed from what it had been, as though someone had sprayed the air with dejection. The two of them sat there, sunk silently in it for a long moment. "Do you intend to ever quit them?" Gainer asked.

No reply from her. Instead, she smoothed back her hair with both hands, this time so severely that for a moment her eyes were elongated.

Gainer didn't allow the sidestep. "Do you?"

"I've mentioned it to Darrow," Norma said offhand.

"When?"

"A while back."

"But not lately."

"Not lately."

"What did Darrow say?"

"He thought it would be crazy for me to walk away from such a good thing."

"In other words no."

"No what?"

"You can't quit."

"That's not exactly what Darrow said."

"It's what he meant."

"I only mentioned the matter, didn't press it. In fact I didn't even put it to him in a way that called for a yes or no. If I ever really wanted to I'm sure I could quit. The choice is mine. For the time being I'd just as soon leave things be." She wasn't rankled, said it in a normal tone.

"You're hooked on the money."

"That's for sure," she said, "I'm an addict."

Gainer put two Neccos in his mouth and immediately bit down on them. Once, to do that would have been a transgression. They were supposed to be sucked on until they melted.

"Drew, do you know how much I'll clear this year?" She heard his crunching the candy. "Two hundred eighty thousand. For only six days' work, if it can be called work. Two hundred eighty I get to keep." After a beat, she added, "What's more, I've come to enjoy Zurich."

Not cold-blooded, overmethodical Zurich, Gainer thought, all those people with adding machine eyes. What was there to enjoy?

Norma sensed his question, was tempted to tell him. Instead she moved forward in her chair, leaned to him, awkwardly gave him a hug with both arms around. His hand matched the round of the back of her head as he momentarily held it. He hoped she didn't think he blamed her. He could never blame her for anything.

They heard his stomach growl.

"Deep down anger?" Norma asked lightly.

"No lunch."

She got up and went into the kitchen.

His kitchen was as neat as hers, everything in place. While she was making the Brie and tomato sandwiches, she glanced out at him. From where she stood the doorway was reduced to a horizontal slit, but it allowed some of Gainer in profile. Norma thought how caring it had been of him to worry about her situation with Number 19. Although by now, after ten years of it, he should know that making carries was a safe, easy business and there was certainly no reason to be concerned about Darrow. Darrow might not be as straight as he tried to impress but he was far from being a heartless mobster.

She sliced the tomatoes as thin as possible to please her Drew.

And also, she thought, it had been sweet of him to try to get her

25

interested in that lawyer he'd met. She'd responded a bit flip but he wouldn't mind that. She might tell him her reason soon, would have to if ever her body and mind became convinced that it definitely wasn't a passing thing. Which at the moment it certainly didn't feel like.

From where Gainer sat he caught glimpses of Norma moving about in the kitchen. At times, observing her was like looking into a mirror, seeing a ten-year-older feminine version of himself. They looked that much alike. Same dark hair and hairline, same green eyes, faces identically shaped. He also had the resolute mouth and unyielding gaze and while those aspects somewhat diminished Norma's beauty, for Gainer they were considered masculine and attractive.

The physical resemblance had come from their mother. The only photograph of her was kept by Gainer on his dresser in a recent frame. A black and white professional portrait that she had signed with love and, later, perhaps to fit another frame, had cut away nearly all her love and signature. The mother's face in the photograph was so retouched it was as unrealistically without lines as a movie star's publicity photo. Still, her features were there and, no doubt, sister and brother, Norma and Gainer, had mostly taken after her.

This was not, though, the extent of Norma's and Gainer's alikeness. Many of Gainer's ways were masculine translations of Norma's ways. Not to suggest he was effeminate, but some of her was apparent in his posture, his turn of head, his stride, his transitional movements from one physical attitude to another.

The similarity even carried over into the more abstract. It was often possible for them to be together, hardly exchange a word and still feel as though they'd had a long informative talk. That much affinity.

Norma and Gainer.

When she had just turned fifteen, he was about to be five. They lived on West End Avenue in a twenty story building that had the year 1923 cut into its cornerstone. Theirs was an apartment of ten rooms, most of them immense with twelve foot high ceilings and poor light. A remnant of those who determined such fashionable camps as the West Side and moved on, leaving behind prodigal ghosts, abused elegance and reduced rents.

The apartment was because the mother had wanted space, not to suffocate, she'd said. The father had held back, saying it wouldn't be comfortable. Their largest sofa seemed a miniature of itself against the living room wall and no single rug they owned or could afford would be good and large enough to satisfy the dining room. All the hardwood floors were left bare and waxed, scattered with rugs that were constantly slipping out of place, having to be corrected.

Gainer would get a running start down the entrance hall and slide on the copy of a prayer-sized Kashan as though the floor were ice. His big bedroom was as deep into the apartment as it could be, his bed cringed in a corner and in the night his playthings searched for one another across the waxed expanse.

Gainer would put his feet up and thump on the wall, not too loudly, with his heels. Norma's room was adjacent, her bed in the abutting corner, closer than anyone to him. She would respond, tap the wall with her fingers and help bring everything down to his size.

The father was employed by a major advertising agency as its personnel director. He had a degree in Business Administration from Colgate. At least it sounded Ivy League. The father's office did not have a window but it was on the executive floor and vice-presidents sometimes said hello or good-bye to him by name.

Presumably it was the father's job to assess potential employees, decide if they would do. The father took it seriously. He believed his judgment of people was an infallible litmus. True character was not always on a person's front page but more often in the finer print of his want ads, the father claimed. Those, his words, were framed on the wall behind him to let an applicant know straight off that he was about to be thoroughly read.

Most of those hired by the agency were as good as hired before the father ever set eyes on them. A shapely female marketing assistant was a desirable prospect, a clever television writer was a prize already brought in by one of the "head hunters," as the employment agencies were called. The father was aware of the circumvention, but never let it be known, went about his departmental procedures as though the hiring, final yes or no, was up to him. He also seemed immune to starting salaries that usually exceeded his own by five to thirty thousand.

The father appeared to have a perpetual smile. It was the way he'd conditioned the flex of his cheek muscles, causing the corners of his mouth to be ever so slightly upturned. For that reason alone he was thought of as a pleasant person, though he rarely laughed and when he did it was never full out. Not once in his life had he experienced such a release. It just wasn't in him to let it out.

Neither was it in him to quarrel. Any argument with the mother was her argument. First, he would remove his eyeglasses as though intending to fight. She would rant around him, thrust pointed insults while he sat there behind his small smile, waiting out her battle. Then, as though it had never been waged, he'd put on his glasses and fix his attention again on the racing section of the *News*.

That was the most incongruous thing, his playing the horses. Four years back he'd given up the *Wall Street Journal* and following the market every day for the *Daily News* and the horses. He played mentally, just as he had with the market, made *mind bets* of five dollars a unit and kept a running tally to know how he would have done if he'd actually bet. There really wasn't much difference between National Copper at thirty-four and a quarter and Light Warrior in the fourth at six to one. Except, at five dollars a unit, betting the horses was within his investment range.

The father asked around about a bookie.

One of the elevator starters in the agency's building arranged for him to meet Manny.

Manny was a fair-haired George Raft with camel-haired coat, kid gloves and all, but no hat. His territory was around Madison and Fifty-seventh and he had a fairly large handle out of the hotels: the Plaza, the Pierre and the Sherry Netherland. Of course, he was not as interested in the father's five dollar action as he was the prospect of larger bettors once he got a foot in the door of the agency. To that end he showed the father some special treatment, even to the extent of once in a while steering him off a bad thing and, at his own expense, onto a winner. Manny insisted on taking the father and the mother to dinner at any place they chose. The father thought perhaps somewhere Chinese. Manny took them up to the Rainbow Room. For Christmas Manny gave the father a case of Canadian Club. He gave the mother an eighteen karat gold Cuban link chain bracelet he'd bought from a fence.

The mother was never contrary about the father's horseplaying. Actually, it became an agreeable thing for them and every so often she'd ask him to make a bet for her. The father thought she liked certain horses only because she liked their names, and it was incredible, the luck of the ignorant, that even quite a few of her hopeless longshots came in. Manny was not unhappy to pay off.

Practically every day the mother was done with the house by eleven, made-up, dressed and out of it by noon. Sometimes she went to museums or a show, but more often it would be Altman's or Saks. Bonwit's was her favorite with Bergdorf's a close second. "Today I'm doing Bonwit's," was the way she'd put it.

Rarely did she abuse her charge accounts, although it wasn't unusual for her to buy as though she were Jackie O—without even a peek at a price tag, load up on dresses, coats and whatever. She'd return them for credit to her account the following day. Evidently she found such gratification in looking, trying on and buying that keeping was anticlimactic. Normally, she wouldn't head home until the stores closed. On Mondays and Thursdays that was nine.

The father thought it absurd that she spent so much time shopping. While he was at the office where he should be, she was out there anywhere wandering aisles and try-on areas. A shame she couldn't find something better to do was the opinion he kept to himself.

One night in April the mother didn't come home. The stores had been closed for hours and the father didn't know where else she could be. He was worried but too embarrassed to phone the police until the following morning before leaving for the office. The police gave him some fast reassurances. She'd show up. That was what happened ninety-nine out of a hundred times. She'd show.

Apparently the police were used to the husbands of straying wives.

But the mother didn't return.

She became officially missed.

The police believed it significant that she hadn't taken any of her personal things, not even her hairbrush or jewelry.

Gainer asked if the mother was dead, not really knowing yet what *dead* meant.

The father left everything of the mother's exactly as she'd left it. Her make-up by the bathroom sink, nylon nightgown on the hook on the back of the bathroom door. He only put the cap on a tube of lipstick so it wouldn't go dry.

After two weeks Norma received a postcard from the mother. Postmarked Miami. It said she was all right, would be all right. She promised that someday everyone would understand. It was signed with all her love.

The father emptied the mother's closets and dresser drawers. Put all that remained of her into four footlockers and had the superintendent take those down to the building's storage area. The father said he intended to have the Goodwill people come pick them up.

He didn't miss a day at the office. However, the first to go was his small smile. His cheek muscles gave way and the corners of his mouth inverted on him. People began thinking of him as a bit of a grouch for no particular reason. He had never looked well in clothes because he was bow-backed, an exaggerated erectness with shoulders tensed and chest forward, which caused his suit jackets to strain across the front and bunch loosely behind. Now, his body underwent a rather sudden transposition. His back bent the other way, shoulders stooped, chest sank. His clothes fit him differently, worse. They seemed resigned to be on him.

He drank vodka and Seven-Up from a styrofoam coffee cup at ten

29

in the morning. And he no longer held to his noontime ritual of picking the horses. That, along with all else, had become uninteresting for him. Besides, the bookie, Manny, was no longer around.

The connection never occurred to the father. He would never know that the day the mother went was the day Manny went. Manny had collected his accounts (except the twenty the father owed), emptied his safe deposit boxes and flown.

"Don't take nothing with you," Manny had told the mother.

"Not even a few things?"

"Nothing. Whatever you got I'll get you better in Miami."

If the father had known about Manny, naturally it would have made a difference. He would have felt more of a fool—all those afternoons since Manny first came into their lives that the mother was supposed to have been *doing* Bonwit's or Saks. At least the father would have been offered a reason not to turn it all in on himself. Much of the father's hurt came from having his self-illusions exposed. How could he accept that he'd been such a bad judge of character? She'd been his wife and he'd not even seen a hint of it coming. His ability to know people had made him sure of them and, therefore, sure of himself. Belief in that had been his private glue.

He came apart.

Tried mending with vodka, and soon enough Smirnoff 100 proof gave way to the greater number of drinks per dollar of a Jersey City brand that had a skinny blue and silver eagle and Russian-like lettering with backward Rs on its label. It got so he would pour a drink in the refrigerator last thing each night so first thing next morning all he had to do was reach in for it.

At the agency he was assigned an assistant who had the eyes and attitude of a replacement.

By then the mother had been gone almost a year. It was April. A day that came gray and went wet. The father had no umbrella. For the first time ever he left his attaché case at the office. He walked partway home, to a bar on Seventh Avenue in the fifties, a serious, stand-up drinker's place. His toes squished in his shoes, the soaked wool on his shoulders smelled unpleasant. Perhaps he was shaking because he was chilled. He stood at the hard bar and had three of the best, Stolichnaya, lifting his glass slightly before downing them, as though in acknowledgement to something inside him. He bought one for the drinker next to him.

At that moment the father became four inches taller. He stood straight, drew his shoulders back and bowed his spine as before.

He walked from the bar with a stride that was inconsistent with the rain. Head and eyes up he crossed the sidewalk, sidled between the bumpers of two illegally parked cars. Never hesitated. Continued out into the rushing stream of the avenue. One-way traffic flowing north. The father didn't even glance into it. If anything, his head turned in the opposite direction, to not see it coming.

Of all the ways to go, he'd chosen that to get around a clause in his life insurance policy that said death by war or suicide was worthless but accidental death paid double.

The insurance company held up payment.

No matter that the father had never in twenty years been late paying the premiums. There were sworn statements from people at the agency that the father had been depressed. Not merely despondent but bottom-of-the-heap depressed. And there were dispositions from two witnesses saying the father had intentionally lunged out in front of the fast taxi. Indeed, he had stepped out so deliberately it might have appeared that he lunged.

The insurance company said it regretted to say it found in its favor. A New York State judge had signed the decisive document along with others in a stack. A lightly-penciled red check on its upper right hand corner told him he should.

After the father's funeral Norma and Gainer remained at the apartment on West End Avenue. Norma cooked whatever they wanted and Gainer slid on the rugs a lot. The lady who lived across the hall looked in on them. Norma told her an aunt was coming to live with them, an Aunt Helen from Spokane.

Next morning, when Norma was doing dishes and Gainer was pushing a dust mop around, another lady was at their door. From the Bureau of Child Welfare. A fieldworker named Miss Phelps, who showed her official identification. Norma pretended to examine it carefully while thinking ahead about which things to say.

Miss Phelps asked if she could come in after she was already in. She went through the apartment as though not expecting to find someone else there, and her silence seemed to be belief when Norma told her an Aunt Carol was on her way from Akron.

Miss Phelps helped Gainer pack his things. Norma packed her own. They went downtown to 70 Lafayette Street where Miss Phelps turned them over to Miss Gurney. She was a caseworker and they were now a case. They sat on hard city chairs in Miss Gurney's cubicle and Norma gave true answers.

"Do you have any idea where your mother is?"

"Last we got was a postcard from her, from an island. It was a hotel postcard that showed a swimming pool and palm trees." The ink in the mother's handwriting had gotten smeared, on its way or at poolside.

31

"When was that?"

"Just after Christmas." Which was months before.

"Nothing since then?"

"Nope."

"You have grandparents, don't you?"

"They're dead."

"How about aunts or uncles?"

"An Uncle Howard lives in San Diego."

"Howard what?"

"Howard is his last name."

"What does he do?"

"I'm not sure. I think he sells Chevrolets or something."

Five phone calls and Miss Gurney had the right Mr. Howard on the line. She explained the situation and asked: "Do you know where Mrs. Gainer is at the moment?"

"No, but I'm damned concerned. This is a terrible situation. Those children are my flesh and blood . . ."

Miss Gurney's expression anticipated the *however*.

However, Uncle Howard was about to move to Hawaii for his health. He'd recently been divorced and his blood pressure was dangerously high. Otherwise . . .

Miss Gurney understood, said good-bye to Uncle Howard *after* she hung up.

Was there anyone else?

No. Norma decided not to mention an Aunt Marion in Someplace, Illinois, who had never been more than a name to her.

No one.

Miss Gurney placed them.

In a home for such children. The Mission of the Immaculate Virgin better known as Mount Loretto. Located on the southern tip of Staten Island, it faced out on Raritan Bay. Few places were so distant from the city and still a part of it.

Gainer enjoyed the ferry ride over. But at Mount Loretto the sisters, in their habits and headpieces, seemed to be hands and faces without bodies. Gainer was fascinated by them but not sure he shouldn't be frightened. He didn't like having so many people telling him what to do, instead of just Norma.

He saw her every day but not enough. Often he got the feeling she wasn't there, that she'd been taken away, until to his relief she came in sight. Some days they'd sit outside on the slope of grass and watch big ships in the Red Bank Reach, as the channel off there was called.

One morning they counted seventy-three sailboats, although the way the boats cut and tacked across and around one another there must have been some they counted twice.

Another morning Norma took Gainer for a walk.

"Where are we going? he asked.

"Just keep walking," she told him.

They crossed over Hylan Boulevard, beyond the grounds of Mount Loretto. Kept to back streets all the way to Huguenot Station where they caught a local electric train that took them to the end of its line: the ferry terminal. A ferry was just then pulling out. It growled contemptuously at those who'd missed it and its seething wake looked as though it could boil anyone who fell in. But soon another ferry headed into the slip, a friendlier ferry, its bow smiling at the waterline. For only a nickel each it skimmed Norma and Gainer across New York harbor and deposited them on the toe of Manhattan.

They had eleven dollars to go on. And hope in the address of a girl named Dolores Hart. She had been at Mount Loretto the year before, was now out on her own with a nice place of her own, Norma had been told.

400 East Eightieth Street.

It was a six storied building, fifty years older than those on either side of it, apparently depending on them for support. In its entranceway were twelve abused mail boxes, each with a mail slot and an intercom buzzer button. Only four of the boxes had printed names. The others had names scratched over names on the bare metal.

There was no Hart, not even a Dolores.

Norma checked several times. She couldn't even tell which was apartment 6-R because the numbers on the buzzer buttons were so worn. Perhaps, Norma thought, the girl at Mount Loretto who had given her Dolores Hart had made a mistake on the address. Or maybe Dolores Hart was only a fancy, a haven invented out of the girl's own wishful thoughts.

Gainer was chewing on his thumbnail, a sign that he was hungry.

Norma pressed all twelve buttons, causing voices so faint they seemed from distant, tiny people.

"It's me," Norma said in a register lower than normal.

At once a raspy buzzer sounded, enabling the inner door to be opened.

Norma and Gainer climbed. Steps covered and re-covered with linoleum. The metal edgings nailed on the front of some were loose enough to trip on. There was an inconsistent lean to every flight and landing, a slant one way and then an opposite list. The entire stairwell had long ago settled as much as it ever would and so was more reliable than it appeared.

On the sixth floor the only apartment had a door painted baby pink. The high gloss paint, amateurishly sprayed on, had run in places. There was no name or number or doorbell.

Norma knocked politely.

She thought she heard movement inside but no one came to the door. She knocked again, several times and certainly loud enough, but still no one came.

Gainer put his ear to the door. "Someone's in there," he said.

Norma doubted it. She was full of misgivings. They should leave now, forget ever having heard of Dolores Hart. They should take the long ride back to Mount Loretto, back to sure beds and meals.

"Wait here," she told him.

She hurried down the six flights and in twenty minutes came back up bringing a pizza in a box and four cold Pepsis. They sat on the landing. The string on the box cut white into Gainer's hands but he broke it, while Norma opened the drinks and put straws in them. She'd brought extra napkins but could have used more with the melt on their chins and fingers. When they'd had enough, two slices of the pizza were left. For those, possibly for later, Norma made a smaller box out of the larger, tied it neatly with the string.

There they sat. With their backs against the wall. Norma put her arm around to have Gainer truly next to her. The bare bulb in the fixture above was only twenty-five watts but still it exposed where wet moppings of the linoleum had turned dust into dirty cake at every corner and angle. Norma pictured where they were in relation to the city, and expanding further, the city to her mental map of the coast and ocean. Her imagination returned so suddenly to being there on that tilted landing it seemed to her she was surely too small to be protection for him, smaller yet, whose boychest and heartbeat she felt on the flat of her hand.

Scratching sounds. On the inside surface of the painted pink door. A cat, Norma thought, that must have been what she'd heard before. She doubted a Dolores Hart lived there.

The hour that passed seemed like four.

The pink door opened and a man came out. He hardly glanced at them, stepped over their legs and went down the stairs. A girl was in the doorway. She had on wrinkled pink cotton, a two-piece nightie with panties like bloomers and a brief gathered top. Her face was nearly hidden by too much overcurled hair.

34

"I'm looking for Dolores Hart," Norma said.

"No one here by that name," the girl said.

"We're from Mount Loretto," Norma told her.

"Christ, come on in."

The apartment was one long room made into two by a bookcase and drapes that were tacked up. There was a bed at the windowless end and at the other end an old sofa with fat arms. The two windows above the sofa had roller shades with little nude plastic dolls tied to their draws.

Norma explained quickly how she and Gainer happened to be there.

"I'm not Dolores Hart," the girl said. "I used to be but now I'm Vicky Harris." She proved it with a social security card.

A gray and white calico cat jumped up on the table for the single purpose of rubbing against Norma's hand. It was encouraging.

Vicky used a length of red Christmas ribbon to tie back her hair. Her face was round, her features indefinite, as though they hadn't yet completely emerged. Her mouth promised to smile more than it did. "I'm eighteen," she said, "actually . . . almost seventeen."

Gainer hadn't said a word, not because he was timid or apprehensive, but because everything was talking to him. An emaciated geranium in an aluminum saucepan, an empty Modess box in a metal wastebasket that had on it a dented hunting dog holding a pheasant in its mouth, an ashtray used for a bowl to contain foil-covered Easter candies.

Vicky made tea.

The stove and refrigerator were in a closet that had no door. Vicky italicized the word borrowed when she said she'd *borrowed* tea and cups from where she worked. Substantial cups that clanged against one another when she handled them. "I have to be at work at four," she said.

Norma didn't have to ask if they could stay.

Vicky didn't have to ask if they wanted to. She made up the sofa with one of the sheets and two of the pillows from her bed. In tune with Norma's thoughts, she volunteered that the fellow who had been there was no one special. In other words, don't worry, he wouldn't be back that night.

Norma and Gainer went to bed earlier than usual. With their heads at opposite ends, the sofa was roomy enough and its high back reinforced their sense of security. Norma lay there with tomorrow in mind. No matter what she tried to put into tomorrow it seemed empty. Gainer propped his pillow against the sofa's fat arm and thumbed through magazines, recent issues of *Harper's Bazaar* and an August 1933 *National Geographic*. When the light was turned off he scrunched down and hugged Norma's feet.

The following day Vicky had more vitality, more to offer, as though she'd been regenerated. She gave advice like an old-timer who'd been through it. She told Norma: "The worst problem is age. You can't be sixteen."

"But that's what I am."

"Everyone thinks a sixteen-year-old out on her own is an easy hustle. Can't have experience, can't be reliable. You got to be eighteen at least, not just say you're eighteen but *look* it."

The transformation took three days.

Norma, at Vicky's suggestion, went down to Thirty-fourth Street to a school for hairdressers. The students needed practice. Norma managed to get with the swishiest one there, a young man who at once became a confidante and conspirator. Norma didn't understand all that he chattered on about and none of the jargon, but she made it seem that she did. He snipped her plain long hair away a little at a time, using a style in *Harper's Bazaar* for reference. He also insisted on doing Norma's make-up and when he was through he appreciated his work so much he was carried further, shoved all sorts of cosmetic devices into her handbag.

That same night she went blond.

Did it herself with Gainer looking on. She read the Clairol directions, closed her eyes and applied. Didn't face the mirror until she was done and then wasn't sure she looked all that much older.

"Do you think I look older?" she asked Gainer.

"Yeah."

"You're not just saying that?"

He winked his best wicked wink at her.

Then there were the mother's things.

Vicky went with Norma to get them. The Puerto Rican superintendent at the West End Avenue apartment building didn't recognize Norma immediately, nor did he believe anything had been left in storage. Norma insisted. The superintendent muttered idiomatic Spanish obscenities that he was sure they didn't understand as he opened the storage area and found two footlockers. Norma recalled there having been four. The superintendent turned resentful, as though he was being deprived. He left Norma and Vicky to cope with the heavy footlockers. They dragged and shoved more than carried them out to the sidewalk.

Four available taxis wanted nothing to do with them. Vicky walked down a block and got one. The driver was an older Irishman with a whiskey complexion. Not a word of complaint from him about the footlockers and he even helped carry them in and up to Vicky's place. He was redder in the face and puffing hard by the time he was done.

Norma wished she could afford to give him more than a dollar tip but he looked into her eyes and saw that, and as though he had God's ear, he told Him aloud to bless her.

Norma hurried to have the footlockers open. But seeing their contents made her pause. Things she'd never realized occupied any corner of her memory now seemed so familiar, and evocative. What could be more inconsequential than a brown tweed skirt or a white ribbed sweater? Except that they had been *hers,* the mother's, and although Norma couldn't recall any particular instance when they had been worn by the mother, she still saw her in them.

She handled all the mother's things with great care at first, certainly with much more than they'd been packed with. As Norma removed layer after layer, the effect lessened.

She tried some things on. They were only a bit large and long, could be made to fit. Vicky tried on a Bergdorf dress she loved but it was small for her, especially across the bust and hips, would never do.

One of the footlockers contained shoes, boots and handbags. The shoes were also small for Vicky, however Norma fitted them perfectly.

Norma stayed up late altering a dress, a beige, light wool challis. She had to seam and hem it by hand, difficult because the fabric had such give to it. Gainer helped. When she had to do over a side seam, he pinned it as she told him to. He got down and squinted at the hemline to make sure it was straight. He also threaded the needles, licked the thread and was able to get it through the eye first time every try. While Norma stitched, they sang Rodgers and Hart songs, practically the entire score of *The Boy Friend.* Gainer didn't miss many lyrics.

Next day he went job hunting with Norma. He told her she looked beautiful at the perfectly timed moment, just before she entered the first employment agency. He waited down in the lobby.

On the first application Norma only lied about her age and made up a social security number. She printed neatly that she had two years of high school, no special skills, no previous employment and that she desired a clerical position or whatever was available. The only space she left blank was where references were asked for.

The employment agency lady behind a heaped desk assessed the application in an instant. She gave the favor of her appraisal to Norma from thigh to forehead and dismissed her with an automatic promise.

Norma went to two other agencies and got similar reactions. What had started out as a hopeful attitude had been turned into a feeling that she was a bother to people.

By then it was midafternoon. She and Gainer sat at a counter at Chock full o' Nuts for grilled cheese sandwiches that weren't grilled

37

enough and milk shakes that were mostly milk. She tried to hide her disappointment but Gainer sensed it, so instead of asking if she was getting a job, he told her: "While I was waiting in the lobby of that last building this man came up to the newsstand. He was dressed better than the President. He slipped two cigars into his jacket and only paid for a newspaper."

"Probably it wasn't like that," Norma said for his sake.

"If I had the money I'd take us to a movie," Gainer said, and when she didn't pick up on it he brightened and said, "Why don't we go to a music store and play some Cole Porter or someone?"

At that moment Norma was thinking of the father, wondering how he'd treated job applicants, those without all the qualifications trying for their first niche. Had he ever knowingly let one slip through? She wanted to believe he had, more than one.

One more employment agency.

At 30 Rockefeller Plaza.

Norma smoothed the legs of her stockings and went in, chin up, with a faint smile. She asked for an application as though she were asking to pass the salt at her own dinner party, hesitating before adding a please. She didn't print, she scribbled, gave her age as twenty-one. She was a Bachelor of Arts graduate of Bennington, had majored in both Visual Communication and English Literature. She had worked two summers, one at BBD&O, the other at Doubleday. She would accept an editorial position in publishing or, second choice, a programming assistant's job at one of the major television networks. For references she gave two names she had memorized from the copy of *Fortune* magazine she'd purposely glanced through at the newsstand on the way up.

The employment agency woman considered the application and smiled. She offered Norma a chair, a cigarette, a cup of coffee, another smile. Did Norma have time to go on an interview that day? Not today, Norma told her, or tomorrow either for that matter, because she had so many interviews. She used the glass that framed a Mondrian print to approve her hair and went out before the woman could ask another word.

If nothing else, it put some altitude into Norma's spirit. It was just good to know she could pull it off. In a way, she'd helped herself to a compliment, she thought, but from another side of it, didn't she wish it hadn't been an impersonation?

She found Gainer outside on Fifth Avenue talking to a man about Saint Patrick's Cathedral across the way, the possibility of its spires falling and killing a lot of shoppers on their way to Saks. Those high old stones appeared loose and when last had anyone climbed up to inspect them? The man did a straight face and said he'd take it up with the cardinal. He was a vendor of big pretzels and Norma felt obliged to buy one. She and Gainer shared it on the walk home. Up Park Avenue, past all the money, brass water hydrants polished for the better dogs, doormen wearing white gloves as though they might contaminate.

Going crosstown between Third and Second avenues Norma's nose led her eyes to a neighborhood bakery that had a penciled sign taped to its window.

Help wanted.

Norma went in and the baker-owner, a Mr. Larkin, said nicely that he doubted she'd want the job. It wasn't just selling cookies, the hours were bad and the pay wasn't even union scale.

No matter to Norma.

Almost as clearly as she'd seen the *help wanted* in his window, Larkin read the *help needed* in her eyes. He told her to wear white.

She would have to wait until her first pay to get the required white outfit. However, next day when she showed up to work, Larkin let her wear one of his white shirts and a pair of trousers from a linen supply company.

The trousers were overstarched, ironed with such pressure the fabric stuck to itself. Norma had to force her feet down into the legs of them and, of course, they were too large in every way. She cuffed them up four inches three times, used several turns of twine for a belt.

Larkin also provided a white cotton hat with a puffy crown to contain her hair. She had to safety pin a large tuck in the band of it. Her shoes were from the mother's trunk. The only comfortable enough pair. Medium high stacked heels in a navy suede from Bendel's. The first smudge of flour that got on them Larkin made her take them off.

The problem with going barefoot was that the floor around the sink was somewhat wet and by stepping there and around Norma's under-feet picked up flour. It was like walking on paste. More and more of it accumulated, hardened and became a sort of sole.

Larkin was a good, practical baker. Eclairs and Boston cream pies were about as fancy as he went. No flaky pastries, not even a strudel. He did everything in a hurry.

Norma felt that she had to match him. Part of her job was to keep all the utensils clean and all the mixing vats, baking pans and trays. As fast as she scrubbed them, Larkin put them back to use. The air there always held motes of flour and fragrances. Loaves baking. Whenever Larkin removed them from the oven and turned them out of their tins, Norma stood close, all the more to enjoy breathing. Then there was the

39

wonderful sweeter smell of layers for cakes cooking and sugar cookies getting their bottoms browned.

Norma's work hours were from four to midnight. Two-fifty an hour. That came to eighty a week after taxes and everything. On the W-2 forms she claimed one dependent.

The first work night she walked home barefoot because she couldn't get her shoes on.

Gainer had been waiting for the sound of her on the stairs. He was standing in the open doorway. She climbed the six flights up to him. He had his best smile for her and tried not to look sleepy. He hugged her around the hips. She patted the back of his head, which was like kissing with her hand.

Larkin had given her a couple of eclair mistakes and a lopsided loaf of rye to take home.

Gainer exaggerated his delight and she loved him for that.

She ran some water in the bathtub, sat on the edge and put her feet in to soak. The flour and water and now street dirt were like a hardened plaster. She could hardly flex her toes.

When she told Gainer what it was, they laughed. He took off his clothes and kneeled in the water in the tub. She tried to stop him but he wouldn't. He scraped and rubbed with his fingers until the flour became doughy and broke away and her feet were clean.

"What did you do while I was at work?"

"Read mostly. The television was too snowy."

"Just read?"

"For a while I sat in the window and watched. Saw a woman kick a man and then kiss him. Before that I saw a girl in a bathroom pull something out of herself."

"You promised to stay in. Did you?"

The fib was in his mouth but he didn't tell it. "I went around the block a couple of times. I talked with a guy who said he was a police-man. I don't think he was because he had on a dirty T-shirt and an old leather vest. Another guy lying in a doorway asked me for a cigarette."

Norma couldn't reprimand him. Not doing so, she realized, was permission. Serious, eyes to eyes, she made a rule for whenever he was out on the street and anyone got mean, started acting crazy or tried to touch him.

"What should *you* do?" she asked, testing.

"Run!"

That first job of Norma's as flunky to a kind baker helped them get the first place of their own. Like Vicky's it was the highest to walk up to, situated at the rear of an older building. One long everything room

40

that Norma and Gainer scrubbed down and rolled yellow paint onto. Yellow because it seemed the happiest of all the little sample chips, but when painted it was too much yellow and they couldn't get used to it.

They bought what they needed to cook and eat with. And a pair of twin size mattresses. Whatever else went into the apartment came from the streets, from the unwanted furniture and other things people put out at the curb on a specified night every month for the city sanitation department trucks to take away.

Each month, on that night, the seven-year-old Gainer roamed the streets on the lookout for anything usable. From Fifth Avenue over to Lexington in the Sixties, Seventies and Eighties was the high yield district, where better quality unwanted things might be found. Gainer would make his way back and forth from block to block appraising the heaps of discards. Whenever he could manage alone, he lugged something home and then returned to continue looking where he'd left off.

It got so Gainer could imagine people according to what they threw away. Books, for example. No one would throw out good books unless the books had belonged to someone no longer liked. The same went for nice souvenirs of places and perfume bottles that still contained more than just a little. Normally, when there were a lot of men's shoes in a pile, there were also a lot of neckties and maybe eyeglasses and a hairbrush. Some man had died. A lot of women's shoes didn't mean that, nor did any amount of cosmetics. But a bunch of women's hats could. From such hats Gainer collected unusual pretty feathers that he used as bookmarks.

Whenever he came across something worthwhile that he couldn't manage alone he'd meet Norma when she got through work at the bakery and they'd heft it home together. Often by the time they got back to where he'd spotted something, it was gone. They weren't the only ones around after street stuff.

They lost out on a lacquered table that was only slightly chipped and an armchair that was only very wobbly. But they didn't lose a wicker love seat with its seat broken through and a desk with one fractured leg that needed a wall to stand against.

Mirrors with their backs scratched, lamps wanting shades or shades wanting lamps, clocks that refused to run until Gainer vigorously shook a tick into them. Stacks and stacks of magazines and all kinds of professional journals. After Gainer went through them he carried them down to the street on that particular night of the month and left them to be picked up by the sanitation department. Pieces of furniture also went to the curb as Gainer and Norma upgraded their finds. As the cycle would have it, many of the things they discarded were wanted and taken away by someone before a city truck could get to them.

After two years of such a life Gainer had learned more than if he had gone to school. He was supposed to be in the fourth grade but Norma didn't enroll him. She feared trouble from the Bureau of Child Welfare. Those people would put Gainer back in a place like Mount Loretto, which would be a waste of everyone's energy, because first opportunity Norma would steal him out. Still, Norma felt school was the best thing for him.

She mentioned the problem to Vicky, who by then no longer had a regular job but was somehow living in a new highrise. Vicky thought she might have an answer. One of her boyfriends, whom she knew only as Arnie, had boasted that he could come up with any kind of document. Vicky called him on that. What did she want, Arnie asked, a diploma from UCLA or maybe a British passport?

How about some school records from a small town? Vicky asked.

A week later Arnie delivered.

Andrew Gainer had attended the Pearson School in Winsted, Connecticut, for the last three years. He'd earned mostly Bs, but a few As, but never an F. A letter from the school principal on doubtless letterhead stationery commended Andrew's learning ability and deportment. There was even a properly imprinted manila envelope to contain it all.

Norma put on her much older look.

Gainer dressed in his best and combed his hair a bit more forward for the part.

Norma was Aunt Norma. She affected a tighter mouth that hardly moved as she spoke to the school's admission clerk.

Gainer blew his nose not to laugh.

The story was his parents were divorced. His mother was not well, suddenly. An uncertain diagnosis. She was in Arizona for treatment.

Gainer met the admission's clerk's eyes with the right measure of innocent despair.

He was in.

Eventually twelve New York City schools would try more or less to educate Gainer. Twelve because of the moves he and Norma made. From Yorkville, better known as Germantown, to Morningside Park, where Columbia University integrated with Harlem, from the fringe of Chinatown and Little Italy to Woodside, not far from LaGuardia Airport, where Irish cops and their families were the neighbors above and below.

Gainer didn't seem to be the worse for so many changes. As far as he was concerned another school was only another school, a place where he had to spend time and appear attentive. Early on he developed a way of assuming an interested expression, fixing his gaze on the teacher while his mind turned over extraneous, usually more complex subjects. His acute mental reflexes allowed him to get away with it. When asked a question, he could snap his thinking back to the classroom and give a reasonable answer.

The books he was required to read were so dry he had to splash his eyes with water to get through them. And what the hell use was it ever going to be for him to know, line for line, the map of Europe before World War II?

The subject he enjoyed was mathematics. That was spoiled for him later on when it became trigonometry and calculus. At that point he branched out on his own into the area of mathematical probability and chance.

He went to school only because that was what Norma expected. He went as seldom as he could. His absence record was flagrant, would have been unacceptable had he not done so well on examinations and deserved his high grades. Whenever called to account for his truancy, he never offered an excuse. Told how much better he'd do if he tried, he doubted it.

Norma wasn't unaware of his attitude toward school. Her talks with him about it reassured her that he was doing fine even if he wasn't staying in line as everyone wanted him to. As time passed, the more Norma learned of what Gainer did when he wasn't in school, the less she worried about him.

"What did you do today?"

He wouldn't lie, not to her. "I was at the Pierre Hotel."

"Doing what?"

"Watching."

He'd sit in one of the plush silk chairs in the lobby of the Pierre as though he had every reason to be there. For hours. Comparing those who checked in or out, overhearing, remembering. Other times it was the Regency or the Saint Regis.

On a sixth grade school day he might go for a swim at the East Twenty-third Street municipal pool or be somewhere midtown observing a monte game or some other scam. He was even more likely to be at Dunhill's or Cartier's, roaming around, keeping his hands off the glass display cases.

"May I help you?" Meaning, he knew, what the hell are you doing here.

"I'm waiting for my mother. She's coming in to buy something."

He had a way of getting into special places, all the way in. For that purpose, his air was detachment, as if being there was the last thing he wanted. He'd enter the most direct way and just keep going. Being alone helped. Being alone he was taken for the kid of someone, perhaps someone important.

It got him into a closed rehearsal of the New York Philharmonic. The conductor, Gainer noticed, scratched himself with the baton several times, his back and bottom, and swore at the various instruments categorically, as though musicians weren't playing them.

It got him into the upper corridor of a fast-trick hotel off Times Square. Watching the comings and goings, not altogether innocent about it.

Into the executive offices of Universal Pictures on Park Avenue, through a reception area and down the hall past offices where practically everyone he saw was on the phone. He wound up sitting softly in the projection room to see a movie that wasn't yet finished, but already, from what he heard, had too many mistakes in it.

Another time, into a leather chair in the reading room of the Harvard Club, only because it was raining for a couple of hours. And, same day, a hard city chair at the Nineteenth Precinct police station in view of the holding pen that had in it a man who had killed two people just that morning. The man seemed more relaxed than anyone there, including the policemen.

It also got him into the kitchen of "21," the cellar of the Metropolitan Museum, a better dresses try-on room at Lord and Taylor, where he was made to feel invisible. Yankee Stadium and Shea and Madison Square Garden were all regular easy places to slip into without a ticket.

So were Broadway shows.

Gainer, with any old rolled up *Playbill* in hand, would simply step into the thick of those out of the theater at intermission for the air or a smoke. When intermission was over he'd flow back into the theater with them. Nearly always there was an unclaimed or vacated seat for him, but if not, he'd stand in the back with a lost look and watch from there. Seeing only the final act of plays and musicals had its drawbacks, but he enjoyed them.

The city.

He used it to prepare himself for it.

"Hey kid."

A man with a horse face. Wearing a suit that couldn't be wrinkled.

"You live around here? I always see you around here."

Gainer didn't say anything.

Horse Face told him: "You can make money today."

All Gainer had to do was go uptown to the Seagram's Building and pick up an envelope. A sturdy five by eleven envelope, surely sealed, that Gainer put inside his shirt and buttoned from sight because he thought he knew what was in it. For doing the errand Horse Face gave him ten dollars.

Gainer ran that same errand again for Horse Face and from then on, it became a weekly way to make ten. Horse Face asked offhand if Gainer knew what the envelope contained. Gainer made sure the way he said no also said he didn't care. One week the envelope wasn't well sealed and Gainer saw it contained hundred dollar bills, about a quarter inch of them. That time, when he handed over the envelope he had to go with Horse Face into the men's room of a coffee shop and wait while Horse Face was in the toilet booth with the door closed. He didn't blame Horse Face for counting the money.

That ten a week was the first money he could almost depend on. He also earned when he could by posting, upon any possible surface, posters for politicians and Village plays. Sometimes he helped wash cars at the Rolls and Bentley dealer's on Third Avenue.

For quite a while he was a shill for a tattoo artist. He'd roam around midtown on the lookout for servicemen, long-haired guys and motorcycle types. Aside, in a low voice, Gainer would ask: "Want to get a tattoo?" It was against New York law for anyone to tattoo, so Gainer would lead the customer to an apartment on West Forty-sixth, where the artist and his needles waited. Guys who got that far seldom balked, but at the first sign of misgiving Gainer would bare his chest or shoulder to show his tattoo. An elaborate eagle with a bolt of lightning in his talons, or a pair of doves in flight with a furbelow displaying the word MOTHER. Having LET ME in blue on the tip of his tongue was always good for a laugh. That a thirteen-year-old had the nerve was enough to shame any grown man into submitting. Gainer's tattoos, of course, were done with watercolor brushes and inks that only required some hard scrubbing.

Shortly before Christmas of that year a guy Gainer had seen around put it to him that the going price for a set of license plates was five dollars. Gainer gave it about a week's thought and then borrowed the screwdrivers, a regular and a Phillips. He went out at two in the morning. Keeping low between parked cars he worked systematically, removed the front plate of one car, merely turned around and removed the rear plate of the next. All the way down an entire sleeping block of East Seventieth Street.

Twenty sets of plates.

A hundred dollars.

It had been so easy Gainer almost wanted to go for more.

He spent twelve of the hundred on a wallet for himself at Dunhill's.

The rest went for presents for Norma. He had a great time buying a wool hat, a new hairdryer, and a number of other nice things for her. He wrapped and tied them individually and wrote some serious and some funny inscriptions on the tags.

Norma was overwhelmed, truly, and she didn't spoil it by asking where he'd gotten the money. He knew, of course, she wondered about it, and he wanted to tell her, but they both put it off and kept putting it off until it took an unessential place in the past.

Gainer was so much in and around the city he could easily have chosen to fall into trouble, but the opposites in his character gave him a sort of balance, like the weights on the tips of a tightrope walker's pole.

Trouble.

Inevitably, it did fall on him.

"Help me."

The plaintive voice came from behind Gainer. It was not a plea that always got total immediate attention in the city where those two words were commonplace. So, Gainer kept walking, merely glanced back. He saw a boy near his own age, skulking in a doorway.

Gainer stopped, turned.

The boy rushed to him. He was taller than Gainer and better dressed, had on a navy blazer with a school crest sewn on its breast pocket. A packsack of school books was strapped to him. "I'll give you a dollar if you walk me home." he said.

They were on Central Park West at half past three in the afternoon, the lull time before work let out. There was scarcely anyone along the street, no one within a block on either direction.

"Please walk home with me."

The boy's voice, elevated by hysteria, was more like a girl's.

Gainer noticed four toughs standing across the way at the edge of the park. He asked where the boy lived. It was only a block out of Gainer's way.

The boy walked beside Gainer with a short sort of tiptoe step, as though even with his longer legs it was an effort to keep up. He was so relieved to get home he forgot the promised dollar. Gainer told himself he probably wouldn't have accepted it anyway. He crossed over at Seventy-eighth to cut through the park.

The toughs came at him.

No chance for Gainer. Because they were four and older, heavier boys. He couldn't fight in every direction. When he went down they held him up to hit him and when they let him stay down they kicked him.

46

Gainer was taken by police ambulance to Mount Sinai Hospital. He was still unconscious when Norma got there. His condition was listed as serious. Norma signed the required hospital forms, assuming responsibility. She would have signed anything.

She remained all night in the waiting room of the intensive care unit. Gainer became conscious the next morning and she was allowed in to see him for a moment.

His eyes were almost swollen closed, the areas around them bruised purple and green. It didn't seem his eyes could see her so she wasn't sure her smile got through until she saw a trace of a smile in response from him. She told him it was a miracle his nose wasn't broken and he opened his mouth so she could see he still had all his teeth. She didn't cry until after she left him.

A doctor told Norma it was too early to know the extent of Gainer's injuries. There could be internal traumas. Numerous X-rays and tests were needed. Blood had already shown in Gainer's urine, his blood pressure was erratic and his white count was up. The doctor was by no means a hand-patter, didn't say not to worry, which would have been a waste of words anyway.

No matter that the hospital wasn't sure Gainer would be all right, Norma felt she knew. She drew her reassurance from the same well-spring that produced her fear—her deep love for Gainer. He would get well. He *would*. She refused to think otherwise, as though such a dreaded thought might be an influence transmitted from her.

And Gainer began mending. Even before it was determined that he had two cracked ribs, a concussion, spinal contusions and bleeding in his right kidney. He was recovering so rapidly that Norma had the impression she could see minute-by-minute changes for the better. His spirit helped. It was as resilient as his sixteen-year-old body. During the hours when Norma wasn't visiting, he'd lay there and whistle, a faint, thin, nearly self-contained whistle. Fragments of obscure show tunes. Some from third acts he'd seen of shows that had failed and been forgotten by almost everyone after a single first night.

Perhaps another reason for Gainer's quick repair was the mounting hospital bill.

Norma coped with that.

At the time she was working at a restaurant in the financial district. As a waitress her salary wasn't much, but not paying taxes on her tips made up for that. She wasn't yet resigned to doing whatever brought in the most money, even though this was her third restaurant job. Over the past seven years she had clerked at Korvette's, given shampoos at

47

Kenneth's, and been an assistant in the showroom of the wholesale furrier, Theodor Beecher.

She had hoped the job at Beecher might lead to better things, give her some special experience. There were two Theodor Beechers, a senior and a junior, ages sixty-five and forty. The day Norma started, Theodor Junior started on her. Not with his hands but with his words, told her what he would do to her sexually, as though the favor would be his.

Norma mentally sidestepped it, thought that was the best way to handle it. But that only seemed to inspire Theodor Junior. His verbal approaches grew more lewd, more explicit.

It was impossible for her to avoid him. Each workday from first minute to last he seldom missed a chance to speak in one obscene way or another. Still, he hadn't physically touched her, not once. He seemed to avoid contact, gave her a wide right of way whenever they passed, and there were times when he reacted as though he risked being the cornered one.

Probably, Norma thought, Theodor Junior was incapable of anything beyond talk. If so, the threat was out of it. All she had to contend with was her own repugnance.

Even the worst words were harmless, she reasoned. Words couldn't draw blood. Unless she herself gave meaning to them, words were babble, nonsense syllables. That, she decided, was how she would hear Theodor Junior.

It worked, to some extent, when she was extremely preoccupied. When whatever he said to her included a word such as *cunt* she tried to intercept and scramble it before it registered. Naturally, her brain's associating process was too quick for her. Besides, such a word was always issued in context with other active words that insured its meaning. She got tired of trying.

One morning in the vault, surrounded by pelts. With him.

"Theodor . . ."

"Yeah?"

"Give me a break."

"How do you want it?"

"Please?"

A silent moment like an emotional hyphen. She was almost sure she saw a flicker of compassion in his eyes.

"Okay," he said compliantly and, after a beat, added, "I'll let you suck me off for lunch."

Her quitting check was made out by Theodor Senior. No apology from him, so she insisted on being paid right up to the hour.

From that job and the others Norma wasn't able to save much. Usually it was a stretch to come out even month by month. However, when there was extra money, no matter how little, she banked it.

The balance in her passbook was one thousand two hundred and some.

Gainer's hospital bill was already over two thousand, on the way to three.

Norma had nothing to sell or use as collateral. Four banks approved of loaning the money to her if she brought in a qualified co-signer.

She turned to Vicky.

They had kept in touch over the years, phoned one another often and occasionally met for lunch. Norma remained grateful for the advice and help Vicky had given at the start. Vicky referred to Norma as her only *straight* friend. She made no secret of what she did for money. She never discussed it in detail with Norma who was never the one to bring it up. Norma knew what Vicky meant when she mentioned having to take care of business on a trip to Jamaica or wherever.

Vicky's most recent name was Danielle Hansen, but Norma didn't have to call her that. The name, Vicky claimed, suggested shameless Swede and practical French. She was much changed from the Vicky Norma had first known. Thinner, for one thing, and prettier for it. Smarter-looking, and not nearly as able to be enthusiastic about anything.

She sat there in her own place on a dark brown velour covered sectional beneath a slightly magenta light with her back to an expensive downtown view. She heard Norma out, then told her: "Two thousand isn't much." While those were her words, her mind was converting two thousand into fucks and it came to a more arduous number. "I've got the money," she said, "but I'll have to ask for it."

The reason for that contradiction appeared within minutes. His name was just Charlie. He was in his early twenties, underweight, dressed snugly to flaunt his build. His eyes appeared locked in their sockets, never moved without his entire head moving with them.

Vicky was both pleased and intimidated by his presence. She got him a drink he didn't have to ask for, and instead of extending it to him she placed it in his hand. She didn't look at him while she explained Norma's predicament.

Charlie seemed to already know it, had heard it before, many times. Norma had the feeling that he was pricing her.

"Stop worrying," Charlie told her with his slow-motion voice, "you've got the two large." He took hundreds from his pocket, counted off twenty that he tucked beneath the edge of an ashtray on the table. Halfway to Norma.

She was about to thank him when he told her: "I expect you to bring me four by the end of the month." Three weeks from then.

"Four thousand?"

"Okay, make it three."

"I can't possibly . . ."

"Sure you can. You'll do a thousand a week easy."

"I can't . . ."

"Any working girl, even a dog on the stroll, could do three," Charlie told her.

Norma was taken aback but managed not to show it out of deference to Vicky.

Vicky was a spectator, but her silence endorsed the proposition.

"Take it or leave it," Charlie said.

Norma left it.

She went to visit Gainer at the hospital, brought him the *Village Voice* and some huge black grapes.

He sensed her worry, hit right on it.

"Bring me some clothes," he told her. "I'll just drift out like I don't belong here. I'm probably as good at getting out of places as I am at getting in."

He was serious but they laughed about it and his ribs hurt, and after visiting hours, Norma stopped in at the hospital accounting office for the latest total due.

From there she walked twenty-five blocks, slowly, not truly convinced that her legs were independent from her better judgment. All the way to Vicky's place.

Charlie wasn't there.

But the two thousand was still under the ashtray, expecting her.

CHAPTER
THREE

I T was a juncture for Norma and Gainer, a time point.

Norma would always think of it as the year of the three weeks.

After the hospital, as soon as he regained his street legs, Gainer went out to find regular work. It was imperative to him that he pull his share, not on a hustling maybe basis, but dependably. No doubt, Norma's bailing him out of Mount Sinai was the influence. Gainer was about eighty percent sure he knew how the money had been raised by her. He didn't try to put it out of mind, the idea that she loved him that much.

The job he got nearly suited his school hours. He went around in a panel truck with a man named Jim, servicing instant photo machines. Those four-poses-for-a-quarter machines located in Grand Central and LaGuardia, Woolworth stores and other such places.

Gainer lugged the heavy containers of developer and fixative and refilled the tanks inside the machine. Jim checked the automatic mechanisms and emptied the coin box.

Jim was a horseplayer. The sort who considered not losing much almost the same as winning. While riding around between stops, Gainer read the *Daily Racing Form* and handicapped. After hitting five out of eight, including a forty-some dollar horse, he had Jim's confidence. He also had the key to the coin boxes of the photo machines. But he never used it.

One summer Gainer worked for Parke-Bernet, helping handle the items that were sold in sequence to and from the lighted auction stage. One day it would be weighty Boulle commodes and gigantic Regence bronze doré chandeliers or rugs such as an Isfahan with over seven million knots that needed three men to display. Next day it might be antique faience from Choisy or eighteenth-century Canton porcelains requiring delicacy and absolutely sure hands. He came in touch, literally, with many of the world's most precious paintings and got to see the backs of those as well, the scribblings, codes and seals on the canvas stretchers, cross-braces and frames, like decipherable commercial histories.

Another summer he cooked fifty-two thousand hot dogs at the cafeteria of the Central Park Zoo.

For quite a while, when he was nineteen and going to City College, he worked at the New York Public Library, the main branch on Fifth Avenue. His duties were down in the stacks, locating books and sending them up the conveyor or returning books to the shelves where they belonged. He liked it there. One reason was that at any time he could reach in almost any direction and learn something. The other reason was Edna Scott.

Edna Scott was thirty-two. A career librarian with a degree from the University of Vermont. She was in charge of the stacks, serious about their order and intolerant when a book was mistreated. She had straight brown hair and a face with fine features unenhanced by make-up. When she wasn't wearing her eyeglasses, they hung from a plaited brown ribbon around her neck.

Edna Scott was indeed bookish.

Hands plain as blank pages. Clothes linear and concealing as the conservative bindings around her. Her speech was almost uninflected. She pronounced Gainer's name like a book title, always both his names. Andrew Gainer.

It made him wince inside.

One morning he was pushing a cartload of returns along one of the deadends of *Biography* when he saw Edna Scott alone down an intersecting aisle. It was a moment unexpectedly meeting a moment. She had her skirt lifted, was reaching up in under to tug her blouse neat.

Gainer continued on. She'd been so preoccupied he doubted she was aware that he'd seen.

He was wrong.

It was like an activating switch.

That night, as usual, he left the library by way of the Forty-second Street access. It was snowing, large floaty flakes. Edna Scott was standing on the library steps, apparently waiting. A brown wool cap pulled over her ears, low-heeled rubber boots. Waiting for Gainer. She told him that right off.

He kept his balance, not a blink from him. Smiled his best smile and said what was right in an easy way, so they could walk together.

She lived in the Murray Hill district.

He was surprised to see a pair of Head skis standing in her entrance hall and even more unexpected was the carnival red bulb in the socket of her bedside lamp. The red took the innocence from her skin, exaggerated its warmth.

Edna Scott's body was a completed woman's body. Unlike those Gainer had previously experienced, girls with intermediate shapes.

Edna Scott uncovered.

All her well-done planes and affiliated parts were, Gainer realized, what his own had been wanting. He believed she was beautiful, the way she insisted on pleasure through him, entirely relinquished herself to it with him. He was only slightly diffident about her open-leggedness and then only at the beginning.

Edna Scott's body seemed pleased. She had anticipated vigor and quantity, but not the quality of his lovemaking. Only a little of it had been technique. He just knew how.

Never again would she call him Andrew Gainer.

He carried on with her every possible night and weekend for eight months. Until Edna could not refuse a better library job in San Francisco.

At that time Norma and Gainer were living on East Eightieth Street between Park and Lexington in the third and fourth floors of a brownstone with high ceilings, three fireplaces.

Money was no longer a problem.

It hadn't been since Norma's year of the three weeks.

During those three weeks one of the arrangements Vicky had made for Norma was Laurence Davidson. Two hundred for most of a night.

During the course of that night, actually when the purpose of it was accomplished, Davidson wanted to know about Norma and she told him the truth because it sounded like fiction.

Davidson believed her. "Try something else," he advised.

"I know I'm not very good at this . . ."

"Have you ever considered becoming a broker?"

"What kind?"

"Stockbroker, you can take courses to get a license. There's a school downtown on Pine Street especially for that." He jotted the name of the brokerage school on the back of one of his business cards. "If you're really interested give me a call."

"Here?"

"At my office."

Only later, from the card, did she realize he was an account manager with L. E. Horton, the prestigious Wall Street investment firm. She chalked it all up to just talk under the circumstances.

Davidson called Vicky again, wanting to arrange another evening with Norma, but her available time didn't coincide with his and when he next called her three weeks were up.

It was purely chance that Davidson saw her again. At the restaurant in the financial district where she waitressed. When she was serving him he said, "I want to see you again."

"I don't work there any longer."

"I still want to see you."

"No."

"As a friend . . ."

They got together the following night. A pleasant, casual dinner with no mention of their previous piece of business. Davidson still believed she should try being a stockbroker. He'd be her mentor. His firm, L. E. Horton, would pay for the courses.

"Do well, get your license and there may even be a spot for you at L. E. Horton," he told her.

"Why should L. E. Horton pay my way?"

"It's not unusual. Like most other large firms it has a fund set aside especially for that purpose, rather like a scholarship. Besides," he shrugged, "it's deductible."

She went to school.

Three nights each week from five-thirty to eight. The courses assumed that one would have some relevant background and the language was technical. Norma felt out of place, but she kept at it and soon found that stockbrokering, like many professions, was made to seem extremely special and complicated to protect the self-importance of those in it. She had to learn the precise answers to many questions that would rarely, if ever, come up.

In three months, under the sponsorship of L. E. Horton, she took the examination required by the New York Stock Exchange and the National Association of Security Dealers. She passed the exam easily and received her broker's license.

In her twenty-six years, she'd never been more delighted with herself. L. E. Horton took her on, as Davidson had said they might. To start, her draw was fifteen hundred a month. Within a year, her commissions averaged twice that.

Davidson remained her friend and business confidante. Now strictly a platonic relationship. She trusted him. He never disapproved of her being so ambitious. To the contrary. He encouraged it, advised her to take some advanced courses at a school in Boston where she could learn the intricacies of foreign trading. No loss of income while she attended, he assured her.

After doing exceedingly well in Boston, Norma was assigned by L. E. Horton to deal exclusively with foreign stocks and commodities. It was then necessary for her to make frequent trips to London and Paris and she was so often in Zurich she maintained an office at the L. E. Horton branch there.

ON a late autumn day in 1971 she went for a country drive with David-son. The leaves were at the peak of change, blazing, the roadsides layered gold. As they drove along Norma fell into a reflective mood, thought how ironic it was that the high in her life had come as a consequence of such a low.

They stopped in Banksville for a dinner at Le Cremaillere. They ordered extravagantly and about two hours later, when their hands were warming and swirling Remy Martin, Davidson complimented her on how well she'd done with her career.

"Thanks to you," she said.

"I only saw to it that you were always headed in the right direction."

"Only?"

"Those advanced courses you took in Boston positioned you perfectly."

She agreed.

"As a specialist in foreign trading for L. E. Horton you have the most credible sort of reason to make trips overseas, now *and* for years to come."

"I enjoy the traveling."

"Good. From now on that's just about all you'll have to do."

She thought he was exaggerating.

"From now on you don't have to give any attention to brokering or otherwise servicing your accounts or, for that matter, concern yourself with making an impression with your supervisors at L. E. Horton. Just act the part, make it look good."

"What the hell are you talking about?"

"To be blunt, I'm saying you'll use your L. E. Horton job as a front," Davidson told her.

He was straight-faced.

"A front for *what?*"

"To carry money."

Norma still wasn't sure he was serious. She kept her eyes on him, hoping she'd discern some contradiction to his words. "What do you mean carry?" she asked.

"Exactly that. Every time you go out of the country you'll take cash along with you. Large amounts. Cash that needs to be, as the saying goes, laundered."

Norma took two deep breaths to let it sink in. Her color left her and then returned, an angry flush. "I don't want any part of it."

"You're already in it, Norma, you've been in from the start."

"That's not true."

"I recruited you, saw that you got along. Consider yourself fortunate."

The bottom was dropping out. "Are you saying that I was set up, that I couldn't miss, that all along it was arranged that I do well?"

"No. Your accomplishments were mostly genuine. Allowing that the way was cleared, you got where you are on your own."

"Then surely you don't expect me to *carry,* as you call it. I don't have to."

"You must." A shade of threat in his tone.

"Okay, I'll leave Horton. As a matter of fact I was approached just recently by another firm."

"You won't get a reference. L. E. Horton will see that no one in the business will touch you.

"This is *your* sideline, not L. E. Horton's," she said.

Davidson answered with a slow shake of his head.

Norma was stunned.

It was difficult for her to accept that L. E. Horton was part of such an arrangement. Not old-line, ultra-respectable L. E. Horton. Large, powerful L. E. Horton.

"L. E. Horton is no more than a leaf on the tree," Davidson told her.

Norma felt deceived, smaller. What it had come down to again was take it or leave it.

Davidson, as though nothing had changed between them, ran down some of the advantages that would be in it for her. He didn't try to sell her, merely stated that as a carrier practically all her time would be her own, and, of course, anywhere she went she'd go first class.

"This cash that's . . . laundered, where does it come from?" Norma asked.

"Don't concern yourself with that."

"But how dirty is it?"

Davidson's shrug said money was money.

"Just out of curiosity," she asked, "how much would I make?"

"At least a hundred thousand a year. L. E. Horton will continue paying you what you're now making each month and that will serve as a plausible income. You'll only have to declare that much for taxes. Whatever you receive from L. E. Horton will be deducted from your other, real earnings. The difference you will receive out of the country and will not report."

"You still haven't said how much."

"If you're conscientious you can clear two hundred, two hundred fifty thousand a year."

Good lord.

Davidson seemed to hear her. He nodded.

"I'll think it over," she said.

"I have to have your decision."

"When?"

"Now."

"That's ridiculous. It isn't something one could just jump into."

"Now."

"The big money involves a big risk, no doubt."

"Practically all the risk has been programmed out of it."

"I need time to consider what I'm getting into, for God's sake," Norma protested.

Davidson pushed back his shirt cuff, glanced at his thin-as-possible watch. "Some people are expecting us. Tonight."

Norma brought her brandy beaker up, inhaled from it. As though that cleared her head, she gave her decision. "No," she said crisply, definitely, "no."

She wanted to hear how it would sound as much as she wanted to see how Davidson would react.

Davidson merely patted her hand, signaled for the check.

Minutes later they were gone from the restaurant and under way in the car and Davidson's conversation was on a different, casual subject.

Norma noticed that the dusk was taking the color from the autumn leaves. The rock walls didn't look charming now, the rocks just hard worthless hunks piled up. She remembered the first night she'd worked at the bakery with Mr. Larkin, the dough caked on her bare feet, and then all the sweat, the bowing and scraping for tips in so many restaurants . . . even Theodor Beecher Junior's face came back to her for review.

After three or four miles of all *that,* Norma looked intently at Davidson. "Okay," she told him, "I'll . . . carry."

"Good for you," he said, and turned the car around and headed for Harrison.

Within a half hour they were turning in at the drive of 19 Purchase Street.

It was a kind of paragraphic point for Norma, so much of a shift in her life it made her think of all other events as having happened either before or after it.

FOR Gainer, a similar important time mark was his quitting college. It didn't matter that he was on the dean's honor list, he was plain bored with it. Over the past three semesters he'd switched his major study four times. At that rate he might have gotten a degree in another few years, but by then it probably would have been a degree in something that no longer interested him.

He enjoyed history, all periods; but he figured that the going rate for historians was never likely to be much. Psychology was his choice for a while and maybe he could have lived with the theoretical aspects of it, but sitting on his ass soaking up other people's twists and turns was hardly his idea of adventure.

So, he quit college. Went into a business of his own. Something he believed he was one of the best at, already had a good amateur reputation for around town.

Handicapping.

He became a professional handicapper, for anyone who wanted to wager on sports, especially football.

Gainer himself was not much of a bettor. Less active than most. The bets he'd made on some ballgames had been like finding money and a number of times he'd gotten down fairly heavy on horses that might as well have been running alone. Usually, however, he'd gotten enough out of it from just handicapping, making mind bets, a good feeling from just knowing he was right more often than wrong about these contests that perplexed so many people. (Like his father.) It was satisfying to prove again and again that he had the mental control and objectivity to keep out of range of blind enthusiasm for a certain team or horse. Also, it was certainly no harm to his ego to have people going out of their way to ask his advice.

Once, when he was eighteen and only mildly regarded as a handicapper, an old guy Gainer hardly knew had handed him a ballpoint and a football betting card and implored with the eyes of a tired loser. Gainer circled ten choices on the card, casually, as though he were checking a shopping list. The payoff for picking ten out of ten on such a card was three hundred to one. The actual odds against it, possibly ten thousand to one. A sucker's bet. Nevertheless, the old guy heeded his gambler's inner voice that had so often deceived him and put fifty dollars on that card. As it turned out, Gainer's picks were right all the way down the line. The old guy won fifteen thousand and tried his best not to lie that he'd done it himself.

Word got around. Then practically everywhere Gainer went, football betting cards were thrust at him. It was almost like he was being asked for his autograph. He refused politely and appeared modest. Smart. He realized how impossible it was that he could repeat his ten out of ten feat, or, for that matter, five out of five. No reason to spoil the image.

As time went on, Gainer was presented with numerous other more likely chances to live up to his reputation and, eventually, the smart money, that most skeptical core of big bettors, became convinced that he deserved to have an opinion. He was included in the coterie they referred to as "the talent."

Such was the equity Gainer brought with him when he turned professional. He could have operated out of his pocket as did most handicappers, but with Norma as his backer and silent partner, he opened a regular place of business in a commercial building on Forty-fifth Street, just west of Fifth Avenue. No name on the door and nothing fancy within. Two ordinary desks face to face in front of partitions that created two rather small offices. The desks for the two girls who did the paper work and relayed incoming calls to one another as though they were floors apart, the extra office for Gainer's sideman, a glib but honest enough guy named Billie who had been performing in the trade for a dozen years. The place was unified by a nearly indestructible gray carpet, an elaborate telephone system, including two Watts lines and the letterhead-logo that said:

POINTWISE, INC.

Gainer had plenty of confidence, and competition. Practically every sports journal was thick with ads of handicappers trying to induce bettors to call for information. Invariably the wording of the ads implied the handicapper had inside knowledge, knew which team or horse would win because of access to those who manipulated such things. It was never said straight out that a game or race was fixed but that was the inference. Such an appeal was well-aimed at the bruised, the cynics, the losers who needed something to blame other than their own bad judgment.

Also, the largest type in the ads made the apparently generous proposal:

WIN FIRST—PAY LATER

A subscriber was not required to send a fee until *after* the game or race, *after* the handicapper had delivered a winner as promised. The handicapper was that sure of his sure thing, it seemed. Fair enough? Actually, it allowed the handicapper to take unfair advantage. For instance, say the game involved was the Rams versus the Cowboys and, say, two hundred subscribers called in. The handicapper gave the Rams as the winner to half those people and the Cowboys to the winner to the other half. That way, no matter which team won, the handicapper could count on his sixty dollar fee from at least a hundred subscribers, make six thousand in absolutely sure money. And he would have those hundred subscribers hooked, eager to send in the following week.

Gainer would have none of that.

He took a full page ad in the sports journals such as *College and Pro Football Newsweekly.* Announcing the inception of Pointwise, Inc. and his affiliation with it. There in print he pledged there would never be any one-way gimmicks or double-dealing with Pointwise. To get acquainted and demonstrate that his handicapping was as good as his word he offered his "best play of the week" free, without qualification. Also, for starters, a bettor could call Pointwise and ask about any game being played that week. Gainer would personally give his opinion. No charge.

Thus, he really put himself on the line, bare ass out in the open. If he didn't come up with a winner straight away he'd be out of business, at least relegated to the category of just another handicapper on the hustle.

He got a lot of response from that first ad, and he could feel every other handicapper in the country pulling against him. No doubt many had called to learn what he was giving out.

His winner won.

He was in business.

Pressing, he ran the same sort of introductory ad for the next two weeks, made the same offers.

Winners, both weeks.

Three in a row made believers out of a lot of people. It made Gainer hoarse from talking on the phone almost constantly fourteen hours a day.

From then on it was for money. Never, however, did Gainer stop reassuring his subscribers that they weren't being double-dealt. He displayed his losers as well as his winners in ads where everyone could verify them, and each week he put his best selection in escrow, so to speak, placed it in a sealed envelope that he left in the care of Price Waterhouse, the same who kept secrets for the Academy Awards. It was a nice piece of ethical showmanship, and effective.

Within a year, Pointwise, Inc. was grossing two thousand a month and the following year, half again as much. Most of it came in as money orders, good as cash.

Too much cash. The crime would have been to report it all, so five hundred and thousand dollar chunks of it went into a bank deposit box.

Still, Gainer needed tax help, some secondary business that would help him keep more of his money by seeming to use up a lot of it.

Several such propositions found him. Most suitable was the one proposed by Ruth Applegate, a woman who had worked part-time with Gainer back in his library days. She was fifty, not attractive, but persistently pleasant, an honest brightness about her. Her squat, waistless figure gave the impression that she might very well be awkward, even clumsy. However, she was surprisingly agile and had quick decisive hands. Applegate, as Gainer called her and she rather enjoyed being called, wasn't married, never had been, wasn't looking to be. The one thing that occupied and preoccupied her, that she believed in right down to her bones, was herbs.

Herbs.

Gainer opened a shop for her. The ground floor of a narrow brownstone on East Sixty-second Street just around the corner from Lexington Avenue. The rather small place was decorated in weathered barnwood and used brick. Not too well-lighted, the atmosphere was cozy, special. One would feel good about having discovered it. Shelf above shelf of antique, glass-lidded jars contained the various herbs and displayed their names.

Some were familiar. Sorrel and coriander, fennel, cumin, saffron and sarsaparilla.

Then there was maidenhair and pennyroyal, stargrass, sweetflag, coltsfoot, devil's-claw, beggar's-blanket and witch's-candle. Wake-robin, deer's-tongue, snakeroot and even one called Lizzie run-in-the-hedge.

For cooking, for teas, medicaments and cosmetics, but by no means limited to those uses. There seemed to be a herb good for just about every imaginable thing.

Gainer, with Applegate's approval, gave the shop an easy name:

HERBIES

Announced in handlettering on a swinging wooden sign outside, just left of the entrance.

It was a small, important pleasure for Gainer to go to the shop and breathe. The air, its equivocal fragrance, seemed to reach all the usually obscured portions of his senses. Applegate took his frequent visits as indications of interest or perhaps concern. He reassured her, told her not to worry about overhead and the lack of customers. He was delighted with the shop. Truly was.

Herbs and handicapping.

NORMA and Gainer

Now they sat in Gainer's top floor apartment on Roosevelt Island. The sun was weakening, could almost be directly looked at. Before long it would turn its cast from amber to orange and like the mere disc the Egyptians believed it was, drop behind the New York skyline.

Norma had her shoes off and feet up on the same chair as Gainer. Their toes were nearly touching. The tomato and Brie sandwiches Norma had made were gone but the plates remained on their laps. Gainer wet his second finger with his tongue and dabbed up some crumbs.

"Still hungry?" Norma asked.

He was.

"Why don't I call and have the Foodworks pack a basket for you? You know, that place on Third where I got the lemon mousse you liked so much."

"Don't bother, I'll stop somewhere along the way."

Norma took Gainer's plate and her own into the kitchen, from which she said, "I love you, Drew."

He was noticing a sixty-some-footer going down river as white and brassy as could be with a party aboard and gulls tagging along in hopes of leftovers. "I love you too," he said. Was what he felt in his throat a fragment of little boy crying?

Norma returned to him with a suggestion. She'd go to Zurich, take care of business in a couple of hours and catch the first available flight out. That way she'd be back tomorrow night, late, but back.

Gainer didn't want her to put herself through that, the rush and strain.

"All right," she said, "tell you what. I'll stay overnight in Zurich and fly back Thursday. When I get in I'll cab straight to LaGuardia for the one o'clock to Edgartown. Air New England has a one o'clock, doesn't it?"

"Yes." He'd taken that flight a number of times.

"I'll be on it," Norma promised brightly and gave him a hug, a punctuation to end any chance of disappointment.

"Better not," Gainer told her. "It's only okay for them to break their rules." He meant their rule about coming back. A carrier was supposed to stay over for a reasonable length of time, a week at least, so as not to be obviously shuttling. Norma had always abided by it, supporting the appearance that her trips were for L. E. Horton legitimate business. And recently her stays in Zurich had been longer, two weeks to a month.

"They shouldn't mind this once," she said. "Besides, I'll have a good excuse ready if it's ever brought up."

But he talked her out of it, told her they'd celebrate twice as much sometime soon, she should just make the carry as she normally would. Please?

She seemed both sorry and relieved.

That settled that, Gainer thought, put it out of mind. Still, there was one thing about it that didn't quite fit. If the bastards at Number 19 had an unexpected carrier problem, surely there were numerous others on their rolls they could have called on. Even given that she was their star, really, why Norma?

CHAPTER
FOUR

SWISS Air Flight 101.

It was lined up with runway 31 left, held there by its brakes while all four of its engines were being brought to half speed. The number one starboard engine was last to get to half. When all four were stabilized, the Boeing 747 was let go.

The runway offered eleven thousand feet.

The plane needed ninety-five hundred of it.

Up it nosed into the night sky at a positive rate of climb of a thousand feet a minute. At once, as though self-conscious of evidence that it had ever been earth-bound, it hid its landing gears.

Left turn over Canarsie, old Floyd Bennett field. Under the charge of Kennedy departure control. Left again over the ocean just south of the Long Island shoreline. The next checkpoint was Hampton, then would come Nantucket Island. Boston center control assumed responsibility at twenty-three thousand feet.

Norma was in the raised spine of the jet, the upper forward area that sets off the conformation of a 747. Originally that overhead section had been a lounge for first class passengers. Now it was put to profitable use, installed with special reclining seats the airlines called "slumberettes." Available for sixty dollars above first class fare, the seats could be let down to nearly a horizontal position, providing plenty of room for a passenger to stretch out and snooze. The atmosphere and attitude up there were as conducive as possible to sleeping. No movie. Dinner only

64

if requested. Eyeshades, extra pillows and blankets.

Even before the plane leveled off to cruise, Norma was snuggled down for the short night. Her stocking feet warm in Swiss Air booties and the music system providing faint Debussy preludes.

Eyes shut, her mind chose first her carry for its subject. The three million dollars contained in her thirty inch suitcase. As always, there hadn't been a hitch getting it out of the States. When the limousine brought her to the curb at the International Departures Building, a skycap was immediately there to tend to her baggage. The same black skycap who had been there for her numerous times before. Perhaps that was coincidence but Norma thought not. For a moment at curbside, while the skycap was tagging her three bags, checking them directly through to her flight, her eyes and his had caught in what seemed a subtle, conspiratorial exchange. Norma was almost certain of it. She'd been told there were people to look out for her along the way, and after so many carries she ought to be able to determine who they were. What, she wondered, would have been the skycap's reaction if she'd hyphenated their connection with a pertinent remark? Probably he would have gone on tagging and scribbling as though he hadn't heard. That would have been the same as an admission. Anyway, now again, the three million was aboard, the one-hundred and twenty banded packs of hundred dollar notes, two-hundred and fifty hundreds to each pack, was somewhere in the belly of this giant and the most crucial half of her job was done.

A pleasant Debussy phrase moved her to the theme that recently seemed to take over all her other considerations. She lay face up with the airline blanket to her chin, her arms underneath, fingers laced, and her mind ran with it.

She told herself she should sleep for tomorrow. When she would be held.

Not contained, but surrounded. Held against that particular length by the pressure of her own willingness. Such a new need, that touching. The hand flat on her back, skimming as though to remove its normal surface, exposing skin far more responsive. Hand cupping her shoulder, fingers traveling one way, then the opposite, circumscribing her breasts, momentarily disappointing the nipples, giving attention to usually neglected places for a long while. Such a new need. She hadn't known her body until it was discovered for her.

She should sleep for the tomorrow she was flying to.

To those particular fingers, the tips tracing the rises and dips of her, repeating their course whenever her breath was made to catch or a grateful sound came from her. Wise fingers. She had cried more than

65

once from the stir, the mercilessness of them. And often, animallike sounds had escaped from where she had them trapped.

She opened her eyes. Debussy had given way to Schubert, she realized, a symphony for piano that to her honed sensibility at that moment was like fine leaded crystal striking together. She removed the headset from her ears, let it drop beside her seat. Perhaps she should have some wine.

Two hours out.

The 747 was over Sable Island, Newfoundland, its final checkpoint this side of the Atlantic. It reported to Oceanic control and proceeded eastward as directed on North Atlantic track three.

The trouble in number one starboard engine was not immediately apparent. A defect had developed in the scavenge return line leading from the oil reservoir to the engine. Constant vibration had caused the fitting on that line to crystallize and crack, allowing oil to leak. The crack had become worse, and now oil flamed out into the slipstream. The oil pressure dropped below thirty pounds per square inch, and that electronically lighted up the corresponding low pressure warning signal on the flight engineer's panel. When the oil pressure continued to drop, the number one starboard engine was shut down.

The plane descended to twenty thousand feet. It was already banking in a full turn when the announcement came over the intercom system that it was returning to Kennedy. With reduced power and prevailing westerly headwinds the return took nearly three hours. The time was straight up three A.M. when the 747 docked and the passengers were let off to wait in the International Departure Lounge.

Norma telephoned a Zurich number but it was busy. Moments later when she tried the number again, no one picked up.

The plane was repaired right there on the apron. The troubled engine was mobilized with a starter and the oil leak located. The scavenge return line and its fittings were replaced. It only took an hour for the engine to be made right, but just as much time was needed to service and reprovision the airplane, and for a new crew to come aboard.

At five-ten A.M., New York time, Swiss Air Flight 101 again lifted off for Zurich.

Again Norma could begin counting the hours.

CHAPTER
FIVE

I N the official atlas of Westchester County, New York, the town of Harrison can be found mainly on page thirty, map ten.

According to its boundaries, the shape of that township is remarkably penile. Like a flaccid organ of considerable length it hangs between White Plains and Rye and down nearly into Long Island Sound.

Possibly the surveyor or whoever determined what was to be Harrison had had a roguish sense of humor. It seems somehow more than coincidence that the southern end of the town is rounded off as though a bit swollen and at its very tip is a familiar indentation.

Purchase Street is like a vein running the shaft of Harrison. It goes north-south for about seven miles.

Most streets on the map are indicated in common black and white, and the names of many are in such tiny, crammed type that magnification is needed to read them. Purchase Street is outstanding yellow, shown much wider, lettered large enough for easy reading. At least four lanes, and considerable commerce are expected of it. But Purchase Street turns out to be only two regular black-topped lanes minimally shouldered. A typical suburban way with old maples and elms in touch with one another high above. No sidewalks and surely no Exxon stations or Grand Union markets; not even a doctor's shingle is allowed display.

Giving prominence to Purchase Street is the force of a pattern, a prevailing tribute to an earlier time when along there all the houses were *important* houses—twenty, thirty or more rooms on as many acres. Places of such quality and detail they could not be put up today at any price. The fine materials are still available but the craftsmen are gone, along with their patience and conscientiousness. They had no apprentices. Their lines were abruptly ended by greed—the doing of things not nearly so well and as quickly as possible for much more money.

The houses, their last, are left to stand and speak for them. Especially those situated where Purchase Street is proximate to the Westchester Country Club and farther north where it continues beyond the Hutchinson River Parkway. Anachronistic, these houses that refuse to decay at the current going rate. They require too much heat and help for these times. Many of the people who live in them are caught in them, caught between pride and property taxes. Gatehouses are rented as well as the quarters above ten-car garages. Frontage is sold off with condition of a right-of-way. Orchards, vegetable gardens, even raspberry patches are taken seriously.

Still, *some* do not give ground. Wild sumac is not allowed to overgrow their walls and any tumbled-down rock is hefted back into place. The grandchildren of the children of the original fortunes still occupy and oversee that their charge is mowed and pruned, plowed and replanted. The slightest wound, outside or in, is swiftly healed, despite the pain of the price to do so.

But most of the homes along Purchase Street have changed hands numerous times, and there are those living in them now who had only hoped someday they might. An example is Number 16, a huge Tudor occupied by a recently promoted officer of IBM. Number 18 is a tall, columned Colonial now owned by a marketing executive for General Foods. Across the way, Number 17 is either authentic Mizner or Mediterranean, pale but grand, arches and terra cotta. The man of the family who lives there is quite a ways up at American Tobacco.

Those Purchase Street neighbors do not see one another, not even from their highest windows, never socially. They have too much in common, and there are forty-some country clubs within a five mile radius.

Such cultivated insularity suits Number 19.

Number 19 was constructed in 1906 on a site which at that time was truly country. It was built for a John MacFarlan, whose wealth came from hardware, the making and selling of all the things that made the things to make the things. The house remained MacFarlan until 1925. From then to 1965 it changed hands eight times.

A man named Gridley bought it in 1965. Paid cash. He was ostensibly in the shipping business, which was high-sounding and ambiguous enough. The letterheads of his business stationery listed offices in New York, San Francisco, and ten foreign seaports. Gridley was only in his late forties when he died suddenly of natural causes in 1970.

The Number 19 house was never put on the market. Real estate dealers, who watched the daily death notices hoping to get a jump on an estate settlement listing, were told by Gridley's executors that the house had already been bought. Taxes had been paid on the sale and everything was legal and tidy.

The buyer was Edwin L. Darrow. He also paid cash. His visible source of income was his law practice. Maritime law. That was, apparently, the explanation for his having been acquainted with Gridley and the reason why he had been able to acquire the house in such short order. Being a maritime attorney was also at once nicely abstruse and substantial. To help matters, Darrow was genuinely a Yale graduate and a member of both the New York and Massachusetts bars. His name appeared as a senior partner of one of the oldest highly regarded law firms in Boston.

Number 19.

Last, northernmost house on Purchase Street. Its property lines on two sides were adjacent to the Westchester County Airport. Not the airport proper nor any of its runways or hangars but the far outer reaches of airport-owned land, overgrown and serving as a sort of buffer area. If anything, it enhanced the privacy of the house. For further insurance all twenty-seven acres of Number 19 were enclosed by a red brick wall that averaged about eight feet in height.

The only interruption of the wall gave to an entrance on Purchase Street. Tall gates of iron, elaborately worked. A pair of outer gates, with another identical pair immediately beyond.

On the left, adjoining those second gates, was the gatehouse, a pleasing two-storied structure that nicely prefaced the substantial style of the estate. From there the paved drive went up, but back and forth so as to nearly neutralize the steepness. Clipped holly hedges lined the drive so high on both sides that anyone coming or going felt somehow irrevocably committed. At the crest a slight drop formed a shoulder for the expanse of level green the imposing main house was situated on.

Thirty rooms in the style of an eighteenth-century Georgian manor house constructed of brick and limestone. Two and a half stories with a pitched roof of silvery blue slate from which dormers stood out like so many identically raised eyebrows. Numerous chimneys capped by copper turned green. Spacious upper terraces, balustrades. Ivy not really allowed to have its own way up the brick wall. Rather, carefully disciplined to appear unrestrained, as did the trees, the lindens and elms. The grounds, every foot, were conscientiously attended to, the grass of the wide lawns kept taller-bladed, plushy, textured with white clover so bees were always working in it.

The house was designed in the shape of an extended uppercase letter H with the bottom half of its first vertical leg missing. So, the north wing was only half a wing. That asymmetry enhanced the structure, helped it appear not so formal, somehow more hospitable.

Off the south wing ground floor was the most important terrace. It ran for over a hundred feet, the entire length of the wing. The surface of the terrace was composed of beige granite blocks a yard square and a half-foot thick, laid out so there was precisely all around a one inch space between them. Within those planned crevices fragrant white alyssum was set out, encouraged to squeeze up and cluster, determining one's stride there.

Thirty wide steps below the terrace and across a half acre of lawn was the swimming pool. Off to the left was the fenced and lighted tennis court, a clay court that required and got daily attention.

Altogether the atmosphere around Number 19 was tranquil appreciation for the finer things, a place where venality and violence would be foreign.

ON the last Wednesday in that July, Edwin Darrow stood at the open french doors of his study. For the moment he watched a purple finch go from a begonia bed that bordered the outside walkway to its nest in the ivy on that side of the house. The tiny ball of a bird made trip after trip, nervously carrying twigs and fibers.

"Yesterday's flow," Darrow said still looking out.

"On your desk."

"It wasn't there when I came down."

"You were early."

"No matter." Darrow refused the excuse, turned to Arnold Hine but didn't give him his eyes. Hine was Darrow's thirty-five-year-old nephew, the son of Darrow's older sister who had married and divorced well. Darrow seldom exchanged looks with the man although he frequently observed him.

On the huge directoire desk was a single sheet of paper. Darrow made a ritual of cleaning his gold wire-rimmed glasses with his breath and a tissue.

Every day, Hine thought, same damned thing.

Darrow sensed the impatience, took his time putting the glasses on, careful not to resmudge them. He remained standing, leaned over and read from the paper without touching it.

There were two figures, one above the other on the paper, hand-printed about twice as large as normal. The upper figure was five comma eight. The figure below was four comma seven. They were what had come in and what had gone out yesterday. *The flow.*

Darrow was slightly pleased, at least not upset. He didn't show it.

Hine didn't expect Darrow to show it. He hitched up with a smile, said how much he admired Darrow's navy flannel blazer, asked was it new.

Darrow nodded once. No need for reassurance that he looked well in clothes. He always had. Even any old shirt and slacks seemed upgraded when he put them on. It was something he'd taken for granted all his life, just as it was natural for him never to be without a sun tan regardless of the season.

He was sixty and lean, ten pounds under for his height. His posture made good use of all his five foot eleven. It was erect, effortlessly erect without even the suggestion of a stoop. His face was consistent with that. Square shaped. A slightly aggressive jaw set with lips somewhat thin, a strong forehead and narrow nose.

The immediate impression of Darrow was a man of means, one who had benefited from conscientious breeding and omnipresent wealth. The sort who could make it through the guarded gate of any yacht club in the world, without question.

Old eastern money?

Actually, Darrow was only two generations away from Nebraska farmland athough he had never stood in a field of wheat. His great grandfather had never seen a lobster.

"Do you want to go up today?" Hine asked him.

Darrow was undecided. He held up his right hand and examined the back of it while he made up his mind. He was especially proud of his hands, the unusual length of them. He tensed his fingers, to define their ligaments and appreciate seeing them work. No, he thought, he didn't want to go up. He would rather leave all that to Hine. However, if there was a discrepancy, he as Custodian, not Hine, would have to face the consequences. That was the established code, the thing his predecessor, Gridley, had not taken seriously enough. "Of course," he said, as though it had been ridiculous of Hine to ask, "I'll go up." He folded the sheet of paper with yesterday's figures on it, put it in his jacket pocket.

Hine led the way from the study and down the wide ground floor hallway. Persian runners underfoot, a Gainsborough and a Sir Joshua Reynolds among others on the walls. When they reached the main entry they went up the triple-wide staircase to the second floor landing, turned left, headed for that half-wing at the northern extreme of the house.

Walking behind, Darrow's eyes were level with the strip of white that was the back of Hine's shirt collar. Hine was that much taller, about two-thirds of a head. Darrow resented the fact Hine was able to look down on almost everyone. He also noticed the younger man's dark hairline, evenly trimmed, neck skin showing. Hine always wore his hair cut short, parted high and combed to the side like a good schoolboy. It emphasized all the more his knubby and somewhat elongated features and it also made the most of his eyes. His pale blue eyes with a soft, benevolent quality to them that Darrow knew was a lie.

At the end of the hall the grinding sound of a motor stopped Hine. He looked out of the window to the service area directly below. There was a garbage truck and three men. The truck had *Santiano & Son* and a Bronx address lettered on its housing. The men worked with an automatic efficiency, detached from their task. They raised the hatches of the enclosed garbage bins situated along that rear side of the house. In the bins were six regular garbage containers, green plastic with black covers. The men emptied the trash and garbage from five of the containers into the jaws of the truck. The sixth container had nothing in it. One of the men shouldered an ordinary black plastic trash bag. It was full, bulging, but securely tied. He dropped it into the sixth container, put the cover on. They slammed the bin hatches shut and got aboard the truck that growled down the drive in second gear.

"The northeastern 'bring'," Hine said.

"Get it," Darrow told him.

"I'll have Sweet go down."

Darrow let it go at that. In his estimation, Hine and Sweet were of the same cut.

Hine continued on down the hall of the north wing. Darrow followed. Past secondary bedrooms to a closed door at the end of the hall that appeared identical to all the other doors in that area, solid wood with several inset panels. Hine, tall as he was, hardly had to reach for the upper right corner of the door trim. He placed his fingers lightly there and electronically snapped the door open.

It gave access to two adjoining rooms, each about twelve feet by twelve feet. No windows.

The first room had two long counters, waist-high. Several electronic calculators were plugged in, and there was various other office equipment for collating and packing, including an electronic scale that could weigh from a thousandth of an ounce to three hundred pounds. Underneath the counter stood ten suitcases of various types, leather and canvas, men's and women's styles. Each had a red and white identification tag attached to its handle. In the center of the room were two canvas bins, like those used by the U.S. Postal Service. One of the bins was half full with money, loose bills, some fifties and five hundreds, but mostly hundreds.

Two older women in pale blue housekeeper uniforms were at work. The second fingers of their right hands were almost a blur as they counted the bills into twenty-five thousand dollar sheaves nearly an inch thick. It was something they were very skilled at. They dropped their finished work into a wire basket, turned and dipped a similar basket into the loose money bin for more. A man in olive drab slacks and shirt, suitable for a gardener, placed the counted money, one sheaf at a time, on the scale to check it, then bound each sheaf with a wide, self-sticking paper band and tossed it, as though it were a mere brick, into the second canvas bin.

F. Hugh Sweet was supervising.

He was as tall as Hine but about seventy pounds heavier. Round faced, sandy haired. Like a huge football lineman. He said hello to Darrow with a *Mister*. His voice didn't match him, was too small and high for his size.

Hine told him: "The garbage came."

Sweet hurried out.

Darrow smiled and nodded to the two women and the so-called gardener, told them not to let him interrupt their work. He and Hine went into the second room.

Darrow stood in the middle of it and inspected, slowly turned a complete circle. All appeared to be in order. Of course, there was no way he could be certain without counting. Someday, he thought, perhaps soon, he'd call for a count of The Balance and see if Hine's total jibed. For now, as usual, he'd just transmit by his attitude that he had his own way of knowing whether or not it was all there.

The Balance.

That upper room contained it.

On floor to ceiling shelves that took up half the space.

A hundred hundreds is three-eighths of an inch thick.

A thousand hundreds is three and three-quarters inches thick.

A million dollar stack of hundreds is only thirty-seven and a half inches tall.

The ceiling in that room was ten feet high, so each single stack, floor-to-ceiling, amounted to three million.

There were twenty-four such stacks in each row on the shelves. Seventy-two million dollars.

Twelve rows to each wall. Eight hundred and sixty-four million.

Times four and allowing for the doorway.

Three billion, two hundred and forty million dollars.

In cash.

In that room above the servants' quarters of that house at 19 Purchase Street.

It came there in the most inconspicuous ways.

On the average, thirty million dollars each week.

Brought by practically anyone who came and went for any commonplace reason. The groundkeepers brought it along with their equipment. The men who kept the swimming pool clean and those who tended the tennis court brought. Two maids, the cook and the handyman lived away from the premises and were able to bring everyday in the satchels that were supposed to contain their personal things. There were deliveries by what appeared to be United Parcel and Parcel Post and a "bring" at least once a week by the dry cleaners. Even the newspaper boy also brought this other kind of paper.

Three billion, two hundred and forty million dollars.

The Balance.

At times it had been more than that amount, as much as four billion and some. At other times it had gotten down as low as two billion. Never less.

Where was it from?

From banks, mainly.

Many of the most prominent and highly respected banks.

But before that: from the losers, the chumps, the sickies, those bettors who phoned in their convictions to voices they'd never seen the faces of, and every following Tuesday in bars and coffee shops and other such places they passed to men who were practically strangers more cash money than they'd ever thought of giving to a close friend. From the tricks of cold hookers on the hot streets around every downtown. From the high price of admission into narrow theaters for close-ups of glistening membranes. From the turned-downs, the discredited, marked by their own names and social security numbers. The great computerized memories never forgot to disqualify them, so they had to borrow from the sharks and pay twenty percent interest per week. From the tooters, those who got up by the nose, didn't want to do without snort, blow, snow, even at a hundred dollars a smidgen. From the vendors of the cigarettes trucked up by a steady convoy from the cigarette states,

74

avoiding all the taxes. From the one-third-the-price brand new stolen television sets, furs, air-conditioners. Entire vanloads pulled over, taken over, most often not actually by surprise, and pushed out into the effluvia of swag. Who wouldn't come up with two hundred for a Beta-max still in its shipping carton?

Goods and services.

All cash business.

Dirty money.

The three billion, two hundred and forty million in The Balance at Number 19 Purchase Street wasn't even the half of it. The larger, total amount was put before the eyes of America in the May 16, 1977, issue of *Time* magazine. A ten-page article dealing with crime and showing how much money it was making each year. The breakdown went:

Gambling	7 billion 600 million
Loan sharking	10 billion
Narcotics	4 billion
Hijacking	1 billion 200 million
Pornography & prostitution	1 billion 200 million
Cigarette bootlegging	800 million

These weren't figures out of the air. They were compilations based on the data from the National Gambling Commission, the Drug Enforcement Administration, the Tobacco Tax Council, the Senate Small Business Committee, the New York State Commission of Investigation and various other law enforcement agencies.

Twenty-four billion, eight hundred million a year.

For a comparison, General Motors in its good times made only three billion, five hundred million and Exxon only two billion, seven hundred million. With the profits of Ford, Mobil, IBM and General Electric thrown in, it still came to about half as much. By many billions, the most profitable business in the country was crime.

Organized crime.

That's what the *Time* magazine report called it, along with such familiar synonyms as the Mob and the Mafia. The report wasn't really an exposé as much as it was another rundown on the latest in the underworld, who had been recently killed and who of that element most likely did the killing. A rehash. Who had passed on and who was coming on. The struggle for territories and various rackets. It was the hanging of enemies on meat hooks and the puncturing of informers with ice picks. The usual stuff, sort of low-life gossip that those criminals who rated being named in the article probably called attention to

75

with pride, while those not mentioned felt slighted.

Was the *Time* article accurate?

As far as it went.

However, was it supposed to be accepted that twenty-four billion, eight hundred million in cash ended up in the hands of those guys with the funny-sounding Italian names who so frequently made headlines and gruesome messes of one another? What could they do with all that dirty cash money? They had bad language, bad teeth and bad old hearts, and they held sway while winding pasta or slurping clams in linoleum-floored restaurants in Brooklyn. They would drown in that much money. Five hundred thousand pounds of it. It would overflow their dark walk-ups down around Mulberry Street or their overdone houses faced with false brick, close as a spit to everyone, on less than a half acre in the Bath Beach section. Were the Luccheses and Gambinos, Genoveses, Colombos and Bonannos of *Organized Crime* really that much organized? It was ridiculous to think that any of them possessed the executive mentality, the business acumen to create the sophisticated financial structure needed to receive an average of over two dirty billion month after month and make it come out clean.

Who then?

THE answer reached back to the year 1935 in New York City.

A bad February night of freezing rain, a coat of ice on everything.

Gordon Winship and Millard Cabot were pleased with the weather. It provided an unassailable excuse when they phoned home to Larchmont to tell their wives they'd be staying in town that night, not to worry.

Winship and Cabot were senior account men with seats on the New York Stock Exchange bought for them by their fathers when they had graduated from Harvard fifteen years earlier. They were right next to the top at the New York branch of Ivison-Weekes, considered to be the most prestigious and powerful investment banking firm in the world. The home office of Ivison-Weekes was in Boston.

Winship and Cabot had been looking forward to that particular February night for the past two weeks. Winship had let Cabot in on it. At a crowded Christmas party up in the East Seventies, he had been introduced to a man named Frank Costello and within minutes someone's whisper had informed him that Costello was a gangster. That was the term used, gangster. Winship saw it as a chance to stock up on some colorful conversational material. After two more Old Fashioneds he sought out Costello.

Winship never got Costello onto the subjects that intrigued him. Once or twice he tried to delicately steer their conversation to the areas of gangland killings and other aspects of underground life, but Costello sidestepped. Mainly they talked about foreign-made limestones, Renaissance art and even some of the machinations of Wall Street. Winship nearly forgot the kind of man he was talking to. Costello was charming, as well-mannered as he was well-dressed. No flash to his personality or appearance. He had a large oblong face with a slightly prominent nose. His voice was naturally a bit hoarse, deep-timbered, as though everything he said came through a congestion from his chest. He was at the party with his friend, the father of a President, he said. He asked for Winship's business card. Winship didn't think twice about giving it. What possible harm?

The first week in January, Costello sent Winship a gold-tooled leather portfolio containing hand-tinted lithograph prints of the most elaborate foreign-made limousines. Winship, being correct, learned Costello's address and got off a thank-you note.

The first week in February, Costello called Winship. Said he and a few friends needed some advice regarding an investment. Could they set up a meeting?

Winship pictured a line of gangsters parading down the hall and into his office. Couldn't have that.

As though reading his thought, Costello suggested an evening meeting which would also allow him to arrange for some interesting entertainment.

There was no doubting what Costello meant by that. It caused Winship to create altogether different mental images.

The date was set.

The night had arrived.

Winship and Cabot put on their black chesterfields with velvet collars and their black homburgs and took a taxi from the office up to the Harvard Club on West Forty-fourth. They spruced up a bit, had a nourishing dinner but not as many drinks as usual. They both had the sexual jitters. At nine o'clock, precisely the appointed time, they were in the Fiftieth Street lobby of the Waldorf Towers. They asked for Charles Ross. The attendant at the desk phoned their names up, and they went up express to the thirty-ninth floor.

The door to suite 3907 opened from the inside before Winship could press the buzzer. The apartment suite was six rooms. Charles Ross, also known as Charles Luciano, occupied them. He was there along with Costello and four others: Joseph Adonis, John Torrio, Albert Anastasia and Frank Scalice. All the men were wearing suits and ties. They had been meeting there for the past ten hours but the ashtrays were clean and no one had a glass in hand.

Costello introduced Winship, who introduced Cabot. Winship noted that their handshakes were pro forma, no wasted energy.

Drinks were poured as though they were everyone's first for the night. All sat except Luciano. He did the talking, got right to the point, said he and his associates had in mind to establish an investment fund of some sort and wanted to make sure they went about it correctly. Luciano asked several questions that Winship felt the man already knew the answers to.

Winship and Cabot gave polite, proper advice, as though they were dealing with straight, genteel clients.

Luciano was pleased. When he smiled his mouth seemed much larger. His eyes were narrow, the right one more so. As a matter of fact, the entire right half of his face seemed affected. The knife scar that ran from beneath his chin to halfway up his cheek didn't quite pass for a face line. He flattered Winship and Cabot before asking if they would personally take on the responsibility of setting up the investment fund.

Winship looked to Cabot, who deferred by taking his gaze to his left shoe. Winship's inclination was to say they'd give it some thought. But he knew that wasn't what these men wanted to hear. His better judgment told him not to displease them. He was also listening to his crotch.

Winship said he didn't see why not.

Luciano wasn't interested in what Winship didn't see. Yes or no? Sure.

Costello had to leave. Adonis and Torrio left with him. Then Anastasia and Scalice put on their hats and overcoats and were gone. Luciano asked was there anything he could get Winship and Cabot.

No, they'd have this last drink and be off.

What neither Winship nor Cabot knew was they had just come in on the tail end of the most important conference ever attended by top-level mobsters. Delegates from Cleveland, Detroit, Philadelphia, Kansas City, Chicago and other cities had gathered at the Waldorf Astoria to close once and for all the accounts, grudges and other such due bills left over from the prohibition era.

That very day, crime had become syndicated on a national basis. Territories were redefined to everyone's satisfaction and new codes of conduct were agreed upon. For one thing, within the Syndicate there would be no more indiscriminate killing. The reason for one of them to kill one of them would have to be heard by a commission made up of twelve of their kind. They could walk their streets without fear, shuck their bodyguards. When a killing was allowed it would be carried out in a new, cleaner way. Each region would volunteer the services of six of its hit men, who could be imported from one region by another. They would go in, kill, get out the same day. The police would be perplexed. Murder, Incorporated.

And then there was the investment fund. Everyone's take was getting too large. It wasn't good to have so much cash around, as a matter of fact it was getting more and more difficult to hide. Smarter if they pooled it, kept a fixed percentage and let the rest be invested. It appealed to them, the idea of becoming legitimate, and to that extent more stable.

The second hand of Winship's watch was sweeping around to make it straight up eleven. His drink had been down to its ice cubes for fifteen minutes. Cabot shrugged when Luciano wasn't looking.

The door buzzer didn't ring.

But Luciano got up, went to the door and let the girls in. Four very pretty girls. Luciano himself had selected them out of a dozen of his best.

They were young experts.

THE following day, Winship and Cabot had misgivings, of course. They had overindulged, gotten only a couple of hours sleep, weren't accustomed to such erotic acrobatics. It was all they could do to summon up the spirit to kid one another about it. Not a word about the investment fund they had agreed to set up. The silent hope was that perhaps Luciano and Costello and the others hadn't really been serious.

A week went by. Two.

Less and less Winship expected a call from Costello. He almost believed he'd heard the last of it. Part of him was disappointed . . . that all-night two-on-one at the Waldorf had pretty much receded to a fantasy.

On the Tuesday of the third week Winship returned from lunch and found two packages on his desk. Brown-paper wrapped, about twice the size of a shoebox. He untied them. They were indeed shoeboxes—four of them. Each contained one million dollars in cash. There was no accompanying letter, nothing, but there was no doubt in Winship's mind who the money was from. No receipt requested. Luciano, Costello and the others trusted him that much on such brief acquaintance, Winship thought, and then realized they considered themselves their own guaranty.

The sight of that much cash did not astound Winship. He was accustomed to dealing, though on paper, with amounts of six, seven, eight, nine figures. Besides, he was a Winship, in the direct line of that great old wealth. Huge sums were his first nature. What Winship found fascinating about this shoebox cash was how *dirty* it was.

He took up a thickness of it, riffled it, chose to imagine the very prurience it represented, the many warm, working crotches.

He quickly covered the boxes and locked them in his private coat closet. Considering the circumstances, there was no doubt what he should do. Beg off, apologize and see that the money was returned to Costello.

In a roundabout way he acquired Costello's phone number and several times went so far as to dial all but its last digit. Something pulled him the other way, offset his bluenose, his inbred principles, cut right through his caution. He would not admit to himself that it was anything so inconsequential as his wanting to experience more young experts.

After more than a week of ambivalence he opened an account for his new clients. Kept their identities secret, of course. Put the account in his own name and coded it Ruff and Company. Ran the cash through one of the banks dominated by Ivison-Weekes, not really an uncommon course of action.

Winship's first investment for Ruffco, as it was now called, was ten thousand shares of American Telephone and Telegraph. He reasoned it was the solid sort of buy that would appeal most to the men he'd met, particularly Luciano and Costello. He was anxious to call Costello and tell him.

Costello was delighted. Amiable as ever, he suggested Winship join him and two attractive friends for dinner at L'Aiglon the following night. He understood the hesitancy, the silence that followed his invitation and immediately revised it. Said in case something came up and he couldn't make it, Winship and the young ladies should enjoy the night without him. He'd make the reservations.

Winship had recently read in one of the newspapers that Frank Costello's underworld associates referred to him as "The Prime Minister." At that moment of finesse, Winship believed it suited him.

The cash in the shoeboxes continued to arrive, not regularly but often. Sometimes it was one million, other times four. Winship processed the money into the Ruffco account and made only the surest investments. In a few instances he gave the account the advantage of ripe stock information he was privy to because of his position at Ivison-Weekes. Except for charging the standard commission he treated the money almost as though it were his own.

During the first year not a single demand was made on the account. There were no withdrawals, not even an inquiry. Numerous times in the course of that year Winship phoned Costello using the pretext of business. He would have the Ruffco portfolio right there before him ready for review but Costello always took their conversations as quickly as tact allowed to Winship's real reason for calling. When it came to that, Winship was easily diverted. He had become addicted to the sort of girls that were being supplied, the variety, their erotic catering.

THE following year, the last week in May, Costello phoned Winship. This time it was business. Luciano wanted a meeting. That night.

Winship didn't mind the short notice. He knew Luciano was under pressure. It had been in the headlines for weeks. Special prosecuting attorney for the State of New York, Thomas Dewey, was trying Luciano in the state's Supreme Court on ninety counts of compulsory prostitution. Every day Dewey had whores and madams on the witness stand swearing to how Luciano had exploited them. Winship doubted it. According to the photos in the newspapers, those witnesses were unattractive, low-life whores, not up to the quality of those he'd known through Luciano.

Nine that night was set as the meeting time.

Winship arrived at the Waldorf Towers at five after nine. He'd worked late at the office, foregone dinner, gotten so involved with a problem account that he'd lost track of time, and to make matters worse, the driver of the taxi he'd taken uptown had refused to hurry.

It seemed they were waiting for him in apartment 3907. Luciano and Costello, of course, and Anastasia, Scalice and Adonis. They were seated around the dining table, lights on bright. A lot of smoke.

No handshakes.

The empty chair was for Winship. He sat down in it. Luciano said Torrio wouldn't be there. Torrio was sick in Chicago.

"Sick of Chicago," Adonis quipped.

Costello asked if Winship wanted a drink and Winship picked up from Costello's tone that it was best to decline. He snapped open the catch on his pure leather briefcase and took out a gray legal-sized folio bound at the top by flat metal posts. The Ivison-Weekes logo was printed on its cover in black. Winship placed the folio on the table surface in front of him. He looked to Luciano for permission to proceed. Costello gave it to him.

It wasn't until Winship opened the folio that he realized the mistake. He'd brought the wrong one. All Ivison-Weekes accounts were given that same gray cover and in his rush he'd picked up the folio of another of his accounts, a rather large one code-named Contico. It wasn't like him to do such a thing, not to double-check.

He was about to explain and apologize when Luciano took the folio from his hands. Winship almost protested.

Luciano scanned the first page of entries and the second. Too quickly to be getting more than an impression. The holdings of Contico were summarized on the final page and Luciano impatiently turned to it.

Sixty-eight million, three hundred fifty-four thousand dollars was the bottom line figure.

Luciano was unreadable, no change in his mouth or eyes. He passed the folio to Adonis and it went around the table from man to man. For a look at that last page. Only Costello examined the other pages, noting the shares bought and sold. After he closed the folio, he was grim, eyes-to-eyes with Winship for a moment and then broke it with a smile.

Luciano said he was pleased.

They all were.

Winship should keep up the good work.

"Yeah, keep it up," Anastasia remarked wryly to make Scalice and Adonis laugh.

Winship again said no to an offer of a drink. Said he had to hurry to another business appointment. Costello saw him to the door.

Down on Fiftieth Street Winship tipped the doorman but declined a cab, walked over to Park. To get his legs back. He tried to put out of mind the horrible things they would do to him if ever they believed he was cheating them. Evidently they were satisfied with that sixty-eight million figure. Was it possible they didn't know how much had gone into their account—all those shoeboxes full. They weren't careless with their money. Were they? In his mind he went over exactly what had happened up there, tried to recall the reactions. They'd been either pleased or acting. It had been spontaneous. They were pleased, he decided. Probably no more or less than they would have been with the actual Ruffco total.

Ninety-eight million, four hundred eighty-five thousand dollars.

A thirty-million-and-some difference.

Winship walked slower.

TWELVE days from then, on June 7, 1936, the New York State Supreme Court found Luciano guilty on sixty-two counts of compulsory prostitution. It sentenced him to not less than thirty years. He was taken to Sing Sing and then upstate to Clinton state prison in Dannemora.

In his place, Costello stepped up.

About that time Winship also was moved up a couple of rungs. He was brought home to Ivison-Weekes in Boston. It was assumed he knew he was being given a clear shot at the top.

The packages of dirty money followed Winship to Boston. No problem. Ruffco was acknowledged as his personal account. He handled it as he had in the past.

By then, some of the syndicate bosses had stopped contributing to the investment fund. Just stopped and made no claim on any part of it. However, the majority continued to put in a share of their take, true to the pledge made when the national syndicate was formed. It was a rule easier to live by than the one that said there would be no killing of one another. That stipulation was never in their hearts. So, Calonna killed Forti, so Stassi killed Calonna, so Scarpullo killed Stassi, so Cuchiara killed Scarpullo and that was how it went. The dead were as forgotten as lost hats.

Crime increased.

The profit from crime increased.

The Ruffco account prospered, with its cash influx and Winship's special care. It became important to Ivison-Weekes. When asked about it, Winship said only that Ruffco was a consortium of investors. Presumably, he was one of them.

Winship had at least one meeting each year with his anonymous clients. They were only five without Luciano, and in 1939 they were down to four because John Torrio was sent to Leavenworth on a fourteen year sentence for income tax evasion.

That 1939 meeting was held at night in Costello's place high up in the Majestic Apartments at 115 Central Park West. The men sat around Costello's dining room table with the chandelier on bright.

Winship presented the Ruffco folio that, by then, was diverse and complicated. As usual, Anastasia and Adonis and Scalice tried to give the impression they understood it, but again it was obvious to Winship that they were concerned only with the last page bottom line figure. Also, as usual, Costello was another matter. He looked over every page and asked about certain holdings.

Winship had the answers.

The last page of the folio showed that Ruffco's worth, after commissions, was three hundred seventy-four million and change.

The meeting could have been that short, but Winship placed the folio on the table, pushed it a few inches away from himself to show his detachment and, with care to appear that it did not matter one way or the other to him, he asked: "Do any of you care to draw from the account at this time or perhaps even withdraw from it entirely?"

Anastasia, who was seated on Winship's left, made a face as though he smelled something unpleasant. "Why do you ask that?"

"To reaffirm everyone's position," Winship replied.

"You never asked that before," Anastasia pointed out.

Winship told him: "I just thought it should be stated that you have the option to close out your share of the fund, take your part of the money and no longer participate."

"Sounds like a squeeze-out," Anastasia said.

"Merely a courtesy," Winship assured him.

Anastasia gradually relaxed his face. He turned to Scalice. "What do you think, Cheech?"

"About what exactly?" Scalice asked.

"Want out of this fund?" Anastasia asked.

"Tell you one thing. I'd like for a change to be able to feel my money instead of this having it but not really having it, if you know what I mean."

"Can I speak for you?" Anastasia asked him.

Scalice gave permission with one definite nod.

Anastasia told Winship: "Cheech and me want ours out."

Winship didn't waver.

Costello asked: "Are you serious Albert?"

"I got asked, I answered," Anastasia replied.

Whenever Costello talked to Anastasia he was cautious about how he might be taken. "Do what you want, of course, but if all at once you have that much money, you'll probably end up with Torrio in Leavenworth," Costello told him. "As you are, the federal tax people have you under glass. What is it with you, you need money?"

Anastasia sat straight, stretched his neck to relieve it from the starch in his shirt collar. "I don't need," he growled.

"Then for your own sake, leave the money where it is," Costello advised.

Adonis, who had been seesawing, decided on that.

"Let it ride," Anastasia said.

"Let it ride," Scalice said.

It didn't occur to them that they had just consented to the fact that the money had outgrown them, that by its immense amount, it was no longer theirs, unless they chose to pay the penalty for having it.

After one more drink, Adonis, Scalice and Anastasia left. Winship stayed on. He and Costello turned comfortable chairs to the window to have the lights of the East Side skyline for their view. It seemed to Winship that the tension was gone. It was the frame of mind he'd hoped for. He reached into his briefcase, brought out another gray covered

Ivison-Weekes folio, handed it across to Costello, who didn't ask what it was or bother to go really into it, just appreciated its thickness and turned to the last page, last line.

Five hundred forty-eight million and change.

The actual worth of Ruffco. Two hundred million more, Winship pointed out.

No reaction from Costello. Winship wondered if perhaps the man could be that good at concealing his anger.

Costello now regretted more than ever that he hadn't exposed Winship and that first wrong folio back in 1936. Problem was then he'd only been suspicious, anyway not sure enough to risk spoiling the set-up they had managed to establish with reputable Ivison-Weekes. So he'd gone along with it, no wiser than Luciano and the others as far as they knew. Now, when he rationalized it, it seemed to Costello, he'd never really had a choice in the matter, certainly not one that would save him in Anastasia's eyes. He, Costello, had brought Winship in. Winship was *his* man. According to code, if Winship fucked them over Costello was as much to blame and deserved equal penalty. So, as long as he was holding back for his life, Costello decided he might as well also hold back for an extra few hundred million.

Calmly, he told Winship, "I knew."

"I was sure you did, all along."

"Not to the dollar but my figure was within ten million."

"Amazing," Winship said, playing to it. He was grateful that his judgment had been influenced by his fear.

Still calm, Costello said: "I thought about having you killed."

"Why didn't you?"

Costello did not reply.

"Really, why didn't you," Winship pressed.

Costello sensed that this banker from Boston was making a move, although he didn't see in what direction it could be. He decided to tell Winship part of the truth they both knew. "Killing you," he said, "would have been too expensive. You and that half billion in the fund are too tangled up. Kill you, we lose it all."

Exactly what Winship wanted to hear. He had, by God, control.

"Do the others realize that?" Winship asked.

"It may have occurred to them, but I doubt it."

"How would they react if they knew about the double folios?"

"Anastasia would kill you no matter how big the loss. So would Luciano."

Winship hoped Costello wouldn't let it go at that.

After a long silent moment spent considering Winship's leverage,

Costello threw his loyalty over the fence. "They don't need to know," he said.

WINSHIP was made a partner in Ivison-Weekes in 1942.

The strength of the Ruffco account was a factor in his getting the promotion. Realizing that, he looked and saw how the account, with its perpetually increasing nature, would eventually become too much for him. It was like a spiraling, replicating mass that he was bound to, unable to prevent its rise into a financial atmosphere rare and dangerous. Left on its course, it would overexpand, expose itself, destroy itself and him.

It was vital that he take measures while the account was in a less conspicuous stage.

He decided to stake his fine old name and position on greed.

He went about it methodically. Formed a mental profile of the sort of men who were needed, and over the next three years singled them out.

Nine men.

Some Winship was quite sure of. The others he was positively sure of. The similar eastern establishment backgrounds of the nine already had them affiliated. Their lives went back to the original colony, their ancestors had fought at the bridge. Only Saint George's or Phillips Andover, Harvard or Yale were in them. They had the same double values, the same well-guarded psychological soft-spots, pretty much the same hard old wealth under them.

On the first of November, 1945, Winship invited the nine to attend an early evening meeting in the partner's room of Ivison-Weekes. And there they sat in their English wool vested suits and their shirts that had been starched and ironed just so, at home, by laundry maids. They did not know why Winship had called them there but they hoped it had nothing to do with charity.

Winship did not beat around the matter. Right off, he revealed the Ruffco account, the shady underside of its inception, the basis for its remarkable growth and its present flourishing status. He took special care that it came across as a history, not a confession. He even showed them the double set of portfolios he had been using.

No one walked out.

Winship drew the future of crime for them, as though it were like any business. What he foresaw in the prosperous years ahead. How the growth rate of crime could make it the most profitable of all industries, by many billions. How if the financial power of it were brought to

86

center, those who controlled it would eventually have the wherewithal to control the economy of the country.

They tugged at ear lobes, scratched necks, recrossed legs and picked specks off sleeves, as though motion was needed to cover their thoughts. They did not look to one another. The notion of controlling the economy, farfetched as it might be, was particularly amusing.

Winship noted their receptivity.

He took the advantage, proposed they form an alliance. Clandestine, of course. Their single, mutual concern would be the Ruffco account, all its ramifications and potential.

Did that mean he was willing to put Ruffco into the pot?

Yes.

Ruffco, according to its latest, honest folio, held over a billion dollars.

They would each share equally. As they would also each contribute whatever special service or influence that was needed for the well being of the account.

Winship had read them accurately. Except for one thing. He had thought they would take leave at that point in the meeting. Just short of commitment. Straighten their backs and ties, pull tight their puritanical coats and say they would think it over. They had long cars and obsequious chauffeurs out on the street waiting to carry them to a decent night's sleep. However, at two in the morning, they were still there, wrapped up everyway in it, assuming responsibilities, suggesting strategies.

It was decided they would refer to the body they now were as the High Board.

That meeting gave Winship the backing and the underpinning needed to make the most of the business of crime. It gave access to the facilities as well as the money muscle of the three largest commercial banks. It opened the way in several prominent Wall Street brokerage houses, their most inner doors. And it supplied a direct reach into the government, such agencies as the Justice Department, the Federal Reserve, the Securities and Exchange Commission, and the Internal Revenue Service.

The only essential Winship didn't have covered through the High Board came into place as a consequence of World War II. During the war numerous men with eastern establishment backgrounds chose to serve in intelligence. The OSS, Office of Strategic Services, was to some extent their own elite corps. It was by no means a sheltering niche removed from the action. Most often it meant being deep in danger, moving behind enemy lines for information and working with resistance groups in enemy occupied countries. Strange, that fellows from the east with their more rigid, offish ways should choose such a tenuous and dramatic part of that war. Perhaps they had the well-schooled cunning for it or perhaps being on constant edge, not knowing from one moment to the next there would be another breath offset the inevitable security they were born and blessed with. Anyway, they did their duties and killed in the efficient ways they were taught to kill whenever they had to and sometimes when they really didn't have to.

The OSS was discontinued after the war. Many of those men were left stranded, unable to return to a predictable routine. Some ran to Allen W. Dulles and the newly formed Central Intelligence Agency. Some went with Winship. Winship simply ran a modest two-column-by-six-inch advertisement in the Boston *Globe* and the New York *Times* saying that Ivison-Weekes was looking to employ several experienced people for security work. At the same time Winship made certain that word got around that some of Ivison-Weekes stock-and-bond messengers had been held up at gun point and that what the firm wanted was not someone just to go around checking doors and identities as though danger had a particular odor that they found irresistible. Former OSS people flocked to be interviewed. Winship had more than enough to choose from.

On behalf of the High Board, he enlisted those most addicted to jeopardy and deadliness. He immediately put them to work gathering information on the national crime syndicate and all those who belonged to it. They went at it systematically, and it was not difficult for them, so experienced in covert operations, to travel about and learn what was what and who was who in each of the syndicates' territories. Winship's *boys* compiled fat dossiers not only on the bosses but also on those second in command, the underbosses or *sottocapo,* those who had the elbows of the bosses and whose duty it was to pass messages and orders down to those lower in the order. Winship's boys also learned each and every *consigliere,* those elder powerful confidants to the bosses, and, as well, the trusted, clever go-betweens, *buffers,* who were precisely that, who saw to it that a boss never need be directly involved with underlings and their dirty work, thereby insulating the boss from the police. More on the working level there were the *caporegime,* to whom a number of soldiers, buttons, wise-guys, were responsible. Winship's boys were interested in them all, every *made* guy from top to bottom, and before long they had an exquisitely organized file on them. Identities and whereabouts, professional credits and personal habits were noted and kept up to date. Winship could reach into that file any minute and know, for example, where Scalice had his suits made, or if the preferred weapon of a certain soldier in Cleveland was an automatic, a revolver, a .45, a .38 or whatever.

In mid-February of 1946, the High Board decided it was time to move.

Winship met with Costello. This time on Winship's ground. An afternoon meeting at an apartment on Fifth Avenue, almost directly across the park from Costello's place.

Costello was in high spirits that day. "Luciano's been deported" were his first words.

"So I heard."

"Now I won't have to make that goddamn trip every month up to Dannemora. He was crazy. No one can run things from prison."

Winship agreed. He was strictly business, abrupt, not out to solicit or appease Costello. In fact, it did not really matter what Costello's reaction might be. The words had to be said, had to be heard. That was all there was to it.

Winship informed Costello that he and his people, the High Board, intended to take over the national syndicate and the greater part of its income. They naturally would not be involved in its day-to-day operation. That would be left to the district bosses and their subordinates, who would be compensated for their efforts in two ways.

First, by being allowed to continue in business.

Second, by being permitted to keep ten percent of everything earned through gambling, loansharking and other major activities—plus every cent of whatever came in from garbage hauling, linen supply, olive oil, funeral homes, restaurants, vending machines and other minor things such as extortion on the neighborhood level.

The bosses would make more than enough to live as well as usual and keep up their fronts. There would still be hundred dollar shoes and fifty dollar hats and cash in the pocket to hand out for respect. The remaining ninety percent from the higher profit areas, gambling and so forth, would go to Winship and his people. Their end was much greater, but all things considered, it was, Winship said, fair. There could be no holding back, he made clear. A ten year projection had been worked out of how much he and his people would expect. No amount less than their figures would be acceptable.

Briefly, that was it. A ninety-ten split.

For the time being the Syndicate need only acknowledge its obligations, Winship said. It had three days, until three-thirty Friday afternoon, to respond.

Costello said nothing.

Not even good-bye.

He felt if he questioned it, it would lend credibility to what he had just heard.

He pulled up his coat lapels and headed across the park. The wind cut through the camel hair fabric and the silk lining. No matter, he was already numb.

Only one reasonable explanation for Winship's behavior, Costello thought. The man had lost his mind. And, if that was so, he had lost his share of the Ruffco holdings. Counting both portfolios, his share came to over four hundred million dollars.

No good fucking horny Boston banker . . . should never have gotten mixed up with him. His sort married first cousins, had too much of the same blood in them. There was no telling when their brains would flop over. The crazy bastard Winship, the way he'd sat there and said all that shit about taking over the Syndicate. Straight faced and serious. As though it were possible.

What, Costello thought, was he going to tell Anastasia? And the others. Couldn't expect them to just smile good-bye to their money. It was his mistake, he'd brought Winship in, he'd advised Anastasia to leave his money in the fund. Anastasia would make a point of that. Anastasia might take it all out on Winship, but more probably not. There wasn't much satisfaction in killing someone crazy.

Costello couldn't manage the long strides that would have suited his mood on account of the icy patches along the way, and the leather soles and heels of his polished black shoes made the going all the more slippery. He had to take short, cautious steps, slide his feet along. Like an unsure, old man.

By the time he reached the west side of the park he had settled on how he'd have to handle it. For his own sake, for the time being, he would not mention it to anyone. On the chance that Winship might snap back to reality, stop playing boss of bosses. If only just long enough for everyone to get their split and to hell with the IRS.

AT three-thirty the next Friday afternoon, Sabato Nani was on One hundred-sixth Street just east of Second Avenue, parked in his gray Plymouth sedan. Nani was one of the survivors of the Masseria-Maranzano gang war of the early thirties. His record was eleven arrests and two convictions that he took as though he couldn't pronounce any name other than his own. As a result, he was being taken care of, a *made* guy. He wasn't in the upper echelon of the New York organization, nor was he merely a soldier. A sort of permanent in-between who could be relied on to do a killing or trusted with more complicated tasks. Such as being the field man for the "numbers" in that section of lower East Harlem. Every day at that time Nani was at that spot where runners brought their collections to him. Nani was waiting for it, just sitting there without a fear in the world, when the fat gray .45 caliber entered the base of his skull, tore on through and exploded out of his face.

That same Friday afternoon, Rosario Tarditi was at 130 West Twenty-ninth Street, a ten story building in the fur district. He had just lined things up with the wholesale furrier who would handle a shipment of Canadian pelts that had been hijacked earlier in the week. Tarditi was alone in the sixth floor corridor, his attention above on the arrow of the elevator indicator, when the .45 caliber piece of metal slammed into him, just above the nape of his neck.

There were two killings in each city. In New York, Philadelphia, Detroit, Chicago, Saint Louis, Miami, New Orleans and Los Angeles. Altogether, sixteen. They could not be accepted as coincidence. All sixteen were Syndicate men, *made* guys of about the same standing in their districts, experienced soldiers. All were shot in the back of the head with a single bullet of the same caliber. All were killed just after three-thirty.

The reflex of the district bosses was to blame one another. At once the points of old grudges were brought out and sharpened. Actually, the bosses did not know what to make of it.

Except Costello.

Costello found it hard to believe that he could have been so off the mark with Winship. He remembered clearly that three-thirty Friday had been Winship's deadline, and so it followed that the sixteen killings were the penalty for not having met that deadline.

What most concerned Costello, and convinced him, was the tidy, professional way the killings had been carried out. It meant Winship had an organization to deal with such matters, a formidable one. More efficient even than anything the Syndicate could call on. The typical Syndicate killer was not a marksman, never practiced. Which was why he used a shotgun or machine gun whenever he could. To make up for his poor aim.

Winship's gunmen, however, had used only sixteen shots to do away with sixteen guys in eight cities like clockwork. Such competence was to be respected—in another word, feared.

Costello decided it was past the point when he could lay it all out for Anastasia and the others. He was in too deep. It would be burying himself. His one possible advantage was from not telling them, staying ahead of them. Maybe he could cover himself, even come out of it with his Ruffco money.

He got together with Winship, saw Winship in a different light. No longer was he manipulatable or deranged, or a man with a cock for a brain. Winship was extremely intelligent, shrewd and remarkably lacking in conscience. He was, Costello thought, the most devious man he'd ever met.

Winship, answering before he was asked, said that he and his people had confiscated the Ruffco account.

All of it.

All but a fourth of Costello's share.

The opening was evident.

Costello put his life into it. He offered to be Winship's man within the Syndicate in return for that twenty-five percent, that hundred million, and any possible future considerations. It was, Costello pointed out, a perilous, straddling position, but fortunately the Syndicate and Winship's side were worlds apart.

Winship agreed. He set another deadline.

Costello was to deliver the ultimatum.

Costello did not. Partly because he wondered how strong Winship's next move would be, but mainly because he was afraid of the task and so procrastinated, could not get himself up to delivering those words that still at least *sounded* insane to him.

Eight *consigliero* were killed.

Eight of the right hands of the bosses, the well-known, counselling shadows of the bosses in those same eight cities from New York to Los Angeles . . . the victims died almost identically, same trademark, shot once in the base of the skull by a .45.

The funerals of the eight were not held with closed coffins. However, opaque linen squares had to be placed over their blown-away faces.

That was enough for Costello. He called for a convening of the bosses, explained that he had just been contacted to act as intermediary. He conveyed the terms of the High Board.

The bosses were shocked, stunned. Hated the idea of being forced to give anything to anyone, being on the other end of extortion. They were so enraged they couldn't speak English, and spat on themselves as they raved. It was almost as though they were competing to determine who could express the most fury. However, below the surface of all their angers lay their fears—the prospect of sudden death, as already demonstrated. That simmered them down to some reason.

Grudgingly, shaking their head, they gave in to the High Board.

The transition that followed took many months but was surprisingly tolerable for the bosses. They would never be obliged totally to adjust to being subservient because their arrangement with the High Board was so improbable, so invisible that their noses would never be publicly rubbed in it. As for the money, they wouldn't miss it except in their minds. Actually, there was too much money. Ten percent would still be more than enough. They were still the bosses. They would still stir up a current of fear and a wake of relief wherever they went.

The strategy of the High Board was to keep itself as removed as possible. It would remain where it was, innocent and dignified, while it pushed the criminal element even further out into the limelight.

A perverse public relations campaign.

Its purpose was to instill the public with the idea that there was such a thing as the Mafia. Believe in it like a faith. A perfect diversionary front.

The campaign got underway in 1950 with the Special Senate Committee to Investigate Organized Crime. Senator Estes Kefauver led the committee, but it was the High Board that set it up.

There had never been anything like it. Television cameras captured everyone, banks of lights increased the sweat. There in black and white, in the actual moving flesh, was crime. Costello, Anastasia, Profaci, Scalice, Adonis, and whoever else might play well.

The senators knew a certain line they were not to exceed.

The witnesses testified with self-incriminating vagueness.

The audience was convinced that crime was indeed organized in some intricate, evil way called the Mafia and that these men were head and heart of it.

It never occurred to anyone that they were really the foot.

Those hearings were also used by the High Board to shake up the bosses, show them the sort of pressure that could be brought to bear.

There were six hundred subpoenas.

Over a year of probing.

But not one conviction.

The bosses were made to understand they could thank those on the High Board (whoever they were) for that.

From then on the campaign to promote the Mafia fed itself with nearly every crime that was committed. There seemed always to be some piece of Mafia melodrama for newspapers and television to make the most of it. If things got quiet, the High Board saw that they were stirred up.

On June 17, 1957, the High Board had Frank Scalice murdered.

The blame went to Albert Anastasia.

On October 25, same year, it had Albert Anastasia murdered.

Who would believe Carlo Gambino when he said he'd had nothing to do with it.

The bosses realized who was in truth responsible. It made them very nervous. They decided to try to help themselves with a conference. They took extreme care to keep their meeting secret, passed the word only from privileged mouth to privileged ear and chose the most unlikely out of the way place for it. A little hill town in northern New York State called Appalachin, at the remote home of Joseph Barbara, who was suitably a remote fellow.

All the bosses showed up, from every part of the country. Although they arrived in thirty-four black limousines, when just one in that rural area would have been out of place, it appeared as though they had pulled it off. Possibly they could combine their intimidations, transform them into resistance. They were fed up with having a knee on their necks.

They had hardly had a chance to light a cigar when the hand of the High Board descended on them. In the persons of a dozen New York State Troopers. The High Board had known of the meeting from the start, had only allowed such conniving so it could take advantage of it.

The bosses reacted like naughty children caught.

They ran.

Mainly for the woods, which was, of course, out of their element. Branches switched them, poked at their faces, seemed to be trying for their eyes. Fallen leaves tricked them, made the footing appear solid while the humus beneath was so damp and giving they went in over the tops of their delicate shoes, soiling their silk socks. The woods multiplied their desperation. They lost hats, sunglasses, jacket buttons and one another as they ran.

It was humiliating for the bosses. They felt less effective than ever. Self-consciously they retreated to their respective territories and let it be known they did not want to hear a word about it, not another word.

NEWSPAPERS and television made as much as they could of the Appalachin meeting. It would go down as a milestone. However, no one dug into it enough to question whether or not the State Police were really what had caused all those top Italian tough guys to run as though for their lives. Many of them had stood up to grand juries without a qualm. They weren't breaking any law by just being there, nor were they wanted men trying to avoid capture. So, why hadn't they stayed in place, thanked the police for looking in and gotten on with business? Obvious questions, but never asked. Instead, the angle that got played up was these men had gathered at Appalachin to take part in secret Mafia rituals. And to accept Don Vitrone Genovese as the *capo di tutti capi,* boss of all bosses.

Those reasons for the Appalachin meeting were verified a few years later by Joseph Valacchi.

The informer, Valacchi.

He wasn't created from scratch by the High Board, but he was its product. The moment Valacchi let it be known that he was suffering with loose mouth, the High Board saw that he was properly used.

Valacchi was never anything more than a knock-around guy, satisfied to be doing just this and that. His name had never once come from the mouth of any boss. So it was no wonder that when in 1963 he was transferred from Atlanta Federal Penitentiary to comfortable private quarters in the Westchester County Jail he felt immediately bigger.

Valacchi enjoyed every minute of his importance. What the newspapers said he said made him sound as though he really knew, as though he had really been up there, and he liked making that impression. He would never admit words were put in his mouth. They were his words. He'd swear to it.

When he testified in Washington before the Senate Rackets Investigating Committee and its chairman, Senator John McClellan of Arkansas (another in the continuing series of such dramas the High Board cooked up), it was Valacchi's peak moment. For the occasion, he was dressed in a suit that was at least a hundred dollars better than any he'd ever had on. A pure silk tie that he knotted badly. He wanted a manicure but that was too much bother. A girl would have had to be brought in to do it, so they just promised the manicure to him right up to when there wasn't time enough.

There couldn't have been anyone more convincing than Valacchi. He refused to see that all the time they had spent on him was rehearsal. Like a greedy actor, he took possession of the dialogue and the stage.

A number of charts had been prepared for him. Like cue cards. Huge charts mounted with full face FBI and police photographs of the bosses and underbosses and everyone all the way down to the lowest soldier. The way Valacchi told it to the McClellan Committee, he knew them all, top to bottom, personally. Knew their records, habits, criminal specialties. He was a veritable archive of the Mafia. And, of course, it was all up there on the charts.

No one doubted Valacchi. Because no one wanted to doubt Valacchi. There were no convictions as a result of him and the bosses never really offered to pay a hundred and fifty thousand to whoever killed him, as the newspapers reported. The bosses just squirmed some, soaked up the notoriety and truth be known, did not entirely dislike it.

Valacchi was promised that he'd be kept in custody only as long as it took the commotion he'd caused to settle and smooth over. He would be given a new identity and, in other ways, be provided for. Meanwhile, he spent much of his time thinking up luxuries for his future. His keepers agreed to everything.

On the morning of April 14, 1968, in his private quarters in the Federal Correctional Institute in LaMesa, Texas, Valacchi rolled up his shirt sleeve and received his weekly intravenous injection of vitamin B complex, which he believed he needed. The 50cc syringe contained vitamins and also live liver cancer cells. Within three months Valacchi was dead.

Costello also died.

But of a natural cause, out of the limelight and far wealthier than any of his confederates knew.

Winship had 16mm motion pictures made of Costello's funeral. He viewed them alone in his study, his way of attending.

All the old bosses were dead and gone.

The underbosses stepped up, already conditioned, aware of what they should fear most and their accountability to the High Board. Not one of them had ever seen Winship, and the few who knew the name did not really believe it.

The High Board never let up on them. Disobedient Carmine Galante met death sitting in the sun on July 1979 on the rear terrace of Jo and Mary's Italian-American Restaurant in Brooklyn. Frank Tieri, at age seventy-six and suffering, had to endure being wheeled by two registered nurses into Federal District Court in November 1980 so, although too feeble to zip his own fly, he could be charged with being the most powerful of all. Tieri sat there in his sallow, age-spotted skin, his old dog eyes seeming to ask, "Why now?" The district attorneys chewed on him and fed him to the press day by day. Innocence was never a question. Actually, the proceedings were like a premature eulogy, reviewing the crimes of Tieri's years as though they were accomplishments. Funzuola Tieri, age seventy-seven, IQ seventy-nine, died six months later. Attention was immediately shifted to one Aladena Frattiano, who claimed to have been forty years in the organization, an acting boss out west. According to Frattiano he chose to be a born again informant because he found out he was about to die. His deal with the government was that he receive suspended sentences for two confessed murders, thirty-five thousand dollars every year and all the other amenities of the federal witness protection program. However, if that was truly the arrangement why was Frattiano allowed to appear on television talk shows with such forthright brashness. Would he, trying for a safe profile, really flaunt his face while naming such names as Dragna, Buffaleno, Persico?

The Mafia.

It was essential to the High Board that whenever the public considered organized crime, it should think no further. To whatever extent the High Board went to cultivate and keep up that impression it was well worth it.

Over the years, the income the High Board received from crime increased. There were those on the board who believed the original projections of profits were exaggerated. However, the money came in at a rate that exceeded even Winship's expectations.

Probably no group of men in the world were more capable of surreptitiously dealing with such enormous cash sums. They had both the financial knowledge and clout for it. Their banks were most useful. Three vast commercial banks with branches throughout the country where the various bosses and underbosses made regular cash deposits into accounts that existed solely for that purpose, accounts coded in such manner that they were automatically kept separate and never entered into the books at the end of any day.

At regular intervals that cash was sent on to the main branches of those banks. The actual handling of it was not a problem. There was no need to be self-conscious about it. Who was to know which cash was which in all those bulging cloth bags transported apparently by Brinks or Wells Fargo trucks. As for holding the accumulated cash in the vaults, many millions were not discernible from other many millions. Besides, the traditional concern was a shortage, not a surplus.

Bank examiners came in each year.

From the Office of the Comptroller of the Currency or the Federal Reserve.

The examiners usually spent a week poking into every column and corner, hardly speaking to anyone. It was assumed they were looking for discrepancies; actually they were making sure for the High Board that there were no loose ends. They seldom found one. When they did, they trimmed it off with their accounting expertise and tucked it cleanly into place.

The dirty cash in the main vaults moved steadily from limbo. Some of it seeped into the bank's regular excess reserve. And from there, out in the form of loans. (By 1982 the High Board held two hundred and twenty-five billion dollars in residential mortgages, one out of every five in America.)

Some of the dirty cash was put into certain business accounts, where it showed as legitimate profit. Typical was a string of three hundred and twelve motion picture theaters in the midwest that, on the average, had about half its seats unsold but its income reflected capacity audiences. The same sort of cash take on a much larger scale was facilitated by two fast food chains with their thousands of outlets. And by service stations, amusement parks and supermarkets. The intention, obviously, was not to avoid paying taxes on the money, rather to place it in conduits where it would be taxed and thereby cleaned. (A legion of lawyers for the High Board were continually finding and opening such ways to accommodate the cash.)

Wash.

The most significant way the High Board pulled it off was with its strength on Wall Street. Never mind the laws that prohibited banks from dealing in or owning corporate stocks. The Banking Act of 1933. The Bank Holding Act of 1956. Both had such large holes in them they weren't even a squeeze for the High Board. As well, whenever the Securities and Exchange Commission or the Office of the Comptroller of the Currency happened to look in the High Board's direction, they did so with such self-serving myopia, they saw only the impeccable foreground.

Sizable chunks of the dirty money were regularly passed through the trust departments of the banks to be converted into stocks and other securities. The powerful investment banking houses owned by the High Board were in on it, especially Ivison-Weekes. They bought large blocks of issues, often from stock offerings they themselves packaged for important corporate clients.

As the stock was acquired, it was registered to Hartco, Ninco, Vasco, Bostco or any of forty-some such entities. These were corporate code names, or *street names,* as they were called. For hiding behind. The real beneficial owner, of course, was the High Board, but there was less than a speck of a chance of anyone being able to determine that. A look beyond any of those front companies would find only another front, and beyond that, still another. Like the amusing futility of one of those hollow Spanish toy figures of wood that opened to reveal only a replica of itself, that in turn opened to reveal only a replica of itself, and so on, until what it got down to was nothing.

The dirty money never stopped flowing in.

Stock was continually bought with it.

Not even a hesitation when it came to the law that limited an anonymous investor in a corporation to five percent. The High Board exceeded that amount in nearly every instance. Got around it by simply slicing its share into such portions and arranging for them to be owned by one or the other of its investment firms and certain individuals not apparently affiliated.

By the early 1980s the High Board had its hold over many of the largest industrial corporations in America. Out of the leading five hundred in *Fortune* magazine's directory, the High Board had fifty, was close to having fifty more, and none of those was very far down the list.

This was what Winship had foreseen early on, that his eastern establishment accomplices had found so compelling.

Not the profit so much as the control.

Power over the being and well being of so many.

Most people sensed it was there, over them, but they couldn't say really what it was, or who. Something omnipresent but elusive in the upper reaches of the American system was moving their destinies more than they were led to believe. It was too vast to get one's mind around.

The High Board. By way of crime, seven hundred and fifty billion dollars had come into its system so far.

It made the three billion at 19 Purchase Street seem a pittance.

That house at Number 19 was a thread in the High Board's tapestry. Important, but not vital. It served to take care of The Balance, whatever amounts of cash were left over from all the other ways of washing. The place had been set up for that particular purpose, and the way it should operate had been well thought out in advance. No need to deviate from those ways, the High Board said. Nor was there margin for incompetence. An error would remain an error, despite excuse. It was to be understood.

Edwin L. Darrow, the Custodian of Number 19, was well aware of the High Board's inflexibility. It was something he tried to keep in mind. He did not believe the fatal heart attack of Gridley, the man who had been Custodian before him. No one seemed to know exactly how much of a mistake Gridley made, but rumor had it in the neighborhood of a hundred million.

Darrow begrudged Gridley's death. Believed it had impeded him. If not for it, by now he, Darrow, would have been at least a director of one of the High Board's conglomerates. Out in the public sun, basking in philanthropy, Penobscot Bay, Palm Beach and America's Cup. That had been his direction until Gridley's heart attack and he was told to take over at Number 19. It wasn't at all what he wanted, being on the shady underside. It required too low a profile and relatively modest lifestyle.

Temporary, they had said.

But now, eleven years later, there he was. With his nephew Arnold

Hine. Making his daily visit to those two upper rooms where The Balance was kept.

He told Hine firmly now: "We'll have none of that."

"What?"

"You know the rule against having food up here." He indicated two cartons of groceries set aside on the floor.

"They're not just groceries, they're a bring. One of the security men found them this morning down by the gate."

"I know all about that. I'm talking about eating up here." From one of the cartons, he took up a tin of Carr's wheatmeal biscuits. Its lid was on crooked and half its contents was gone. He showed it to Hine and then, to reinforce his case, brushed some crumbs from the nearby counter surface.

Hine glanced at the man who looked like a gardener, and the two women dressed as housekeepers. They were pretending total concentration on their work. Hine thought they had probably eaten at least one biscuit each. And Sweet had eaten the rest. It wouldn't do any good to mention it to Sweet. It was just his way.

"Minor things add up," Darrow cautioned, and to impress the point, tapped with his second finger on Hine's upper arm.

Hine reacted as though burned, jerked his arm out of range.

Darrow had done it purposely, knowing full well about Hine. Hine would rather shove his fist into a public toilet bowl than shake hands with anyone. He avoided crowds so as not to have others brushing against him.

Sweet came back with the bulging trash bag the garbage men had left. He put it down on the scale, untied it and spread it open.

Sheaves of hundreds.

The electronic scale registered a fraction over one hundred and twenty-two pounds. "Six million, one hundred thousand," Sweet quickly figured, evidently very accustomed to converting weight into sums. It was one of the few things he was mentally quick at.

"Don't just weigh it, count it." Darrow ordered. "There may be fifties in there."

Sweet nodded and went about it. He would count until Darrow left and then, as usual, he and the others would randomly go through the heaves for fifties.

The man in gardener's clothes pardoned himself to Darrow, who moved aside so the man could get at the suitcases under the counter. He brought up a two-suiter of leather that was considerably soiled and scarred, much traveled but still sturdy. He placed it on the counter, unbuckled and zipped it open.

Darrow observed as the man packed the bag with individual banded sheaves of twenty-five thousand dollars. Eighty of them, neatly placed to make two million dollars altogether. There was room to spare. The man distributed small white-peanut shell shaped styrofoam around the edges and a layer on top to fill out the bag. He closed it and checked to make sure the red and white identification tag was securely attached to its handle. He set that bag aside and went to work on another.

They were two of the thirteen carries that would be made that week. That was the weekly average, thirteen.

There were one hundred and twelve carriers on the active roll and twenty on standby.

Each carrier made about six carries a year.

At an average of two million a carry, the yearly wash of Number 19 was one billion, three hundred forty-four million.

Carriers worked on commission. One and one-half percent.

On two million, that was thirty thousand. In a year, six times thirty was one hundred and eighty thousand to the carrier, in cash and paid overseas.

The high pay was not because of high risk. It was to make it seem that way. When a carrier felt he was in a precarious legal situation, his mind would more likely be on that rather than on thoughts of running greedy. Besides, who would bite the hand that fed so well? During Darrow's eleven years as Custodian, only two carriers had tried to make off. Both had made elaborate preparations, changed identities and headed for remote places. It had taken Hunsicker's people less than a week to find them. And deal with them.

Take the dirty cash from here to there. Nothing more was expected of a carrier. No transactions, no receipts, merely deliver to a particular bank in Zurich or Geneva or Lucerne, in Lichtenstein or Andorra, or most recently, in Vienna, since Austria had gotten into secret banking. Numerous banks were owned by the High Board, fronted for them by nationals of the country in which they were located. The cash a carrier brought to those banks was converted into gold and held, or it came back clean, as bank-to-bank loans.

Darrow watched the packing of another two million in another bag. Enough, he decided. He had displayed his conscientiousness for the day. Surely they believed he was too interested and aware of what was going on to try to get away with anything. It was a small matter that every day the two housekeepers folded two of the newest hundred dollar bills into a three-quarter inch square that they placed beneath their tongues like wafers and stole away with. As long as they limited it to that, Darrow was not concerned. When they stopped it would mean they were filling their bodies. Then he would call for a physical inspection. It was something he had had to contend with every now and then.

He left The Balance, went with Hine down the wide upper hall. They paused on the landing above the main stairway. A dark-haired young woman was coming up, taking the steps two at a time, not so much in a hurry as to satisfy her energy. She had on silk evening pajamas of a pale peach shade that made them look all the more like lingerie. The pajamas were wrinkled, the bottoms especially creased around the crotch, and the cuffs were dragging and getting underfoot, too long for her now because she'd taken off her four inch high gold evening sandals, had them slung by their ankle straps over the first finger of her left hand.

She was Hine's wife, Lois. Her maiden name was Whitcroft, which was a High Board name.

Lois was very pretty without trying. A fortunate look with fine bones in perfect place. Blue eyes with a drowsy quality to them. An aggressive mouth, not tight, but soft and slightly forward and parted.

At the moment her lipstick was fresh, her eye make-up was not. She said one good morning for the two men and made it sound like more than they deserved. Went right past them, headed for her room in the south wing.

Hine caught up with her, stopped her with: "Where were you?"

"When?"

"Last night."

Lois shrugged one shoulder.

She'd been away three nights running but Hine was concerned only with the last. Because they were supposed to have had dinner in Greenwich with one of her Whitcroft relatives. Hine had gone alone and lied for her, and felt he'd gotten nothing out of it. Certainly he hadn't made points.

"You cunt," he said, down to her, and repeated it more gutturally, as though it was a bad taste he had to get from his mouth.

She agreed with a small smile.

He had to turn from her.

She started for her room, had a second thought. Noiselessly, crept back to him. From behind, careful not to give herself away, she thrust her hand in between his legs, around and up. Got his genitals, the flaccid bunch of them, gave them a quick squeeze.

Not nearly enough of a squeeze to cause pain.

Hine screamed. Like he'd been terribly wounded. It threw him off balance, and he barely avoided sprawling over a nearby bergere. He was drawn with rage, an animal violated.

Lois anticipated his fury, which didn't faze her. She continued on down the hall with an insouciant, barefoot gait, and she spun once slowly all the way around to let him see the mockery on her face.

CHAPTER
SIX

I N Zurich the day was practically over when Flight 101 landed at
Flughafen Floten.

Norma came from the plane feeling the twelve hours she'd spent
in it. Her face was stiff from those many hours of recycled air and her
feet felt large for her shoes. She had managed to help her appearance
to some extent, brushed and reorganized her hair, freshened over her
make-up, but there was nothing she could do about her dress, the pale
green cotton that was so terribly wrinkled.

There was the possibility that she might be met. She hoped not,
wanted to feel and look better, go straight to the hotel and repair.

At the baggage claim area it was ten minutes before the conveyor
started presenting bags from Norma's flight. Her two smaller bags were
among the first to come, so she expected the thirty-incher would not
be far behind. She kept her eyes on the opening from which the baggage
was being tossed up. Vuittons and Guccis and Fendis rubbing sides with
Samsonites and American Touristers. People pressed for position at the
conveyor to grab and heft up what was theirs, using the bags like
bumpers to make way through the crowd.

Five, ten, fifteen minutes passed. Norma's thirty-incher still hadn't
appeared and now there were not nearly so many bags on the conveyor.
Some, Norma noticed, were coming around for the fourth or fifth time.
Could that mean there were no more to come from Flight 101?

The thought caused a clutch of panic in her.

That precious thirty-incher might have been misplaced, she thought. Put aboard the wrong flight, was this moment in Dakar or Bahghazi or someplace even more remote where it would stand aside unclaimed until a baggage agent got tired of seeing it there and took it home for whatever might be in it.

Norma imagined how Darrow would react to the explanation *lost*. Three million. She wondered if anyone had ever tried to pull that off.

Or, possibly this time someone who was not involved had looked into the thirty-incher, some straight authority back in New York who had the power to seize it. If so, would Darrow and his people have the weight to extricate her? Would they even try? They had never promised that much, and she had always thought if ever it came to such a situation, she would be expected to take the fall and keep her mouth shut. No doubt, the three million would be regarded as drug money, and she would have to pay accordingly, doing time inside.

Hold on. Why such premature concern? It wasn't like her to be paranoid. Perhaps, she thought, this was a remnant of her talk with Gainer about quitting, or it could just be the late flight over had thrown her off. All sixty-four of her previous carries had been relatively uneventful.

Her bag with the red and white name tag.

It bucked up and out of the conveyor opening as though anxious to come to Norma's relief. Her fears were at once chased. Everything was again routine.

She put the thirty-incher and her two other bags into a wire cart that she pushed out and down the passageway to "Immigrations." Her passport was good for two more years, but she needed a new one. It contained so many entries and departures that now the Swiss Immigration Office had to settle for the lower right hand corner of page seventeen, where the blue ink of his stamp partially overlapped the red of one that had been pounded at DeGaulle months earlier.

At customs there were four pass-throughs in operation, a line at each. Norma did not immediately commit to a line. She sought out the faces of the customs inspectors, couldn't recall having seen any of the men before. Usually, she went through in the morning when the inspectors on duty could be relied on to recognize and acknowledge her in some small, reassuring way.

She got into line at pass-through four. It was the longest line and the slowest moving, but it was intuitively her choice. Looking ahead, she noticed the customs inspector was, as usual, asking only Swiss nationals to open their luggage for examination.

Just then, pass-through five opened and the customs inspector there was beckoning Norma to it. She couldn't ignore him. A fair-haired younger man in a newish uniform. His gesture was emphatic, his eyes right at her, almost as though he had singled her out.

She placed her bags on the counter and was asked if she had anything to declare. Her reply of no would settle it, she thought.

The inspector told her to open her smaller bag. He felt around inside it without much disturbing it.

The medium-sized bag. The same. And then the thirty-incher.

Norma unzipped it, didn't flap it open as she had the other two. She reminded herself there was no restriction on the amount of currency one could bring into Switzerland. She would not be taken into custody or even detained, but she was about to attract three million dollars worth of attention that would mark her everywhere from then on.

The customs inspector's hand froze when, for the first time, he noticed the red and white name tag. He tried not to show that he had come within an instant of making an expensive error. Methodically he zipped the thirty-incher closed and chalked a Z-like stroke on the ends of all three of Norma's bags. He dismissed her by taking his attention to the person next in line.

AT that moment two "middlemen" were in room 438 of Zurich's Dolder Grand Hotel.

The one with the waxy complexion, the taller, bony middleman, was Eugene Becque. He was forty-seven, had brown thinning hair and large, unpleasing features. The sunken bruise-colored circles beneath his eyes pronounced the sockets, made him appear both tired and cadaverous. There were patchy networks of burst capillaries on the skin over his cheekbones, on the bulb of his nose and behind his ears. Becque wore a black-on-gray woven pinstripe suit that he had bought less than two weeks ago on the Boulevard Malesherbes. He did not seem comfortable in it. He'd had the trouser bottoms cut off too high so when he was standing, his socks showed. His black tie was carelessly knotted, pushed up unevenly into the shirt collar that was a full size large. The collar hit so low Becque's Adam's apple stood out like something sharp stuck in his throat.

The other middleman was in his late thirties but looked ten years older. Emil Ponsard. He was in charge. His hair was fuzzy and flying from his temples to his ears and his overgrown brows had no particular direction. He could have been taken for a doctor or perhaps a professor. He was a little less than medium height, thick in the chest, shoulders and neck. His round face and fall-away chin added to the impression that his heaviness was fat. Actually, he was rock solid.

Ponsard was seated on the yellow damask-covered sofa, hunched forward on the edge of it with his forearms on his knees. He was using his fingernails to clean beneath his fingernails.

"Keep watching," he told Becque.

Becque had taken his eye away from the peephole in the door. He was tired of having to squint, being alerted to everyone who passed down the corridor. He disregarded Ponsard, and went over to a room service tray on the dresser. The coffee had gone cold hours ago and the cream in the pitcher had a scummy yellow coat on it. Becque was hungry again. They hadn't planned on eating there. Perhaps he'd call down again, have something more sent up. He shoved what was left of a poppy-seed roll into his mouth and drank the cream, was still chewing when he went into the bathroom to urinate. He didn't bother to close the door.

Ponsard lighted a cigarette with the half-inch stub of the one he'd been smoking. His brand was Galoise, the strongest. He smoked with his mouth far more than his hands, kept the cigarette between his lips and sometimes between his teeth so that he was inhaling to some extent with every breath. His clothing, such as the dark blue wool twill suit and vest he was wearing, was permeated with the odor of burned black tobacco. Ponsard was surprised to hear Becque in the bathroom washing his hands. It irritated him a bit that Becque was not even that predictable.

Becque came out and lay on the bed with his shoes on. No respect for the fresh white linen coverlet.

"Off the bed," Ponsard motioned. "Get off."

"I'm tired."

"We can't mess up this room."

The room was registered to a reputable man and wife from Stockholm who had motored to Lugano and would not return until they got word that it was all done.

Becque remained as he was. From his jacket pocket he took a folded half page that he'd torn from the Paris newspaper, *Le Matin.* From the sports section. A listing of that afternoon's entries at Longchamp racetrack. Becque had circled a horse in the eighth race with such emphasis that the paper was perforated. He believed that horse owed him. He'd bet and lost on it three times, but today he'd not been there to bet and now the eighth had been run and that horse was the winner. Becque didn't actually know the results of the eighth but he believed that was the way luck would treat him if he gave it such a chance.

This "order", Becque thought. If it had come off on time he would have been back in Paris at Longchamp. He crumpled the piece of newspaper and tossed it at the wastebasket beside the dresser. It fell short.

"Pick it up," Ponsard said.

Becque's expression said *fuck you*.

Ponsard let it pass. He puffed up a cloud around him. There was already a layer of smoke in the contained atmosphere of the room, like an elongated phantasmagoric tissue made visible by the window light. "Can you think of anything we've overlooked?" He put the question to himself more than to Becque.

Becque shook his head irritably.

"Let's go over it again." Ponsard opened a black leather satchel that was on the low table in front of the sofa.

Becque said *no*. He just wanted to do the order and leave. He didn't like Ponsard just as he hadn't liked the middleman he'd worked with on his most recent order in Nice. He preferred doing any order alone. He'd never seen or heard of Ponsard until they'd joined up yesterday at the airport, and he probably would never see him again. He did not even wonder what Ponsard did on the outside. He rolled over and used the other pillow to shield his eyes.

Ponsard went to the door, sighted through the peephole. He carried the desk chair to the door. Sat there for Galoise after Galoise. Whenever he heard someone in the corridor he stood and peeked out.

Nearly an hour passed.

Ponsard shook Becque awake.

It was time.

They put on white cotton gloves. Ponsard picked up the black satchel and they went out.

The room directly opposite was Number 450. Ponsard stood to one side of the door to that room, Becque across from him, both out of view of its peephole.

Becque gave the door two official raps.

"Yes?" From within. Norma's voice.

"Message," Becque said in an appropriate voice.

"Slip it under the door," Norma instructed.

Becque slipped an authentic sealed hotel message envelope under the door and said, "There is also a package."

Norma turned the knob.

As soon as the door was unlatched Becque shouldered it all the way open. In nearly the same motion his hand went to Norma's throat, driving her backward. His powerful bony fingers clutched, squeezed her windpipe and voicebox.

Ponsard stepped in and closed the door.

Norma was in panties and bra.

Becque shoved her against the wall, his arm straight out, keeping his hold on her throat.

They did not want a struggle, no lamps or anything else broken.

Norma couldn't scream. She flailed, her fist beat futilely on Becque's arm and shoulder. She couldn't reach his face, and the way he was standing, sideways, his crotch was out of range of her barefoot kicks.

"Be quiet," Becque said.

Norma told herself they were thieves. After the money. When they didn't find it they would run.

Becque told her: "Don't struggle and we won't kill you. Okay?"

She nodded.

But Becque didn't believe her, didn't let up on her throat. He turned her partly around, for Ponsard to undo her brassiere and pull it off.

That changed Norma's mind about them. They meant to rape her. She was no match for them. Worse for her if she fought. It would be over that much sooner if she didn't. Good thing there were two of them. One alone would be more likely to do something more terrible. She'd try to blank her mind. She stopped resisting.

From the black satchel Ponsard took a canvas restraining belt about ten inches wide. It was lined with soft flannel to prevent bruising and friction burns. He wrapped it around Norma, around her arms at her sides, fastened another smaller restraining belt around her lower legs. They sat her down on the floor. All the while Becque had not lessened his grip on her throat. He didn't believe she'd scream now, seeing the fear and apparent give-up in her eyes, but he wouldn't count on it. And Becque was now glad he hadn't filled this order alone. He could have done it but not the way they had specified.

Ponsard brought out a loaf of ordinary bread. He broke it open and dug out its soft interior that he compressed into a doughy ball nearly the size of his fist. He set that aside and gave his attention to an unlabeled pharmacist's vial containing eight Methaquaalude tablets, 300 mgs. each. And a bottle of Martell cognac. Using his thumb and forefinger he put such inward pressure on Norma's jaw, left and right, that her mouth and teeth were forced to open. Her head was angled up, lips protruding. Ponsard dropped five of the Methaquaalude tablets into her mouth. One would have been enough.

Norma felt them hit and stick beyond her tongue. She could not get enough force in her cough to dislodge them.

Becque used his free hand to pinch her nostrils closed.

Ponsard poured cognac into her mouth.

She managed to spit out some of it, but it was poured and poured and eventually she had to swallow in order to breathe. The five Methaquaalude tablets were washed down by five to six ounces of the brandy.

Ponsard picked up the doughy ball of bread. He worked it a little more and then used the same thumb and forefinger pincer technique to make her open her mouth. He forced the doughball into her mouth, stuffed it in, filled her mouth to its roof and all around, kept stuffing until her cheeks bulged.

Becque released her neck.

The dough served as the most efficient gag, better in this case than a tied cloth or adhesive tape, avoiding the possibility of any binding marks or irritation or foreign substance on the skin. The crammed lump was congealed almost like plaster. There was no way Norma could disgorge it. The sounds she made were choked back, and if overheard they would be taken as the sort of sounds often generated by passion.

Norma, of course, now realized only too well that these men were neither robbers nor rapists. They were there on account of the money she had skimmed from her carries over the past few years. Oh God, how foolish of her. She had skimmed the first time only as a sort of self-dare. When she had gotten away with it she couldn't resist skimming the same amount the same way the next time, and then time after time. She certainly hadn't done it entirely for the money, but she had done it. These men intended to punish her. This was the punishment. The beginning of it. Gainer and his warning advice came to her mind. Too late for now.

They lifted her onto the bed, pulled down the sheet and coverlet. Becque got some tools from the black valise and went into the bathroom.

Norma's dress was where she had tossed it over the back of a chair. Ponsard put it on a hanger, straightened it and zipped it up, placed the belt she had worn over the hook of the hanger just as she would have done. Hung the dress in the closet. Picked up her shoes from where she had kicked them off, stood them up in a neat pair on the floor of the closet beneath the dress. Folded the panties and bra he had taken off of her, put them and her stockings in one of the dresser drawers.

Norma continued to scream inside as she watched Ponsard. He appeared so naturally preoccupied when he opened her bags, the small and the medium, and transferred things from them to the closet and dresser drawers. He did it with haste but also with care, folded tidily, smoothed with the back of his white-gloved hand.

The cognac combined with the Methaquaaludes. Norma felt her

extremities tingling as though grains of sand were blowing on them. Her feet and lower legs seemed too heavy. The dough impacted in her mouth was causing her jaws to ache terribly.

Ponsard placed her hairbrush and comb on the vanity top, was very precise about them, their relative positions. Also her clear plastic kit of make-up and a believable scatter of bobby pins and the tortoise combs she used to hold back her hair. He brought her hand mirror to the nightstand by the bed. On the mirror's face he emptied a two gram vial of cocaine. He called for Becque to come help him.

Becque moved Norma so she lay across the bed, facing upward, her head over the edge. He pulled downward on her hair, harshly so as to have her head inverted.

Ponsard rolled a brand new hundred dollar bill, formed it into a narrow tube like a short sipping straw, tamped the end of it into the cocaine, forcing the white powder up into the shaft of the bill until he had about a half inch of it in. He inserted the tip of the bill into one of Norma's nostrils and blew on its other end, blew the cocaine into her. He repeated the procedure five times. Norma was left lying across the bed. The upper part of her face became numb.

Becque returned to whatever he was doing in the bathroom.

Ponsard used a razor blade on the surface of the mirror to separate a portion of the cocaine and form it into two lines. He leaned over to it with the rolled hundred dollar bill and, keeping an eye on the bathroom for Becque, drew the white lines up into his nostrils. He placed the razor blade and the bill on the mirror, adjacent to the remaining cocaine. Also, next to the mirror he set down the vial of Methaquaalude tablets, purposely dropped the top of the vial to the floor.

Two empty but used glasses. Ponsard poured some cognac into each and spilled a small pool of it on the marble top of the nightstand. He placed one of the glasses in the spill and then elsewhere on the marble so it left several wet rings. He stood the other glass up beneath the bed and knocked it over. The cognac soaked onto the carpet.

The final item from the black valise was a vibrator, the sort not customarily used for a legitimate massage. Its motorized element was housed in its ten-inch handle and attached to that was its vibrating end, a pliable plastic sphere about two and a half inches in diameter. It had two speeds, moderate and intense, a choice that depended on the condition of nerve ends. Ponsard plugged the vibrator into a coily extension cord, plugged the cord into the socket nearest the bed. He put the vibrator into Norma's hand, closed her fingers around the handle of it several times at various places.

Becque returned, saying he was finished with the bathroom.

III

Ponsard told him to go back in and get some tissues.

Becque didn't mind because he knew what would be next. The woman was the sort that appealed to him, fair skinned with an abundance of dark pubic hair, slightly heavy breasts and hips. He didn't like swarthy women. Even if they came from families that had been French or Italian or Spanish for ten generations, they had some African in them, Becque believed. The only fault with this woman on the bed was her face. It was too handsome for his taste. He preferred a pug sort of face with less definite features.

Becque rolled Norma over roughly and pulled her by the feet so that she was not quite half off the bed, her buttocks just on the edge of it.

Norma's senses were now confounded. She felt cold except for her skin that now seemed hot, as though it had been sandpapered. Every inch of her was perspiring. Her heart felt like a fist inside her, opening and closing at a strenuous rate, and yet her breathing was shallow and slow. One moment her mind was so sharp she could recall anything, the next it was so hazed over she lost hold of the immediate circumstances. Her fingers and feet were twitching uncontrollably and the sounds of protest she had been making were now impotent, guttural moans.

Ponsard removed the restraining strap from her ankles. That act stirred up a resistance in her that really was no more than a fragment of the notion of resisting. She grasped at the thought of moving her legs, kicking, but it seemed the very air held them down.

Becque took off his jacket, shoes and trousers. He was not wearing undershorts. He held his cock with his right hand, flopped it as though to shake it out of itself, larger. He pulled back the foreskin, braced himself and leaned forward over Norma, rubbed his cock over the back of her thighs and across her buttocks and after a while could no longer do that because his cock was hard, angled upward.

Ponsard tried not to look at Becque's cock. It made him both angry and respectful. It was, he thought, exceptionally large, the head of it like a huge magenta mushroom cap. He parted Norma's legs for Becque.

She began to slide off the bed.

Ponsard hurried around to the opposite side, pulled her back in position. To prevent her from sliding off again he got on the bed and lay down across her.

Becque spread Norma's legs wide. He worked his tongue around in his mouth for saliva and spat onto his fingers, used the saliva to slicken his cock. Parted her with the thumbs of both hands and shoved his cock into her, all of it all the way in on the first stroke.

Ponsard, from his crosswise position, could not see as well as he would have liked, but his imagination was active.

Norma knew what was being done to her, and then she did not.

Bacque made it last a while. When he came, after the first two spasms, he removed his cock and quickly found her anus with it. He then wiped himself with a couple of the tissues, which he dropped at bedside. He dressed, sat in the chair across the way, waiting for Ponsard to take his turn.

Ponsard used the vibrator, pressed it against the base of his cock while his free hand stroked. He did it while sitting beside Norma, every so often interrupting himself to take hold of Norma's buttocks or to run his finger the length of her vagina. He came into the sheets and a hotel tissue, which was the purpose in his coming. He crumpled the tissue and tucked it beneath the mattress.

Becque took the wide restraining belt off of Norma and carried her to the bathroom. A large bath tiled white, with a separate enclosed stall shower. The shower door was clear, of heavy gauge safety glass. Ponsard held the shower door open. Becque put her in, propped her up in the far corner of it. For a moment Norma looked right at Becque, and he felt her eyes transfixed on his. Her knees gave way, locked, gave way again and locked. She tried for the chrome handrail, missed it by inches. Ran her hand along the tiles and managed to get the rail, but her fingers wouldn't mind, kept jerking and losing it. Her head dropped, again and again.

Becque avoided her eyes.

The shower control was the rotation type with a single white porcelain handle and indicator that worked in conjunction with a fixed chrome plate. It went left to right, from cold to hot. Becque had altered the mechanism so it would lock in the extreme heat position and appear to be a malfunction.

Ponsard reached in and turned the handle as far as it would go.

The hot water sprayed down.

Upon Norma.

She could not avoid it. Even if she had been able to react normally it still would have hit full on her.

Ponsard shut the shower door, leaned against it.

The water was scalding. The interior of the glass became coated with steam so that they could not see it. Norma hit against it, weakly. The cry in her now was unmistakably one of pain, but it wasn't loud enough to be heard. Five minutes after her cry ceased, Ponsard opened the shower door.

She was down in the near corner in a stiff, contorted position.

Eyes open but set.

Avoiding the water, Ponsard forced her teeth apart and dug out the doughy wad, including what was lodged between her gums and cheeks, upper and lower, all around. He handed it to Becque, who flushed it down the toilet.

Ponsard was about to try for Norma's pulse when her hand twitched. It startled him.

A little closed-mouth laugh from Becque.

Ponsard gave her a shove. She toppled to the far corner of the shower, more directly in the scalding stream.

Her skin was splotched. Bright crimson and glaucous, already rising into blister sacs in large areas.

The hotel, with its two hundred rooms, had an endless quantity of boiling hot water.

Becque and Ponsard waited another fifteen minutes before looking in on Norma again. Ponsard took her pulse. He believed she was dead. She was.

CHAPTER
SEVEN

T HE morning of that same Wednesday.
From Woods Hole to Vineyard Haven the ferry was five minutes early. The Sound was as calm as it ever got, but the wind from
the east was blowing high up for some reason, not scuffing the surface.

Aboard was Gainer. Outside on the upper deck, sighting shoreward,
he saw ahead off to the right the white painted cylindroid that was West
Chop Lighthouse. He heard the buoy bells, lazier than usual, and
the cries of the gulls seemed closer with scarcely any wind to carry
them. He imagined they were announcing him, not to everyone, just
to her.

All the way into the harbor Gainer remained there on the upper deck.
It was the best possible vantage. He told himself he shouldn't expect
to see her. Their arrangement had been she would wait at the cottage.
Still, as the ferry approached and maneuvered broadside to the landing,
he searched among those there to meet it. The color of nutmeg was
what he looked for, the shade of her hair, and when he didn't find it
he tried to make up for the letdown with distractions: the private boats
tied up directly across the harbor; an overtanned woman in a white
bikini polishing the brass of one of them. But he was drawn back to
again scan the crowd on the landing.

And there she was.

Leslie.

His insides did a catch.

How could he possibly have missed her? She was so outstanding. Her eyes were right on him, and she had both hands as high as possible, waving. A stray breeze chose that moment to take her hair across her face. She made no attempt to discipline it. That was so much like her.

Gainer hurried down to the lower deck and got into his car. He was the sixth to drive off, and not to hold up those cars in line behind him he could stop only long enough for Leslie to jump in.

No hellos. In their entire year and a half they had not said either hello or good-bye to one another, as though in that small way refusing to submit to the time they spent apart. It had been only four days this time, but seemed longer for them both. Leslie's kiss missed, got mostly the right corner of his mouth and a lot of cheek. Her bare arms were quick and tight around his neck, almost yanking him to her, and it was particularly cruel that he had to resist, pay attention to the Main Street traffic, vacationers on foot, assuming right of way, darting between and across.

"Where's Norma?"

Gainer told her of Norma's unexpected carry. Matter of fact.

She read through his tone, would do her best to offset his disappointment, and her own. She had a limited but accurate understanding of what Norma did for a living, was the only one Gainer had ever confided in about it. It was the sort of chancy, across-the-grain thing that rather appealed to her. A few times she had tried to pry Gainer for details but had gotten nowhere. Her excuse for being so inquisitive was that a dozen years back a man she had met and known not very well for a brief time had obliquely proposed she do the very thing Norma was doing. At the time she was twenty-six and a very busy model with the Ford Agency. Not the highest paid nor the most in demand, but close to it. She was always flying somewhere, to Europe practically every month, for *Vogue* or *Harper's Bazaar* or some other fashion client. Being a carrier of money would have been easy for her, and, perhaps if she hadn't been making a hundred an hour then, just for being herself in someone else's brand new clothes, she might have given the offer more than a mere in-and-out thought.

"It was wrong," she said incredibly.

"Hmm?"

"My intuition told me you'd be on the ten o'clock."

"You were there for the ten?"

"And the nine," she gladly admitted.

Gainer took that for all it was worth. He smiled, a nice one for her.

"You have winning ways," she said.

"But you're the champ."

"What time did you leave the city?"

"Around four."

"You look sleepy. Aren't you sleepy?"

"No."

"Let me drive."

Before she said it he was already looking for a place to pull over. They were out of Vineyard Haven proper by then. The road did not have much shoulder so he had to continue on quite a ways before he came to a place to stop.

There, by a rock wall at the roadside, as though especially for their eyes, was some Bouncing Bet in bloom and some cosmos with pink exclamation points arranged around a large drop of yellow. Gainer got out. Leslie could have just slid over into the driver's seat but she also got out.

They met halfway around the front of the car for what the haste at the ferry landing had denied them. Went against one another and felt their fit to each other. Leslie was tall, in heels nearly the same height as he, so their holding was effortless, reciprocal; breast against chest, center to center, presses and rubs, some not so subtle. They did not kiss right away, put off the kiss and just held, nuzzled one another's neck skin and hair like sweet animals, and breathed one another.

The air around them was also disturbed, although that was caused by cars passing. They kissed and kept on kissing through several good-natured honks.

When they were again in the car and under way the first thing said came from them both at the same time, word for word.

"I love you."

They laughed at the nice coincidence.

Leslie pushed the car right up to seventy-five. It was a rental, a this year's Chevrolet, already overworked. Leslie considered herself a much better driver than passenger. She couldn't take anyone's obedient poking along, and even when riding with Gainer, who, in her opinion, was a better than fair fast driver, she wasn't satisfied until she took over the wheel. She drove with admirable authority but with such alarming abandon that Gainer often found himself involuntarily bracing with his legs and hanging on.

He remembered Leslie telling him about an instance when she was being chauffeured in her husband's Rolls-Royce Silver Wraith on the way home from a long weekend at his place in Bedford Hills, unable just to be luxuriously taken, to sink in all that plush and smell the freesia that was placed fresh daily in the tiny crystal vase attached to the window post. She'd had the chauffeur stop and exchange places with her. Made the Saw Mill River Parkway her Le Mans. The engine of the Rolls, she rationalized, was in need of a blowing out. A hundred and twenty miles per hour would do more for it than any thousand dollar tune-up. Over the short distance from Mount Kisco to the Elmsford toll station she got three speeding tickets, and was damned aggravated by those interruptions. The chauffeur quit that evening. Rodger, her husband, was amused. What else?

Now, on the island of Martha's Vineyard, she had just driven through North Tisbury Village at a speed that for her was quite humane, whipping grass and top-heavy Queen Anne's lace around the nearly ninety degree curve at Priester's Pond.

Gainer took a quiet, deep breath and slackened his neck and shoulders. He began humming any song to convey how loose he was. "So the mosquitoes really got to you?" he said.

"In unlikely places."

"For instance."

"You'll see. Did you go to Zabar's?"

"I forgot."

She didn't believe him for a second. "All I had for breakfast was some sprouts."

Gainer reached to the rear seat for the orange printed Zabar's bag with the unsliced loaf of raisin pumpernickel in it. The bread, as usual, was crusted hard, wouldn't be easily torn. Gainer managed to get his fingernails into it, broke off a hunk larger than he had intended, nearly a third of the loaf. She took it from him, didn't say it was too much, went right at gnawing on it.

A raisin had fallen onto his lap. It eluded him. He dug at his crotch for it, lifted and felt and finally got it. Tossed it in his mouth and went to humming again as she was doing a one-handed eighty-five.

It was easier for Gainer if he kept his eyes off the road and on her. She was, he thought, his perfect distraction. Wearing hardly anything at the moment—white shorts of a soft cotton and a matching drawstring blouse that had an extremely deep-cut neckline and no way to keep it closed. Gainer stole glimpses of her left breast all the way to its nipple, pink and firm like the tip of a baby's finger.

Leslie caught him at it.

His shrug said he couldn't help himself.

She was the most beautiful woman to have ever shared anything with him, Gainer believed. He would never tire of looking at her. Such as now, her profile. He noticed she lifted her chin slightly to lengthen the line of her throat and knew she wasn't actually all intent on the road ahead. It was for him, he thought, generous of her, allowing him to appreciate. He could do that with his eyes closed, often did.

Knew her by heart.

Her hair, baby fine but abundant, a soft parenthesis for her face. She wore it most often not quite shoulder length, full and choppy with strands that seemed wayward, not intentionally mussed. Her nose was straight as could be, narrow and perfectly related to her mouth and eyes. Her mouth had a natural *moué* to it, so it was never slack or without expression. Her eyes were particularly special, a variegated blue, like polished lapis, encircled by a fine line of black. As though the black was needed to contain such liveliness.

She was born and reared in Wales, far out on the westernmost tip in the town of Milford Haven, where the damp weather was like an atomizer. Which accounted for her complexion, its incredible fine texture all the way to her toes. Her nutmeg-colored hair was another matter. Both her parents and their parents and everyone else in her family, for as many generations as could be remembered, had hair as black as the coal of Carmarthenshire. The only acceptable explanation for Leslie's hair was that it was a throwback from centuries ago when the Norsemen had come down the west coast of Britain, grabbing up everything, enjoying the women.

"Two miles more," Gainer thought aloud.

A large summer bug was killed by the windshield.

"Been taking your Remedy?" Leslie asked.

Gainer, with the tolerance of a true lover, had constantly put up with her so-called flower remedies. It was one of her holistic beliefs—that the essences of certain flowers could alter the mental outlook and thereby help keep the body in a healing state.

"Well?" she plied for his answer.

He nodded so it seemed less of a fib, asked, "How was it being alone?"

"I wasn't."

"Oh?"

"I seldom am. You know that."

"Who was it this time, the Lady or the High Priest?"

"Lady Caroline."

"Where was the Egyptian?"

"I've no idea. He hasn't been around lately."

"Maybe he got promoted—for doing so well with you."

She liked that. "Think so?"

"That would explain it."

"Are you sure you don't have a guardian angel?"

"I'm sure."

"How sure?"

His immediate mental figure was a hundred percent, then eighty-twenty in his favor. He stood fast on sixty-forty. "Anyway," he said, mine is probably a guardian devil."

"I doubt that. You have it too good."

With her, he thought.

"It's not impossible, you know," she said. "Some people even have both, guardian angel and guardian devil."

"Anyway, thank heaven for good old Lady Caroline," he said.

"She's not old."

"Ninety. Over ninety."

"She's my age," Leslie contended.

Gainer's estimate of Lady Caroline's years was based on the claim that she'd served as an ambulance driver in the First World War. That was, of course, according to what he got from Leslie. Her Lady Caroline, she said, was a lovely person from Devonshire, somewhat severe but in a feminine sort of way, who had wheeled all round no man's land in the thickest thick of it. Until a day during the Battle of Belleau Wood when the largest of German shells had blown her to irretrievable pieces. The good Lady's spiritual self remained intact, however, and, instead of merely ascending, it chose to hang around and be both there and here. Leslie couldn't say exactly when in her life she'd come under Lady Caroline's influence. She thought most likely it was soon after she married Rodger because since then she'd been so much more able to cope, and like Lady Caroline, unafraid of anything except boredom.

Leslie's greatest interest, close second only to Gainer, was what she called the *super sensible*. That included everything from iridology to Tantra. She'd read extensively on psychic healing, mysticism, Zen, transcendental meditation, I Ching, the works. Even an entire book devoted to pargaritomancy, a way of predicting the future by means of pearls. Leslie didn't believe pearls could do anything more than be pearls, but she didn't put the book down until she'd taken in its last word. She had read all of William Blake and Edgar Cayce and Madame Blavatsky, as well as Carlos Casteneda, and every month read every page of *Prevention* magazine. She accepted a little from this and some from that and what got synthesized was a personal sort of orthodoxy that gave the body and the spirit a lot more combined credit than did any of the organized religions. No doubt many of Leslie's concepts were inherited from her Druid ancestors, who felt there was more of God in a tree than in a cathedral.

Regarding life after death, Leslie believed in it religiously, and to avoid crediting death with as little importance as possible, she called it life after life. In line with that, she was sure everyone had lived previous lives. She considered her relationship with Gainer a vital aspect of their mutual destinies. They had, according to her, chosen one another while in spiritual limbo, and the ten-year difference in their ages was explained by Gainer having been confused. He'd hung back for that long, which in the ethereal dimension was no more than a blink, really.

Gainer never ridiculed her beliefs. He himself had never experienced a spiritual presence, an invisible someone like Lady Caroline, whose single purpose in afterlife was to hover around watching out for his well-being. But, he was wise enough to know he didn't *know* what was true. Besides, he had no better philosophy to offer. At times he envied Leslie's faith, wished he could believe as strongly in anything. Because he seldom challenged and never denounced her convictions, she tended to assume they thought mostly alike.

Concerning Lady Caroline's age, however, Gainer decided not to let the point go by. "What you're saying is those on the other side stay the same age they were when they died."

"Some do, some don't."

He should have expected the ambiguity. He leaned forward and looked out the window on her side, to the southern horizon that had a roll of blue-gray clouds all along it. "It's going to rain," he said for a different topic.

"That'll be nice." And after hardly a pause: "You haven't really been taking your remedy, have you?"

"Don't nudge."

"It's not nudging, it's caring."

"I couldn't take my remedy."

"Why?"

Think fast. "The bottle broke, fell and broke." As soon as those words were out, he wished he had them back unsaid. The bottle containing his remedy was of glass so thick it would have taken a hard throw against a wall for it to break.

She knew that, of course. She drew in a breath so deep it made her breasts rise very noticeably. She sighed it out. "All right," she said, "I'm not going to help you anymore. From now on I'm not even going to try."

She sounded really irked. He hoped not. It had been four days and he didn't want that kind of friction between them. He tried to think of the perfect mending thing to say.

Her carryall was on the seat beside her. She felt around in it, brought out a small brown bottle with a medicine dropper cap. It wasn't a prescription or over-the-counter drug product. The self-adhesive label had *Rescue Remedy* on it in her printing. With one hand she unscrewed the cap and squeezed four clear drops into her mouth.

Gainer took the bottle from her.

He pretended to be replacing the cap. When he was sure she'd notice, he opened his mouth, wider than necessary, didn't bother with measuring drops, just squirted in as much as the dropper could hold. Leslie remained unimpressed just long enough to worry him, then allowed a closed-mouth grin that surely had her wonderful smile behind it.

By then they had crossed the bridge over Nahaquitsa Pond. They turned off the main road and soon were on a dirt track with stubborn grass and a few cornflowers along its middle. For nearly a half mile it led round sandy humps and marshes to where it ended at the cottage.

Nothing else man-made in sight.

The cottage was situated on solid ground. Above the beach with a name that was fun to say: Squibnocket. No steps were needed to get from the cottage to the beach because the sand had formed an easy slope all the way up. The cottage was a saltbox in its fifty-third year. Like most beach cottages set out in the open, unaccessorized and battled by weather, it did not appear friendly. The bleached shingles of its siding were like the scales of old skin and the stark geometrics of its white painted trim added to the impression.

At the moment, however, all that was being contradicted by three fat gulls perched contentedly on the peak of the roof. Leslie skidded the car to a stop, left the motor running, hurried inside. Gainer surmised she was urgently bound for the bathroom. He got his canvas bag and the other things from the back seat and carried them in.

The interior of the cottage was altogether amiable. It was six rather small-sized rooms, three down, three up. All the walls and ceilings were paneled in four-inch width tongue-in-groove cedar that was painted so high a gloss it looked to be porcelain. Not painted plain white, as might be expected, but white tinted just enough so those surfaces influenced the entire atmosphere in a subtle way. The living room, for example, enjoyed the congenial benefits of the merest hint of persimmon, the kitchen a pervasive suggestion of leaf green and, appropriately, the bedrooms had the faint cast of incarnadine. Throughout, the floors were of pine, wide boards that Gainer and Norma had stripped clean so they could be stenciled with Japan paints and other penetrating pigments. Not a rug on any floor. Just those huge created bouquets, the pastel to vermilion peonies arranged with pink nicotinia and windings of mauve morning glories. All on a transparent green-washed field bordered by leaves with their veins contrastingly detailed. The floors were by far the most intricate aspect of the cottage, all else in it gave way to them, simply stood aside. The chairs, and tables, the dresser bureaus and beds, all carefully chosen and carefully kept, but not allowed to be ornate. The paintings on the walls were watercolors, all sizes hung here or there without concern for alignment or spatial balance. Each painting had been put up practically anywhere the moment after it entered the cottage. Such impulsiveness suited them, their own spontaneity. There were watercolors to be found in unusual places—unframed and push-pinned up on the inside of a closet door; a very small, unfinished one fixed to a window frame; and, of course, others tucked along the edges of mirrors.

The cottage was inviting, pretty, comforting and comfortable. But above all, it was romantic.

For Gainer, a favorite place.

He set down his bag at the foot of the stairs and went into the kitchen. Everything, he noticed, was in place the way Norma liked, and there were some current touches by Leslie: red geranium petals floating in a shallow crystal dish on the table, a circle of fine old lace beneath the dish, sort of presenting it. A fat, new Boston fern hung in the kitchen. Fresh creamy candles around. Small light blue Tiffany boxes, several such birthday gifts placed where they couldn't possibly miss being discovered by Norma.

Not thoughtful of Leslie, however, was her six carat diamond ring and her Buccelatti ruby and gold chain necklace left in an ordinary saucer on the kitchen counter by the sink. Gainer had often admired the ring. It was difficult not to, the way it flared at him and the way she so casually wore it. Once, by chance, he had seen its pedigree papers from the Gemological Institute of America certifying the diamond was a D color flawless round cut, worth well over three hundred thousand dollars. The ruby necklace was at least a fifty thousand dollar piece. Leslie had received both from her husband Rodger. Perhaps, Gainer thought, that wasn't the reason she'd left them there with the back door wide open and not even the screen door hooked where anyone could just look in, reach in and snap them up. He let the water run from the kitchen tap until it was cooler, drank down a tall glassful without stopping. It crossed his mind that he was miles from crime. Told himself he should, could safely, adjust his outlook. Still, he put the ring and necklace in his pocket and hooked the screen door before he went upstairs.

Leslie was in the front bedroom.

"I was beginning to think you wanted me to come down," she said.

She was standing on the other side of the bed, her back to the windows that overlooked the beach. The window shades were up and midday brightness was reflected in. It wrapped around her, came through her hair and between her bare legs. Gainer thought of telling her she had an aura.

"Are you honest to God sleepy?" she asked.

"It's warm up here."

"Not too."

There was an electric fan on the dresser nearby. Gainer switched it on, and at once it began rotating back and forth sweeping the room, animating the pages of an open book on the nightstand by the bed. The bed was like a fresh envelope with its immaculate sheets precisely folded down. Four pillows were plumped and waiting. The bed seemed very dominant at that moment and Gainer imagined Leslie making it, tucking and smoothing and making it just so for when they would share the pleasure of messing it up.

She crossed the room and was within his reach when she opened his canvas bag. She quickly unpacked the few things he'd brought, hung and placed them beside hers, and it occurred to Gainer that she was getting rid of loneliness. In the bathroom while she placed his personal necessities in the cabinet and on the window sill, Gainer sat on the covered commode and watched her every movement.

"Are you going to shave?" she asked.

"I thought I would." He hadn't since the morning of the day before.

She ran the palm of her hand over the thick beaver bristles of his shaving brush, asked herself if this wasn't one of those times when she preferred impulsiveness, bypassing ritual and preparation. No bath or shave, no drink or music or applied fragrance. Not even the holding off for such minor interventions as closing the door or drawing the shades. An immediate heated course between them, taking them into one another, burrowing with sensation to where their creature furies lay caged. She had never been capable of that until him. Sex without a lot of hygiene, being aroused by odors that were normally offensive. Any initiative on his part of hers, no matter how abrupt, enough to wet and unfold her. Whether or not that was how it would be this time was up to her.

She placed the brush on the brow of the sink. "I'll shave you."

It was another of those things she had never done with anyone else. Early in their time together she had gone with him to a regular old barber shop on Fifth Avenue near Twenty-first Street. A place called Frank's. She was supposed to wait and read but she couldn't take her eyes off Gainer. So, while she waited, she watched, and it was evident to her that being shaved was something he greatly enjoyed. The next time she was there with him, she paid closer attention, stood by the chair at Frank's elbow, taking in his professional techniques. Picked a lot of them right up and the first time Gainer let her try she only nicked him once, a tiny but quite bloody wound that she so regretted she couldn't say enough how sorry she was and tried to make up for it by surprising him with six shirts from Andre Oliver.

Gainer was tempted to have her shave him now. His face, especially around the eyes, felt starchy from all those hours of concentrating on the road. However, he reasoned it would be quicker if he shaved himself, told her that.

"No hurry," she said, archly blasé and then contradicted that by kissing him a very slick, promising one before leaving the bathroom.

She was gone less than five minutes, returned carrying a silver tray.

By then Gainer was all lathered up and making a face in the mirror to help the blade of the straight razor get at an awkward area below his nostrils.

"Need help?" she asked.

"Nope."

Leslie imitated him with a Quasimodo.

"I'd still love you," he said.

"Hell you would." She placed the tray on the toilet seat. It held Beluga caviar, iced in its original half-pound tin, a pair of Baccarat goblets and a chilled bottle of Le Montrachet '78 that according to its label and price was from the chateau of one Marquis de La Quiche.

Leslie poured, handed Gainer his glass. He got lather on it as he took some long sips that went down into him like heated silver wire. His eyes were on the caviar. She fed him a heaping spoonful. Straight, no garnish of any sort. After a second helping for him, Leslie sat on the edge of the tub and helped herself.

A jet plane was heard, miles up but still audible along with the repetitive thumps and fizzes of the Atlantic breaking.

"There's a chance Norma may show up tomorrow," Gainer said.

"Only a chance?"

"I think I might have talked her out of it." Now he wasn't so pleased with having done so. He had a notion to take a run over to Chilmark to a pay phone, call Norma and tell her to hell with everything, hurry on back. To keep from doing that he went on shaving and asked, "How's Rodger?"

"Who?" As though the name meant nothing.

"Heard from him?"

"He's in San Francisco. At least Walsh mentioned that he was." Walsh was one of her husband's pilots.

Silence told Gainer that for the time being Rodger was not to be a topic. He glanced around at Leslie. "Only one thing wrong with you."

"Since when?"

"You have rotten teeth."

She craned up for the mirror, then stood up beside him and gave it the sudden phony model's smile. She saw the black, like cavities.

"From eating too many sweets," he said.

"You are that," she said, purposely flat and without looking at him. She took a mouthful straight from the Montrachet bottle, swished it around before swallowing. Then, caviar remnants eliminated, her fullest smile quickly on and off was once again equal to any advertisement.

Gainer was almost through shaving, had only beneath his chin to do. Leslie took over the razor for the finishing touches. Which left his hands free. He undid the drawstring of her blouse and put both hands up in under, skimmed her breasts, barely brushed them, traced duplicate sensations all the way from the ladder of her spine around to her nipples. Cupped her breasts as though extracting from them.

He noticed the first signs of flush apparent on the fair skin of her throat, a pink mottling that he knew from the many times before was evidence of her arousal. She had always considered it a disadvantage, having such an obvious giveaway. But not with Gainer. She liked that he could know how little was needed from him to begin her.

In spite of his hands, she remained apparently intent on shaving him, kept up the same firm sure strokes using a page from a magazine to wipe lather from the blade. She held back warning him that such erotic distraction might very well cause her to nick him—or worse. His hands on her while hers with the blade were on his throat created a disturbing circuit that he was not unaware of, she figured. She prolonged it, spent more time than needed on his Adam's apple.

At the same time Gainer had the urge to pinch her nipples.

He withdrew his hands, took the razor from her, cleaned it and put it into its special leather case.

The mottling on her neck had spread and was deeper pink. She carried the tray in to the bedroom.

He took a very brief shower, did not dry thoroughly, went out to her.

She had undressed, was on the bed. Not posed, just there, faced up in an ingenuous waiting position.

He stood beside the bed.

She stayed still, had to control her legs because they wanted to part.

"I love you," he said, giving each word equal importance.

They seemed like inscriptions on white silk floating down to her, those words. Her lips were dry but she would wait for him to wet them. She knew she had hands in her eyes. She watched him become hard while just standing there.

"Beautiful cock," she thought, so caught up by it she did not realize those words had come out. Her hand went to it, led him down to her by it, spread and found herself for it. She tried not to come quickly. At least not as quickly as usual but her mind as well as her body was full with him. He caused flowers to open in her belly and her thighs, and no sooner had they begun to fade, he would blossom them again.

Gainer came.

He stayed inside her after he came, and within a short while she felt him become as hard as before in her and go on.

They loved, one way or the other, for most of that afternoon. Dozed in between times and finally slept. Usually it was difficult for Gainer to sleep with Leslie. She was such a determined snuggler. They would start out compatibly positioned with an equal amount of territory on either side. Before long Gainer would come half awake to find he was on the edge with, for example, a knee cantilevered way out or his hand braced on the floor not to fall, and Leslie pressing to get still closer. Rather than shove her away, he'd get up and sleepwalk around to the other side of the bed for the ample space there. Right away she would begin to close the gap. Gainer complained about it. She was most apologetic. She did not, however, suggest separate beds. Nor did he. It was, he figured, a small enough price to pay.

GAINER and Leslie.

They had first laid eyes on one another two Novembers ago. A miserable day, drizzling and cold.

Gainer was at his herb store on Sixty-second Street, minding it while Miss Applegate was out having a chiropractic adjustment. He was seated on a high stool behind the old, long table that served as a counter, going over yesterday's racing form, searching between its rather cryptic lines for a reason why yesterday's unlikely winners had won.

Leslie entered.

Gainer looked up and kept looking.

She was in sable, Barguzin sable. Rain looked as though it enjoyed being on it. Her hair, all but a couple of disciplined wisps left and right near her temples, was contained within a sleek cloche of tiny iridescent black beads. The collar of her coat was pulled up so that it nestled her face, made it appear small, recedent. The tip of her nose was reddened from the cold.

She looked like some exceptionally elegant woman who had somehow stepped over all the years since 1920, Gainer thought. He said his best "may I help you?"

Leslie acknowledged it with an almost indiscernible nod. She surveyed the place while taking off, finger by finger, her black kid gloves and tucking them in her handbag.

A large diamond and a wedding band, Gainer noticed.

"By chance do you have mouse ear?" she asked.

Her voice was British flavored.

"Mouse ear," she repeated.

"Probably," Gainer said, glancing up at the rows and rows of jars on the shelves. "What's it used for?"

"Perhaps you know it as cudweed."

Cudweed didn't ring a bell.

"You *do* work here," she said dubiously.

He admitted he knew practically nothing about herbs. "I only own the place," he told her, downplaying that.

"Oh." Her lips formed a perfect little circle. She released the collar of her sable, which almost floated from around her face.

For Gainer it was as though the curtain had gone up on an exquisite opening number. He didn't give a damn if he was staring. She'd be gone in a moment. He'd enjoy her while he could.

"I use it to make mouthwash," she said.

"Mouse ear mouthwash?"

"It's true."

"Everything you say is true."

Gainer thought that caused a slight break of a smile. He started looking for mouse ear or cudweed among the labels on the rows of bottles.

"How about some pokeroot?" Gainer suggested, choosing an herb at random.

"For a mouthwash?"

"Whatever."

"You're dangerous. Pokeroot is a poison."

She searched the labels with him, stood closer. The fragrance she was wearing seemed to be going off in tiny explosions around her. "To hell with it," she said. "I'll come back another time."

Think fast. "May I put you on our mailing list?"

She said her name and address only once and so rapidly Gainer wasn't sure he got it. Then, without bothering with her gloves, she pulled the sable close around her face and was gone.

Later, when Miss Applegate returned, Gainer learned that mouse ear was also known as everlasting and they had plenty of it in a jar on the topmost shelf. He emptied all they had into one of the store's printed brown paper bags and went out. He couldn't get a taxi because of the rain and rush hour so he walked the nine blocks up Lexington and the two longer crosstown blocks over to Madison and the neat blue awning with her desirable address on it. It wasn't a huge apartment house, but it had two formidable doormen on duty in white gloves, little white bow ties and dark blue uniforms that fitted them as though tailored.

Gainer was soaked, rain dripping from his ear lobes. Affluent people were rarely caught in such a rain.

"For Mrs. Pickering . . ."

A doorman took the paper bag from him.

Gainer thought he could get past them, get in there if he really wanted to. He put a folded ten into the white gloved palm and went out into the rain again, thinking Mr. Pickering was one lucky son of a bitch.

Over the following few days Gainer spent more time than usual at the herb shop. He didn't entirely admit to himself it was on the chance that she'd come in again. His style wasn't to stand around waiting for a married woman to throw five or ten of her many leisure minutes his way. Nevertheless, there he was.

And on the bright, nippy afternoon of the next Tuesday, there was Leslie.

She looked different. All her nutmeg-colored hair was exposed, suggestively, a bit wild. She had on western boots tucked with straight-legged tan slacks that fit precisely, a plaid wool challis shirt and a loose-fitting antelope jacket lined with lynx.

She smiled right off, an honest to friendly smile, thanked Gainer for the mouse ear. Promised when next she made up a batch of mouthwash with it she'd give him some.

Gainer picked up on the future that that implied. He was suddenly aware of an urge to know her immediately all the way down to her most personal marrow. He imagined her answering his most intimate questions. His next thought was how unfair and unromantic that would be.

That day Leslie bought enough herbs to supply a small naturopathic army. Miss Applegate was overwhelmed to the point of tears. Gainer carried the packages out to Leslie's car, a black Rolls-Royce Corniche defiantly parked in a tow-away zone. Seeing her so casual at the wheel of it, using it as though it were a Toyota, subdued him.

Leslie visited the shop twice more that week. Once for a sprig of vetiver, which seemed a pretext, considering she stayed over an hour.

Exchanged viewpoints with Gainer on a number of subjects such as the marvelous compensation for enduring New York City and some of the possible explanations for *déjà vu*.

Saturday she came in again, starved.

Gainer, careful to sound offhand, suggested lunch.

Her eyes got him by the eyes as she told him: "I'd like that."

They lunched at Le Relais.

For four hours.

Held hands beneath the table and then, with her initiative, in plain sight.

That was the start of them.

There were never any trading lies or need for other such synthetic excitements. Not even the usual purposely bewildering omissions. Leslie believed right off in the quality of what she felt for Gainer, and instead of cynically chalking it up to a mere phase of latter-day naiveté, she opened to it and allowed it to lead her.

She especially wanted Gainer to understand her marriage.

She'd been twenty-eight when she married Rodger Pickering. He was in his fifties and wealthy beyond count. His business was heavy construction on the international level. Hung on the walls of his study were photographs of him at the sites of huge projects in various parts of the world—of him stripped to the waist, chunky, hairy, wearing a hardhat and looking as though he could break rock.

Rodger didn't marry Leslie to camouflage his homosexuality. He no longer gave a damn who knew about that. His cock and ass were his cock and ass and he'd do whatever he wanted with them, was his attitude. He married Leslie to satisfy, in the least oppressive way, an older man's innate gravitation toward domesticity. Also because he liked her, liked her spirit and coveted her style and knew they required expensive upkeep. She hadn't saved much from her thousands of hundred dollar hours in front of the cameras, and it was imminent that her booking charts at the modeling agency would become spotty and then go blank. She'd seen other slightly older models suffer through that and she knew it was something to avoid if at all possible.

Marriage to Rodger saved her. The convenience, as she said, was more hers than his. Naturally, Rodger protected himself, had his New York lawyer draw up a tight, antenuptial contract that said she'd get nothing from a divorce other than what personally belonged to her. But also legally provided was an escape clause for Leslie—divorce papers prepared in advance, signed by Rodger and kept current. Anytime Leslie wanted out, all it would take was her signature.

What most made the arrangement comfortable was that she liked

Rodger. He was delightfully frank, had a well-honed sense of humor and was, so far as she knew, always honest. Leslie saw relatively little of him, but their time together was usually rich with funny wicked anecdotes, particles from the cracks and crevices of their separate societies.

Where they lived was in keeping with their relationship. The twenty-room penthouse on East Seventy-fifth Street, for example, was divided equally, a sturdy partition separating Rodger's space from hers, designed to slide open and out of sight only when mutually activated.

All in all Leslie had the wealth of advantages that came with being married to big money. And none of the restrictions. She could do whatever whenever she wanted, was not even required to be all that discreet. It was, in many ways, a perfect setup, one that most women would have traded their souls for.

Gainer was relieved to learn these were Leslie's circumstances. He would have preferred that she was unmarried, of course, but this was the next best thing. At least he wouldn't have to feel like a sexual trespasser and keep looking over his shoulder.

What did bother him, though, was all that money of Rodger's. And Leslie's apparent need for it. Early on, only once, Gainer discussed it with her. He told her exactly what he did and what he had. He didn't ask her to give up a dollar for him nor did he pledge to make an all-out run on the fast track for her. She didn't volunteer to give up or even check her extravagances, nor did she want him to try hard to be rich. She meant it when she said she thought it would be a terrible waste of both head and heart if he struggled to make millions.

They made a pact. Never to let money come between them. His or hers, or anyone's, no matter, they'd just use it.

That had worked out fine.

However, recently Gainer happened on a hint of a complication. In the margins of several of Leslie's books on psychic healing she had doodled, among other things, her first name together with his last, and put a "Mrs." larger in front of them.

Now, in the bedroom of the beach cottage, that same sort of image came sliding across Leslie's mind. She let it go by. She was bare, scrunched down in a chair by the window, her feet up on the sill. Outside, dawn was nearly finished. Only a little of the lower rim of the sun remained below the sea. The water was so calm the horizon looked as though it had been cut with a scissors.

She had gotten up before any sun, rather than lay there half awake

131

and disturbed by premonition. It was like being maliciously teased by some force that already knew what would happen. Why not let her clearly in on it instead of prodding her unconscious with vague unpleasant intimations?

Gainer was still asleep, lying face up diagonally across the bed, as though claiming all of it. Poor love, Leslie thought, probably she'd oversnuggled him most of the night. She held her breath to hear his and be grateful for it. Felt sorry for the ocher and blue bruises and scabbed-over abrasions on his shins. She scratched a new mosquito bite just above her pubic hair.

There were the dry clawing sounds of gulls moving about on the roof.

She went over to the bed, stood absolutely still beside it for a long moment to, as she would say, center herself. Closed her eyes and asked for protection, asked for the help of Lady Caroline and any other guardian angels who might be around. Extending her arms above Gainer, she made her wrists and fingers resolute, placed her left hand an inch or two over her right, palms down. She started at his feet. Made vigorous, clockwise circles in the air, like she was scrubbing, worked all the way up to his head. There she interrupted her scrubbing motion, seemed to push a lot of something undesirable off and away. She shook her hands as though snapping a nasty substance from her fingers.

Resumed at his feet again.

Gainer, in the shallows of an REM state, experienced several images, including a cyclone funnel, a helicopter and a dragonfly. When he opened his eyes Leslie was intently churning the air above his groin. Had he been more awake, he would have pulled back.

Thickly, he asked: "What are you doing?"

"Cleansing your aura."

"Is it dirty?"

"Very."

"Filthy." He nodded.

"You've picked up an awful lot of negativity."

"Better than a cold or a social disease."

No comment from her.

"Can you see negativity?" he asked.

"No."

"So, how do you know it's there?"

"I can feel it."

"Really?"

"It's prickly."

Maybe she can, he thought. His stomach grumbled. He'd only had her and an apple and some cheese since the caviar. Still, he was patient, remained on the bed for her to cleanse him the required three times front and back.

He jumped up then and ran to the bathroom.

She needed something to offset any negativity she might have absorbed, she said. Hugging a tree or walking barefoot in grass would do it, but neither was possible there at the beach. So, she chewed on some juniper berries and washed her hands thoroughly with cold water.

After a long breakfast on the porch, they walked the beach. Gainer brought along a soccer ball. The day was burning so bright it seemed to put a glaze on everything. There were a few clouds, like frayed silk. Leslie enjoyed the sun, but it betrayed her whenever she trusted it, so they made it a short walk, only around the point to the Bight and back.

Leslie retreated to shade on the porch, sat there behind blue-tinted sunglasses with gold wire frames. The brim of her blue cotton hat was a foot wide and very floppy.

Gainer stayed on the beach to kick the ball around where the tide had left the sand harder. He assumed Leslie was watching so he practiced some fancy dribbles using his ankles, heels and insteps. Also did some fairly good headers and a couple of reverse scissor kicks that he badly mistimed.

His showing off amused and touched her, brought a crowding up into her throat.

He took off down the beach, running full out, pushing the ball in front of him without breaking stride, as though headed for a goal, unstoppable.

Leslie went in to make a pitcher of iced rose hips tea.

From the kitchen window she saw a car pull up.

It was Charlie Colt in his white Cutlass Supreme. Charlie was perhaps a three-fifths Wampanog Indian who lived on the other side of Squibnocket Pond up toward Gay Head. The nearest neighbor with a phone. He was by no means the archetypical stoic Indian. Charlie told jokes, was an easy laugher and usually even at the most serious times, he had trouble keeping a straight face.

This day he was grim.

CHAPTER
EIGHT

THE *Kanton Spolezei Zurich.*

Located at Number 29 Kasernenstrasse, six blocks from the main railway station (Zurich's most commonly used reference point) and directly on the River Sihl.

An older structure built to last and kept to last, it takes up all of a long block. There are five stories to its roof line. Dormer windows indicate two more stories above that. Dark stone exterior, red and white crossed flags flying, it appears efficient just standing there.

Gainer was with Inspector Zeller, in the elevator going down. Zeller had used a key to open the control panel so he could hold the elevator on express all the way to the lowest level and a wide, vacant corridor painted gray. Zeller led under fluorescent lights through disinfected air to a pair of thick doors with a sign on each: *Do Not Enter.* Through those into a long room, cool, concrete floor painted white and slightly slanted, punctuated with a drain.

Everything clean.

No one there.

A wall of stainless steel hinged compartments, three by two.

Zeller consulted a listing on a clipboard before opening the compartment that was second from the bottom, fourth from the left. The seven foot tray slid out easily. He partially unzipped the plastic bag, pushed it aside for Gainer to see another Gainer.

It's not you, Norma. It doesn't look enough like you.

A long look at the face, seeing all the times not taken, care not shown, things unsaid. Oh, Norma, never now.

Zeller asked, "Do you identify her?"

"Yes."

Zeller began to close the bag.

Gainer stopped him. "I want to see all of her."

Zeller thought he shouldn't but he unzipped the bag entirely to reveal the skin looking reptilian where the massive blisters had been lanced and had dried, the fingers flexed unevenly as though to grab anything, the medical examiner's incision from her pubic hair up to her throat unevenly sutured with large stitches, like a child's sewing.

"Okay?" Zeller asked.

"No," Gainer said, and walked out.

He had not cried. Not one tear from the moment on the beach when Leslie told him, right up to now. He had wanted to cry but his grief was so intense it would not let him. His mind's way of protecting him. Otherwise, no telling what he would have done. He was changed, though. The way he saw things was different. His surroundings seemed out of register, removed. When he first noticed that sensation he shook his head to try to clear it, but it stayed with him.

Leslie had come to Zurich with him. He never once mentioned making the trip alone. On the flight over she tried to hold him but he insisted on holding her.

She was waiting for him now in Inspector Zeller's office on the fourth floor. When Gainer came in she searched for any visible change. He seemed the same, in control, coping. He sat in the hard official chair next to hers.

Zeller went behind his desk. There was nothing on it but a manila file folder and a meticulously sharpened yellow pencil. Zeller was a dry-looking man in his late fifties. He had a conscientiously tended gray mustache, was dressed in a sincere blue wool suit.

Zeller tugged his suit jacket neat, smoothed his tie and examined both its ends to see that they matched in length.

Delaying tactics. It was always distasteful for him to deal with matters of this sort, cases in which lust was so prominent. Lust to any degree was as much a transgression as any crime he could think of. He had wanted to become a pastor before he won the *Knabenshiessen* one September and became the champion marksman of all schoolboys.

He glanced out the window to Saint Jacob's Church, its spire an acicular finger pointed heavenward. It was his usual reinforcing view.

He flipped open the folder. Wasted no words. Did not spare Gainer. Showed him photographs of Norma's room at the Dolder Grand.

Various angles and numerous detailed close-ups: the nearly empty bottle of cognac, the vial containing Methaquaalude tablets, the vial containing cocaine, her hand mirror with cocaine on it, the vibrator, the tissues. The shower stall with her in it as she'd been found by the chambermaid.

Gainer remained steady, or seemed to.

Zeller went on to the laboratory and medical examiners' reports, which stated that there was spermatozoa on the tissues and on the sheets, and in her vagina and rectum. Cocaine crystals in her nostrils. High percentage of alcohol in her blood. The scalding had not brought about her death. She had died from the combination of the alcohol and the Methaquaalude, which in its effect upon the brain, specifically the medulla oblongata, had prohibited the automatic responses of her lungs and heart.

She had died of lust, Zeller felt, but he said it was the official conclusion of the Kanton police that her death had been accidentally self-induced. No further investigation necessary.

He closed the manila folder.

Gainer considered telling Zeller he was full of shit, it was all shit. He realized, however, he would only sound like the bereaved brother who had been kept in the dark. Besides, no doubt all it would get him was another Zeller.

He signed a receipt for Norma's personal effects and a form confirming positive identification and another form with which he assumed responsibility for the body.

I'm responsible for you now, Norma.

Out on Kasernenstrasse Leslie asked, "We're taking her home with us, aren't we?"

"It's not her," Gainer said.

"But darling—"

"It's not her."

In another moment Leslie understood.

The Mercedes at the curb awaited them. The driver put Norma's two pieces of luggage into the trunk and drove to the hotel. They were staying at the Savoy in a quiet suite on the Waaggasse side. Leslie had taken it on herself to handle such details. As much as she could she would try to smooth things along.

Up in the suite Gainer watched and heard her on the phone. He had not told her what arrangements to make, but she assumed and he confirmed by nodding while she talked to the necessary people.

It had to be done that afternoon.

At four o'clock they were driven back to the Kanton Police Station.

A hearse was there. They followed it out Badenerstrasse for about fifteen blocks, then into the Friedhof Cemetery and past field after field of dead to the crematorium.

Two men from the hearse and two from the crematorium carried the casket and Norma inside. It seemed crazy to Gainer that there was a casket, but the undertaker had insisted on it.

No ceremony.

Gainer and Leslie waited in the car for nearly an hour. One of the crematorium men came out with a brown cardboard carton ten inches square, carried it with both hands as though it were heavy. Or sacred. Gainer rolled down the car window to receive it.

Back in the hotel suite Gainer opened the carton, removed the shiny metal container. It resembled a paint can, two quart size without a handle or a label, and the same sort of pry-open lid.

"It's not her," Gainer said.

He shook the container, felt its contents shift and wondered if they really had cremated the casket. Probably they'd saved it to sell again. He placed the container on the writing desk. Turned on the television. Got a soccer match in progress. Bayer-München playing Ajax-Amsterdam at Munich Olympic Stadium.

He sat there, trying to concentrate on it.

Leslie took Norma's luggage into the bedroom, opened it and found everything messily crammed in. She went through Norma's carryall, removed from it whatever might be important: keys, address book, airline ticket, receipts, every slip of paper and stub. In one of the bags was a pair of leather-framed photographs—a recent one of Gainer alone and another of him with arms around Norma.

The next morning over breakfast Leslie asked should she make reservations for the flight home.

Gainer told her: "Not yet."

She believed she knew why. Here in Zurich was where it had happened and leaving here would, to a certain extent, close the book on it. He was not ready for that.

They went out for a walk. Their hotel was practically on Bahnhofstrasse, the street Zurich is most proud of. Along there the sidewalks are wider, the shops finer, the way lined on both sides by plane trees and decorated from above with Swiss flags.

Gainer and Leslie walked up one side as far as it went, then crossed over to return on the other side. They looked in store windows, bought a huge chunk of bittersweet chocolate at Sprungle that they passed back and forth as they continued on.

It was Saturday. The crowds along Bahnhofstrasse had a liberated attitude and most of the outdoor tables of the cafes were occupied.

Gainer sidestepped to avoid a little girl enjoying a momentary escape from her mother. At that instant a woman brushed by Gainer and pressed a folded note into his free hand. It took him so completely by surprise he almost threw the note away. He stopped to read:

> I have information
> regarding Norma. Come
> to Kirchegasse 28. Please.

Gainer searched for that woman in the coming-and-going crowd ahead, caught a glimpse of her. She had paused, turned toward him, no doubt to assure herself that he had gotten the message. Then other heads and shoulders cut her from view.

Kirchegasse was a minor street in the older section east of the River Limmat. Number 28 turned out to be a coffee house of a dozen tables. Seated alone in the deepest corner was the woman.

Gainer and Leslie sat down with her.

She appeared to be in her forties, quite pretty, had baby-fine hair of a medium blond shade, conservatively styled. Her eyes were inflamed, the dark semicircles beneath them made all the more apparent by her pale skin. From crying and too little sleep.

"My name is Schebler," she said, "Alma Schebler."

Gainer introduced Leslie. "It seems you already know who I am."

"You are Drew," Alma said warmly.

Norma's name for him. Hearing it made his insides react as though cringing from the hurt. "You're sure of that."

"From photographs."

Gainer assumed Norma had shown them to her.

Alma told him: "Even if I had not seen them I would have recognized you, the resemblance."

"Norma spoke of you often," he tried.

"No," Alma said. A thoughtful pause. "But she might have soon. It was planned that I should go with her to America."

"To stay?"

"To stay."

They ordered coffee and pastries. Leslie took small bites from each kind and gave the impression that she was detached from the conversation. Actually she was silently trying to interpret it.

"Norma always stayed at the Dolder Grand," Alma said. "I have a position at the Dolder. Senior bookkeeper." Alma's coffee spoon stirred round and round, as though on its own. "At first Norma and I saw one another merely in passing. We exchanged proper automatic greetings, employee and guest. I knew her by name. No, that is not true. I made a point of learning her name. One evening at early dinner on the terrace just by chance our tables were adjacent." Alma took a deep breath that hitched as if it had caught on something. "That is not true either," she said. "I arranged to have the table next to hers, hoping she would invite me to join her. She did. We talked for hours and became friends."

Alma decided to stop at that. She would not say and he would not know how delicate the first intimacy had been, the first of its kind for both Alma and Norma. And what a long, uncertain hunger they had created in one another before daring to risk it. The embarrassment they had anticipated but not felt. Their lake boat rides to shoreline villages such as Stafa and Rapperswil, where they stayed at the smallest, plainest inns and doubted anyone really believed they were close cousins. But it did not matter. They sank nearly out of sight in down-filled mattresses and one another.

What came to Gainer's mind at that moment was Norma having remarked how fond she had become of Zurich.

"I was in the vestibule of the police station yesterday," Alma said. "I saw you come and go. I called all the good hotels, located you at the Savoy and waited there in the lobby this morning."

"Why didn't you just come up? Why the note and all this?"

"Fear."

"Who are you afraid of?"

"I am not sure."

"The police have decided Norma's death was her own doing. Drugs and alcohol."

"What do you believe?"

"Someone killed her." It was the first time he had said it. He hated it.

Alma finally drank her coffee, emptied the cup and signaled for a refill. She immediately went to stirring again. "I have a son," she said. "His name is Karl. He is twenty, a student at the university. During the summer he works at the Dolder Grand as a room-waiter. Wednesday last, around lunchtime, Karl carried a tray of food to room 438. That is the room directly across the hall from the one Norma regularly stayed in." Alma told it slowly, deliberately. "Karl was instructed by a man in the room to push the tray in through the partly opened door. It was not an unusual request and Karl tried to do as he was told. The tray accidentally bumped the door open wider and Karl could not help but see the two men who were there. He recognized them because he had served their breakfast that morning in room 280 and one of the men had stuck his fingers in the orange juice and complained that it was not cold. Karl acted as though he had never seen the men before, because that is the conduct the Dolder expects of its waiters, to be polite but remain impersonal."

Alma paused to get a cigarette from her purse, lit it with a hefty black and gold lighter. She took a heavy first drag, and there was smoke around her words as she went on. "Karl thought nothing of it until he heard what had happened to Norma. He told me about it, asked if I thought he should tell the police. I advised him to stay out of it. Naturally, as bookkeeper I have access to the hotel's records. I looked up room 438 and room 280. On Wednesday a man and wife from Stockholm were in 438. As a matter of fact, they were still there, staying on, so that seemed in order. The registration card for room 280 showed it had been occupied on Wednesday by a woman and her daughter from Vienna. It occurred to me that someone might have tampered with the records. The Dolder is such a large hotel, it would go unnoticed. I called the telephone company and pretended there was a dispute regarding Wednesday's charges to room 280. I was told that three calls to France had been made from that room. Two to Paris, the other to Vernon."

Alma handed across a slip of paper.

Gainer studied her Germanic numerals.

"Those are the telephone numbers that were called," she said and waited for his comment before asking: "What will you do with them? Will you go back to the police?"

"No. Did Karl describe the two men to you?" Gainer asked.

"They were French."

"He's sure of that?"

"Karl is very observant, especially of people."

She gave the second-hand descriptions in such detail it made Gainer dubious. Nevertheless he paid strict attention, mentally constructed the two men as she talked.

Until he felt he could almost reach out and waste them.

CHAPTER
NINE

L ESLIE would not listen to any reason why they should stay in a hotel.

Not when there was husband Rodger's house on Avenue Foch with all its comforts ready and waiting. It was so much better than the Plaza Athenée or the best at the Ritz, for that matter, and it would make a much more convenient base of operations. Besides, she said, the house was half hers, in a way.

Gainer did not put up much of an argument. What mattered most to him was being in Paris where he could get a hold on the leads Alma Schebler had provided.

Those telephone numbers.

They had caused a small chink in the wall of his remorse. Relieved some of the pressure. No longer was he being asked to just accept Norma's killing, to go home and go through everyday motions and hope some normal feelings returned to him.

Leslie, attuned to him as she was, sensed the shift. It was also obvious to her what had brought it about.

"Leslie?"

"What?"

"Do something for me."

"Anything . . ."

"Take a flight back to New York."

". . . except that."

"Please. I'll be better off alone."

"You'll need me. You know how much you need me."

More than ever, he thought, and let it go at that.

THEY arrived in Paris and at the Avenue Foch house very late. Went directly to bed and sleep. Leslie made the ultimate sacrifice, placed a long bolster between herself and Gainer, hoping that might help him to sleep better.

Still, he woke up at dawn, then tried to slip back under but too many disturbing possibilities kept coming at him. He gave up, got up and wandered about the house.

It was larger and more luxurious than his brief impression of it from the night before. Thirty rooms, was his guess. Intricate giltwood paneling and Scalamandre silks on the walls, countless knots by past Persians underfoot. Authentic Louis *quatorze* and *quinze* everywhere.

The Genoise crystal chandelier in the main entrace hall was so huge and made up so many sharply faceted pieces, to walk beneath it made Gainer uneasy. It didn't matter if he gawked a little, he told himself.

He found the kitchen.

No one there.

Green figs in the early sunlight, resting individually in cotton wool in a little crate stenciled *Fauchon*. They weren't really too perfect to touch, Gainer decided. He took one and, on second thought, two more.

Found the library. Thousands of leather bindings with burnished patinas, as though each was a frequently handled favorite. Gainer sat at the ormolu-mounted *bureau plat* and returned the blank stare of a small Degas bronze that rested on its surface, a pubescent boy with arms out, palms up, evidently to receive something. Gainer placed one of the green figs in the boy's arms. He ate one of the others, except for the hard part at the tip of its stem. He chewed on that.

There was a telephone on the desk. Maybe now, early, was a good time to call, catch the bastards off balance, talk them into revealing their addresses. He'd already thought of a fairly credible routine. He took the numbers from the pocket of his robe, practically had them memorized. He dialed one of the Paris numbers and let it ring twenty times before giving up on it. Tried it again in case he'd misdialed.

He also got no answer from the other Paris number and the one in Vernon. He slammed down the receiver.

Where *was* everyone?

He asked the books to distract him, climbed the sliding ladder to get at some of the high ones. Turned pages for fragments of La Fontaine and a few lines of Rimbaud, got momentarily lost at sea in a passage of Conrad's *Lord Jim*.

When he went back up to the bedroom he expected Leslie would still be asleep. She was seated on the floor with an open fifth of four star VSOP Martell cognac between her legs and a large bottle of Vichy. Several one ounce brown, dropper-capped bottles were scattered around, and, all lined up, as though hoping to be chosen, were thirty-nine bottles that were smaller yet. These contained her stock of essences, concentrates, such things as willow and water violet, holly and heather. Leslie had obtained them (for a price) direct from the Dr. Edward Bach Healing Centre in Berkshire, England.

Dr. Bach himself was long gone but his *Remedies* prevailed. The doctor had been a successful Harley Street consultant with M.B., B.S., M.R.C.S., I.C.P., D.P.H. following his name. In 1930 he gave up his lucrative practices to tramp about in the woods and fields. His colleagues thought him very balmy indeed. Bach would sit for hours on a log contemplating the face of a wildflower. He spent the rainiest days observing the behavior of certain trees. What came of it was a theory that petals and buds contained marvelous medicine, the power to heal a person's very nature, restore psychological vitality and thereby offset the simmering of disease. No one ever bothered to disprove Dr. Bach, which perhaps was the basis for his efficacy.

Leslie was a believer.

"I'm mixing a new remedy for you," she told Gainer brightly.

He sat on the chaise just above her. "What was wrong with the old one?"

"It had cherry plum in it. You don't need cherry plum."

"I need a gun."

"Cherry plum helps control the temper."

Throughout the trip she'd been giving him a special remedy. At any moment she'd bring out the little brown bottle and he'd tilt his head back and open his mouth like a baby bird for her to squeeze in some drops. Not because he believed, he told himself. It was just easier to go along.

"I called the numbers," he said. "No one answered."

"It's Sunday."

"All the more reason for someone to be home."

"Maybe those aren't home numbers."

That had occurred to him. "And maybe Karl Schebler has us carried away with his imagination.

"Be positive. I'm positive."

"Why?"

143

"I asked Lady Caroline."

"Oh."

"She said you're on the right track."

"While she was at it, why didn't she give us the names and addresses to go along with those numbers."

"She didn't have to."

Leslie selected one from her stock of essences, announced it decisively: "Rock rose."

"What's that for?"

"Courage. It's great for courage."

"Think I'll need it?"

"Might."

She also chose gorse, star-of-Bethlehem, olive and clematis. He didn't ask and she didn't tell him gorse was to keep him from becoming despondent, star-of-Bethlehem was to help offset the emotional shock he was still suffering, olive would give him energy and clematis would improve his concentration.

"You're a lovely shamaness," he said.

"Merci, mon bête." She smiled up to him, which was also up into the strong sunlight coming from the tall windows. Out of habit she didn't squint or blink—thanks to the countless times as a model she'd had to look directly into the sun without scrinching up her face. It took a while for the dark spots to go away.

She went on concocting. Into the ounce brown bottle she put two drops of each of the essences she'd chosen. Along with a spoonful of cognac. Filled the bottle with Vichy, put the top on and shook it. Labeled it with a nice, although lopsided, heart and printed a capital G inside that.

Tossed the bottle to him.

"I have to get a gun," he said.

By then the help had returned from mass.

Gainer and Leslie took brunch on the wide terrace overlooking the formal gardens at the rear of the house—precisely laid out paths, topiary and ancient-looking statues enclosed by a high-vined wall. All that could be seen of the house next door were its chimney peaks.

"Who lives over there?" Gainer asked.

"The Mellons. When they're in a Paris mood."

Gainer felt displaced, thought these sumptuous surroundings weren't right for a man set on revenge. He should be in an inconspicuous disagreeable hotel being miserable and hating everyone.

He was poured a third demitasse from a dazzling Georgian silver server.

144

Leslie went inside for a moment. Returned with a Maud Frizon shoebox containing two automatic pistols, a pair of silencers, holsters, extra clips and ammunition. She handed him one of the pistols, grip first.

It was a custom modified Smith and Wesson M39, the sort known among shooters as an ASP, after its maker, Armament Systems and Procedures, Inc. The look of the ASP was all business—black Teflon finish, no frills or nickel plate, a transparent grip that allowed a visual count of the eight 9mm cartridges it held.

Gainer immediately took to the feel of it. Its pound and a half compactness seemed made especially for his hand. Or maybe that was because he now felt so much need for a gun.

"Whose is it?" he asked.

"Rodger's."

She brought out another ASP, a duplicate.

"That one too?"

"Mine," she said.

"Then let me use yours."

"No."

"Why not?"

She didn't reply, was preoccupied with screwing on one of the silencers. Inserted one of the loaded clips and shoved it home.

Gainer kept his eyes on the gun in her hand, ready to duck if she inadvertently pointed it his way. He told her: "Be careful. You'll blow your pretty toes off . . . or something."

"One of the great things about an ASP is its smooth body, so it won't snag when you draw. It's very easy to commit."

Gainer had never heard her talk like that.

She cocked a round into the chamber. Got up and assumed a good solid shooting stance, used her off hand to steady the weapon with the forefinger snugly around the special contour meant for that purpose on the front of the trigger guard. Sighted at a headless, legless statue of a nude Greek among the yews about seventy feet away. Squeezed off three rounds.

Limestone dust and chips flew.

All three shots hit within an inch or so of one another, just slightly right of the statue's left nipple.

Gainer couldn't remember ever having seen anything so incongruously lethal. His own gentle love with her own fierce weapon. It made the hairs bristle on the back of his neck. He expected she'd be at least a little smartass about being a good shot; but she only smiled modesly and explained, "I went to Jeff Cooper's shooting school in Arizona."

"Why?"

"Never know when you'll need to kill someone," she said, not lightly.

Flower remedies and hollow points, Gainer thought. He looked at the statue. "Won't Rodger be upset about that?"

"He paid two hundred thousand to have that piece sneaked out of Greece. But it's a fake. He's been meaning to get rid of it."

They target-practiced with their ASPs for an hour, killed the fake Greek again and again. Gainer got so he could fire an entire clip into a tight pattern. It was the best he had ever shot.

When they went inside, Leslie received a telephone call. She took it in the boothlike enclosure underneath the main stairway.

Gainer wondered who could possibly know she was here. Maybe it was Rodger telling her she'd overstepped her arrangement by bringing Gainer to bed in this house. But then, if Rodger didn't give a damn in New York, he certainly shouldn't in Paris.

Leslie was on the phone only a couple of minutes, came out and handed to Gainer what she had jotted down.

Two addresses:

12 Rue de la Cerisaie

82 Boulevard de Menilmontant

To go along with those two Paris phone numbers.

"I'll have the one in Vernon tomorrow," she promised.

"How did you do it?"

"Yesterday before we left Zurich, I called George."

"George who?"

"Grocock."

"You're making that up."

"No, honest. It's an old New England family name. He's with the American consulate, which probably means the CIA too."

"How do you know him?"

"Rodger gave him to me."

"Birthday or Christmas?"

"As someone I should call on here if ever I was in a bind."

Something else to be grateful to Rodger for, Gainer thought.

THE choice was to take the dark green Bentley, the gray Daimler or a taxi.

Gainer would have settled for a little ten-year-old half-destroyed Renault, all the better to blend in with the rest of the Paris traffic. Leslie didn't believe that would make much difference. Certainly she would rather not have to put up with some grumbling ingrate of a taxi driver.

Besides, she contended, they might need to get from somewhere in a hurry.

So, they took the Daimler.

Leslie drove.

Down Avenue Foch and into the death-defying whirlpool of Place de l'Étoile. Actually because it was August and most Parisians had made *le grand départ,* the usual streams of cars on the wide thorough-fares were reduced to relative trickles, and the lesser streets had practically nothing at all running on them.

That suited Leslie, enabled her to make nearly record time down the Champs-Élysées, whizzing so close by one gendarme directing traffic that she damn near scraped his brass buttons and left him crossing himself. She led with the Daimler's fenders, intimidated her way faster than everyone along the Quai des Tuileries, past the Louvre and on into the Fourth Arrondissement.

Rue de la Cerisaie was obscure and out of the way, but Leslie found it—one short, narrow block that cut across near the point where two avenues converged at Place de la Bastille. Typical of that section, it had older, three-story residential buildings compressed along both sides with lookalike windowed faces all somehow looking distressed.

Number 12 was halfway down on the right. Leslie parked not quite across from it.

Gainer's watch, an Audemar Piquet that Norma had given him, said twenty past three. He was aware of the stretchable straps that harnessed around his shoulders and across his back beneath his jacket, of the ASP in its slip holster there next to his heart. The weight of it against him seemed to exaggerate his heartbeat. It was good that his heart was beating harder and faster, he thought. It meant he was nervous, but the adrenaline would make him sharper.

Number 12. Its entrance was an archway that once must have accommodated carriages. It was fitted with a heavy wooden gate painted a dark green enamel, probably a hundred coats. A door was built flush into the right section of the gate for easier coming and going. Twelve windows above, eight of those covered with metal shutters.

Gainer imagined his adversary up there somewhere, maybe taking a Sunday snooze, unaware that his death was so near. Whoever he was, he'd come out sooner or later and Gainer would make a move. No finesse, no margin for a miss, he'd get out, walk up to the man and kill him. That was the smart street way of handling such a thing, Gainer knew. However, he'd never killed anything except a hell of a lot of New York City cockroaches. Even coming, as it was, from rage, it still wasn't going to be easy. Another thing, he'd have to make sure of his man.

147

What a mess if he whacked out the wrong guy.

Leslie gave him a squirt of Remedy and placed her hand on the back of his neck. Probably it was his imagination, but he felt an assuring energy being absorbed from her.

He started humming a Noel Coward tune.

As though merely making conversation, Leslie asked: "If I wasn't married to Rodger or anyone, what about us?"

"What about us what?" He knew but liked hearing her ask.

"Would you want to marry me?"

"I'd want to."

"But would you?"

"In a minute."

"I'll be thirty-nine next time."

"Yeah, going on twenty-one."

"I'm not sure I appreciate that."

"I meant it nice."

"Okay, I'll take it." She hardly paused. "What did you think of Alma?"

"You mean, Alma and Norma?"

A nod from Leslie.

"They would have been fine with me," he said. "Any kind of happiness would have been fine. I only wish Norma had told me."

"Probably she wasn't ready."

"I guess."

"She mightn't have been altogether sure of it herself. Do you resent that she kept it from you?"

"No, it's just that I didn't get the chance to make it better for her."

Leslie let that sink in, told him: "You know, sometimes I think the only reason I love you is you're exceptional." She kissed him below the earlobe, then whispered for emphasis: "But you wouldn't marry me. I wouldn't let you."

"Sure, you'd be nuts to give up all you have with Rodger."

"See, you're already backing off."

It drew a little laugh from Gainer, very small but the first since Martha's Vineyard.

To celebrate it Leslie went into her carryall, rummaged around under her loaded ASP and brought out a plastic bag. Slices of a bagatelle, some slathered with a well-truffled *pâté de foie gras,* others with raspberry preserves.

A talent for coming up with exactly what a tight moment called for, that's what she had, Gainer thought. He was munching away when the green door of Number 12 swung open.

A man stepped out.

A dapperly dressed old-timer with frail hands and a hanging face. He hesitated on the sidewalk, glanced down at his fly, adjusted his straw hat and set off in the direction of Avenue Henri IV.

In no way did he fit the description of either of the men Gainer was out for.

A girl came down the street, hurrying. She appeared to be about fourteen, had on extreme high heels but was not fazed by them, even when she crossed the cobbles.

She went into Number 12.

Nothing more for an hour.

Gainer decided not to just wait any longer. He went over to the green door, pushed its button. A buzz clicked the door open. He stepped in.

There was a bulging woman in a cheap housedress and felt slippers that her bunions had misshaped.

The concierge, Gainer assumed. He had a name ready as his excuse for being there.

The concierge routinely looked him down and up, as though she had seen him a thousand times before. With a dismissing wave of her hand, she indicated the cobbled courtyard beyond, then left him standing there.

There were glass-paned double doors at the deep end of the court-yard, one of which opened, and a thin blond woman appeared. She beckoned to Gainer, invited him in by stepping aside. He went to her and into the foyer of an attractively furnished apartment.

The blond woman's appraisal of Gainer was different than the concierge's. She took an intense measure of him, greeted him with an overlotioned handshake, along with the name Lewiston, which she mispronounced.

She just missed being chic. On her the expensive clothes did not appear to their best advantage. Her blond hair needed a touch-up. The ruby pin on her collar was real but still somehow unbelievable. She asked how Monsieur White was.

Gainer told her Monsieur White was better.

"Oh, has he been ill?"

"No, but he's better."

She smiled tolerantly, led Gainer into the salon.

Any moment he might be meeting one of his men, he thought. Maybe this woman's husband or the man around this house. He sat in the chair he was offered. The woman left the room, not excusing herself.

Within minutes two young girls entered and sort of collapsed rather than sat on the deep sofa opposite Gainer. They were barefoot, had on simple white cotton panties and camisole tops laced loosely with pink silk ribbons. Additional ribbons tangled in their long hair.

They were very pretty.

Gamins was the word for them, Gainer remembered. Thirteen- or fourteen-year-olds was his guess.

They pretended to ignore him, to be preoccupied only with themselves, but he caught their glances. One sat with her legs drawn up so her chin could rest between her knees. Surely an immodest position from Gainer's point of view. The crotch of her panties stretched tight over her mound, a few little coils of pubic hair showing. The other girl was sprawled on her side, just awkwardly enough to cause her camisole to ride up, exposing her rounded tummy and navel.

No doubt they were posturing for him, Gainer thought. They certainly were a couple of teasers. He tried to look elsewhere in the room.

That caused them to take other measures.

They intertwined their slender legs.

Kneeled and bowed so their bottoms seemed offered.

Stuck out a slow tongue at him.

Decided to exchange camisoles, took them off.

Examined a nipple, touched it with a forefinger and thumb.

Gainer got up.

The girls made room between them on the sofa.

He went past them, out to the foyer.

The blond woman was seated there reading *L'Officiel*.

"Is something wrong, monsieur?"

Gainer decided he'd risk describing one of his adversaries to see where that got him. "I'm looking for a man," he said.

"Oh?" the woman arched.

"A certain man—"

"You have come to the wrong place, monsieur, definitely the wrong place." She was brusque and rude the way most French get when they lose money that was practically in their pockets. She wouldn't hear another word.

When Gainer got back to the car Leslie gathered from his attitude that nothing had been accomplished. He did not tell her what had happened only because he didn't feel like going through it at the moment. All he said was: "Let's try the other address."

Boulevard de Menilmontant.

Leslie took a moment to look it up in the little red book: *L'indispensible Repertoire des Rues*.

The boulevard was in the Twentieth Arrondissement. The most direct way to it was the Rue de la Roquette. Leslie timed most of the traffic lights and disregarded many of those she did not get right. Along the way Gainer noticed all but a few shops were closed *pour les vacances,* windows covered by solid metal shutters. Hardly any pedestrians. Like a city expecting enemy planes, he thought.

Boulevard de Menilmontant gave less of such an expression because of the bistros and tabac stands still open. Leslie cruised slowly while Gainer looked for Number 82. On the east side of the boulevard a high, cut-stone wall ran for several long blocks, so he concentrated on the west side. There was Number 115 and Number 103 and after a short ways, Number 83. Next door to 83 was Number 81.

Where the hell was 82?

There was no 82.

Seemed that Rodger's man at the consulate had come up wrong.

"What's that over there?" Gainer wondered aloud as he looked across the boulevard.

Leslie made a U-turn over to where the high, neatly masoned stone wall gave way to a pair of square columns and a grillwork gate heavily chained and padlocked. Immediately beyond the gate was a stone structure that appeared to be an office.

Chiseled deep into one of the columns were the numerals 82, and beneath that cut in the same manner:

CIMETIÈRE DE L'EST
DIT DU PÈRE-LACHAISE

Gainer sank.

What it had come down to was a minor league brothel and a graveyard.

LATER that night, at the house on Avenue Foch, Gainer was again high up on the library ladder.

Searching for *Lord Jim.*

It wasn't where he thought he'd replaced it and in his frame of mind he blamed the book. It was purposely eluding him, hiding among all its confederates so similarly, smugly leather-bound. To hell with it. He pulled out Camus's *L'Homme Revolte,* opened it to any page. A paragraph held him for three sentences before his eyes went over the crease of the binding to Leslie below.

She was within the central medallion of an eighteenth-century Kashan carpet, seemed to be held afloat by twines of blue flowers. She was wearing a wrap-robe of creamy *crêpe de chine* bordered in matching maribou. She had nothing else on. The silk tie of the robe had slipped its knot several times until now she was just letting it have its way. There were several books around her, and she was presently so engrossed in a large, thick one that she nearly tipped over her wine glass when she reached for it.

Gainer asked what was so interesting.

"I'm boning up on that cemetery," she said, not realizing the pun. "It was named after the Jesuit priest who served as confessor to Louis *quatorze.*"

That really helps, Gainer thought unhappily.

"Père-Lachaise was opened in 1804. Before that, for eight hundred years, the main cemetery was the Cimetière des Innocents. More than two million people were buried there.

"Big popular place."

"Only two acres, actually. People were buried on top of one another. In stacks thirty feet deep, seven feet above street level. Imagine."

Gainer tried. He got World War II concentration camp pictures.

"The parish of Saint Germain was paid a fee when anyone was buried at Innocents. It was the only holy ground around and they weren't about to give up their good thing."

"Figures."

"Then it happened."

Gainer's grunt asked the expected what.

"Innocents had a big landslide. Two thousand of its corpses crashed through the walls of apartments. That was in 1780, and that was how Père-Lachaise came to be."

"I thought you said it was started in 1804."

"The French government argued about it for twenty-five years."

"Call what's his name again."

"Grocock."

"Hard to forget. Call him."

"He'll be calling me. Not to worry."

"I still think he's confused."

"I don't."

"What makes you so sure?"

"Intuition."

"Intuition tells a woman she's right whether she is or not."

"What's that from, the Bible?"

Gainer reached down and ran the hard edge of the Camus over his shins, left and right several times. His soccer sores were healing and itching.

Leslie told him: "All kinds of famous people are buried at Père-

Lachaise. Even Heloise and Abelard. Lots of artists—Ingres, Corot, Pissarro, Delacroix, Daumier, Seurat, Modigliani. Did you know Modigliani's mistress killed herself the day after he died? She was buried in Père-Lachaise with him. Her name was Jeanne Hebuterne. She was only twenty-two."

Gainer read a few more lines of *L'Homme Revolte* but couldn't keep his mind on it. He put it back into its space and reached for his glass of wine that precariously balanced on the top edges of *The Memoirs du Marquise de Montespan,* which, Gainer thought when he noticed, would have been more suitable for warming brandy.

"Here's a map of the place!" Leslie exclaimed, discovering and unfolding it. "Come down and look at it with me."

They took the map of Père-Lachaise and another bottle of Chateau Cheval Blanc 1947 to bed with them. It was their third such bottle from Rodger's cellar since dinner. It got to Gainer, rounded his mood considerably.

Leslie lay inside his arm. She held up one edge of the map while he held the other so that Père-Lachaise was spread in front of them. According to the map, the cemetery covered forty-three hectares, twenty-five centiares, fifty-six acres, which Gainer converted via acres to an area around a half-mile by a half-mile.

Leslie traced its outline with a fingernail. "It's shaped like the head of a man."

"Or woman."

"Or woman," she conceded.

"With a next-to-nothing nose."

"No upper teeth."

"Pugnacious son of a bitch, the way the lower lip and jaw juts out." Gainer imitated it.

Leslie said he didn't look so tough. She indicated the various ways inside the lower half of the cemetery, the *chemins* and *allées* and *circulaires.* "It's like a cross-section, and those are veins."

"Grocock hasn't called."

"He will." Leslie pointed to an area marked Number 89. "Oscar Wilde is buried there."

Altogether the map showed ninety-seven numbered divisions. An accompanying list indicated by division where the most notable were buried.

"Sarah Bernhardt is in 44. Where's 44?"

Gainer found it for her, told her, "Balzac is in 48."

"Know what happened to Oscar Wilde's monument?" She took a quick gulp of wine, spilled a drop on the linen sheet that spread like a live pink sea creature. "I read about it. His monument is a sculpting of a nude winged sphinx. Two very proper English ladies became so indignant when they saw it, they found a stone and knocked its balls off."

"You believe that?"

"Sounds likely. Seems they were a sizable pair."

"The English ladies."

"Uh uh. The *conservateur* of Père-Lachaise retrieved them and used them as a paperweight."

"Everything you say is true." He kissed her as he hadn't kissed her since Martha's Vineyard. But he stopped there.

CHAPTER
TEN

A T eleven Monday morning Gainer and Leslie were at Père-Lachaise.

They had not heard from Grocock, but rather than wait on edge for his call Gainer decided he might as well follow through on this lead.

Leslie was more sanguine about it. She was dressed for a cemetery, in a black Giorgio Armani suit, black stockings and black Frizon low-heeled pumps, a white blouse with a high neckline and a square of white silk chiffon flowing from her breast pocket. The jacket of the suit was amply cut and easily accommodated her holstered ASP automatic. The silencer went inside the waistband of her skirt, where the concavity of her backbone left a little room. It was taped there.

Gainer was also very conservatively dressed and had his ASP harnessed on underneath. For an extra touch Leslie urged him to wear one of Rodger's hats. A black homburg. Gainer never wore a hat and he especially didn't want to put his head under one belonging to Rodger —even if it did fit. But he went along with it.

He brought along the shiny metal container that held the ashes of what had been Norma. With the metal container in the crook of one arm and Leslie holding onto his other, they went in through the main gate of Père-Lachaise and down a wide, smoothly cobbled way. On both sides tall trees stood between impressive-looking private mausoleums that Gainer thought looked like miniature versions of solid old bank buildings. Other people were walking along there with guide maps in hand. Evidently tourists come to hover over fame in its ultimate impotence.

A sedate sign directed Gainer and Leslie to the *Bureau de la Conservateur,* which was a small building in keeping with the funerary monuments around it. Inside, a varnished oak counter ran the entire length of the main room. No chairs and a gritty marble floor. Behind the counter was a clerk, a man with a rodentlike face and overgrown sideburns to make up for the absence of hair from his forehead to crown. At the moment he was impatiently explaining to a Polish couple how they could locate the grave of Frederic Chopin.

Aside, in a low tone, Leslie told Gainer: "Only most of Chopin is buried here. His heart is in Warsaw."

Finally, the Polish couple departed.

Gainer and Leslie faced the clerk, who said the automatic: "Monsieur, madame."

"I want to inquire about a place for my sister," Gainer told him, tapping the crematory container.

"C'est impossible."

The common French reaction. Everything was first of all impossible and, if one accepted that, for the French it avoided all the bother that might otherwise follow.

"She always wanted to be here, at Père-Lachaise."

The clerk shook his head no.

"Surely—"

Another no headshake from the clerk, so emphatic it made his mouth flap.

"Money's not a concern," Gainer said.

The clerk cocked his head, quickly took in the black homburg and the size of the diamond on Leslie's wedding finger and said: "You must see the conservateur." He went into an inner office for a moment, returned, lifted away a section of the counter and showed them in.

The conservateur was standing behind a municipal desk. He was tall, gaunt-featured, about forty. Had sunken eye sockets and a dry, merciless mouth. A very pronounced Adam's apple.

Gainer knew immediately that this was one of them. The man locked right into the description. More, Gainer sensed it, as though his hate provided a special antenna. He had the urge to draw the ASP and blow the fucker away. He might have done that if Leslie hadn't been along, no need to incriminate her to that extent.

The conservateur introduced himself as Eugene Becque.

Gainer introduced himself as Mr. Douglas and Leslie as his wife. He placed the can containing Norma's ashes on Becque's desk, indicated it with a nod. "My sister."

"My condolences," Becque said.

Gainer looked at Becque's hands, and thought what they had done.

"You wish her remains to be placed here at Père-Lachaise?"

"Yes."

"Your family has a plot here, perhaps?"

"No."

"We have not been accepting ordinary internments for twenty years. It is a matter of space—"

"James Morrison was buried here in 1971," Leslie put in.

"Who?"

"James Morrison, the musician, one of The Doors."

"There are always exceptions, naturally."

"This is an exception."

"Exceptions are determined by committee."

Gainer tried to look past Becque's eyes, to see the perverse quirk that had brought him to killing Norma.

What Becque saw in Gainer and Norma was a pair of wealthy foreigners who could provide money for many enjoyable days at Longchamp. He also had another "order" coming up. In London. Between the two he would be able to bet and win heavily. "How much . . . do you wish your sister here?" he asked.

"Five thousand. Dollars, of course."

Becque shrugged as though he had just been paid a small insult.

On the wall above his desk was a huge map of Père-Lachaise, showing by name each grave site. A few were marked with red stick-pins.

"There are certain plots that have gone into default." Becque removed one of the red stick-pins. "Fees for upkeep have not been paid for as long as ten to twelve years. Most often the reason is a family has ended, there are no survivors to continue a line. It happens." He replaced the stick-pin.

Gainer waited.

"As conservateur, only I know which sites are delinquent. Not even the *comptabilité* knows, because out of sympathy, of course, I see that the required fees are paid. From my own pocket."

Big-hearted son of a bitch, Gainer thought.

Becque told him: "It would be a most unusual exception, but perhaps it could be arranged for you to assume responsibility of one of those neglected sites for your sister."

"How much?"

"The site I have in mind is in arrears ten thousand. Cash dollars, of course."

"Let's go have a look at it."

"At closing time," Becque said. "We will have more privacy then. Come back at six o'clock. With the money."

THE ten thousand.

It took Leslie three minutes to withdraw it from the Pickering personal account at the Paris branch of Morgan Guaranty Trust. Gainer was hesitant about her doing that. After all, it was his affair, not hers, and certainly not Rodger's. Leslie counterreasoned that such a small amount wouldn't be missed and it could, if Gainer's conscience was so sensitive, be put back—afterward.

While there at Place Vendôme they had lunch at the Ritz, did their best not to discuss Becque. By then, it was three o'clock. They drove back to Boulevard de Menilmontant, where they sat at an outside table of a bistro opposite the cemetery. Drank *citron pressés*. The bistro was called, *Mieux Ici Qu'en Face* (Better Here Than Across the Way).

At four they decided to go over into Père-Lachaise and walk around. For one thing, Leslie had learned that Alain Kardec was entombed there and she wanted to see the spot.

Gainer had never heard of him.

Kardec, Leslie explained on the way, was practically the pope of spiritualism. He'd done more than anyone to make people realize there were things beyond normal consciousness, such as reincarnation. Also bilocation and contacting those on the other side and all sorts of divining.

"What's bilocation?" Gainer asked.

"Being in two places at the same time." Said as though he should have known.

Now that they were deeper in Père-Lachaise they realized what an incredible place it was. The major walkways and most of the small *allées* that ran from them were vaulted by mature trees. Black walnuts, elms and beeches, chestnuts, sycamores, and cherries transformed the sun into a Pointillism. High, thick hiding places for birds that chattered and sang.

An idyllic atmosphere.

Had it not been for the tombs and crypts that lined each way. Side by side, close to touching, they stood like competitors in a morbid architectural contest. Inert, lifelessly asking for attention: canopied altars, sarcarphogi, basilicas, pyramids, obelisks rendered with every sort of column, gable and frieze. No two alike, yet so identical in purpose.

The statuary was most impressive. A bronze man lay fully clothed and rumpled exactly as he had fallen, top hat tumbled off. Another bronze man was partially out of a sepulcher, in the act of rising, pushing up a thick granite lid. A bronze life-size mother was breast feeding. A carved young woman lay as though contentedly sleeping, nude but modestly arranged, her long hair falling over the tomb's edge. In marble, granite and basalt there were nymphs and dogs and owls as accessories to statues kneeling, prone, akimbo and some just striding nowhere.

The more well-known had the simpler graves. Marcel Proust was just a plain horizontal slab. Sarah Bernhardt had only a little arched niche for flowers. Gertrude Stein was a purely linear headstone overlooking a rectangle of bare earth. Apollinaire was a shaft of ordinary raw stone.

Colette was there. And Piaf and Balzac and Loie Fuller.

"Who was Loie Fuller?" Leslie asked.

"The rage of Paris in the 1890s, danced with veils. Toulouse-Lautrec did her."

"You're trying to impress me with a fib."

He didn't answer.

"Want me to carry it for a while?" The container with Norma's ashes in it.

"No." She's not very heavy, Gainer thought.

The map they had studied the night before helped them now. The labyrinth of *allées* was not as confusing as it otherwise would have been, and they located division 44 with only a little difficulty.

Kardec's tomb was situated in a corner of that division. It gave the impression of a primitive shelter made up of rough granite chunks a foot thick on three sides and overhead. Within it was a life-size bust of Kardec done in black, polished bronze and placed at a height so that it gazed out at eye level.

After a reverent moment Leslie whispered, "They say he has more visitors than anyone." Kardec was surrounded by fresh flower tributes, a garland of camellias on his right shoulder. "They also say that on certain nights he acknowledges certain people by blinking," Leslie added.

Gainer limited his skepticism to a short grunt and the next instant was startled by a brushing around his lower legs.

A ginger and white cat.

It dipped its head and rubbed its shoulder above Gainer's ankles, stared up at him for a long moment and closed and opened its amber eyes several times.

"Poor thing's starved," Leslie said.

"Doesn't look it." Indeed, a fat cat.

"I mean, for attention."

Leslie squatted and gave the cat several firm strokes. In appreciative response it raised its hind end, stiffened and slowly snaked its tail.

Another cat approached.

A huge dark brown tabby tom, striped like a tiger with dense black markings on an agouti background. It didn't come directly to them, stalked back and forth with an air of indifference, as though reluctant to admit it needed anything, but with each move came closer and finally within reach. The moment Gainer extended his hand, the tabby collapsed, rolled over and gave in completely to having its chest and belly rubbed.

Along the cemetery ways Gainer and Leslie had noticed quite a number of cats. One in particular that they had encountered, a white with a gray-patched face and paws, had sat in the middle of a walkway making sure the birds kept to the trees, refused to budge, so Gainer and Leslie had to walk around it. Now they became aware of how many more cats were in this vicinity, seemed to be concentrated around Kardec's tomb.

On the peak of every crypt and mausoleum in sight there was a cat. Or two or even three. Sprawled or sitting. Others were settled on the uprights and transverses of crosses, lolling, so relaxed in impossible positions on the top edges of tombstones it seemed miraculous they didn't fall off. All shades and mixtures of cats. Tri-colors, calicos, blacks and nearly all blacks, nearly all whites, slate grays and gingers. Spontaneous mutations. The one that sat on the roof of Kardec's tomb was the most striking. Its dun-colored fur was sleek, and its points, ears, tail and paws, were of blackest black. It had a stronger, more elegant body with a longer neck and smaller wedge-shaped head. Leather black nose. Orange, almond-shaped eyes. A frayed silky ribbon around its neck held a tiny gold bell.

Someone's darling gone astray, Leslie thought.

The cat sat there on the upper edge of the tomb so still it seemed a part of it. It got Gainer by the eyes. Those lustrous orange eyes gazed deep, held him.

Ten minutes to six.

A bell rang. The closing bell, signaling all visitors to leave the cemetery.

Gainer stepped into the entranceway of a nearby mausoleum for cover. He checked his ASP and the two additional full clips he had brought along. He took the automatic off safety, drew it a couple of times for last-minute practice. The holster was so slick the weapon practically jumped out into his grip.

They went into the office of the conservateur.

The clerk was still there.

Becque was on the telephone.

Gainer and Leslie waited outside the building. People were leaving, headed for the main gate.

Gainer told Leslie. "I'll go with Becque. You stay here, right here."

"No."

"Goddamn, *yes.*"

"I want to shoot him too."

The pure and simple way she said it, he almost gave in to her.

The clerk left for the day with a dour *bon soir.*

Becque called them inside. An obligatory smile. His expression asked for the money.

Leslie handed over the sheaf of one hundred brand new hundreds.

Becque riffled through them once, put the money in his jacket pocket.

They went out. Becque and Gainer, with the container of Norma's ashes, walked eastward along the Avenue Perrier, past the Rothschild family sepulcher. Gainer glanced back, saw Leslie was cooperating, sitting on the steps of the crypt next to the office. She threw him a little wave.

Becque and Gainer were going against the flow of stragglers on the way out. They cut across between graves of divisions 14 and 16 and then up a fairly steep grade. Becque took quick, long steps. He had the money, wanted to get the rest of it over with. *Fou Americain* he thought, but said, "A very old section, very desirable," as they passed division 36 and went up another short rise.

Only a few stragglers now.

Gainer's mental map of the cemetery told him he was on the extreme perimeter just above the jutting lower lip of the figurative face Leslie had called attention to the night before. Division 33.

Becque led the way down a short path of bare ground that was obscured by old ivy. The cemetery wall was on the right. A row of dense bushes seven feet high on the left.

At the end of the path was the mausoleum. Small, made up of smooth-cut stone, slender columns left and right and a gently sloped roof with a winged baby angel on its front peak. A *botonée* cross was carved above the entrance, and above that an elongated stone panel for the family name. It was blank, recently sandblasted. The pair of narrow iron doors of the mausoleum were rusty but interestingly detailed. They were wide open, swung inward. Inside was just room enough for two in separate repose.

Gainer asked if the vaults had anyone in them now.

Becque lied, saying that they didn't.

Gainer stepped inside. He placed the container of Norma's ashes on the surface of one of the vaults, then took off Rodger's homburg and placed it over the container. He stood there with his back to Becque, who was waiting outside. Gainer, head bowed, appeared to be saying a prayer while he took out the ASP, screwed the silencer onto it and shoved it down inside his belt, concealed.

On the way out, Gainer slammed the doors shut, their rusted bolt mechanism locking into place.

"There is no key," Becque said. "No way of getting in."

"It doesn't matter."

Evidently it did to Becque. It would inconvenience his selling that mausoleum again. "You left your hat inside," he said, stepped forward and tried the doors, shook them, shoved his weight against them.

Gainer, behind Becque, took out the ASP. Also, from his inside jacket pocket he removed a leather-framed photograph, the one that had been among Norma's belongings, the snapshot of her and him. He pressed the ASP against Becque's spine, simultaneously brought the photograph around before Becque's eyes.

Becque froze.

Gainer wanted the moment to get to Becque as much as possible, for fear to work its special chemistry. No words were necessary. The hard little muzzle of death pressing Becque's back and the photograph said it all.

Becque was no amateur. He had been in the worst of the French war in Indochina for five years, right up to the end in Dien Bien Phu, as near to death as this a number of times. He knew about infighting. What to do and what was best to do when at a disadvantage, even one so point-blank. This man who had somehow gotten on to him meant to kill him, no doubting that. However, this man was not a professional. A professional would not have stood so close behind.

Instead of moving away, making a run for it, as Gainer expected, in one sudden swift motion Becque backed into the muzzle of the ASP, brought a heel down hard on Gainer's instep. The backward thrust of his weight forced Gainer off balance. At the same time Becque turned to the left so that when Gainer pulled the trigger the bullet went by, though so close it burned the fabric of Becque's jacket.

Still continuing the same motion, Becque lunged for the bushes nearby. They seemed to swallow him up, their branches whipping back into place.

Gainer tried to follow but the bushes would not give, were too thick and woven, sprang him back. He must have misjudged the spot Becque had gone through, it had happened so quickly. He ran down the path to where the bushes ended, caught a glimpse of Becque across the cobbled *circulaire,* hurrying down the grade of division 36. He went after him.

Becque, on an in-and-out course, making the most of the cemetery structures, did not stop until he was two divisions away. He crouched beside the tomb of the Comtesse de Noialles. Took stock. He had immediately recognized the woman in the photograph as the recent order he had filled in Zurich. This man was her husband or lover or something enough to want blood. Probably, Becque thought, that fat little bastard who had done the order with him had somehow fucked it up. Should he make his way out of the cemetery, handle this somewhere else later? He did not like the idea of having it biting his mind and not being able to move around town as loose as he liked. No, he'd deal with it here and now in Père-Lachaise, where he knew every inch, and where, if there was a mess, he had the spare tombs to clean it up.

He took out the pistol he always carried in a belt holster on his right side. A 9mm Astra automatic 600. Normally it was his back-up weapon but it would do. He checked its full clip and the spare attached to his belt. Cocked a cartridge into the chamber.

The compressed spitting sound of a silenced automatic being fired.

A slug clanked the corner edge of the Comtesse's tomb just above Becque's head.

He judged the direction from which the shot had come. Moved away, kept low, using the crypts and grave markers for cover. He wanted his adversary to follow, come straight on. To encourage that, he cupped his hands to his mouth and shouted back: *"Leche moi le cul,"* which could only be translated as "lick my ass."

He altered his direction then, darted off to his right through division 50 and cut back around.

There was Gainer.

About a hundred feet away nearing the top of a long flight of stone steps that led up to division 24. Gainer was faced away, stalking, moving cautiously, his attention on where Becque had last been.

Becque raised his pistol, sighted.

It would not be an easy shot at that range.

He decided not to risk wasting the advantage.

In another moment Gainer reached the top of the steps, disappeared from view.

Becque pressed on, he would close ground.

Gainer kept off the main walkways, only crossing over them when he had to. He was no longer sure Becque was somewhere up ahead. He had not entirely understood Becque's shout but obviously it was a curse. Signs of the man's desperation, Gainer thought.

He paused where he was, at the grave of the artist Dominique Ingres, and because it was one that he remembered Leslie pointing out, he knew his location in relationship to the rest of the cemetery. He was in the center of it. He sat with his back against the stone marker of Ingres, remained still, quieted his breath. Slowly he scanned his view, searched for any movement or irregularity of color among the maze of grave markers, monuments, oversize crosses and statues.

The late-day sun was imposing an amber cast—the green of the bushes and trees was going gray, and the gray of the cemetery stonework was turning jaundice. There were no more stragglers that Gainer could see. Probably all gone by now. Birds were singing their final notes, over and over. And here he was, he thought—in Paris in a graveyard sitting over the bones of a fine artist with a gun in his hand and about to use it. He'd sure as hell botched the chance when he'd had it, wouldn't get another so easy. Becque was smart, say that for him.

Footsteps.

Off to the right about thirty feet away beyond the tall bordering row of azaleas.

Gainer kneeled up, slowly, extended the ASP. Aimed at the motion he saw through the intervals in the bushes, followed it with his aim. Took up the slack of the trigger.

Now, in the clear.

A man. In his seventies at least, dressed nattily in a dove-colored summer suit bought forty years ago but fastidiously cared for. Hat to match, and spats. He was carrying a long white box from Frisard, the most prestigious florist on Faubourg Saint Honoré. The box was opened, lined with green tissue for the gladiolas inside it.

The old gent stopped at a grave site, placed the box on the top surface of an adjacent sarcophagus and helped himself to some gladiolas that had been placed there that day. He chose the most fresh, removed any blossoms that had turned or showed any brown from turning. He added those flowers to those in the box, arranged them in layers, professional-like, overlapped the green tissue to cover them and slipped the lid on. He wiped off any grit that might have been picked up by its underside and, box under arm, continued on to be appreciated for his thoughtfulness by a forty-five-year-old divorcee from Copenhagen who was enjoying the last of him. The old gent did not notice Gainer, would never know he had come within a squeeze of having that natty suit ruined forever.

Gainer resumed his lookout for Becque. He again thought he saw him but it turned out to be a cat. He decided to move up the small incline on the left, would have a better view from there.

He crouched, took three steps.

A compressed spitting sound. The slug ricocheted from monument to monument. It had passed so close by Gainer he had felt the heat and the gust of it.

He went down flat, knew now that Becque had a gun.

That turned everything around.

Including Gainer's stomach.

He crawled between two crypts, front down in the dust, through there and beneath a section of cast iron rail and up into the recessed entranceway of a mausoleum that faced onto a main walkway. He believed from the shot that Becque was somewhere off to the right. Directly across the way now was the rise he'd been headed for. It had a good many shrubs and some large monuments for cover. If he made it over there he could circle around, cut back behind Becque as, evidently, Becque had done to him. But wouldn't Becque figure that? This was his turf, every inch of it. If only instead of Père-Lachaise it was Central Park, Gainer thought.

He made a dash for it across the cobbles, dove into the ivy, fought the undertangle of it until he reached the side of a statue's base.

Becque wasn't one to waste shots, Gainer thought, and told himself to keep moving.

He shimmied along the ground over graves, from monument to crypt, using the shrubs and trees for cover. He got up into a crouch when he reached the top of the rise, paused there beside a gaudy sepulcher.

His throat was so dry that breathing hurt.

His shirt was soaked and stuck to him.

He peeked back around the edge of the sepulcher—

A shot from Becque, so close it blasted grit into Gainer's eye and stung his forehead with stone splinter. Which cancelled out any thought of doubling back.

Becque seemed to be driving him, to a wall perhaps, someplace where he'd be cornered. Should he make a stand here? He glanced around for a better place and recognized what he believed was Kardec's tomb a short distance away. Yes, there was the thick rough granite side walls and roof that formed its shelterlike configuration.

At least to some extent it was a familiar spot. Across from it, on the opposite side of a patch of abused grass, was a line of small mausoleums, nearly contiguous, some with less than a foot separating.

Gainer backed in between two of those structures, had to back in because there was not enough room to turn around. He was face down, shoulders wedged in left and right, arms extended, elbows dug into raw dirt, the ASP in both hands.

Kardec's tomb was no more than twenty feet away. From his point of view the lower part of the bust was obscured so that the shiny black head seemed to be emerging from a shroud of flowers.

Wait.

Listen.

Gainer thought he heard someone in the bushes a couple of mausoleums over, but it could have been birds or another cat. Dusk was deepening, only leftover light now. But Kardec was still shining.

At that moment Becque was at the columbarium about two hundred feet away. He had thought Gainer would head for there, for the safety such a large structure would seem to offer. Becque curled around a corner, noiselessly proceeded along the wall of individual enclosed niches, where the urns of ashes were kept. He avoided the little vases of flowers hung there, especially the many at the niche of Isadora Duncan.

Becque was now convinced that he had bypassed his man, but he was still close. He paused, considered the possibilities, settled on the most likely. He moved low, his back nearly horizontal with the ground, darted erratically so not to be a predictable target, in and out between cemetery structures as quiet and sure-footed as he had once been in a Vietnamese village thirty years earlier.

Going for the kill.

Definitely coming in on it now.

Felt a pleasant tightening behind the bridge of his nose and inside his rectum. He approached Kardec's tomb from the back, changed his mind about going along the protected side of it, he would do the unexpected. He used a small crypt to knee himself up over the back edge. Not much time left, not much light either.

He crept across the roof of Kardec's tomb to the front edge, stuck his head up for only an instant, but in that instant took everything in. As he had been trained to do in combat. And then once again.

Satisfied that he had seen nothing, now doubting his instinct, he stood upright on the stone roof, surveyed the area. Stepped forward to climb off.

His left foot and all his weight came down on something squishy. The squeal of kittens.

The mother cat, the dun-colored cat with the silk ribbon and bell at its neck, leveraged her haunches, her tail helping to balance her so the muscles of her hindquarters could spring. All twenty of her claws were extended when she dug them into Becque's face. One claw pierced his eyelid and went on into his eyeball. Another went all the way through his left cheek.

Becque tried his best not to cry out. Tried to pull the cat away, but its curved claws had hold of him and it kept slashing.

Gainer fired.

Three times.

The first 9mm slug hit Becque just above the navel. Doubled him over as it drove him back, tore through the intestines, nicked a branch of the abdominal aorta and continued on to lodge near the middle of the third rib, shattering vertebrae.

In the next instant Becque snapped up stiffly and spun, his arms flailing grotesquely, as though his sleeves were stuffed with rags. He fell backward off the tomb.

Gainer extricated himself from between the mausoleums.

The dun-colored cat was still on Becque's face but on seeing Gainer it released him and leaped to the roof of Kardec's tomb.

Gainer examined the spreading splotch of blood on Becque's lower shirtfront. That was the shot he had carefully squeezed off. He'd jerked his second and third so badly they must have missed.

But there, higher up on Becque's chest, was another entry wound, just left of center, where it must have blown away half the man's heart.

Hell of a shot, Gainer thought.

He took the ten thousand from Becque's jacket pocket, as well as his wallet. He turned all Becque's pockets inside out. There was nothing in them but a few francs.

He twisted the silencer off the ASP, put it away and put the ASP in its holster. He then ran full out down the main walkway as straight as possible to the office of the conservateur.

Leslie was where he had left her.

But she was out of breath and trying hard not to show it. Her hair was kinked with perspiration around her forehead. Her suit was soiled with dust. She emptied a pebble from her shoe.

Gainer was so glad to see her he scarcely noticed. Or maybe he was too pumped up. He said nothing except, "Come on."

The main gate was still open. Becque was supposed to have closed it later.

Gainer and Leslie walked at a leisurely pace out of Cimetière du Père-Lachaise as though they had just paid some late respects to a late friend.

BACK at the Avenue Foch house, first thing, Leslie squirted a double dose of Rescue Remedy into Gainer's mouth and then drew a bath. She put a cupful of powdered ginger into the bath water and swooshed it around. The water looked to be suffering from old plumbing and had somewhat the odor of a restaurant in downtown Calcutta. Nonetheless, Leslie removed her clothes, let them drop wherever they came off and got in up to her chin.

Gainer paced. From the bathroom through the bedroom to the sitting room and back. Like a marathon runner cooling down.

He hadn't expected such a reaction, but then he'd never killed anyone before or been so close to being killed. His adrenal gland had squirted some of its own sort of Rescue Remedy into his stream and he was still feeling the high of it. He thought of having a drink, a double straight, the way most heroes got out of such a state, but he felt if he did his head would surely leave him.

"Poor love," Leslie said, when he paced into the bathroom for the fifth time.

She got out of the tub, mindless of dripping ginger water. Stopped him. Undressed him. Took off his holster harness and ASP and hung them on a towel hook. He sat on the edge of the bidet so she could yank off his trousers.

She noticed he was half hard.

The tub was an oversize European fixture, long and deep. Leslie got into the slanted end, spread her legs for Gainer to sit between them, his back to her. She put her arms around and brought him to her, so that the top of his head was just beneath her chin.

"I'm heavy on you," he said.

"Relax darling. Relax."

The water buoyed him as, little by little, he let go. Maybe it was the ginger, but more likely the caring of her got to him, calmed him.

"What was at that first address?" she asked.

"Hmm?"

"The one on Rue de la Cerisaie."

"Nothing."

"You were in there too long for nothing."

"Okay. It was a whorehouse."

168

She was not surprised. "Never know what's happening behind inno-
cent-looking doors in this town."

"Or anywhere."

"I suppose there were fat old whores with cellulite and everything
flopping around."

"What makes you think that?"

"I was in a whorehouse."

"Doing what?"

"Working."

A skeptical grunt from Gainer. "When?"

"Years ago, doing a fashion spread for British *Harper's.* I think the
place was on Rue Saint Denis. The idea was to use it for atmosphere
with the whores just as they were. The whole thing ended up pretty
obscene."

"And you walked out."

"If that's what you believe, that's what I did."

"Rue de la Cerisaie wasn't that sort of place."

"What did it have, men for sale?"

He told her about the very young girls.

She dropped the subject, reached with her toes to turn the porcelain
tap designated *chaud* just enough to cause a steaming dribble.

Gainer could almost hear her mind doing some fast arithmetic about
relative ages. Anything that he might say at that moment to reassure
her would be too obvious, he decided. Besides, as usual she made a
quick recovery.

"Tomorrow," she said, "what we ought to do is go shopping."

"For what?"

"Whatever. Maybe you'd let me buy you something at Ceruti. How
about a whole outfit? . . . You've stopped grinding your teeth."

"Was I grinding, really?"

"Like a pepper mill, but the Rescue Remedy took care of it. Every-
time you think of it you should take some Rescue."

"I don't want to get overrescued."

"You won't, I promise," she said with a barely discernible edge. She
took a deep breath for a new start. "Two things I'd like to do for sure
tomorrow. Kiss you shamelessly on the Pont Alexandre and go a little
crazy at the Boulangerie Poilane."

"Did Grocock call?"

"While we were out."

"*Shit.*"

"He'll call back. Ever been to Poilane's?"

"No."

"It's on Rue Cherche-Midi, of all places. Cherche-Midi derives from an old French pessimism aimed at people who chase the impossible: *Cherche-Midi a midnuit,* looking for noon at midnight."

It didn't apply, Gainer told himself. Proof was a dead Becque.

He sat up.

Leslie soaped his back and rubbed it with a loofa.

"Possibly," she said, "what we should do is settle for what's been done. Take the first Concorde home."

"Do that."

"Not without you."

"I suppose that's what your spirit guide says, run home."

"Actually I haven't consulted her yet and she doesn't seem to be volunteering anything."

"I've talked to mine."

"Oh? You've got one now?"

"Yeah."

"Since when?"

He almost said since last week, but maybe the truth was since the day he was born.

Leslie turned his head to her, to make sure he was serious. She was pleased when he didn't wink or grin or anything. "Who is he, your spirit guide?"

"She's a she."

"Do you know why she chose you?"

"It's Norma," Gainer told her.

Leslie considered it. Decided Gainer might think he was merely saying that without realizing how sensible it was. Often that was the way with spirit guides. "So, what does Norma advise?"

"Norma keeps telling me what I should do is . . . waste them."

A quiver started at Leslie's tailbone, climbed her spine and humped down to her pelvis. She had been testing with her remark about flying home. She would have been disappointed if he had agreed.

They got out of the ginger bath, their skins crimson, took a rinsing shower and put on terrycloth robes. Leslie insisted on cleansing Gainer's aura. "Can't have you absorbing any of Becque's negative junk." She put a lot of effort into her air-scrubbing motions, and Gainer stayed still for it, which was a way of showing his gratitude.

They had dinner in her sitting room at a table by the open french doors. The city humming of Paris was a sort of accompaniment.

Afterward, in just the right amount of light, they lay on the bed. Side barely touching side, silent but with overlapping thoughts. A little while to create a chrysalis that might keep out crematoriums and ASPs.

Leslie was asking things to please be easier on him, to allow once again, soon, the normal easy flow of his emotions, feelings. Whatever he had to go through she'd go with him. Even if it meant walking on shards all the way to one of his old-time genuine smiles.

Gainer was trying to recall Norma as he had last seen her alive, his very last instant of her. The impression should have been easy and clear for him, he thought, but he couldn't get it without getting Leslie too. Leslie and Norma, composite, like two slides together in a projector.

He reached down.

Touched his cock.

His cock was full, hard. It occurred to him that maybe it was a reaction from the excitement of killing, a way of verifying he was still alive, vital.

Leslie's hand traveled down to him, to it.

He intercepted her hand, replaced it on the pillow near her face, as though it were a valuable, fragile object. He rose above her, and without touching any other part of her, placed his open mouth on hers. He asked nothing of her, kept his mouth merely lightly pressed for a long moment and then said into her: "I love you."

Words left unsaid, Leslie thought. She remained dead still. He could do what he needed to do with her.

He was particularly gentle now. The enormous energies of his rage and his love, intermixed and contained within a sort of emotional funnel, came from him by way of only a delicate pinpoint opening. His fingertips phrased his worship, were like whispers, so weightless wherever they traced or skipped on her. His tongue was like a wet brook stone that rolled down the inside of her arms, over her ribs, around the knubs of her ankles.

He did not want her to move for him.

He would move her.

He lifted her legs into arches, pushed aside left and right, their tension gone, so she could not be more open. Her thighs were like thresholds that he shaped his hands to and stroked again and again up to her center, as though accumulating her there.

She had gone wet and was parted long before he traveled her exactly and parted her more.

Please.

CHAPTER
ELEVEN

THE green Bentley turned off the auto route to the west at Cocheret. From that point on Route 181N it would be only five miles to Vernon, across part of the plateau between the River Eure and the Seine, countryside flat and growing, punctuated mostly by cows that could munch nearly anywhere they put their heads down.

Early that morning Grocock had, at last, phoned with the information and Leslie had scribbled it on a bedside notepad, with her eyes closed. As soon as she hung up she covered her eyes with the embroidered edge of a pillowcase to keep the day from beginning. She wanted to snuggle and drift until at least ten and then get up to nothing more pressing than some impetuous spending along Saint Honoré. Last night Gainer had loved a lot of the go out of her, had kept her coming and coming. Not that she complained, but she vaguely recalled having mumbled to him just before falling off that too much of anything could be toxic. Maybe even lovemaking.

With the first ring of Grocock's call, Gainer was out of bed, as though he'd been lying there awake just waiting for it. Leslie did not get up until she heard the mechanical sounds of Gainer checking his ASP, inserting a fresh full clip and clicking a round into the chamber. He was already showered and dressed and had to wait while she did her face and fussed some with her hair. She remarked that the suit she had worn the day before had been too damned confining. For today she got headfirst into a dress of sheer linen gauze that was abundant and free.

And vulnerable to backlight, Gainer noticed.

She shoved the sleeves up and let the front plunge. Took her ASP from its holster, tossed it and the sheaf of ten thousand dollars into her canvas carryall.

12 Chemin des Coquelicots.

That was the address Grocock had come up with for the Vernon telephone number. Also a name:

"Emil Ponsard, Expert."

Humble fucker, Gainer thought. How could anyone come right out and advertise himself as a know-it-all.

"It's a profession, being an expert," Leslie said.

"What is he, a tout?"

"An appraiser."

"What kind?"

"Probably antiques or art."

With that in mind, before leaving the house, Leslie removed two paintings from the upper gallery: *Road to Honfleur in Winter,* signed Claude Monet 1865, and an 1881 Edgar Degas *Portrait of Mary Cassatt.* Both paintings had been acquired by Rodger several years earlier through the Wildenstein Gallery, and there was no doubt as to their authenticity. It was a simple matter for Leslie to unsnap the canvases from their frames. She wrapped them in a cashmere car robe and put them in the trunk of the Bentley. She had no plan, just a notion that the paintings might somehow serve in getting to this Ponsard.

Gainer agreed they might be useful, but he hoped to be more direct. His experience with Becque had forewarned him. He had come foolishly close to being blown away. This time he would handle it in strictly street fashion. Instead of surprise bang it would be bang surprise. Goddamn but that sounded ugly tough, he thought, and promised himself it would be temporary.

Vernon.

They were coming to it now, Gainer navigating with the help of page 153 of a *Guide Michelin* for Normandy. A winding downward grade suddenly became Avenue Montgomery and they were in the town before they knew it. Predictably, like most French towns of modest size, Vernon had its pre-Renaissance cathedral, its Place de Gaulle and its Hôtel de la Poste. But it also had an impressive but not overwhelming chateau, the Chateau Bizy.

"Royalty used to come here a lot," Gainer said, informed by the *Guide Michelin.*

"Probably the king without the queen."

"Or the other way around."

"A royal fucking," Leslie thought, remembering a man in her hometown in Wales who had often used that phrase. Leslie had been old enough then to know what a fucking was but hadn't understood the distinction of one that was royal. It had always brought to her mind a literal, and unacceptable, image of Queen Elizabeth on her back.

The Bentley cut across the street that led up to the chateau.

Gainer imagined some straying queen sneaking into town with her lover, but still going up that street in a gilt carriage pulled by six matched horses and followed by a retinue of fifty, including, probably, a half dozen trumpeters. He again checked the map for Chemin des Coquelicots. It just wasn't indicated.

Leslie pulled over and asked directions from a man delivering wine. She caught him just as he'd heaved a full cask onto his back; his load, though, was considerably lightened, thanks to the way Leslie always drove with her skirt pulled way up. He was most obliging, glad to take the time to repeat his directions, even though his knees were giving way.

Chemin des Coquelicots was on the western outskirts of the town, an unpaved road that was like a green tunnel the way the bushes and trees were so thick around and above it. Every so often a clearing, tall summer grass speckled profusely with the red heads of poppies, made it evident how the road got its name—poppies *(des Coquelicots).* None of the few houses along here had numbers on them, but no matter, Gainer and Leslie could not miss Ponsard's house when they came to it. A professionally painted sign by its entrance announced in arrogant French script:

"M. Emil Ponsard, Expert."

Leslie drove slowly by so Gainer could look the place over. She turned the Bentley around and pulled over to the side of the road a short distance from the house. Cut the motor.

The place, more impressive than the other houses they had seen along the way, was constructed of brick and isolated by a corresponding eye-level wall. Two stories in the style *Regence,* with a blue-gray slate roof. Not a very large house, ten rooms at most, but it was pleasingly set, umbrellaed by mature trees and surrounded by well-tended shrubs and perennials.

The only sounds at the moment were birds chirping and Gainer's and Leslie's breathing. They watched for five minutes. Then, Gainer got out.

"I'm going with you," Leslie whispered.

"Be ready to drive," Gainer told her emphatically, and took off for the house.

He thought about going over the wall. It would have been easy, but he reminded himself to keep it *street,* simple, right through the main gate. He would know his man on sight, but his man would not know him.

Gainer walked in as though he belonged there, right up to the front door.

Pulled on a bronze knob that rang a bell inside.

No one came.

Knocked loudly on the door.

Still no one came.

He went around the side of the house to the rear, where the grounds ran quite deep. Far back were several apple trees. A ladder was propped up against one of them, and Gainer could detect movement among the branches. And the white of a shirt. He slipped the fingertips of his right hand in under his jacket, advanced to the apple tree until he was only some twenty feet from it.

He saw the black trouser legs of the man up in its branches, and called out: "Monsieur Ponsard?"

The man climbed down the ladder with some difficulty. He had a manual insecticide pump in hand. He was frail, old. He did not fit the description at all. He looked back up the tree, cursed the caterpillars and then acknowledged Gainer quizzically.

Gainer told him: "I'm looking for Monsieur Ponsard."

"He is not here."

"Do you know where he is?"

"I am the gardener, and the carpenter and the cook," the man complained.

"Where is Monsieur Ponsard?"

"At this moment?"

"Yes."

"He is painting."

"Painting what?"

"Haystacks." The man followed that with a nasal scoff and made for the house.

Gainer had to get the directions to Ponsard from him, and just did manage to get the last, most vital part of them as the man went inside, slammed the door and, as an afterthought, bolted it.

Gainer hurried back to the Bentley, immediately recited the directions out loud to keep them straight. He applied them to the *Michelin* map and found the way, navigated for Leslie, back to the town and through it, and up a grade to open countryside.

The first sign they saw of what might be Ponsard was a silver-gray Citroën sedan parked on the side of the road adjacent to an open, sloping field. About a hundred yards out in the field was a heap of something white that Gainer couldn't make out exactly. It didn't seem to be a person, the way it just sat there.

Gainer got out and started off into the field. The grass was taller, thicker than it looked. He had to wade through it with high steps. As he got closer to the white image he saw it was a figure in a white smock coat and a white cap seated beneath a white umbrella.

A man painting.

He had an easel up and a canvas on it. He did not notice Gainer, intent as he was on dabbing with a long brush.

It had to be Ponsard, Gainer thought, and continued on. The noontime sun was glaring, striking so intensely on the white figure that Gainer could not clearly make out the man, but he kept his eyes fixed on him and at a range of about fifty feet the figure in white locked in, correlated with the description Gainer had been carrying in his mind since Alma. The chunky build, the round, almost chinless face, a wrestler's neck.

This was his man, Gainer was sure of it, felt it. He put his hand in under his jacket, gripped the ASP. But could he just kill the man without warning—?

Goddamn right he could, Norma.

He took a few more steps, decided he would get closer, as close as he could, point blank if possible, at least until the man noticed him. Only twenty feet to go.

Gainer was about to draw the ASP, have it aimed and ready.

Something came up out of the grass between himself and the man.

A young girl.

She got to her knees, stood up, squinted at Gainer. She was entirely nude. A girl in her early teens with breasts that were mere promises and a sparse triangle of fine blond floss at her crotch. The hair on her head was gathered back and held by a number of narrow pastel-colored ribbons, long ribbons that flowed down her skin. She was pretty, had a full, slightly pouty mouth and large eyes. Her hello to Gainer was a question.

The man looked up.

Gainer's hand released the ASP and came out from under his shirt.

"Monsieur Ponsard?" Gainer said.

"Yes."

"I was told I'd find you here."

Ponsard quickly took Gainer in, and rejected him for the painting. He chose a different, smaller brush to make a few small commalike strokes of yellowish white, careful with them. "Haystacks are very illusive," he said.

Gainer glanced further out in the field to a mound of hay, pale and dry under the sun. It was only remotely represented by what Ponsard had put on the canvas: a stringy ocher lump set nondimensionally on an attempt to capture the texture of the grass. Gainer thought it looked more like the top of a lopsided head emerging from green ooze.

"Monet's haystacks were only a little better," Ponsard said, mostly to himself. "Monet was extremely fortunate with his haystacks." He had a dead Gauloise stub between his lips, it stuck to his upper one as he spoke. "Who sent you to me?" he asked Gainer.

Gainer glanced at the naked girl, who stood there as though she was too young for modesty.

Ponsard noticed and told her to get dressed.

Which gave Gainer time to invent. "A dealer in Paris recommended you. He said you were the most dependable expert on Monet."

"You are writing a book?"

"We have a painting."

"You want me to appraise it."

"Yes."

"My fee is one percent of the value," Ponsard said as he squinted at the haystack. "Oh well," he sighed, "the light was changing anyway. Most people cannot discern such subtle changes in light and its effect on color." He tossed his dirty brushes into his palette box, didn't bother to put the caps back on the used tubes of paint. However, he was very careful with his bad, wet painting.

The girl had put on a simple white cotton dress that was next to nothing. Ponsard said she was Astrid, his niece.

Gainer did not believe the niece part. Astrid was too similar to the young girls he had encountered at that brothel on Rue de la Cerisaie. Her precociously erotic attitude . . . that would explain the phone call from Zurich to that address. It fit.

Gainer said his name was Crawford. Mrs. Crawford was waiting in the car.

Astrid took down the umbrella and the easel, carried them to Ponsard's car.

Ponsard stuffed himself behind the wheel of his Citroën and abused its ignition. Astrid rode in the rear seat like a privileged passenger. All the way to Ponsard's house she kept glancing back at the green Bentley, as though such an expensive car could not be disregarded.

Within ten minutes they were at Ponsard's house, in the large room that he called his studio. Gainer had brought the two paintings in from the car for Ponsard to examine beneath a skylight. He studied them from across the room and close up, front and back; inspected the canvas frames and stretchers and used a magnifying glass to examine the brushstrokes.

There was no need for all that, really. Ponsard knew the paintings were genuine and worth a fortune the moment they came before his eyes. He was using the time to decide whether he should go for his appraisal fee, which would be a considerable amount in this instance, or . . . "Where did you get these paintings?" he asked.

"My grandfather," Leslie replied quickly. "He died last month and we found them among his old junk."

"Has anyone else looked at them?"

"No."

Gainer appraised the appraiser, who was evidently a different sort than Becque. What was their connection? Gainer wondered. Why had they been in Zurich together—a cemetery keeper and an art expert? Why would they have shared a room at the Dolder Grand? Something about it didn't jibe, Gainer thought.

Ponsard's overgrown eyebrows went up. He ran his palms over his incorrigible hair. These were gullible Americans, he assured himself. He turned his back on the paintings, to demonstrate their unimportance. He sat in a leather armchair that was conditioned to his weight and shape. Astrid lay on the floor at his feet like some obedient pet.

"Excellent attempts," Ponsard said, "especially the Monet."

"Attempts?"

"Whoever painted them should have had more confidence in his own ability."

Leslie acted disappointed. She went into her carryall, felt beneath her ASP for a tissue that she used to dab at her eyes.

Gainer wished Astrid would disappear. Had the girl not been there to witness right then, he would have silently put a 9mm hole in Ponsard's forehead. He watched Ponsard light another Gauloise and exhale the first puff from his nostrils. He imagined Ponsard's brain was on fire.

"I'm sorry," Ponsard said, "your paintings are not worth what you expected."

"It doesn't matter," Leslie said, turning blasé.

The lying bastard, Gainer thought, and anticipated what would be coming next from him.

"You know . . . actually . . ."—Ponsard glanced around at the paintings as though condescending to give them a second thought— "they are not authentic but they are also not intolerable."

"There's nothing I hate more than a fake," Leslie said.

Ponsard did not catch her double edge. "I could use them as examples in my profession."

Leslie gave them away with the back of her hand. "They're yours," she said.

Ponsard said he couldn't accept them.

"Well, I certainly can't be bothered with lugging them around," Leslie said, nose up.

"Then . . . I insist on paying you for them. Shall we say twenty-five hundred francs?"

"How much is that in dollars?"

"About five hundred."

"For both paintings?"

"Twenty-five hundred each."

"Oh, I'd say that's most generous of you, Monsieur Ponsard." Leslie beamed her best model's smile. "Isn't it, darling?"

"Most generous," Gainer said.

Ponsard had trouble downplaying it. God, but he wanted those paintings, so much his balls ached. The Degas would fetch a half million, at least, the Monet even more. These two Americans were uncultured assholes, probably *nouveau riche* from selling breakfast cereals or canned soup or something. Served them right.

Ponsard got out some of his letterhead business stationery. He composed a detailed, binding bill of sale. Took ten five hundred franc notes from a desk drawer, handed the money, the bill of sale and the pen to Leslie.

She stuffed the money into her carryall, signed the bill of sale without reading it.

Ponsard checked the signature of Mrs. L. G. Crawford, folded the bill of sale and put it in the desk drawer, locked the drawer and made a tight possessive fist around the key. Done, he thought, done! He was so elated he felt like having Astrid use her mouth on him again, and would as soon as these Americans were gone. Meanwhile, he'd throw them a couple of tidbits. He felt expansive. "You know, of course, Monet lived in this area."

"Did he really?"

"In Giverny, just a few kilometers from here. Lived there for thirty-six years, died there."

"He's probably still there," Leslie said.

Ponsard gave her the benefit of not having said what he'd heard.

"In spirit," Leslie explained with a quick little smile.

"As a matter of fact," Ponsard told her, "Monet's house and gardens

179

have been restored to the way they were in his time."

"All the more reason for him to be around."

Ponsard lowered his head and sneaked a look at her through his eyebrows. "The place has been declared a national site," he said.

"Oh, I'd love to see it!"

Ponsard felt himself saved by the day. "It's Tuesday," he said. "It is closed on Tuesday." The last thing he wanted to do with the afternoon was play personal guide-to-Monet for these two.

"Won't someone be there?" Leslie asked.

"No one."

"Wonderful! We'll have the whole place to ourselves."

"But—"

"Surely you can arrange for it, Monsieur Ponsard. After all, you are an expert."

Ten minutes later they were in the green Bentley headed for Giverny.

The problem was still Astrid. No matter how pointedly Leslie and Gainer told her she'd be bored, she would not be left behind. For one thing, she wanted to experience the green Bentley, so that she wouldn't have to make a total lie to the other girls. She'd already thought up for them an elaborate memoir of the lurid things she'd been required to do in the car. Even more important, however, was her practical reason for going along. Madame Brossolette, the woman who ran the rendezvous at 12 Rue de la Cerisaie, had taught her never, under any circumstances, to allow a client to leave without first settling his account. The client in this instance, of course, being Ponsard.

So, there was Astrid in the rear seat. And Gainer in the rear with her. Ponsard had thought it best that he sit in front where he could more easily give directions. Leslie had the window all the way down on her side and sat so close to it she was nearly sideways to the steering wheel. Because Ponsard smelled of Gauloise cigarettes and roses. His clothing was permeated with smoke, and before leaving the house he had splashed his cheeks and neck with a heavy cologne. So heavy, it made Leslie's eyes water.

They drove through town. Ponsard pointed out puncturelike indentations on the walls of some of the buildings where bullets had struck. "The Germans wounded Vernon badly when they came in 1940, and I must say the Americans did worse to it in 1944," Ponsard said and, as though it was the most important thing that had happened since the ninth century when Rollo established the town, Ponsard added, "I was born here."

He's about to die here, Norma, Gainer thought.

They crossed over the Seine to the satellite village of Veronette and stopped there at the house of the government-appointed Monet estate caretaker. Ponsard went inside. Across the way was a pâtisserie with its door open and wonderful baking fragrances wafting out. Leslie's mouth watered. Astrid stuck her head out and inhaled through her nose several times. They could see the reds of things raspberry and the yellows of things lemon and the white of sprinkled powdered sugar on the tops of things on display in the pâtisserie window. Leslie sent a strong mental message to Gainer, urging him to jump out and get some. But just then, Ponsard returned, jangling a ring of keys, holding them up rather victoriously to convey that he had been able to make the necessary special arrangements.

Leslie expressed her frustration by pressing the engine up to nearly 5000 RPMs and leaving black traction marks on the cobbles of the street. The road to Giverny had the Seine and a single set of railroad tracks running beside it. Here and there were the lighter green droops of willows or the higher spears of poplars. Wild bushes grew dense along the way, competing for the sunlight that was somewhat demure now, hiding behind a haze. Leslie drove the road as though she knew it, at high speed with no letup for any dip or turn.

She was doing nicely until a curve deceived her, and the Bentley swerved around it, momentarily out of control. The centrifugal force sent Astrid flying over onto Gainer. It could not have been more opportune as far as she was concerned. Her right hand braced on his crotch, grasped it, and while the sensation of that overwhelmed him, her left hand went in under his jacket to remove a leather case from his inside pocket. Recovering, she slipped the case beneath her right buttock, sat on it for a while and, when no one was looking, dropped it out of sight down the front of her dress. She'd done it almost instinctively, as though only her hands were responsible. It was something she'd learned early from her mother, a whore in Hamburg. Any day she picked a pocket she didn't have to go to school—those had been her mother's terms. At the moment, however, Astrid almost regretted her behavior. The wallet hadn't felt fat, felt thin in fact. Still, *maybe* it contained brand new hundreds, or even better. She knew that certain people carried only new money because they were afraid of germs. She glanced over to Gainer and said the word *fuck* to herself. This one didn't look as though he was afraid of anything, let alone germs.

Leslie parked the car on the Chemin du Roy, right at Monet's front gate. Ponsard made a minor ritual out of unlocking the gate and, acting as host, stood aside for them to enter.

The house was situated on the north side of the road, set back about two hundred feet. It was on three acres, rectangularly shaped and walled all around. In the far right corner of the grounds was Monet's main studio, high-peaked with much more skylight than roof. In the opposite corner was his second studio overlooking the thousands of panes of his greenhouse. Between the two studios was the house itself, a long, two and one half story structure somewhat resembling the architectural personality of an army barracks. It was saved, to some extent, by the creeper vines that overgrew its rough pink-cast surface, softly disguising corners, obscuring most of the repetitive eaves and sills.

From the porch of the house all the way to the road was garden— as true as possible to the way Monet had originally laid it out. The trellises that spanned the wide center path were climbed upon by pink and crimson roses, and bordering that path were creeping nasturtiums, daisies, white, pink and violet asters, delphiniums, dahlias and anemones. Although there was a certain symmetry to the spacing of the beds and walkways, the attitude was by no means formal, a far cry from Le Notre, this garden of Monet's, where mats of nasturtium were allowed to spread beyond their territories and wild geraniums, abrietta and pink saxifrage were disciplined as little as possible. One had to walk with care not to step on them.

Irises stood up with their tongues out.

Gladiolas looked as though if shook they would ring.

Hollyhocks were attentive, listening in all colors.

Gainer and Leslie had expected a pretty garden but not this. They were struck to the point of near-reverence.

Ponsard suggested that they begin their tour on the other side of the road. A passageway tunnel ran beneath the road and the railroad tracks, and when they were in it Ponsard's echoing voice told them this convenience had recently been installed with the money of some wealthy American. Monet, he was certain, would have detested it.

Gainer didn't think so. From what he'd read, Monet had appreciated advantages when he could finally afford them. Monet had owned a motor car in 1901, a Panhard-Levassor, and had had a chauffeur. He had eaten his share of *foie gras* from Alsace and truffles from Perigord, had worn suits made for him of fine English wool, the trousers fastened at the ankles by three bone or gray pearl buttons. His boots were of the best leather, made especially for his feet, his shirts were of intricately pleated cambric with ample elaborate cuffs.

Emerging from the tunnel, the first thing Gainer's eyes came on was the Japanese bridge, the same that Monet had rendered on canvas so many times in so many different moods of light. The bridge spanned about thirty feet over the narrower end of Monet's pond. The pond was about two hundred feet long and at its widest point fifty feet. It was the soul of that piece of land. On its bank was a mirror forest of bamboo, enormous ferns, masses of rhododendrons and azaleas, tall blades of iris guarding soft purple blossoms half in and half out of the water all along the edge. And water lilies, great gatherings of them with their white faces wide open at this time of day, their leaves like flat, floating hearts.

Leslie recalled having seen some of Monet's water lily series years ago at the Louvre. She had been entranced by the nuances Monet had caught, the simple qualities, and had thought at the time the man must have been blessed with special, unusual eyesight that enabled him to see the aura of the blossoms. *Des Nymphéas,* the water lilies, had been Monet's subject for thirty years and were the last thing he painted. There, on the bank of his pond, on the very spot where Leslie now stood, was where he had set up several easels in a row and worked on canvases in sequence according to the changes in the light.

It seemed to Leslie she could feel Monet's presence. She turned her head slowly, and would not have been surprised if there had stood Monet with his white Santa beard and round crowned straw fedora. Instead, she saw Ponsard, who was urging them to press on.

They walked along the path that duplicated the pond all around.

Gainer was not so caught up in the esthetics of the place. He had at least an eye and a half out for a good spot to kill Monsieur Ponsard, the *expert.* At one point, when he and Leslie were far enough from the others, he whispered, "Get the girl away from here." Leslie kissed him near his ear and told him she'd try. They went back through the tunnel and up the center path to the porch of the house. Ponsard was relating a piece of trivia about Monet when Astrid interrupted: "I have to pee," and she went into the house.

Ponsard started to go on with what he had been saying, then left the sentence unfinished and also went inside. He did not know Astrid well, had been with her only twice before, but he knew her well enough not to let her wander alone among precious things. He could too well imagine her lack of resistance to an irreplaceable Monet memento, such as the Japanese ceramic in the glass cabinet in the drawing room. Ponsard called out for her.

No reply.

Aha, she was up to something! He went from the entrance hallway, through the main salon to the drawing room at the extreme east end of the house.

There was Astrid. But she was not paying any attention to the glass cabinet or anything else in the room. She was reaching up in under her skirt past the sash that she had knotted at her waist. On seeing Ponsard she immediately let her skirt drop, sat in one of the wicker chairs, her hands laced in her lap and with a slight, innocent upturn to the corners of her mouth.

"What were you doing?"

"Nothing."

"You have something inside your dress."

"I had an itch you know where."

"Let me feel."

She expected him to go up between her bare legs, but he frisked her above her waist, found the leather case she had concealed there.

She resorted to the truth, only because lying was now useless, and told him how she had lifted Gainer's wallet, hoped that Ponsard would see the justice of poor her having done that to a rich American.

What Ponsard saw was a possible threat to the transaction he had just made for the two paintings. Astrid's petty thievery might cast suspicion on his own honesty, and although he had the bill of sale all tidy and tight, the two Americans could make a legal fuss.

He grabbed Astrid by her hair, pulled her head up by it and slapped her with a forehand and a backhand, sharp, powerful slaps that caused her cheeks to blotch red.

She didn't cry out or struggle. She had been slapped as hard and more on other occasions. Slaps didn't last so long.

Ponsard shoved his hand down the front of her dress, so harshly he ripped the neckline. He brought out the leather case.

It was not a wallet.

Ponsard flipped it open, saw the photograph it contained. A man and a woman with an obvious family resemblance. The man was this American, Crawford. The woman was . . . the order in Zurich. It was her, no mistaking it.

It wasn't a coincidence.

Becque, the careless son of a bitch—Becque was somehow to blame, Ponsard was sure.

His mind rapidly replayed the day, and he now realized that all the while these Americans had been looking down his throat. Well, he thought, Astrid, the undeveloped whore with the practiced mouth had inadvertently shifted the advantage in his favor. Instead of expressing his gratitude he told her he wasn't going to pay her—unless she did exactly as he said. She was to take the leather case and, unnoticed, place it on the floor of the rear seat of the green Bentley. In the event it was missed it would be found there and he would still have the edge.

Astrid agreed, took the case, deposited it again down her neckline and ran from the rooms as though reprieved.

Ponsard stayed there. He reached in under his suit jacket, around the back of his trousers to where the seam of the seat met the waistband. Located there was a concealed pocket, tailored to hold what Ponsard called his *bébé doux,* his sweet baby.

A .25 caliber Browning automatic. Made in Belgium, so compact Ponsard could practically palm it. It actually had the word *Baby* trademarked on its grip.

Under other circumstances the Baby would not have been Ponsard's first-choice weapon. He had never relied solely on it, carried it only as a backup. However, he was skilled with it, and its deadliness had served him efficiently three times in the past. It would do. He released its clip, checked that it had eight hollow-nose cartridges, rammed the clip home and slipped it into his jacket pocket.

Ponsard was a very experienced killer, an expert at art and death. He'd been extensively initiated at the age of nineteen during the Algerian revolution when the French soldiers seemed to be creating new, excruciating ways for people to die. With that behind him, Ponsard became a middleman in the system when he was twenty-five. His profession and his slightly fatuous manner were a perfect cover, helping him to fill orders in almost every major city in Europe.

Without a hitch.

Until now.

Ponsard turned to leave.

Gainer was standing in the doorway.

How long had he been there? Had he seen the Baby? Ponsard had to assume not. He smiled, "You've been exploring on your own."

Gainer nodded twice, thought he should return the smile but couldn't.

"I thought we would start upstairs," Ponsard said, "perhaps with the bedroom where Monet used to sulk whenever he disliked his work or whenever the asparagus was overcooked."

Ponsard passed Gainer, nearly brushing him, then led him through the salon and up the main stairs, all the way chattering on the subject of Monet. How the artist always began his day at four in the morning with a cold bath, how when success came to him he was not loyal to the art dealer Durand-Ruel who had subsidized him through the many desperate years, how overcome with doubt he would often pile his paintings in a corner of the garden and burn them.

At the door to Monet's bedroom Ponsard stopped and gestured for Gainer to precede him. Gainer stepped into the room, scanned it perfunctorily, turned to Ponsard.

Ponsard was not there.

Nor was he in the hall.

Gainer went from room to room. No Ponsard. Why would he disappear like that? Gainer looked out a closed second story window. Below, off to the right were Leslie and Astrid, strolling between beds of snapdragons. Gainer saw them pause and lean over to put their noses into some blossoms. He saw Leslie's lips move, saying something. Leslie offered her hand. Astrid took it. They were like a pair of excited youngsters as they ran down the path, across to the gate and out to the road. Gainer watched them drive off in the Bentley.

Good. Thank you, Leslie.

Which was also Ponsard's thought, as he observed the same tableau from a small round ventilating window in the attic area. Now he could more easily cope with the situation, with this amateur. And the woman later. His plan included the river that ran close by Monet's pond—a body in the Eure would be taken to the Seine in an hour. The Seine, with its increasing width and undercurrents, would carry it to the sea, never to be found. It had, after all, happened to cows.

Gainer went to the far end of the second story hall, found a narrow stairway down to the kitchen. He peeked into the adjacent dining room. The large table in the center of the room was set with blue and yellow Limoges porcelain on pale yellow linen, everything, including tiny-footed open salt cellars, in its place, as though any moment Monet and friends Clemenceau, Rodin, Cézanne, Renoir and Sargent would be taking their chairs for a meal. It was a little eerie, Gainer thought.

He went out the east end of the house, where a sort of sideyard open area was punctuated by several lime trees. On the lookout for Ponsard, he passed through the shade of the trees and entered Monet's main studio.

The afternoon sun was striking through the skylights. Gainer stood in a trapezoidal block of it, scanned the huge room. It was immaculate, not even a cobweb in the lattice of steel beams that supported the roof. In the center of the room was a soft sofa and a long hard bench, the two of them back to back. Here, according to his mood, the old Monet had rested his legs and fixed his failing but painfully critical eyes on his *Decorations des Nymphéas,* those nineteen oversize panels were his final important work.

Gainer sat on the bench. Felt the wood of it warm on his buttocks. As though Monet had just risen from the spot. Gainer told himself it was either the sunlight or his imagination. Actually, the sun wasn't hitting there. Gainer sat for a long moment. Part of him said he was wasting precious time, but it seemed he was bound to the bench.

Don't worry, Norma, he whispered.

He stood up abruptly and went out to the long path that ran parallel with the front of the house. At once he saw Ponsard at the opposite end of the path, about a hundred and fifty feet away.

Gainer did his best to appear as though he was merely strolling, relaxed. He kept his eyes on Ponsard.

Ponsard waved to him with his left hand, his right hand in his jacket pocket. He started walking toward Gainer.

Wait, Gainer told himself, as he advanced. Wait for a sure shot. At fifty feet, forty, it was difficult for him to resist the ASP. He could see Ponsard's fixed smile, the lock of Ponsard's eyes. The smile was not in the eyes. The eyes were changed, cold, etching into him.

Thirty feet.

Gainer's street mind and legs came suddenly into accord. He jumped aside, off the path. Heard a cracking report. Felt a burn across the back of his left shoulder as though a hot wire had been drawn across it. Rolled twice over in the packed dirt of that adjoining path and lay prone, concealed behind the density of tall marigolds. The ASP was in his hand, although he didn't remember having taken it out.

A second cracking shot.

A bullet cut through the leaves and stems a foot away. Another missed by more.

Ponsard was firing blind. He was on his knees two paths over, peering through the flowerbeds, hoping to make out the contradictory gray that would be Gainer's suit. Directly in front of Ponsard was a profusion of pink roses, enormous blossoms. He remained absolutely still, taking shorter, quieter breaths, certain that Gainer would make the nervous amateur's mistake of moving. Ponsard had his Baby ready for that moment. He listened for Gainer, heard only the summer afternoon sounds, predominantly the humming of the wings of the bees busy in the flowers of Monet's garden.

One particular bumblebee queen was working very hard, lifting the overlapped petals of a half-opened rose to reach its center. The black and yellow bumblebee queen rubbed her hairy body over the rose's stamen until she was covered with pollen. This was a fresh rose. No bee had been there before her and there was so much pollen she would have to make several trips. She squeezed between the tighter inside petals, made her way out, paused, perhaps to get her bearings so that she would be able to locate this particular blossom among so many. She started her wings and took off, intending as direct as possible a flight to her nest beneath the tool shed. However, she had flown only ten feet when the concentration of rose fragrance attracted her. The attar of rose so strong it was as though a hundred blossoms had opened at once and were blowing their sweet breaths at her.

She lighted on the back of Ponsard's hand, the one he had used to apply his cologne. His gun hand.

He felt a tickle. Saw the bumblebee, fat and black. Tried to brush the bumblebee off, but its legs had been in nectar and they stuck. Distrubed, the bumblebee bent its four front legs, straightened its two hind legs and jabbed its barbed stinger into Ponsard's flesh and, as it did so, into a superficial nerve end.

Under other circumstances Ponsard would have yelped, but now he stifled it so that it came out guttural, more of a growl. He could not, however, stifle the pain that shot up to his shoulder and down his fingertips. His fingers lost their grip, went rigid.

Baby was flung into the air and down into the rose bushes.

There it lay, on the ground among fallen petals, the blue-black of the Browning .25 caliber automatic, its business end pointed directly at Ponsard. He got down on his stomach, reached for it, was unable to avoid the thorns. The more he stretched the more the thorns pierced him. He put his shoulder to the bushes on the perimeter, but they were meshed, would not give enough. He looked at Baby, only about a foot out of reach. His right hand was going numb and swelling from the bee sting. His wrist and knuckles were bleeding from the rose thorns. The damned garden had become his enemy. He'd be lucky to get out of there alive.

The gate.

If he could make the gate, run to the nearest neighbor's house about five hundred feet down the road, he'd be all right. Unlikely Gainer would shoot him with anyone as a witness. Otherwise he'd have done so before, Ponsard reasoned. He sucked hard on the bee sting. Took four deep breaths. Got into a crouch and ran down the path.

Gainer heard movement before he saw the man. Saw through the gladiolas and hollyhocks the gray of the top of Ponsard's head bobbing as he moved. Gainer didn't know what to make of it for a moment, and then he realized Ponsard was making a try for the gate.

Gainer figured he was a dozen years younger and seventy pounds lighter. He went full out, made up for Ponsard's head start, was first to reach the end of the paths where the front wall was interrupted by the gate.

Ponsard knew he was cut off. The gate was impossible now. The only way to go was the tunnel, which was just to his right. He made a zigzagging dash for it.

Gainer stopped and got the flat of Ponsard's back in the aim of the

ASP, but when he squeezed the shot off he did not have him, and the bullet chipped into the wall beyond. Ponsard was at the mouth of the tunnel. Another shot by Gainer apparently did not hit anything because in his hurry he had jerked it.

Gainer paused, tried to take stock. Ponsard was now across the road and railway tracks somewhere in the area of Monet's pond. From what Gainer remembered of it, that meant Ponsard was cornered. Unless he swam the river, and Ponsard didn't impress him as the swimming type.

We've almost got him, Norma.

The back of Gainer's left shoulder throbbed as though it was a separate, hurt part crying out for attention. He touched the place, felt the sponginess of the fabric of his jacket and brought his hand down red. How bad was it? He flexed the shoulder to test it, realized the wet that was running from his armpit down his left side wasn't entirely perspiration. His shirt was sticking to him there, the blood already turning gelatinous.

I'm okay, Norma.

He entered the tunnel, proceeded slowly and kept flat against its wall. He did not know Ponsard had lost his gun, and when he reached the opposite opening of the tunnel, he slipped out in one swift motion, keeping low. Surely Ponsard had been watching the tunnel. Better move. He used some thick azalea bushes to go off to the left, careful with every step, putting his weight down only where the ground was soft. Every moment expecting to confront Ponsard, he worked his way around the upper shore of the pond, all the way to the sluice at the eastern end. Near there he crawled to the edge, remained concealed behind a huge patch of iris. Belly down, he parted the tall green blades for a view of the pond. With the concentration of a hunter, he scanned its banks for any giveaway sign of Ponsard, could not see clearly the opposite end of the pond where the Japanese bridge was located because the sun was now partially west and reflecting off the surface of the dead calm water. The water lilies seemed to have spectral images rising from them, undulating in the brilliance.

Gainer decided to press on. With the same care, he moved around the lower edge of the pond, going from iris to agapanthus to petasites, thankful for their cover but aware of how little protection they provided from a bullet. Close to midway above the lower edge at a rose tree, he flushed a bird. A female wild canary that made a fuss as it flew up.

Ponsard was in the thicket of black bamboo at the western end of the pond, had been there all the while, remaining still, moving only his eyes. He had a professional's patience. (Once in an apartment in Brussels he had stayed put in a small utility closet for eighteen hours until conditions were right for filling an order.) From his vantage in the bamboo he had seen Gainer come from the tunnel but had lost sight of him after that. Now, a bird had given Gainer's position away.

Ponsard estimated his advantage was about a hundred feet. He was that much nearer than Gainer to the Japanese bridge. It was enough for him to cross the bridge, get through the tunnel and out of the gate. However, with his opponent coming on, the longer he waited the less his advantage would be. Fortunately the man wasn't much of a shooter.

He stood up, broke through the bamboo, ran for the bridge and was encouraged when he felt the hard wood of it under his feet. The bridge was a gently arching span constructed of boards butted laterally with similar narrower boards evenly spaced on it for treads. Wooden railings wound by wisteria vines duplicated its curve on both sides.

Ponsard was halfway across.

He stopped short.

The woman. She was on the other side of the bridge.

Ponsard's impulse was to run right through her, except she had an automatic pistol held out by both hands straight at him, and her squared-off, wide-legged stance told him she knew how to use it, and her eyes said she would.

Ponsard turned quickly.

As he did, the heel of the shoe on his right foot slipped on one of the bridge's raised treads, caught on it. His right leg stiffened, locked while the rest of his body continued turning. He grasped for the railing for balance but couldn't get it. Like an overweighted top he was spun once and then half again around, and he saw in succession the pond, the trees, the sky, the woman, the trees, the pond and now—the man with gun in hand at the other side of the bridge.

Ponsard's rump smashed against the railing, struck it at precisely the spot where wisteria vines over the joint of two sections concealed a bolt that the weather had corroded and weakened. The wood rail creaked in overture to a loud cracking as it gave way. The wisteria vines could not hold Ponsard.

He went over backward.

Fell the ten feet into the pond.

Fell into the middle of an expanse of water lilies.

He sank and came up spewing, thrashing the water, trying for a hold on anything substantial. There were only the water lilies. Their stems, thick and strong as ropes, grown all the way up from the bottom of the pond, were covered with algae. Ponsard felt their sliminess in his grip as they refused to support him. He kicked to keep his head above the surface, tried to raise his legs in order to float, but the stems of the lilies prevented that. They were wound around his ankles. The more he kicked the more he became entangled. The stems of Monet's lilies seemed to be coiling, tying themselves around his lower legs and then his thighs, tightening. And soon he could not move his legs at all.

He saw Gainer above.

He thought, stupid amateur.

He went under and began breathing water.

A SHORT while later, under way in the green Bentley, Gainer was bleeding on Rodger's leather seat, though Leslie had not yet noticed.

"What did you do with Astrid?" Gainer asked.

Took her to the pâtisserie. Bought the little tart a whole bagful."

"Then what?"

"Gave her Ponsard's five thousand francs and pointed her toward Paris. How are you?"

"Okay."

"Take some Rescue," she got the bottle from her carryall.

He didn't bother with the dropper, unscrewed the cap off and drank the bottle down to empty.

Leslie scowled. "You shouldn't have done that."

"Why not?"

"I needed some."

He doubted that. "How about Rodger's paintings?"

"They're in the trunk."

He was glad to hear that, had thought she just might not give a damn. "You covered a lot of ground," he told her.

"So did you."

"No more expert."

"He died from Monet." Gainer only shrugged, and Leslie thought better of what she'd said. She shouldn't deprive Gainer of any of the revenge he needed. "Well," she adjusted, "at least it seemed that Monet helped you some. I mean, he didn't like Ponsard either."

She glanced over to see how Gainer took that—and saw the blood on the seat. Her insides went hollow. If anything happened to him she'd give up. "Are you . . . shot?"

"Yeah."

"How bad?"

"I don't know."

She pulled the Bentley over and stopped.

He took off his jacket and his sopping shirt.

The wound looked as though it had been made with a knife rather than a bullet. Not deep but a four-inch swath of skin laid open. Still oozing.

Leslie wiped away a lot of the blood with the dry half of Gainer's shirt, then tore off part of her gauze dress for a bandage. She did not daintily use the hem the way women did in Western movies. She ripped off a wide piece from it straight up the front and used it to compress and wrap the wound as best she could.

"Say 'Ezekiel sixteen-six.' "

"Sixteen-six what?"

"From the Bible, the sixteenth chapter sixth verse of the Book of Ezekiel."

"Why?"

"It's good for the good guys on this side like us when they get hurt. Helps stop the pain and the bleeding."

"I don't know it."

"You don't have to say the whole verse. Just saying 'Ezekiel sixteen-six' gets the point across. Damn it, *do* it."

"Ezekiel sixteen-six," Gainer mumbled.

CHAPTER TWELVE

THE late morning sun struck on the Tiffany chafing dish and reflected onto Darrow's bare chest. It seemed to beatify the gray hairs that formed a curly cross on the front of him, from the notch below his throat nearly down to his navel and horizontally from nipple to nipple.

Darrow was not aware of it. He nudged his sunglasses down enough for an inspection of the sky above Number 19, approved it and pushed them back into place. The frames of the glasses got smeared with the white sun-blocking substance Darrow had applied to the bridge and tip of his nose. A peeling nose was a vulgar, plebeian trait and he couldn't have that. Some of the white also got on a finger. He wiped it away with his napkin and examined the finger closely to make sure it was as impeccable as before.

The man seated around from Darrow decapitated his three-minute egg and spooned out the part he had lopped off. His name was Donald Hunsicker. He was sixty. He had an ingrained serious look, the sort one might expect, for example, from an insurance executive, someone who knew too well the chances for disaster in practically everything. His mouth was a straight, thin-lipped affair with neither down nor up lines at its corners. Also somewhat hyperthyroid eyes. Two-thirds of his hair was gone and at least that percentage of the teeth in his mouth were not really his.

"How's Eleanor?" Darrow asked, as though paying a verbal debt.

Over the ten years that he had been seeing Hunsicker he had never met the man's wife, but he would not think of referring to her as Mrs. Hunsicker.

"She's fine."

"When you were here a few weeks back you mentioned that she wasn't feeling well, had to go under the knife for something."

"Just some female trouble. She's recouping now."

"No worse than having a tooth pulled these days, I suppose," Darrow said, and allowed a mild, private curiosity about the hollow a woman must feel after being all cut out below. The word that came to his mind was *cavernous*. It closed the distasteful thought.

Hunsicker put a dab of butter into the crater of his egg. "Marjorie-Anne comes out this year," he said.

Darrow asked "who" by raising his head.

"My granddaughter," Hunsicker told him.

"Where?"

"Grosse Pointe."

Nice enough but a long ways down from Boston, Darrow thought. If it had been his granddaughter he would have arranged for Boston. A few of his conscious dreams were of a young girl of his own, exceptionally pretty and personable, winning everyone for him at the annual presentation cotillion in the main ballroom of the Copley Plaza in Boston. That would never be now, of course. One way or another his wife Barbara had always prevented whenever he'd raised the possibility of a child to her, and at the time he'd let it go because he hadn't foreseen how useful a child could be.

"Barbara still in Antibes?" Hunsicker asked.

"No." Darrow thought back to his last sitdown with Hunsicker and was sure he hadn't said where Barbara was. In fact that meeting had been very brief, no more than ten minutes, no small talk. It didn't alarm Darrow or surprise him that Hunsicker had special knowledge of his personal life, but he resented the way Hunsicker had slipped it in, obviously demonstrating his advantage. Darrow unscrewed the lid of the Wedgewood egg coddler that was on the saucer in front of him. He glanced into the coddler, as though to discover something other than the two eggs and bacon crumbles it contained. He told Hunsicker, "At the moment, Barbara's in Spain."

"Hell of a place to be in August."

"Exactly what I told her."

"Especially Madrid," Hunsicker said, casually.

Darrow took it as another little prod. Hunsicker and his people probably even knew how much Barbara had paid whatever young man or men she had probably slept with night before last. No matter. "She likes the bullfights," he said.

"A lot of people used to."

"She still does."

Hunsicker bit a corner of toast. "Remember how squeamish people used to be about seeing the bulls killed, how outraged they were on behalf of those *poor* creatures?"

"Hardly hear anything like that sort anymore, I agree."

"People shifted their indignation—to whales and baby seals. And even those causes never really caught on. They're good for a moment of conscience on some street corner while signing a petition but that's about as much thought anyone gives them."

"I guess everyone's too preoccupied these days . . ."

"I agree," Darrow said.

". . . with their own survival. People have come to feel perhaps they're the endangered species," Hunsicker said.

"Is that how you feel?"

"No."

"Nor I," Darrow said with, he felt, just enough emphasis.

They were on the broad raised terrace at the south end of the house at 19 Purchase Street being served brunch at a round outdoors table that had a pale yellow umbrella up through the middle of it. The table had about a quarter-inch wobble because of the unevenness of the terrace surface. A servant had repositioned the table twice and finally slipped a fold of cardboard beneath one leg. The problem was solved until Hunsicker happened to kick that leg.

Darrow avoided as much as possible putting any pressure on the table, spooning lightly into his coddled eggs and setting his drink down with care. Hunsicker, meanwhile, went about eating as though nothing was wrong, even put his elbows on the table, Darrow noticed. After Hunsicker had caused numerous wobbles, Darrow had the urge to tell the man to be more careful. Instead he put down the urge, taking two swallows of his Mimosa, orange juice and champagne, and extending his legs so that his calves as well as his thighs were exposed to the sun.

Darrow wore lightweight cotton trunks of a faded khaki color that went appropriately with his tan. Also, in the same shade, a pair of canvas deck shoes. Darrow—color-coordinated.

Hunsicker had also put on trunks, borrowed green ones with a wide gathered elastic band that nearly came up to his rib cage and ballooned out, leg holes gaping, exposing the built-in nylon jock.

Hunsicker was uncomfortable being that undressed. He had only consented to it, out of prudence, so as not to appear out of place.

Actually he hadn't been to a beach or pool in forty years. His skin was so pale it looked as though it had just been unbandaged. There were hardly any contours to his body. His upper arms and forearms were nearly the same measurement around, and his legs were like posts, ankles thick, thighs thin.

It was the obvious peasant in him, Darrow thought. Competence was one thing, grace another, and for that reason Hunsicker had never risen above his present slot, never would. He was a mere implementer.

Hunsicker was the Distributor.

At least that was the name for him used by those on the inside. Officially, for any public purpose, he was vice-president in charge of client accommodations for a firm called Intelco. That company represented itself as a management consultancy firm specializing in all types of intelligence services—from getting proof against disloyal or sexually indiscreet executives to providing security for those of particular value. Well known was Intelco's system of protecting large corporations from infiltration by organized crime. Nothing unnerved a board of directors more than Intelco's pitch about the possibility of a gradual takeover by the criminal element. To prevent such a thing, Intelco offered sophisticated psychological and electronic methods of interviewing anyone considered for a key position. The complex ways it interrogated, analyzed and collated was reassuring and more often than not its recommendations were followed. Two hundred of the bluest blue-chip corporations were Intelco clients. Never did it occur to them that Intelco was in a position to promote exactly what it was supposed to deter.

Why should it? On the advisory and the active staffs of Intelco were nearly seventy-five percent of the most notable figures of the intelligence law enforcement communities—those of the recent past who had chosen to leave government employment for the greater rewards of the private sector—and so when a corporation bought Intelco it was also buying a former director of investigations of, say, the National Security Agency, a former deputy director of the Central Intelligence Agency, a former senior security advisor of the Department of State, and so on. It was a list so extensive it had to be set in six-point type to fit down the entire left-hand border of Intelco's engraved letterhead. It certainly appeared as though Intelco was an independent firm, owing subservience to no one. Who could possibly possess the clout to compromise such eminence?

The High Board.

Intelco was its satellite. An organization descended from that cadre of OSS fellows Winship and the High Board had enlisted to make the crime bosses bend in the forties. Of course, there was no way of tracing that; the thread that tied back to them was so purposely tangled and even broken at times that no one could follow it. Besides, anyone trying could dig forever and find nothing. Unlike most surreptitious affiliations, the one between Intelco and the High Board was not all dirtily honeycombed and burrowed. The connection was overhead, direct and uncomplicated, from the top to the top. Intelco had a hundred persons on its staff, not including clerical help. But at least ten times that number around the world were clandestinely connected, and many of them were so far out on the edge of things they had no idea for whom they were actually working. In many respects Intelco operated like a government intelligence agency, with the same sort of high-handed attitude and methods that put it a step ahead of everyone. No red tape, though. Throughout Intelco only the most prosaic matters were put to paper, all else was verbal—no matter how crucial a situation might be. In fact the more crucial, all the more reason to mind the rule. It might seem an archaic way of doing business, but in this instance, in this business, very effective, and secure.

Intelco especially served the High Board by seeing to the behavior of everyone within the organization. According to the codes prescribed by Winship himself, behavior was never gray, circumstances were never extenuating. Either a line was stepped over, or it was not. No one was exempt from such judgment. Especially not those in charge of the various divisions.

Darrow at Number 19, for example.

The eye and the pressure of Intelco were on him.

Any foul-up within his area was his foul-up. If it was a serious matter, he would answer for it, and the High Board would accept only one answer. Darrow, of course, knew that. His predecessor Gridley had known it too. Gridley himself hadn't skimmed a hundred million from The Balance but he had been responsible for it. When the shortage was found, Gridley did not try excuses or explanations. He just took it, and died.

Whenever Darrow thought of the terms, the pit of him shuddered. Sometimes he woke up in the night with the consciousness of the consequences squatted on the top of his mind, poking at him, warning him to be more thorough, more exacting with everyone. He would lay there with his neck dampening the pillow and make a pledge to himself. It was the only way he could get back to sleep. Come morning, however, the anxiety would recede to a more reasonable level; not leave, but at least draw back into a crouch. Darrow would shave one more shave, appreciate himself in the mirror one more time and go down to breakfast at a Chippendale table that could seat eighteen.

Most breakfasts he sat alone at the end of the table, the polished length of it like a dark icy surface that the servants hurried around. When Hine's wife Lois ate with him, they would sit mid-table facing one another, and Darrow would enjoy letting his imagination have her fix him immodestly with her eyes, scrunch down and reach across underneath with her bare foot to play her toes at his crotch. Lois, more than anyone, had the power to ease his chronic apprehensions—she with her mix of wickedness and High Board blood. Once she had admired Darrow's hands, said the things he himself liked about them; it had instantly aroused him.

Lois was one reason why it was impossible for Darrow to be more tolerant of his nephew Hine. Another was his dependency that Hine had constructed, taking advantage of Darrow's laxity by making up for it himself—filling in, smoothing things over so that with him there, Number 19 ran like a veritable money machine. Darrow knew it was not loyalty that motivated Hine, and every so often when Darrow took stock of his position he thought he should do something about it. But then his second thought was to let things be. Hine's inroads wouldn't get him anywhere, would lead to nothing. Cunning he might be, but Darrow trusted what else he read in him. Hine did not have the starch it took to be a thief. Probably Hine's count of The Balance was within a thousand of being right on the money, Darrow thought. And that alone mattered.

Besides, Darrow held the ultimate edge.

Like the ten other men who headed such divisions or installations for the High Board, Darrow had absolute authority over those under him. Could not be gotten around. Along with that, he had access to the faction of Intelco that dealt particularly with punishments. So Darrow was able to wield the same sort of final, irresistible power over his people that the High Board held over him.

Darrow was certain he caused Hine to come awake nights. Sometimes he purposely sounded disgusted with Hine just to intimidate him.

When someone committed a wrong, Darrow did not need to argue the case or even present it. All he had to do was put in a call to Hunsicker at Intelco, ask him to drop around.

Hunsicker came to take the order but not to discuss it. It was the way the High Board wanted things handled.

An order from Darrow was as brief as any Hunsicker ever got. In the course of their sit-down Darrow would maneuver to a pause in which his eyes would harden and convey that the next words heard from him would be the order—the name.

This time was a bit different. Darrow was not altogether sure how he should deal with it. It involved outsiders, and another touchy complication. There was no one but Hunsicker that he could talk to about it, yet he didn't want to come right out and ask Hunsicker's advice. He placed his sweating cold glass against his sweating hot cheek. "It could all be coincidental."

"We doubt that," Hunsicker said.

"Your people must have bungled the order somehow, otherwise I wouldn't have to be bothered with any of this."

"They weren't my people."

"All right then, your people's people."

"The middlemen."

"Has such a thing ever happened before?"

"Not exactly."

The moment was underscored by the pock-ta-pock of Hine and Sweet playing tennis on the court down from the terrace. Darrow had observed snatches of the match and noticed Hine wasn't up to his usual superior game. He believed he knew why. Hine was well aware of who Hunsicker was.

Now Darrow told Hunsicker: "Run it down again for me."

"I'm not supposed to."

"As a favor."

"You know, Darrow, it doesn't matter to us how it's resolved or whether it is or not. The loss to us isn't all that great. The world is full of middlemen. It's entirely up to you. It's on your account."

"Mine," Darrow agreed.

"I would think you'd take into consideration the three million."

"You're convinced he got it?"

"I have no opinion."

"Your people believe he did."

"They lean toward that."

"The middlemen probably had a better chance at it."

"They're gone. The point is, do you want to clean the rest of it up or what?"

Darrow wished Hunsicker would stop coming right at him for a decision. "A three million loss won't kill me," he said.

Hunsicker nodded.

Darrow didn't know which way to take that. "The woman is the hitch."

"She is."

"If it were only him, if she weren't involved, I wouldn't hesitate."

"I believe that."

"Thank you."

Darrow glanced to the tennis court again. Hine was looking up to the terrace. Darrow casually gestured as though he was pointing out Hine. Hine stood stock-still for a long moment, then turned and slammed a ball over the tall tennis court fence. It landed in the rose garden that occupied most of the area between that fence and the perimeter wall. Darrow had the delightfully gruesome thought of Hine trying to retrieve the ball at two in the morning. "I've decided," he told Hunsicker, "if I order anything the woman won't be included."

"All right, not her."

"But she'll still be affected. Damn it!" Darrow was back to his ambivalence.

"What kind of plant is that?" Hunsicker asked.

"Which one?"

"The blue lacy one in the urn over there."

"Lobelia."

"Eleanor put some in this spring and they didn't do well, dried up."

"It doesn't like sun."

Hunsicker moved his chair a bit to his right, his left shoulder and arm had been out of the moving shade. He sipped from his cup of coffee now long gone cold. "When you order him, you more or less order her as well, don't you?"

"I gather that's how it is from what you've told me," Darrow said.

"I'm only repeating."

"Couldn't she be talked to?"

"Possibly."

"After the fact."

"But is that what you want, Darrow, for it to get up into that level?"

"No, definitely not."

"The three million lost could become an issue."

They wouldn't treat me that way, not me, Darrow thought, never.

"She was your carrier, and your order," Hunsicker reminded him with a trace of satisfaction.

A conceding grunt from Darrow. He flexed the fingers of his right hand, studied the backs of them. A tiny shred of cuticle flawed the moon of his thumbnail. He wouldn't think of biting it off. Later, with the help of a magnifying glass, he would very carefully clip it. He glanced over at Hunsicker, imagined him at his granddaughter's debut, white-tied and -tailed, hiding all that sick-looking skin, imagined Hunsicker's Eleanor, pigeon-chested, a garden club type. He closed his eyes slowly, as though lowering a curtain on Hunsicker. He wished the problem could be made to disappear that easily. Keeping his eyes closed, he turned his head, opened his eyes abruptly. His view was on Hine, whose tennis game was still suffering from the distraction of Hunsicker's presence.

As soon as he'd given his decision to Hunsicker, Darrow thought, he'd go to Boston. That very afternoon, if they'd see him on such short notice. It had been six months since his last request. Perhaps they would respond to a different tack, a smattering of humility and lesser expectations. No gripes about how much he disliked being there on the shady underside, or why he deserved better. He would sit and balance on his knee a bone china tea cup on a napkin and convince them that he was owed. He would recommend Hine as his successor, praise Hine to the high heavens. They might go for it, Darrow thought. If not, the next best thing that might come of it would be his retirement, with a substantial financial pat on the back. From where he was sitting at the moment, that didn't seem so bad.

Yes. Boston. While he was there he'd spend another time with that special friend, the little black one who never made him feel she would ridicule him. Never made him feel ridiculous.

"Well, what shall it be?" Hunsicker was asking.

CHAPTER
THIRTEEN

GAINER had been back in New York City for two weeks.

It seemed to him there should be several urgent things for him to do, but then nothing seemed important. He still had the feeling that he was off-register with his surroundings, and now being in the city where everything was more familiar only increased that feeling. For example, a mere taxi ride had an element of illusion to it, and the view of the city skyline from his Roosevelt Island apartment was like a cardboard cutout mounted under glass, not something he could go over to and fit into. Fortunately this sense of detachment was not as constant as it had been, which made him believe it would eventually leave altogether. Sometimes it was there, other times it wasn't. The only time it left for long was when he was making love with Leslie.

She was wonderful. There for him, understanding him, as though she had some special emotional gauge she could read. Such as the way she reacted to the plants in his apartment. They had died. All of them. Even the huge favorite fern that had appeared so vigorous. She did not mention that he should have arranged for someone to water them while he was away. Nor did she immediately set about to get the plants out of sight. She left them where and as they were until he thought they were beyond hope and was about to say so. At that moment she picked one up and headed for the incinerator chute. Gainer was only faintly aware that perhaps the plants had died more from a sympathetic act than from lack of water.

He was careful not to brood too much in her presence. When he felt a bad one coming on, he got away from her. No matter what the hour . . .

"Going out?"

"Yeah."

"If you happen to be near that all-night stand on Fifty-third get some seedless grapes?"

From her it was never *where*.

Gainer walked alone a lot. It seemed to relieve the tightening in him when he was on the move. He hadn't gotten much out of his system with the killing of Becque and Ponsard. It put some on his side of the scale but nowhere near a balance. Strange about those two, Becque and Ponsard. As together as they'd been, it was impossible to accept them as a pair, Gainer thought. They couldn't have been buddies, graveyard keeper and art expert bullshitter. The only things they had in common had been their guns. And Norma.

And, of course, their motive.

What had brought them to it? Gainer was convinced it was something more than just sexual. Men who raped together usually had a lot in common. The sure giveaway, though, was the coke and the ludes. Definitely not Norma.

Her carry. The millions she took over the last time.

That could have been the connection between Becque and Ponsard, what they were really after together. Perhaps they got it and then set up all the sex and drug evidence to throw everyone off. Including the people Norma worked for. Make it appear to them that she was the blame, her irresponsibility, hoping not to have to contend with them, especially not them, the ones she worked for.

Mostly, Gainer accepted that scenario.

But not entirely.

It walked with him, as though asking to be kicked full of holes, and, after a while, when he knew he could never entirely accept it, another explanation took shape for him, one that fit the irregularities and circumstances of Norma's death in so many ways it had to be the truth. It wasn't a revelation. Rather, step by step it eased forward in Gainer's mind, as though it had been there all the while and he hadn't wanted it out: what Becque and Ponsard had done was their *job*. They had hit Norma, not just murdered her. Had done it for some reason, for someone. Surely the people she was carrying for had everything to do with it. But who exactly? Who immediately came to mind was that man Darrow. Maybe he was the one, Gainer thought, but more likely the word had been given by someone beyond and above Darrow, one of the upper-level mob guys Darrow fronted for. How the hell could he go up against one of those? But Darrow . . . he'd think on that . . . And he wanted to know *why* Norma had been killed. He remembered her as being so good he was nearly able to convince himself that they'd made a mistake, taken her for someone else.

Gainer tried to get back to routine. Went over to Pointwise, Inc. Business was good. The phones were ringing and a half a shoebox of money orders and certified checks had already come in. The start of the regular season was only a couple of Sundays off. It would be best to begin with a winner, demonstrate right off that he was worthy of confidence. All the better if his pick was an upset.

He sat in his office with his feet up and the air-conditioner unit blowing the back of his neck cold and paged through the recent issues of *Pro Football Weekly,* looking for some helpful information. He might as well have been reading the *Wall Street Journal.* Nothing. To him the Chargers were going to be as bad as the Cowboys were going to be as bad as the Saints. After an hour of that sort of reading but not seeing, he signed enough blank checks to take care of his payroll and went out to walk some more.

All the way down through Soho, all the way up along Madison, around the drives of the park to get away from exhausts, and even resenting the runners, skaters and bikers. He spent most of one afternoon at the Fifth and Forty-second Street library on a hard chair at one of the long hard tables in the main reading room. Just sat there watching the numbers on the call panel above the in-and-out counter light up like a literary bingo game, wondering what it was like now down in the stacks and who was down there, maybe with an Edna.

From there he went up to Fifty-seventh to an imitation Chinese restaurant where some male gays hung out, heavy bookies and loan-sharks. There were five at the bar in similar tailored gabardine and Countess Mara neckties. Playing liars' poker. Each of the men had a stack of dollar bills in front of him. They were just using the singles, not to be flashy, actually were playing a hundred a hand. One of the bookies, the one whose territory took in the Plaza, the Sherry Netherland and the Pierre hotels, declared nine nines so often it got to be a joke, but the one time when he was called he had five of them and the others had four between them. That made the Chinese bartender laugh. The four losers tipped their drinks over on purpose.

A woman came in. Young but going brittle. She sat two stools down from Gainer, ordered a Chablis spritzer. With the briefest possible glance she decided Gainer was neither vice nor a trick, so she ignored him. From her shoes that were wrong and too cheap for her silk dress, he took her as a working girl. Hookers usually saved their better shoes for their own times.

It seemed as though he just opened his mouth and it came out—asking her did she know a woman named Vicky.

Maybe fifty Vickies, was her answer.

Then how about a Danielle Hansen?

The hooker rotated her silk-covered ass and the rest of her a half turn away from him.

From the Chinese hangout he took in windows down Fifth, cut west on Forty-seventh where all the diamonds were hidden for the night, and on to the upper part of the city pool that was Times Square.

He had not been around there on foot for years. There were changes, but the place had the same hustle to it. Anything for money. Standers off to the side looking to pull some out of the flow. Gainer felt a little insulted when a young black tried to sell him, of all people, a *hot* Cartier watch for two hundred that was a bad plated copy with no works in it. That old scam. Gainer checked his reflection in a store window, didn't think he looked from out of town.

About nine-thirty he was on West Forty-fourth, where the lights of all the legitimate theaters put a flattering glaze on even the beat-up taxis while it defeated every woman's make-up. Gainer's sense of unreality was suddenly heightened by it. Pretty soon it was intermission, and just like old times he chose a musical, drifted inside and old luck sat him in an empty on the center aisle. He half heard a couple of apparently happy and sincere songs and vaguely saw dancers be vigorous and enthusiastic one more time. Most distracting for him were the curtain calls, applauding until his hands hurt. Like old times.

Afterward, headed back across Times Square, he had an urge to get a tattoo. The name *Leslie* needled in the most elaborate scroll forever across his upper arm.

Instead he went home to her.

HER, in a white cotton tie robe, snuggled into the corner of his couch. Without the television or any music on or a book or even a magazine near her. As though she'd been held there waiting exactly in that space.

She put her arms around him as far as they would go, hugged for a long while before kissing. Her mouth, as usual, spoke in many tongues. Often it conveyed reminders that she loved, and other times that she wanted. Now her lips were just slightly slack and her tongue not as softly plumped up as it could be.

"Hungry?" she asked.

"No. You?"

"I had a huge lunch at La Grenouille."

No one goes to Grenouille alone, Gainer thought. He put toe to heel and removed his shoes, unbuttoned his shirt all the way down and pulled out the tail of it. He went into the bathroom, washed the city from his face, neck and hands, returned to her. "Anything good and rotten on TV tonight?"

"I didn't look."

He picked up the television schedule saved from last Sunday's *Times*. "Rodger's in town," she said.

"So, hang out a flag," Gainer mumbled.

"What?"

"Nothing."

"He wants me to go with him to Boston for a couple of days."

Nothing from Gainer. He kept looking at the television schedule.

"I'll bet you didn't take any Remedy today, did you."

"No."

She dropped some into him. "How about your cayenne?"

"A couple of capsules," he lied.

Ground cayenne pepper was her newest natural cure-all. Good for cleansing the system, the sinuses, blood pressure, heart problems, head-aches, even stomach ulcers. Gainer doubted that anything so scorching could help an ulcer unless in some way it cauterized it. He didn't tell her that, just washed down the cayenne capsules she gave him whenever she was looking, and when she wasn't, palmed, dropped, tucked them anywhere he could that was out of sight. She was constantly finding them in his pockets and down between the cushions of the couch, but she was patient about it. The cayenne was supposed to counter his depression. She took hers straight, from a spoon, as though she relished it. Her eyes watered. Her tongue needed air. Which made Gainer suspect that whatever the benefits derived from cayenne might be they were related to doing penance.

"When do you have to go?" Gainer asked.

"Day after tomorrow. But I really don't *have* to."

"How would Rodger take it if you didn't?"

"It sounded important to him. God knows why. All I do is sit around crossing and recrossing my legs, flashing for a bunch of wealthy old hypocrites."

"Karen Akers is on later."

"It doesn't seem to matter to you one way or the other."

"What?"

"Actually, Rodger hasn't been very demanding of me, has he?"

"No."

"Fair's fair, I suppose."

"Yeah."

"I couldn't have spent altogether more than a week with him, since you and I . . ."

"Eleven days, ten nights," Gainer said. He rolled the television section into a tube, held it like a bludgeon.

Leslie was pleased that Gainer knew exactly. To keep from showing so with a grin she kissed him. "You know," she said, "in the heart of my heart I'd much rather stay and be with you—even if it is only part-time these days."

"I know."

"You need me."

"You need Rodger."

That wasn't said resentfully by him, nor did she deny it.

"You're my love," she said, and began massaging the back of his neck. With one hand and then with both, really going after his tension. And while doing that she said: "Sometimes I believe I could easily do without having a lot of money. After all, practically everyone does and I couldn't possibly be all that weak. We could have children. It's not too late for me to have at least one child. I wonder what it's like to have sex trying to make rather than prevent. Must be marvelously fulfilling, don't you think? Perhaps what I ought to do someday is to go to a shrink and get the monies treated out of me."

"Some day," Gainer agreed, though they were words that he'd heard from her numerous times, a sort of litany that seemed necessary for her.

It was time for Karen Akers.

Gainer took off his shirt and Leslie her robe and on the couch she snuggled in the cave of his arm while their favorite singer was on Channel 13. Red, straight-to-the-shoulders hair that was banged to make her pale, very pretty, well-boned face incongruously diminutive. Wearing black *smoking* and a white silk shirt open at the collar as though the atmosphere she created around her was too warm for a tie. A long white silk scarf hanging left and right from under her lapels. Key-lighted and singing it right at everyone:

> . . . *Oh, and she never gives out,*
> *And she never gives in,*
> *She just changes her mind . . .*

What would it be like, Gainer wondered, to be able to give someone —no, not just someone—to be able to give Leslie a new Rolls Corniche for her birthday, dark brown, initialed, a phone in it and an eighteen karat key for her to start it with. To be responsible for all the softest available gloves that she ever put her hands into, and all her shoes. Every inch of silk that would ever touch her. Walk into Harry Winston's and say for her you wanted something better.

> . . . *hot lips brushing,*
> *hot cheeks flushing,*
> *Strictly entre nous . . .*

Maybe, Gainer thought, it would be good for him to have her away for a while, give him a breather.

But he doubted it.

The Thursday morning Leslie wasn't there he slept later than he'd been sleeping recently. He woke up with a very hard hard-on and an awful emptiness. He didn't bother with breakfast, not even coffee, hastily washed and dressed, although there was no reason to hurry.

The safety deposit key was inside its own special envelope among collar stays and other such things in a porcelain box on his dresser next to the Tiffany framed photograph. As Gainer removed the key and put it to pocket, he caught on that image of the mother. He hadn't caught on her like that in quite a while. The old thought came back that it wasn't much of her.

Norma's safety deposit box was in Manufacturer's Trust, the big branch of that bank on Avenue of the Americas. Gainer had never been to it, although he had signed the signature card that gave him access, and Norma had reminded him every so often that in any case of emergency he should go and get into it.

There wasn't much there. Eight thousand dollars in hundreds with a rubber band around them. The deed to her United Nations Plaza apartment with Gainer named as owner. A moderately valuable art deco diamond and sapphire bracelet she'd bought at Parke-Bernet in response to an auction whim but had never worn because, as she said, it wasn't enough to be killed on the street for. And a single sheet of white paper folded twice with 3L-18R-6L-5R-3L typewritten on it.

Gainer took everything with him and went directly to Norma's apartment, which actually was his.

He had been putting off going there, but felt up to it today. He still wasn't sure how he would respond to coming into touch with so many things that had been in touch with her. The dresses and blouses and . . . he was relieved to find all that had been taken care of. By Leslie, no doubt. The closets and dresser drawers and cabinets were empty and freshly lined with paper. All of what had been in them was packed in cardboard cartons stacked against the wall in the entranceway. Prominently scotch-taped to one were the telephone numbers of the Goodwill and the Salvation Army.

One carton was open and set aside.

It contained Norma's various papers. Receipts, cancelled checks, records and such. Placed in on top of those was the purse Norma had taken to Zurich; left for him by Leslie to go through, he assumed.

He wandered around, sat in Norma's bedroom chair for a moment, looked into the refrigerator that was spotless and had only an open box of Arm and Hammer baking soda in it.

Yes, Norma, I love Leslie.

He went back to the bedroom, kneeled down and flipped back a corner of the rug and its rubber undercushion, used a quarter to pry up a square foot section of the parquet floor and uncovered a safe.

Norma had once shown it to him. Not its contents, only its location. The series of numbers and letters on the sheet of paper from the safety deposit box were, of course, the combination. He opened it right up and removed a sheaf of letters bound by a lavender grosgrain ribbon. He noticed the Zurich postmarks, the Germanic handwriting, the name of Alma on the return address. There were also about ten old postcards, those from the mother, that Norma had preserved despite so many changes of place. Nothing else in the safe except Gainer's and Norma's birth certificates and an envelope containing an engraved business card:

PRIVATE BANK WALDHAUSER
BAHNHOFSTRASSE 12–24
8022 ZURICH, SWITZERLAND

On the back side of the card in Norma's hand was written in ink the word *Necco* and beneath that SF-1259. Diagonally across the card in pencil, smudged and evidently written previously, was the notation: min. dep. 50.

It was, of course, the private bank in Zurich that Norma kept her money in. She had once pointedly told Gainer that she did. A numbered account—SF-1259, access code *Necco*, he now knew.

Gainer put the things he had gotten from the safe into the carton that held Norma's other papers and her handbag. He took the carton home with him and placed it by his chair at the window. He opened the window, let in the harbor water smell, the spoil of the city, blended with the fresh of the sea. He drank a Heineken and didn't answer the phone twice. His thought had been that someday soon he would tend to the carton of Norma's papers, but he was drawn to it now, sat and reached into it.

Her letters from Alma.

Gainer tugged the ribbon loose. Hesitated. These were meant for Norma's eyes only, he thought, and was about to retie the ribbon when something told him he should not feel like a meddler. Something outside himself, it seemed, invited him to look into the first envelope.

He read all the letters, slowly, taking in as much as he could, the feeling, flavor of each sentence. Read them chronologically, one side of a tender history from which he was able to gather reflections of the other, lost side. Many of the amorous passages were so unashamedly direct they came off as defiant. In the lines and between them was the desperateness of lovers apart, victimized by distance and convention. Frequently mentioned was the eventuality of Alma and Norma being together permanently in New York, and in that regard Gainer seemed to be the obstacle, would first have to be dealt with, informed. Alma was understanding about that but, naturally, impatient.

How simple it could have been, Gainer thought as he read the final "lovingly" of a closing and slipped that letter back into its envelope. Maybe if he hadn't tried to make all those matches with men for her. It pained him to think that ever, even for a moment, he had stood between Norma and happiness.

He put the letters along with the mother's postcards in the top drawer of his dresser. Made room for them by removing some packets of off-track betting slips, losers that a fellow had picked up from the floor day-by-day for Gainer to use to offset any income tax in case he happened to win a large triple or something.

Then, after uncapping another beer, he got back to the box.

Norma's purse.

It was a soft, roomy leather one from Bottega Veneta. In it, among the usual make-up implements and such was her Swiss Air ticket, the unused portion. Gainer read the face of it and would never cash it in. Also, Norma's passport indelibly rubber-stamped with all her arrivals and departures. He noted the most recent and final Zurich entry.

He removed everything from Norma's wallet, examined each item as though it were a fragment of her. Her driver's license, her L. E. Horton business cards, a merchandise credit receipt for $67.50 from B. Altman's. A snapshot of him at age eight, sitting on the street steps outside that first Vicky apartment. Another snapshot of Norma and Alma taken by the rail of a boat, a large-looking boat under way. Norma squinting into the sun. Alma with a hand up shielding her eyes. Wisps of hair across their faces, fair hair and dark being whipped up and entwined by wind. Both wearing casual summer dresses. A charming photo for its candidness, Gainer thought, a loving picture. He would have it reproduced, enlarged. Alma would surely like to have one.

Tucked in the smallest, tightest pocket of the wallet was a slip of paper. Gainer nearly overlooked it. A page from a notepad, cheap off-color paper like newspaper, folded twice into little more than a one-inch square. It had the Dolder Grand Hotel imprint on the bottom right corner. Scribbled in dull pencil above that was what appeared to be a date and a number and an initial that was either J.M.P. or G.N.B. All of it was almost undecipherable. It didn't appear to Gainer to be anything important. He continued with his looking.

He didn't stop until he'd finished the entire box, sorted aside whatever papers might be important, threw nothing away. By then it was dark. His stomach let him know he hadn't sent anything solid down to it all day. He didn't feel like eating at home. He freshened up and changed into clothes more appropriate for night, went over to the city, overtipped the maitre d' at Il Monello so he got a table for four. Ate too much bread and butter before the pasta arrived, six kinds of pasta with six different sauces. Sipped away a half bottle of a 1971 Ruffino. Decided not to go home yet.

At one o'clock he was at Xenon. Sitting on the perimeter of the dancing with some house wine in a highball glass. He wasn't actually at a table, he had pulled a chair up to that vantage point.

Gainer never danced. There was something about all those jerks and gyrations that didn't appeal to him, at least not as a participant. But he enjoyed being the spectator, so there he sat, more or less passing judgment on the moves being made out on the floor. He began making composites of the girls. Mentally put that one's great legs with that one's spectacular ass. Those tits with that belly. That hair with . . . that face . . .

He recognized that face. Did not know it personally but had seen it practically everywhere.

Her name was Harrie. Short for Harriet, everyone assumed, and it didn't seem her last name mattered. There was only one Harrie. She was currently the model who had it made the most. Every working hour of every day for four months in advance on her booking chart at the Ford Agency was filled in, and there were just as many secondary bookings in case a client cancelled. She was averaging three thousand a day including commercials and product exclusives. A certain facial expression had become her trademark. Her variations on it were slight: up a notch for arrogance, down a couple for sultry evil. She could do no wrong in front of a camera. Even the most blasé photographers said she had a tremendous *motor*. She was, indeed, an extraordinary twenty-year-old creature. So beautiful she seemed an anomaly.

That face.

That body.

Harrie danced them right to Gainer. She extended her hand to have him up and dancing with her.

He shook his head no, left her hand stranded.

She dismissed him with a flick of it, danced away.

Gainer didn't think much more about it until during the next number she came skimming and turning his way again, stopped abruptly and stood still, eyes to eyes with him about a reach and a half away. The music was so loud she resorted to charades.

Pointed at Gainer.

Held a make-believe phone to her ear.

Pointed to herself.

You . . . call . . . me.

She conveyed her number by holding certain numbers of fingers up in succession, ran through them twice to make sure he got it.

THE picture of Harrie doing that was in and out of Gainer's mind around two o'clock as he walked to catch the tram over to Roosevelt Island. He admitted he was flattered, in a way. Harrie could have anyone. Maybe, he thought, it was what he needed, would do him good to crash against her. He clearly remembered her number.

His legs kept going for the tram.

Two minutes after he arrived home he was in bed reading a recently reissued Nabokov novel. Within twenty minutes he was asleep.

His phone rang.

His immediate thought was Leslie.

Harrie's opener was a complaint that it had taken her over an hour to get his private unlisted number.

A sleepy grunt from Gainer.

"Come over and fuck me," Harrie said.

That woke him more.

"Just half dress," she said. "I'll send a limo for you. I've got one on standby."

"It's three o'clock," Gainer said instead of okay.

"I thought it was four."

"I'll call you tomorrow maybe."

"Can't. Got a booking."

"Sleep," he advised.

A little protesting whine from Harrie. "Christ, have I ever got the wets for you. You should feel me."

He visualized those words coming from that face. She had him leaning, thinking he could easily put on jeans and shirt and slip bare feet into loafers. With the telephone receiver still held to his ear, not to miss whatever else she might say, he rolled over and cantilevered off the edge of the bed, located the telephone outlet on the wall behind the nightstand and pinched out the connector.

LESLIE returned Friday morning early. She let herself in quietly, found Gainer in bed. She did not know he was so anticipating her key in his lock that he came awake with the first click, and while she was undressing he pretended sleep, watched through the diffusion of his lashes. She eased herself carefully onto the bed, fit lightly against him. Then he came awake all at once and it was obvious he'd been faking it. He practically attacked her. She couldn't keep from giggling against his mouth.

Everything was all right now.

They were together again.

A serious kiss with a lot of missing in it, followed by several around one another's necks.

Would he like some orange juice? Leslie asked, and without waiting for his "yes" went to squeeze it.

The kitchen sounds were a joy to him because they were caused by her. She returned with the juice of ten oranges in two large glasses. "Mind the seeds," she said.

"How did it go in Boston?" Gainer asked.

"About as I said it would."

"No fun."

"Croquet at the Myopia Hunt Club was the high point."

"Did you have to flash much?"

"You mean often?"

"Both."

"Only when it seemed the thing to do . . . or wanted to."

"Shame."

"Never. What have you been doing? Still got the walks?"

"Not so much."

"Did you do anything exciting . . . meet anyone, or whatever?" She looked up to nothing in the corner of the ceiling to seem more offhand.

Gainer took a long, slow swig of orange juice, got a seed.

"Hmm?" she persisted lightly.

Don't answer. He could feel her intuition swarming about his head. "Does Rodger ever expect you to do more than flash for those people?" he asked.

"What do you think?"

"He might."

"No, he's smarter than that. They'd put it on his plus side for a night and his minus side forever."

"They're important to him."

"Apparently."

"Who are they?"

"Just money. Tell me, who did you meet?"

Her intuition closed in. "No one, exactly. I dropped by Xenon night before last."

"Oh?"

"For about an hour."

A half-full, all-purpose model's smile from her. "And you got hit on."

"Some."

"Hard."

"You might say that."

"But you walked away from it."

"If that's what you believe, that's what I did."

"*Touché,*" she said, not liking it but taking some of her own medicine.

Gainer got another orange seed, put it in reserve beneath his tongue while he ejected the first one. He tried for the wicker wastebasket over beside the dresser. Missed. He'd pick it up later.

"Who?" she asked.

"Who what?"

"Hit on you."

"No one you know."

"But someone you do."

"Stop cramping."

"It's not cramping, it's . . . caring."

Things wouldn't get back to right until he told her, Gainer thought.

"Didn't you ask me what I did?" Leslie said.

"Sort of."

"Well, fair is fair."

Gainer yawned twice and told her what had happened with Harrie, played down that it had been Harrie, and if a tinge of self-satisfaction came through it was at least unintended. He recited it in a monotone word-for-word and moment-for-moment so there wouldn't be any gaps to fill in. But there were anyway.

"What was she wearing?" Leslie asked.

"A blue dress, light blue."

"Swishy?"

"Just a dress, not much to it."

"How about her hair?"

"She had it up but it was falling."

Leslie had a set to her mouth, her cheek muscles drawing the corners up ever so slightly. It was all she could do to keep from gritting, and was anything but pleased that Gainer remembered so much about the girl. Leslie knew who Harrie was, of course. Would have had to been blind not to. Just the night before, while watching television from a guest bed in a grand house in Hamilton, Massachusetts, she had seen thirty seconds of Harrie over and over. Harrie peddling some designer's jeans, delighted to thrust her darling ass into the faces of half the country. Harrie selling slick lipstick, shaping her mouth into over-lubricated innuendoes.

Now, without thinking what she was doing, Leslie slipped her feet into her high-heeled sandals. She was reminding herself not to be jealous, that with Gainer the most destructive thing she could be was jealous. She had never been jealous of anyone. Before.

She walked to the dresser. Picked up his seed. Dropped it into the wastebasket.

"Maybe I should clean up your aura," she said.

"Doesn't need it."

"For sure?"

"Positive."

Gainer doubled his pillow behind his head. He remembered Leslie once having said that as a man waited and watched the last thing a really knowing woman took off was her shoes. And there, before his eyes, was the perfect example why. He had the urge to go over and lick the back of her knees, to start with.

Leslie was not really seeing herself in the mirror over the dresser. She plucked at strands of her hair that was as enticingly tousled as ever. I'm not afraid of the competition, she thought. Can handle the competition, upright or however. It was just that if she had to go up against anyone, why did it have to be the goddamn twenty-year-old indisputable all-around champ?

She alerted the angle of her view in the mirror so that it featured

Gainer behind her. She recognized the look in his eyes, the set of his mouth, and if what they said wasn't truth, it was the next best thing.

She turned around and jumped on him.

NEVERTHELESS, that afternoon Leslie called for and got an emergency double session at Janet Sartin. Put her face under merciless operating room lights, a ten-times-one magnifying glass big as a dinner plate and asked for the honest-to-God truth. She was told she had the skin quality of a twenty-five-year-old, partly because she'd kept the sun off it. And, yes, there were just the slightest lines starting at the outer corners of her eyes, not crow's-feet by any means, more precisely the legs of a baby spider. No, no frown lines, nor those vertical above-the-lip lines or any sign of her neck going to crepe. And that was under magnification. She relaxed and had a facial.

From Janet Sartin she went up to East Sixty-seventh to Lydia Bach for an hour on the ballet barre with Lydia herself supervising the exercises. Lydia remarked several times how amazingly limber Leslie was, supple as a twenty-year-old, she said. Leslie accepted that might be a half-truth, which made it a twenty-nine-year-old, only one year older than Gainer. She spent about half the hour doing pelvic pushdowns, Lydia's specialty.

After that she stopped in without an appointment at Davian's and was grateful when David, after the briefest second thought, squeezed her in between two very recognizable models. One he didn't spend as much time on, and the other would just have to wait. Leslie made David promise that while he gave her a trim she didn't really need, he would yank out every gray hair he came across. Unless, of course, it got to be a bit much, she said with a quick poor-me grin. She anticipated any number of painful little tugs but David only kept snipping away. Not because there weren't grays here and there among her marvelous nutmeg red. David was just too tactful to take her seriously.

She was over her anatomical paranoia.

That quickly.

Showed how superficial it had been.

Hell, Leslie thought, more courageous than ever, she could go head on, body on, one on one with any Harrie any damn day.

It was close to eight when she got to Gainer's apartment. A package had been left outside his door, which meant he probably wasn't there. He wasn't. And the inner drop Leslie felt made her realize how much she had been hoping he would be.

AT that moment a man paid off a taxi and got out on the northwest corner of Sixty-second Street and York Avenue. There was a slack in the flow of traffic both ways on the avenue and the man could have made it across easily, but he waited until the light was with him before crossing over.

He headed uptown.

He was in his forties, wearing a fairly expensive summerweight gray suit, a dark inoffensive tie and black lace up business shoes with classic plain tips. He was rather short and slight, and it appeared that his strength would be mental. That impression was reinforced by his sparse dark hair and deep-socketed dark eyes and the chrome wire-rimmed glasses that bridged above his prominent nose bone.

The tasteful simple typography of the engraved business cards in a leather card case in his inside pocket said he was David E. Shapiro, M.D., his specialty was cardiology and his office address was a low number on East Seventy-ninth Street, as attested to on an American Medical Association identification card. His right hand carried a typical black Gladstone doctor's satchel initialed "D.S." A stethoscope was not quite out of sight in his left pocket and in his shirt pocket, as might be expected, was an electronic summoning beeper.

It would have been wrong for him to be strolling. More in keeping was his swifter pace, his passing around others, conveying an important, if not critical, destination.

Dr. Shapiro.

On his way above Sixty-sixth Street he said a hello to the uniformed guard at the grillwork gates to Rockefeller University. As though he knew the man. He also glanced back off to his right to the Rockefeller Research Tower, the seventeen story structure that had been his second choice and was still his back-up location. He had become familiar with that building during the past week. The dining room area on the top floor had been an attractive convenience. The problem had been the angle, not impossible for him by any means, but not as good.

The Rockefeller complex ended at Sixty-eighth Street.

New York Hospital began there.

Dr. Shapiro went into the hospital's main entrance. Administrative offices on the left, dining room on the right, as he well knew. Evening visiting hours were in progress. Considerable activity in the lobby, most of it to and from the back of seven elevators directly ahead. The two on the end were expresses to the tower floors, ninth to twenty-third.

Dr. Shapiro waited for one of these. He removed his eyeglasses and polished them with a handkerchief while he waited. As though his eyes and their fragile reinforcements had already had a long tough day.

When the elevator car came down and emptied, Dr. Shapiro was among the first of the few to enter it. Like most hospital elevators its doors were regulated to remain open longer than, say, office elevators. When they finally, slowly closed, the car was crowded. Dr. Shapiro detected the odor of marijuana in the clothing of the white-coated intern standing beside him. The intern got out on the tenth floor, bound for intensive care.

Dr. Shapiro fixed his eyes on the floor indicator above the doors. When seventeen lighted up and the elevator doors parted, he recalled that that was the tower floor where the late Shah Palavi of Iran had come trying not to die. The place would have been swarming and impossible then, Dr. Shapiro thought.

By the time the elevator reached twenty-three he was the only one aboard. He stepped out and walked down the corridor. Doors to various doctors' offices were along both sides. At the end of the corridor a different sort of door gave access to the stairway up to twenty-four, the top floor. He went up and continued on farther to where the stairwell ended with a short landing and another heavy metal encased door.

Out on the roof.

He immediately heard the pock-ta-pock and saw abrupt movements.

Two doctors at play on the tennis court there.

It was something not entirely unexpected by Dr. Shapiro. He stood by the wire mesh fence and watched them. The green of the court's artificial surface was faded and the canvas strip across the top of the net was dark gray with grime. The doctors were not youngsters, they were both red-faced from the heat and exertion, dripping sweat, their T-shirts soaked. Dr. Shapiro watched their legs, assumed from the way they seemed to need to lock at the knees so as not to give way that they wouldn't be at it much longer. Besides, the daylight was going. He wasn't worried about them leaving him some daylight. He didn't need much. He could do without any if that was how it went.

At eight-thirty the two doctors left the tennis court. They had hardly noticed Dr. Shapiro and were now too tired to pay any attention to him.

As soon as they were gone Dr. Shapiro walked around to check the rest of the roof. Hot air was being blown noisily from a huge air-conditioning exhaust vent. Four pigeons were waddling around the top of the elevator shaft housing.

He was alone.

He used a key from his pocket to lock the roof access door from the outside. He would not be disturbed. He went to a painted black metal standpipe near the northwest corner. The vertical pipe stood four feet above the roof surface. It was nine inches in diameter. Across its opening lay a twelve inch long strip of wood. A cord tied to the wood hung down a ways into the pipe.

Dr. Shapiro took up the strip of wood and the cord, pulled the cord up slowly, hand-over-hand until what it was tied to came up and out to him.

Something narrow and long, wrapped in chamois.

He undid the cord and the chamois.

A rifle.

A special 460 Wheatherby Magnum.

Dr. Shapiro's real name, behind all the layers of other names he had assumed over the years, was Matthew Stemming. He was careful now not to touch the weapon. Not until he had put on a pair of surgeon's gloves he'd taken from his bag. He then examined the Wheatherby, saw it was precisely what he had requested. Single shot, bolt action, a sling on it, the barrel longer by four extra inches. All identifying serial numbers removed. The last time he had used a Wheatherby similar to this had been three years ago in Moravia at seven hundred yards. He had spent most of his life in one part or another of Africa, and trying to recall his first gun was like trying to remember his first pair of shoes. The newer lightweight automatics were his favorites, such as the AR-80 and the Colt Commando. But then, for each situation there was a weapon best-suited. This one, this beautifully . . . as he saw it . . . machined Wheatherby with its slightly deeper seat in the chamber and extra rifling length, was best for this situation.

Stemming looked at the eastern sky and from the mauve going to inkiness of it guessed the time to be a little after nine. His watch that was never wrong told him eight after. Tomorrow night at this time this order would be filled and he would be back on Madeira in Funchal that much richer. But he shouldn't think of afterward until afterward, he told himself.

He went to the east edge of the roof, took off his suit jacket, turned it inside out and folded it. Placed it like a cushion on the raised ledge that ran around the perimeter. The nearest higher buildings to the south were nine blocks away, in the opposite direction five blocks away. No problem. Almost directly below was FDR Drive. Uptown traffic was backed up on it because an old Buick, broken down in the left lane around One hundred-tenth Street, had been just left there.

Stemming spread the chamois and laid the rifle on it. From his bag he removed a Herter telescopic sight with built-in automatic range finder and infrared capability. He rotated its focusing mechanism for the feel of it before attaching it to the rifle. It was his personal sight that he knew he could depend on. He had checked it out earlier that morning, corrected and set it for three hundred yards. The scope would not be discarded down the standpipe along with the rifle when the order was completed, which meant taking a bit of a chance, but the scope was worth it, more trustworthy than any person he knew.

He worked the bolt mechanism, cocked the rifle open and examined the breech, shoved the bolt closed and pulled the trigger. It was something he did not like doing, firing an empty weapon. The crisp hard metal click of it went against his nerves. There would be no more of that.

He went into his trousers pocket, as though digging for change, and came out with a single round of ammunition. He had hand loaded the cartridge and seated the bullet himself, as he always did when he was expected to be perfect at a distance. That way he could be absolutely sure what the bullet would do. This round had a fat case and not much neck. The case contained eighty-one grains of 4831 powder. The slug was a 210 grain spire-shaped Hasler. When fired, the charge would explode the bullet from the muzzle at forty-six hundred foot pounds per square inch. The bullet would be traveling at the rate of thirty-eight hundred and fifty feet per second or about twenty-eight hundred miles per hour. At three hundred yards some of its velocity would be lost, hitting at about two thousand miles per hour. More than enough power to stop, for example, a rhino. Stemming knew because he had done it with one such shot, although killing animals was not to his taste.

He opened the breech again. Inserted the round, ran the bolt forward. It was a familiar pleasure to feel the round slide home into firing position. Next, the trigger. It had two actions. The normal one that required the customary squeezing away of slack and another whereby the slack could be automatically taken up, thereby making the trigger sensitive to the slightest touch. The latter eliminated any chance of jerking a shot. Stemming set the trigger on sensitive.

Brought the rifle up.

Put his hand under and around back through the sling, so that it created tension against his wrist.

Placed his left elbow on his suit jacket on the ledge that was four feet high. He hardly had to bend, merely backed his lower half a little way from the ledge, with his legs spread solidly.

He was going to enjoy this. He thought how fortunate he was to be able to make a living doing something he enjoyed.

He pressed his cheek against the stock.

Snuggled the butt into his shoulder.

Sighted.

Got only sky.

Got one of the three gray, red and white painted three hundred foot tall smokestacks of Con Edison rising from across the river in Queens.

Got the Roosevelt Island apartment complex.

Got the windows of the top floor southernmost apartment. It was as though he were no more than twenty feet from them, couldn't possibly miss. But they had a slight orange flare on them from the last of the sun. As soon as that was gone . . .

Gainer came home with a limp and an apology.

He said he'd been playing soccer up in the Bronx where he usually played, Crotona Park.

"I didn't ask where you'd been," Leslie said as though she couldn't have cared less, threw him a kiss from the couch.

He followed the flight of it straight back to her mouth.

"You've been drinking," she said.

"A couple with the guys. God, I'm tired. I must have run thirty miles."

"Too tired."

His hesitancy said he was.

"Did you score?" she asked.

"Four."

"That's a lot."

"I feel better. Must have run a lot of things out of me. What did you do?"

"Maybe that's what you should have been doing all along, instead of walking."

He pulled his shirttail out and unbuttoned his front.

It occurred to her that he had on his regular clothes, not his soccer-playing ones. She did not mention it. "I did a few chores," she said. "Brought some things from my place, just touched base. We ought to stay over there more."

"Whatever you say." He hobbled into the bathroom, bunched up his shirt and crammed it into the already stuffed dirty-laundry basket.

Leslie told herself she would not examine the shirt later for any blusher or lipstick smudges, but her mouth requested another kiss and in the holding after it she sniffed his shoulders for a trace of perfume. "Did you hurt your leg bad?" she asked.

"It's probably broken." He shrugged.

"Poor love."

"You know how those guys are up there. Those who don't have soccer shoes or sneakers play barefoot but today a new guy named Manuel something, just got laid off by a house wrecking company, he played in his work shoes. Regular heavy leather shoes with a hunk of steel in the toes. I don't know how he could run like he did with them on, and dribble too. The guys threw him out of the game but he wouldn't stay out. Didn't matter to him which side he was on, he'd get the ball and go either way. You had to give him room. Once, I didn't."

Leslie thought if he was making up all that it was too elaborate to cover a mere white lie.

"I didn't know whether or not there'd be a game today. I took my shorts and things along in a shopping bag just in case," he said.

He wasn't perspiration sticky or anything, Leslie noticed.

"Took a shower at Santiago's apartment, left the shopping bag there with my stuff in it."

"Why?"

"Forgot it. Just walked off and forgot it."

Likely story. "Take off your trousers."

"Leslie, I am honestly tired, down to my bones tired."

She didn't doubt that. She smiled and went and got some *People Paste* from the bathroom medicine cabinet. It was a healing salve consisting of slippery elm and golden seal. She had used it to heal his Monet garden bullet graze.

Gainer took off his trousers.

His wounds would exonerate him, Leslie thought, about forty-sixty sure those he had wouldn't be visible. But there was this spreading bruise and awful gash a couple of inches below his left knee. She sat at his feet feeling contrite and foolish. Down there was where she belonged, she thought. She applied the People Paste with light, loving dabs. Then she plumped the cushion of the most comfortable armless chair and had him sit on it, drew a hassock up for his injured leg to rest on, turned on the television, went right past a Bette Davis movie to the sports channel for a pro football game, preseason.

She was about to settle down with the newest edition of *Vogue*, despite it having Harrie incredibly stunning on *both* its front and back covers, when she remembered the package. The one that had been outside his door when she had arrived.

"That came," she said, indicating it.

The package was about the size of a shirt box. He thought most likely it was a gift from her and this was her tricky way of making it a surprise, so he told her indifferently, "Open it."

It was on the side table near her. She tore off its shipping tape and brown wrapping paper to find it was a shiny white box with royal blue edging.

"It's from Porthault," she said, recognizing the imprint of that prestigious little establishment on the cover.

"Oh?" He was distracted by a rookie halfback he had never heard of who was blasting his own holes through the right side of the Steeler line.

Leslie removed the cover from the box.

Beneath the tissue was a three hundred dollar bottom sheet and a hundred dollar pillowcase, in the sort of light mauvish gray usually associated with expensive lingerie. Leslie realized the significance of there being only a bottom sheet and one pillowcase when she read the note that was enclosed.

> Bring these along
> and we'll stain them together—
> Harrie

The noise that came from Leslie was purely female, a combination hiss and growl.

She threw the box and all at Gainer.

He ducked, awkwardly because of his extended injured leg. Went sprawling off the chair.

At that precise instant the bullet shattered the window glass, passed through the space Gainer's heart had just vacated, struck the back cushion of the chair, tore through it and on through the wall to lodge nearly a half-inch deep in the ceramic tile over the bathtub.

CHAPTER
FOURTEEN

P OLICE cruiser.

Seal of Harrison Township on its front doors.

Officer McCatty, alone in the cruiser, brought it to an easy stop at the corner of Stoney Crest Road and New Lake Street. Taking his time, he brought out a fresh box of Dunhill cigarettes, used a two thousand dollar eighteen karat gold Dupont to light one of them. A partial pack of Camel filters and a book of matches were on the flat of the dash, but he never smoked the Camels when he was alone, just as he never used the lighter when he was with anyone. The Dunhills and the Dupont and some Turnbull and Asser sixty dollar shirts from which he removed the labels were the only small luxuries he allowed himself. It helped that he did not appear to be the sort who appreciated such things, that he had the patience to live within the means of his municipal salary while his other money, his "fuck you" money as he mentally thought of it, piled up out of sight. He figured another four years until he retired for his health, and if wife Connie was still around, which seemed unlikely at the moment the way she was acting, he would leave her.

The majority of McCatty's private thoughts were usually on what he had coming. He was just running the days off like mileage on a trip . . . He took a right and went at thirty up New Lake Street, across the bridge over Interstate 684 and then another right for Purchase Street. He was on routine patrol. That didn't mean he should pass by Number

19 once every hour but that was his arrangement and how it averaged out. This was his first time by since coming on duty at eight.

Heading down Purchase he saw the Rolls-Royce Corniche parked in the opposite direction. It was pulled over as far as the street's limited shoulder allowed beside a stretch of tall yew hedge close to where the wall began Number 19's property.

Passing by, McCatty took it all in. Black Corniche, this year's model, impeccably polished. Man and woman in it, the woman at the wheel. New York license plates, initialed plates LMP. McCatty kept it in his rearview mirror as he continued on to Barnes Lane, where he U-turned and went back to it.

Rack lights on, turning and strobing.

Pulled up alongside the Corniche, window to window.

"May I help you?" McCatty asked.

"No thank you," Leslie replied with a smile suitable for a policeman.

"Parking's not allowed along here."

"We didn't realize."

"Are you looking for an address?"

"No."

Gainer leaned across the driver's side to tell McCatty: "We have a problem with the car. It just quit all of a sudden."

"Just like that?"

"Won't budge."

"I'll call for a tow," McCatty said.

"I already have"—Gainer held up the car's telephone—"but thanks anyway."

McCatty decided this wasn't anything, the Corniche helping him to that opinion. He also thought someday he wouldn't buy a Corniche, he'd buy a Silver Spirit. His good-bye gesture to Leslie and Gainer was something of a salute. He then executed a crisp turnaround, using the first driveway on the left, came speeding back by the Corniche as though he'd wasted enough time.

"It's not ten-thirty," Gainer said, taking issue with the electronic digital clock on the instrument panel.

"Where's your watch?"

"Beside your sink or your bed."

"I keep forgetting to have that clock turned back. It still shows Daylight Savings time."

"What would they charge to adjust the clock?"

"I don't know, fifty dollars or so."

Gainer found a ballpoint pen in the glove compartment, used the tip of it to press the tiny button adjacent to the clock, causing its digital numbers to change at a nearly unreadable rate until they reached nine-thirty.

"You're bright," Leslie said.

Gainer was sorry now that he had bothered with the clock. Seeing the minutes and hours go by so fast had made him think his own time was probably running out even faster. He slouched in his seat feeling relatively safe, for the moment.

"They're up by now," Leslie said.

"It's still too early. They're not regular business people, these people."

"Aren't you glad I didn't stay home?"

"I need them to be open-minded, clear as can be."

"Maybe they take uppers."

"We'll give them another half hour."

They had been parked there on Purchase Street since a quarter to eight, within easy view of the entrance gates to Number 19. They had observed numerous arrivals—the servants, the groundkeepers, the swimming pool cleaning service. As far as Gainer or Leslie knew, they were all just showing up for work.

It had been about twelve hours since that bullet missed Gainer but smashed into his life. Both he and Leslie had gone flat to the floor, stayed there below any conceivable line of fire. Gainer had thrown his shoe at the wall switch to turn off the living room lights, but even then they kept down. After an hour that seemed like three, they decided her apartment would be safer, so they crawled out and went there in a taxi, made the driver take the longer but more cautious route by way of Queens and the Queensboro Bridge.

It wasn't until they were in Leslie's bedroom, with the city excluded by drapes, that the feeling of being stalked to death diminished to some extent. Gainer couldn't sleep, sat up in bed—with a lot of pillows behind him—watching television but only really seeing it every other couple of minutes. Leslie was determined not to get any sleep. She sat up in the same manner, but around three o'clock during some of Hepburn's tears in *The Rainmaker* she was gone, tumbled over against Gainer and unconsciously snuggled down.

His mind was going like a shorted-out slide projector. It was terrifying that someone was out to kill him, especially so considering who was behind it.

Zurich, Paris and now New York.

Norma, Becque and Ponsard, and now a high-powered rifle.

If only it wasn't them he might feel he had a chance, not feel so doomed. But his fear, like a compass needle, kept pointing their way.

The mob. If they wanted to whack him out, they'd do it. Now or eventually, one way or another. No matter where or to whom he ran. That was how they were.

Sorry, Norma.

Gainer glanced down at his chest. He could see the left side of it quiver with every heartbeat. His heart was really zapping, as though, like some creature caught in his body, it sensed its end.

All night he'd sat up in bed like that, going over it, his options.

The moves he might make got down to two.

One was leave everything. Leslie, everything. Change himself, fade away to somewhere and to such an extent that he wasn't anyone. It was the street thing to do and probably his best shot, but even if he got away with it, what he'd be getting away with would be almost the same as dying.

His other course was to go right at them. Go neither on the offensive nor on his knees, but straight forward, putting himself at their mercy but also taking them back a bit that he had such nerve. Maybe they would use him. He'd heard the mob sometimes handled matters that way: let the target in, kept him close, wrung whatever they could from him before following through with their original intention to eliminate. If they went for that at least it would save his ass for a while, Gainer thought. It might also give him an inside opportunity to find out who was really responsible for Norma ending up in that Dolder Grand shower stall. Long shot, but what better way was there for him to have a chance at finding that out. God, he wanted to know that . . .

So, now, there he was parked with Leslie on Purchase Street.

She was saying: "Lady Caroline . . ."

"What?"

"Lady Caroline did it. Arranged the whole thing right from the moment she decided you ought to go to Xenon."

"I thought she's supposed to be looking after you, not me."

"Same thing in this instance. Don't you see? She brought Harrie into it, made sure it was Harrie, whipped up her libido and everything."

"You don't really believe that?"

"It makes sense," Leslie said, thought for a moment, then nodded conclusively. What she didn't say was how it also conveniently diminished the power of Harrie's appeal while providing an excuse for her own jealous behavior. "What a dear lady, Lady Caroline is," Leslie went on, "the way she maneuvered Harrie into buying and sending those sheets so I could throw them at you at precisely the right moment."

"To do that she'd have to know what was going to happen."

"She had access. Probably."

"Well, I wish she'd let us in on how this is going to turn out."

"Probably it's only sometimes she has access."

Gainer was contributing less than half-heartedly to the dialogue. His mind was still mostly on survival. He thought Leslie was taking it too lightly, but then, what help would it be to have her shaky and sweating it out? "How do you know it was Lady Caroline?" he asked.

"Who else?"

"Norma."

"I don't think so. There was something upper-British about the way it was done. Tidy yet roundabout. Wouldn't you say?"

"Yeah, sure, why not?"

"You definitely have Lady Caroline to thank."

"Out loud?"

"If you want."

Gainer looked down at his feet. His best shoes. Why had he put on his best? He wondered if undertakers put shoes on the dead, laced and tied them and everything when they got them ready. He remembered a joke about a dead short guy displayed in his coffin wearing Adler elevator shoes. The silence, he realized, told him Leslie was waiting for him to thank Lady Caroline. He wouldn't.

"Then perhaps sometime when you're alone," Leslie suggested. "How about some Rescue? Feel as though you could use a little Rescue?"

"Got a gallon?"

When she went into her carryall for the brown glass dropper bottle, Gainer caught a glimpse of something black-blue metallic. He spread the mouth of the bag to reveal an automatic pistol. An ASP. And another, identical.

"You left those in Paris," he said.

"These are a different pair."

"For New York."

She nodded, a matter of fact nod.

"And no doubt there are two more just like them in Palm Beach and in Bedford and in Vail," he said.

"Among other necessities."

Gainer was glad to see the ASPs. He had gotten so attached to the one he had used in Paris, he'd been tempted to make off with it. And might have if it hadn't belonged to Rodger.

"They're ready and loaded," Leslie assured him.

"You shouldn't have brought them. If you'd asked me, I would have told you not to."

"Hell, I thought as long as someone is already shooting at you, you might want to shoot back."

"Under ordinary circumstances, yes, but . . ."

A truck appeared. Coming down Purchase Street. A huge, green garbage collecting truck grinding along. Possibly it was what Gainer and Leslie had been waiting for. She started the Corniche.

The garbage truck passed, slowed, turned in at the entrance of Number 19, stopped for the gates to be opened.

Leslie got the Corniche under way. Timed her speed so it came up to the rear of the truck just as the truck continued on. Braking smoothly, just enough, she tucked the Corniche into the lumbering slipstream of the truck, less than a foot from its hulking back end, so that as the truck went in through the gates the Corniche, hidden from view by it for that moment, slipped inside behind it and followed it up the drive.

Gainer, looking back, saw the surprise on the face of the man on duty at the gatehouse. The man's right hand went in under his jacket. Perhaps if it had been another kind of car or someone not so well-bred-looking at the wheel he wouldn't have hesitated. His hand came out empty. He hurried into the gatehouse, evidently for the phone.

At the top of the drive the garbage truck went around the service side of the house. Leslie, following Gainer's instructions, brought the Rolls to the main entrance. She had barely cut the engine when a pair of white-jacketed housemen rushed out and down the steps to open the door of the Rolls, as though they were serving expected guests. The men were too large and thick to be doing ordinary butlering, Gainer thought.

"Will there be any luggage, sir?" one of the housemen asked.

"No, nothing," Gainer said, while across the roof of the car his look to Leslie told her to leave her carryall and its contents on the seat.

As they went up the steps one of the housemen cut across in front of Gainer, colliding with him. Their legs especially came into contact. It seemed inadvertent but Gainer realized immediately that it was a well-done frisk. To determine whether or not he had a weapon holstered to either of his lower legs. Otherwise it was obvious that Gainer was not armed. That was the reason he had chosen to wear a pair of natural linen trousers and a creamy pongee shirt, no jacket. As for Leslie, there was no need to frisk her. She only had on four things, two of which were her high-heeled sling sandals. Her dress was a next-to-something plain, loose shift in green *soie de chine*, so pale it was nearly not green. It was slit on the left up to within six inches of her hip, so that it was also bare on top and kept from falling by only the thinnest, most precarious-looking straps. The nature and cut of the fabric teetered the imagination. One moment it hung full, opaque. The next, responding to a stir of air or her body movement, it defined her like her skin.

Darrow was waiting for them in the reception hall, standing there like a confident host come to greet invited friends. Not what Gainer had anticipated. On first sight Darrow seemed posed, with one foot placed at an angle a few inches behind the other, front knee slightly bent to cause a perfect break in his gray flannel trousers that topped white antelope shoes, not new but without a smudge.

Hine stood off to the left on the bottom step of the main stairway, increasing by that many inches his natural height of six and one-half feet. His hands were joined behind his back. Gainer had met Hine twice before but never really met him. The same applied to Sweet, who stood deeper in the hallway, looking like a super-realistic acrylic sculpting of a heavyweight wrestler in street clothes.

"Nice to see you again, Andrew," Darrow said.

His handshake had a calculated firmness and duration to it. Probably learned that in prep school, Gainer thought, and then told himself his background was showing.

When he introduced Leslie he was, as usual, reluctant to say her married last name, but then, he thought, no matter, the name would be unimportant to Darrow or Hine.

Leslie raised her chin and said consecutive how-do-you-dos to them.

Gainer put his hand out to Hine, who pretended not to notice it.

"I was extremely sorry to hear about Norma," Darrow said. "As you know we were all personally fond of her. Weren't we Hine?"

"Indeed."

"We still don't know exactly what happened to her. All we got were some vague bits and pieces. We wondered if there was some way we could help," Darrow said, eyes-to-eyes with Gainer.

"That's why I'm here," Gainer told him.

"Oh?"

"I need some help."

"Of course, whatever, if it's within our power."

It's within your power, Gainer thought.

"Come, let's take this outside," Darrow said. "The weather is certainly warm enough to be used as an excuse for a midmorning tall one, wouldn't you say?" He led the way through the house and out onto the south terrace, where a summer bar was situated in sun, glasses gleaming, slices of lemons and limes contributing color, a white-jacketed houseman ready to tend.

They sat at the same umbrella-shaded table that Darrow had shared with Hunsicker little more than a week ago. In fact, the chair Gainer was now seated in was the very same that Hunsicker "the distributor" had occupied.

Leslie wanted a Kir, not too sweet.

Gainer ordered a beer, any kind.

Darrow took his usual Tattinger and fresh orange juice.

Hine was about to state his preference when Darrow told him: "Perhaps this doesn't concern you."

"I doubt that it does," Hine said, seemingly unfazed by Darrow's rudeness. Hine excused himself, got up and went inside.

Darrow looked to Gainer.

Gainer had thought he might lean forward, say it with a confidential importance. Instead he sat back rather casually and told him: "Someone is out to kill me."

Three furrows of concern appeared between Darrow's brow. "What happened?"

Gainer told him.

"Perhaps it was some city nut taking a pot shot at just anyone," Darrow said. "The city is full of them these days."

"No."

"How can you be sure?"

Gainer's silence spoke for him.

Darrow added more silence to it, took a punctuating sip and told Leslie he was surprised they hadn't met before. "Do you sail?"

"Where?"

"Penobscot, Hyannisport."

"Not recently."

"I believe I saw you once. As a matter of fact I'm certain. Not sailing, but at Parke-Bernet four or five years ago."

"Possibly."

"It was the night they sold a Turner for six million something, May of 1980, I believe. I bought a small Vuillard, nothing important. Actually my being there was more social than anything."

Darrow was all charm for Leslie. So damn oily, Gainer thought.

"As I recall, you bid on a large Renoir."

"Not me."

Rodger, Gainer thought.

"And came within a hundred thousand of owning it," Darrow went on. "Have you been to any of the recent sales?"

"Aren't they closed for the summer?"

"Of course, but there's important jewelry scheduled for sometime early in October. That should interest you."

Leslie said it did.

"I have the advance catalogue if you'd care to look through it. On the condition, of course, that you promise not to bid against me for the things I've checked."

"I break most of my promises," Leslie said without a smile.

It seemed to Gainer that Darrow was trying to draw her out, open her up. Gainer was about to get back onto the subject of the reason they were there when Darrow beat him by saying to Leslie, "There's a sapphire ring in that sale I particularly want."

"A Burmese sapphire?"

"A Ceylon but exceptionally deep and bright. Just over twelve carats. It's an older Tiffany stone."

"How old?"

"Somewhere around 1920."

"They're best."

"Sapphires," Darrow confided, "are rising in value, you know."

"So I've heard."

"As a result of the political situation in Southeast Asia. There used to be sapphire sales regularly in Rangoon but not anymore. The only sapphires getting out now are contraband."

"Your advice, then, is to buy sapphires."

"By all means, as many good ones as you can, and salt them away. Rubies as well. But please, not that twelve carat stone I want."

"You have my word."

"Is there something wrong with your drink?" Darrow asked.

"A little heavy on the cassis for my taste," Leslie told him.

Darrow apologized as though he had stepped on her toe. He signaled the barman for a replacement.

"Don't bother."

"Perhaps you'd prefer something else. Have you ever tried a Savannah Sneak?"

"Only twice," Leslie said with a straight face.

It seemed a cue. The barman immediately brought a tray with all the necessary ingredients.

The bastard obviously had a set routine, Gainer thought. And part of it this time was to leave Gainer out in the cold by fastening on Leslie.

Darrow made the mixture of the drink into a ritual that at least *he* found entertaining. What he proceeded to put together was basically a mint julep in a large sterling goblet using sprigs of fresh mint and what he claimed was pure Chacham County Georgia well water. He muddled mint along with some sugar and water in the bottom of the goblet and all over its inner sides, packed the goblet with ice shaved so fine it looked like snow, then poured in nearly equal jiggers of cognac and peach brandy that seeped down through. He stuck a slice of fresh ripe peach in along the side, garnished it with a sprig of mint, inserted a silver straw and placed it in front of Leslie. "Best to let it sit and frost for a while," he told her.

Within seconds the silver goblet was beaded wet and hazed.

Leslie took a sip. She took two more before commenting, pleasantly surprised, "Delightful."

Gainer shook some salt into his beer to renew its head. He was feeling more and more excluded despite Leslie's wink at him over the rim of the goblet. The whole thing had gotten off track from the start, was now way off. It wasn't intended to be a social visit with all this overbred chitchat. He had the impression that any moment they'd be going out the front door, thanking Darrow for everything and perhaps even with Leslie and Darrow pecking one another on the cheek, for Christ's sake.

Their topics now were people they knew and skiing places.

Gainer stopped trying to appear interested. He pushed his chair farther from the table, turned it at an angle and positioned another chair to put his feet up on. The largest cloud he saw was off to the south, shaped like an English sheep dog or a pig or a dead fat lady on her way to heaven, gradually wisping away. The swimming pool was unbelievable with its water that blue. The tennis court was deserted.

From where Gainer sat he could see the entire rear of the house, from its elaborate long terrace all the way to the brick wall that bordered the grounds. Between the two was entirely garden, not manicured and arranged in a pattern but an uncontrived-looking expanse of flowers like an English country garden. Different kinds were competing for space, foxglove and delphinium taller seeming to win out. The garden didn't ring true either, was not really as untended as it was made to appear, Gainer thought. The whole place was a sort of setup.

His view took in the rear side of the house, all the way to the north wing. It struck him that there was something not right about that wing. A section of the second floor had no windows. Only ivy and wall. It contradicted the house. There should have been two windows up there to balance the two on the first floor. If he was Darrow he'd complain to one of the bosses, he thought, and allowed himself an inner smile.

Gainer's mind was not really so far away. He fully heard the first sound of the first word when Darrow finally turned his way and asked: "What led you to believe we could help you Andrew?"

"It was the first thing that occurred to me, that's all."

"You just assumed."

"Norma once told me if I ever had any heavy trouble, I should come to you."

"When was that?"

"Years ago." Gainer added a lie to a lie.

"I'm sorry, but I find that strange. She knew we prefer not to get involved in matters beyond our control."

Which leaves very damn little, Gainer thought.

"What would you like us to do, Andrew?"

Cut the Andrew shit.

"Whatever you can," Gainer said.

"All right, how much do you need?"

"Money won't help."

"It usually does."

"This isn't usual."

"What then?"

"Maybe you can help me get it straight, so at least I know what I'm up against."

Darrow was tempted to tell him: you are up against termination. You are up against your young balls rotting off. He did not like this young man. Never had. The few times they had met through Norma he'd thought Gainer a good-looking smartass, a sort of social chameleon, *nouveau* nice. Once when Norma had brought him to Number 19 to show him off, Darrow had caught Gainer's eyes taking the measure of him, scouring him deep. Gainer had not taken his gaze away, and Darrow had thought that insolent. At the time, of course, such feelings had been momentary, insignificant. It was only recently that Darrow had brought them forward. Today Gainer had intensified them by coming here. All the worse, coming here with Mrs. Rodger Pickering.

Darrow put his hand on Gainer's forearm, patted it. "Rest easy, Andrew. You'll see now that we're not just fair weather sorts. Mind you, I'm not altogether sure we can actually protect you, but we can certainly do our best. That's what you want, isn't it? Protection?"

"You might call it that."

"You'll have to cooperate."

"He will," Leslie put in, hoping Gainer understood why.

Darrow brought his hand to his chin, evidently deliberating. Actually he was wondering if Leslie had taken notice of his hands, gave her a long moment to do so. He fixed his eyes about two feet above Gainer's head and told him: "I think perhaps what you should do, Andrew, is make this your home base, so to speak. At least for the time being. Come and go as freely as you feel appropriate. Here, or wherever, I promise you will be . . . how shall I say? . . . watched over. How does that suit you?"

"Couldn't ask for more."

"Then that's settled. We'll have accommodations made ready at once."

"What about me?" Leslie asked.

The very words Darrow had expected. He registered mild surprise. "You'll be staying on as well, Mrs. Pickering?"

"Coming and going."

"You're most welcome, of course. Would you prefer a room with early morning sun?"

"It doesn't matter, just as long as it's adjoining."

Mrs. Pickering, Gainer thought. He hadn't introduced her as a Mrs.

She drew on her silver straw and caused the little popping sounds of bottom-empty. "I'd like another Savannah Sneak," she said.

Darrow constructed another but this time lighter on the flourish. As he placed the drink in front of Leslie he glanced toward the house, saw Hine just inside the open french doors gesturing discreetly. Darrow got up and went in.

"What the hell was all that?" Gainer asked, keeping his teeth together.

"All what?"

"You and Darrow and all that social register chumsy crap."

"It helped."

"Yeah?"

"My intuition tells me it helped."

Daniel, Gainer thought, in the lions' den.

Leslie gave up the straw, swigged Savannah Sneak from the goblet, buried the tip of her nose in the shaved ice. Her nose and ears were flushed, Gainer noticed, and thought she should stick to red zinger.

"You didn't really want to stay here alone."

Gainer admitted he didn't.

"Tell you what," she said, trying to sound up, "let's cancel out the thought that someone tried to kill you—"

"Easy said—"

"Hey, I'm at stake too, you know. If anything like that happened to you, it's almost a sure thing I'd kill myself—"

"Don't talk about it."

"Exactly. Let's go at it here as though we're on holiday at some five hundred dollar a day swell place. Swim a lot, play tennis, caviar them to death."

235

He had to laugh a little, despite everything. For all he knew, his beer might have contained a slow undetectable poison. His mind jumped from death to life: the appreciation of Leslie's left leg, her exposed toes and all the way up to where the slit in her dress was as parted as it could be, and ridden up higher because she was seated. He could see where her thigh and buttock made transition. He'd been over every millimeter of that leg every imaginable way, he thought. The idea of not ever being able to again caused what felt like an emotional collision inside him, all drives in him hitting head-on.

"You're terrific when you're jealous," she said.

"I'm not jealous."

"Your eyes get all broody, greener, very attractive."

"When was I ever jealous?"

"Three or four minutes ago."

"You read me wrong."

"Possibly, but I think not. You know, Darrow doesn't seem so dangerous, more like another well-bred old bore—"

"Your intuition needs a major tune-up." Gainer reached for his glass and accidently tipped it over.

Leslie sighed. "Such a heavy number, jealousy. I'm glad I'm never burdened by it." She worked her eyelashes some to let him know she wasn't a serious hypocrite.

He leaned across.

She leaned across.

Their kiss made them both realize they hadn't kissed since the night before.

When they opened their eyes, Darrow was standing beside the table. "Everything has been arranged."

"I'm going to drive back into town for some essentials," Leslie said, and asked Gainer, "How about you?"

Gainer decided he'd better not, not yet.

"Okay, I'll also pick up a few of your things. Anything special?"

"Old shoes and People Paste."

Darrow wondered if that was some sort of code.

"Leave everything to me. I won't be long." She seemed to bless him with her smile before she departed.

She would, as usual, Gainer thought, not let up a single mile per hour at the toll stations, would streak right through the gate kept open for those cars bearing special parkway toll plates, which she didn't have. He should have told her he loved her before she went. He had promised himself, since Norma, never to leave it unsaid again.

"Exceptional woman, Mrs. Pickering," Darrow was saying. "One of

236

the world's great beauties, in my estimation."

"Yeah."

"I suppose you've met her husband."

"Not directly."

Ambiguities annoyed Darrow. "Come with me," he said brusquely, and led the way into the house to his study.

Hine was there.

Darrow didn't sit behind his desk. Casually imperious, he half sat on a front corner of it, his right haunch taking most of his weight. After a pause he said: "Favor for favor is fair, don't you agree Andrew?"

"I guess."

"It so happens at this moment we are short-handed."

"What do you have in mind?"

"Fill in for Norma."

Gainer's heart jumped.

"One carry, two at most."

"Let me think about it."

"By all means, think about it."

Gainer didn't like the italicized sound of that. "When am I supposed to go?"

"You're on the two o'clock from Kennedy to Zurich. That's correct, isn't it Hine?"

"Two o'clock," Hine said.

"Today?" Gainer asked.

Darrow's nod was just barely discernible.

"Hell, I don't even have a toothbrush."

"You will."

"I'm supposed to go dressed like this?" Gainer lifted a trouser leg to show his best shoes but no socks.

"You won't. There'll be a bag containing appropriate things of yours handed over to you at Kennedy. Including a passport."

That meant the shits had been into his apartment or were there now. The pair of locks on his door were probably no more than toys to them. Gainer especially resented their doing that, putting hands on his personal things. He thought of Alma's love letters in the top drawer where he also kept his passport. Somehow the letters were more vulnerable than anything. They didn't deserve to be sullied.

Sweet entered the study bearing a man's suitcase, a thirty-incher, an all leather one that apparently had endured its share of travel. It had a red and white tag attached to the handle. Sweet placed the bag within Gainer's reach.

What, Gainer wondered, would happen if he refused to go, just said

he didn't want to, wouldn't? The carry was very possibly—surely?—
a way of setting him up, certainly it had been invented within the last
hour. Still, for his reasons, not theirs, he'd go along with it.

"How much is in there?" Gainer asked.

"Three million," Darrow told him.

"Not two or two and a half? You're sure?"

Darrow looked to Hine, who deferred to Sweet, who held up three
fingers.

"Three exactly," Darrow said.

Gainer made a dubious face.

"Take my word for it," Darrow advised.

"No." Gainer insisted the suitcase be opened.

The neatly packed hundreds were there.

"We're not going to count it for you," Darrow said, betraying some
annoyance.

Gainer grinned. "I didn't figure you'd even open it. Okay. When I
get to Zurich, then what?"

As soon as Gainer had gone off to the airport, Darrow phoned Hunsicker at Intelco in New York. He told him he wanted his most recent
order changed.

Hunsicker begged pardon, said he did not know what Darrow was
referring to.

Darrow realized Hunsicker was keeping to the strict line, going by
the book. Such business was never supposed to be handled by telephone,
no matter how cryptically. However, Darrow reasoned, in this instance
it was such an uncomplicated thing there could be no misunderstand-
ing, nor was it possible that anyone listening might know what it was
about. He got on with it, told Hunsicker he did not want to cancel the
order, merely hold off on it until he gave word otherwise.

Hunsicker suggested Darrow meet with him to clarify the situation.

Darrow was in no mood for a sit-down with Hunsicker, but if it had
to be . . . "All right, when shall I expect you?"

"I'll be up there next week, Wednesday or Thursday."

"I want you up here this afternoon."

"That won't be possible."

"Why not?"

"I have another appointment here an hour from now, and later in
the day I'm off to Los Angeles."

"This is important," Darrow said impatiently.

"Then I suggest you come here to my office. I'll make time."

Darrow was so furious he very softly and precisely placed the telephone receiver on its cradle. Of all the gall. He shouldn't have to go across the room to accommodate someone on Hunsicker's level. The man was being purposely difficult, sticking so narrowly to an irrelevant rule.

The rule, screw the rules—

The word seemed to hang in the air around him, and brought him up short. He reprimanded himself for having such a risky attitude, even for a moment. Hunsicker was right.

As if in retribution, Darrow reviewed the rules that pertained to orders, mentally recited them.

May only be issued verbally, person-to-person.

May only be cancelled or revised by the initiating party, verbally, person-to-person.

May not be carried forward after the death of whoever issued the order.

The last, Darrow understood, was not only a matter of tidiness but also to avoid having one man inherit the judgment of another. Twelve years ago, when he had taken over at Number 19, there had been two of Gridley's orders outstanding. They were automatically dropped and he, Darrow, had begun with a clean slate.

Now, as much as he did not want to, he would put on business clothes and be driven into town to see Hunsicker. It had become to his advantage that he put the Gainer order on hold.

He had to give Hine credit this once.

It was a splendid idea to have Gainer make a carry. As Hine had pointed out, quite possibly Gainer would take the opportunity to visit the three million he undoubtedly had gotten from Norma's last carry. And, as Hine had not considered but was even more promising, it gave Darrow time alone to impress Mrs. Pickering.

CHAPTER
FIFTEEN

THAT afternoon, while Darrow in New York was four hundred feet above street level putting Gainer's temporary reprieve in Hunsicker's ear, Gainer was at sixty thousand feet in Air France Concorde Flight 002. The plane was approaching the so-called point-of-no-return, a designation Gainer thought appropriate for him personally as well.

So much had happened, changed in just three-quarters of a day. He was not where he should be. He felt displaced. On his way to Zurich via Paris faster than sound.

He might have felt better about it had he been able to reach Leslie. He'd tried, rung her apartment and his from the airport terminal and got no answer. He didn't have the telephone number of Number 19. It was unlisted. Besides, by then he had barely enough time before departure to go into the men's room to change. The matching all-leather bag that wasn't his, but it contained needed things of his. It had been waiting for him when he arrived at the terminal. The skycap had greeted him by his name with a sir after it and informed him that part of his luggage, that smaller bag, had already arrived. The thirty-incher containing the three million got checked right through. What amazed Gainer was not that Darrow's people could pull strings but that they held so many.

Sweet had driven him to Kennedy.

Sweet had tucked a ten-fold of hundreds into Gainer's shirt pocket for expenses.

Sweet had gone all the way to the boarding gate with him and stood at the window until the ramp was disconnected and the Concorde sealed and moving away.

It was obvious to Gainer that Darrow wanted him out of the way, far away, soonest possible. A direct Swiss Air flight leaving at seven would have avoided the hurry, been almost half the fare and put him in Zurich only an hour later tomorrow morning. Darrow's motive appeared to be Leslie. If it was *only* her, Gainer could feel relieved. The old bastard would need a diamond-edged chisel for a prick to get through to her.

But maybe Leslie wasn't it.

Maybe they had decided to deal with him a different way. The three in the bag could be really dirty, dirty millions, marked, identifiable, and he was flying to take the fall. How, in the first place, had they been able to come up with three million all banded and packed and ready to travel in mere minutes? No one had run out to the bank.

Watched over.

Darrow had said he would be.

Gainer had spotted two other passengers who might be doing exactly that, but not necessarily for his protection. One was the thirtyish, apparently well-off woman across the way and one row down. A blond wearing beige and navy. Gainer had caught her eyes on him three times, the third time with a trace of a smile. Probably a styled-up ex-Vegas showgirl, Gainer thought. Then there was the man a couple of rows back with the haggard if polished look of a lawyer. He was reading the *Harvard Law School Journal* but had been on the same page for an hour.

Ignore them.

Gainer plumped his pillow, requested another and filled in the space between the seat and the window for his head. He gazed out at the night, couldn't see the moon or a star or a cloud, just black. Even one star would have helped counter his sense of unreality. To pass the time he tried making a mental list of things he didn't love about Leslie. Got nowhere with that. Switched to the things he loved about her and they were like sweet sheep leaping one after another over a fence.

He napped without dreams until the moment of touchdown at Charles De Gaulle Aéroport, stretched his face and neck awake and filed off the Concorde. He saw the blond fellow passenger being met by a casually dressed, distinguished-looking man who kissed her as though he owned her. The other lawyer-type passenger was met by a sort of young version of himself who gave him a son's hug.

It was midnight Paris time, but six hours earlier Gainer time. Again, he tried phoning Leslie and again, got no answer. He remembered a knockaround street guy in New York who had claimed a couple of times he had the connections to get any unlisted number in the world in five minutes. Gainer reached him, told him what he wanted—Darrow's number. When, as agreed, Gainer called back in a half hour, the guy's wife or woman or whatever said she didn't know where he was, that she thought he had gone over to Meadowlands to the trotters.

So much for that.

The connecting Air France flight to Zurich would not leave until seven-forty. Gainer had all night. He thought of the container of Norma's ashes only a few miles off in that crypt in the Cimetière du Père-Lachaise but was not able to feel any closer to her for that. He bought an Italian edition of *Playboy* and a paperback in English of John Cheever stories. He looked and read at the counter of a bistro while he had a Croque Monsieur and then a glass of *vin ordinaire* for a change of pace. Every so often he would casually glance around for whoever was supposed to be watching over him. No one likely, as far as he could see. Certainly not the slight, brittle-looking old man across the way who had either a bad summer cold or sinus problems.

Killing the night, Gainer wandered the terminal, observed hellos and good-byes from casual to passionate. Also saw a lot of different kinds of waiting. Found a seat and read slowly to make the Cheever last.

Finally he was buckled in and being thrust upward with the rest of Flight 680. The plane climbed for a half hour and descended for a half hour and touched down at Flughafen Floten in Zurich five minutes ahead of schedule.

At customs Gainer had his passport looked at but that was all. He went out to the upper level ramp, disregarded the taxis there, hired a limousine. He kept his smaller bag and the three million thirty-incher with him in the rear seat.

The destination given to him by Hine was a street off the upper section of Bahnhofstrasse. A five story private bank that could not be identified as a bank from the street. Its cut-stone facade needed only a cross or two to make it seem a church.

Gainer told the driver to wait.

He took the carry inside.

Entered a spacious reception area, a hard, traditional atmosphere of varnished walnut, panels and floor. The fringes of an Isfahan carpet seemed combed into place. Not a speck of dust on the crystals of a huge, lighted chandelier. Precisely beneath the chandelier was a receptionist. Her desk and chair were the only furnishings. Evidently they did not care to have anyone else sit. The only thing on the desk was a brown telephone. The receptionist could have been either twenty-five or forty. The most rememberable thing about her was she had very accurately penciled eyebrows in place of her natural ones that were entirely plucked. Otherwise the attempt was to be nondescript, as though if she had a name it was a secret.

Gainer told her who he was. In keeping with Hine's instructions he asked to see a Fraulein Foehr.

The receptionist used the telephone, and then without touching anything with her hands, caused a section of the paneling behind her to slide noiselessly aside. Gainer thought she probably did it with her knee beneath the desk—an interesting touch, ominous and slick. The opening in the paneling revealed an elevator for four, or a close-packed six. With a minimal gesture of her hand the receptionist gave Gainer permission to enter it. He asked what floor he should go to but she did not reply.

The elevator enclosed him. There were no buttons to push, no way for a passenger to control it. Gainer set himself for an upward ride, but only his stomach went up a little when he was taken abruptly down. He waited for the side he was facing to slide away; instead the one behind him opened.

Standing there, anticipating him, was a short, older woman, no more than five feet tall in her solidly heeled shoes. Her white hair was parted in the middle and done up into two buns in back. Her eyes glistened as though she had just been laughing. She said hello with Gainer's full name, seemed please to say it.

Gainer had thought he would be carrying to someone severe and compulsively efficient, not this gnome of a person whose open smile displayed false teeth that were believable except around the gum line. Fraulein Foehr could have been a salesperson in a candy store or a vendor of balloons in some happy park.

She walked just slightly ahead of Gainer down a corridor that had floor-to-ceiling photographic murals along both sides; summer Alps on the left, winter Alps on the right. She inquired about Gainer's flight, his crossing, as she called it, had it been effortless? She also asked if he'd had breakfast, her tone implying she could provide it.

Gainer looked down at her, saw the whiter flesh of her scalp where her hair was parted as he went along with her into a room dominated by an Empire *table de bureau* inset with dark green tooled leather, waxed and buffed hard. On the desk was a white porcelain Yougzheng bowl containing an abundant bouquet of edelweiss.

This was like no bank he'd ever experienced, Gainer thought. Far cry from the sort with waffle iron, AM-FM clock radio, color television set inducements. Not a teller in sight nor an inch of formica and certainly no waiting lines for deposits or withdrawals.

Gainer wondered if Norma had ever been here, perhaps in this very room. He wouldn't have asked if it hadn't been for Fraulein Foehr's seemingly friendly attitude. "Did you happen to know my sister, Norma Gainer?"

"Yes, quite well," Fraulein Foehr said, but nothing more. She indicated that Gainer should place the carry on the desk and as soon as he did she stepped between him and it. She unbuckled and unzipped the suitcase as though she knew it, flipped the top back, exposing the money. The neatly nestled sheaves, tightly wide-banded. Each sheaf containing twenty-five thousand. It was more money than Gainer had ever come face to face with. Benjamin Franklins, he thought, caught more by the gray etched portrait in the repetitive ovals than the numbers in the corners.

Fraulein Foehr went to the paneled wall to her left, folded part of it open. There on a shelf was a scale. She proceeded to weigh the packets of money, was all business now. Her eyes seemed to have gone somewhat dry and her mouth did not appear even capable of a smile.

The scale was an electronic one. Its digital indicator showed to five figures beyond the decimal. Each packet weighed within a few hundred thousandths of 8.125 ounces, Gainer noted. He also noted that instead of one hundred and twenty packets, which would have amounted to the three million he'd been told was the total of the carry, there were one hundred and twenty-four. An extra one hundred thousand. Not an oversight, Gainer thought. Darrow had put it in as a teaser, a tester. Gainer was glad now that he hadn't even considered opening the carry.

Fraulein Foehr transferred the packets into money bags, the sturdy natural canvas type usually used by banks. Thirty packets to a bag. She tossed the bags to the floor as she processed them, forming a disorderly pile. Left them there.

What, Gainer wondered, would happen now to his carry . . . in fact, to all the dirty millions brought over by the people who traveled for Number 19? He had no idea how much it amounted to, but was sure this nice clean bank and others like it in nice clean Switzerland would see that it was washed—loaded a certain way into the big rotating sidewinding money machine that converted it into legitimately earned riches. He had no way of knowing, of course, how systematically it was done. Some of the carried money remained in Europe, where it was soaked up by the financial ends of certain multinational corporations, included in their annual reports as good clean taxable profit. Other huge amounts of the carried money found their way back to the United States in the form of loans. Loans from a High Board controlled Swiss bank to a High Board controlled bank in the United States. Loans that were often written off or only figuratively repaid. It was easy juggling.

"Did you bring along a raincoat and some extra clothes?" Fraulein Foehr asked, becoming once again the amiable stranger.

"No, why?"

"For this bag," she said, zipping and buckling it. "Buy a few things and not all of them new."

Gainer thanked her for the suggestion, took up the empty bag, sixty-some pounds lighter now. She showed him to the elevator, said good-bye.

A minute later Gainer was out on the street. He motioned to the limousine driver that he should stay behind the wheel, he'd get his own door. He tossed the empty bag in ahead of him and was about to duck in when over the roof of the Daimler and the passing traffic he caught a glimpse of something he'd seen before.

It was the white of a tissue that attracted him as it was brought to the nose of the man in the car across the way.

That old man.

Same slight build, brittle-looking old man with sniffles that Gainer had noticed at the bistro counter at De Gaulle Aéroport. Gainer was sure of it.

Gainer stood there, deliberately stared at him.

The old fellow made the most of it. He did not try to slouch down, realizing he had already been spotted. Instead he got out of the car, looked up at the building there as though his destination was above, adjusted his hat and went in.

Gainer, under way in the Daimler, realized now when Darrow had said "watched over" he really, of course, meant *watched*. They were making damn sure he went where he was supposed to with the three million. And now, would they be through with him? He doubted it. Well, he wasn't through with them either. Not yet, Norma.

The carry had been easy. How much had Norma made per carry? Forty-some thousand? It was now easier for him to see why, how she had gotten hooked.

Alma.

He should see Alma while he was in Zurich. He had things to say to her. There was time. Hine had told him to stay at least a week.

At the Dolder Grand.

The room they had for him was an upper floor front room.

Room Number 450.

Norma's regular room, the same that she was killed in.

It could not possibly have been a coincidence, Gainer knew. A sadistic touch. A warning? It did shake him some at first, but he did not say anything, just followed the bellboy up and took it.

There was the bed.

There was the shower.

If they expected room 450 to rattle him, it had the opposite effect. He drew new resolve from showering in that shower, from lying on that bed.

He looked at his watch that was still set New York time—five-forty-five A.M. He should try calling Leslie again. He was tired, hadn't slept more than an hour of the last fifty-two. He'd just close his eyes for a few minutes.

When he woke up he thought it was getting dark. But when he looked out the window, he realized it was getting light. He had slept through from day to day. He felt torpid, heavy-lidded, not refreshed as he should have. He ordered from room service, and after splashing handfuls of cold water onto his face, drying roughly and drinking two cups of hot, black coffee, he started to come around.

Phoned Leslie. Her place, his place. No answer, which at that hour U.S. time meant she was probably at Number 19. Stupid of her. She had no idea what an animal hole it was. Or perhaps she did, which would be worse. She and her penchant for being on the fine line between here and the other side, as she called it. She seemed to want to stretch fortune to just this side of snapping point, as though in that there was some sort of proof for her, a verification of some special karmic prearrangement that she believed in and that nothing harmful could possibly contradict. At the moment, Gainer hoped there was indeed a Lady Caroline looking out for her.

He knew he couldn't take being out of touch for a week, so why should he endure another day? He'd tell Hine he misunderstood, lie to Darrow. He repacked the smaller suitcase and solved the larger empty one by putting the smaller one into it.

Called Swiss Air.

First available space to New York was on the two o'clock. He reserved it. Took one last look at the shower stall and the bed and went down to the lobby. While settling his bill, he asked at the desk for Alma Schebler and was told she was on vacation.

All the better, Gainer thought. He remembered Alma's home address from having seen it so many times on her letters. Rather than lug his bag along he would leave it there at the hotel with the porter, who maintained a special room for such purposes off the far end of the lobby. The room was kept locked but the porter knew which was the key for it among all those on his large ring. It wasn't an ordinary check room. A number of people who were frequent guests at the hotel were above being bothered with bringing or taking away luggage, so they merely left a full set of their belongings permanently packed in the care of the porter who kept them in that room. Gainer tried to imagine what it would be like to have appropriate wardrobes and essentials always ready and waiting at the Ritz, the Berkley, the Carlton and so on.

A very Rodger arrangement, Gainer thought.

The porter scribbled a receipt. Gainer overtipped him.

Alma's home address was in Zollikerberg, a section southeast of the city proper and not far from the hotel. Zollikerberg was like a small town unto itself, and where Alma lived was a modest private house set comfortably between a Lutheran church and a bicycle shop. Two of the upper windows were partly open, suggesting that Alma or someone was there. Gainer knocked and waited, knocked and waited, and then went to the bicycle shop to inquire. A man there told him that Alma and her son were away, staying somewhere down the lake, not expected back for a week at least.

Gainer was disappointed. Realized how much he'd wanted, needed to share time with someone who apparently had also loved Norma. He left a brief note in Alma's mailbox.

From there he went to Zurich proper, sat for a beer at a table under a tree beside the River Limmat. Sipped two of the hours away. From where he sat, he counted the faces of nine huge high clocks keeping up with one another.

A pale, large-eyed young man drinking Chartreuse several tables away misinterpreted the reason Gainer was seated so long there alone. That didn't bother Gainer but it was just enough to get him up and walking.

He strolled the Bahnhofstrasse, looked at windows from store to store, went into one and bought an expensive raincoat for himself and another like it for Leslie. Just to use up his expense money, more than anything.

At twelve-thirty he returned to the hotel.

The same porter was on duty. He recognized Gainer from the overtip and at once hurried off for Gainer's bag.

Gainer overtipped him again. With *their* money, which also allowed him another limousine to the Flughafen Floten.

CHAPTER
SIXTEEN

I T was still that same afternoon when Gainer's homeward flight touched down at Kennedy International. Despite all the odd hours of no sleep, sleep and flying, the circadian clock in Gainer's head was hardly confused. In fact, New York time seemed to click it right back into sync. What little lag Gainer did feel was countered by his anticipation of being again with Leslie and his concern with what he would say to Darrow. He wanted to keep this thing going. He had to if he was ever going to make them pay.

He went directly in a Hertz rental to Number 19.

Stopped at the gate, he causally told the man on duty he lived there and was surprised when that was politely accepted and he was given the go-ahead. The man probably had a mind like a Polaroid when it came to faces, Gainer thought as he steered up the drive.

Numerous cars were parked along the wider area at the front of the house. Leslie's Rolls Corniche among them. Gainer found a space for the rental, backed it in and deliberately caused a deep scar down both doors of a that year's Mercedes sedan.

It helped untighten him some.

He was let in the front way by one of those white-coated former CIA or whatever servants.

"Nearly everyone is down by the pool, sir," the man said.

"Which room is mine?"

The man told him and Gainer went up to it.

It was the sort of bedroom one would assign to a lesser guest. Pleasantly furnished in W&J Sloane versions of Queen Anne but nowhere to stretch out except on the bed, which, Gainer particularly noticed, was a single. An old Sony seventeen inch *black and white* sat on the dresser top and most of the magazines on the lower shelf of the nightstand were middle-aged *National Geographics.* Just one additional piece of furniture, even a side chair, and the room would have been crowded.

Sounds of people down at the pool came through the open windows. One fragment of gaiety sounded like Leslie.

Gainer resisted looking out.

Instead he opened the closet, saw a few things of his, hung too close together, needlessly crushed when there was a whole vacant rod.

The door on the next wall was the connector.

Gainer tried it, went into Leslie's room, recognized one of her skimpy dressing robes tossed over the back of a chair. Her room was more than twice the size of his and done with far more care and taste. Authentic Chippendale and an intricate, needlepoint rug that someone must have spent years on. The bed was king size, its linen fresh and neatly folded. In the spacious bathroom on the marble counter surface was her make-up with its special implements. They were sort of strewn carelessly, as though she'd been hurried; the pink column of lipstick left swiveled up. Gainer disliked the thought of her hurrying for anyone but him, especially not with such things as these. He swiveled the lipstick, capped it, tossed two pink-smeared tissues into the toilet and flushed them down.

Also noticed, in a shallow dish partially covered by a soiled linen and towel, her six carat D color flawless round cut, again carelessly left around. With the diamond were a couple of gold chains and another ring with a large single blue stone. Gainer had never seen that ring before. He examined it, saw the Tiffany mark struck on the inner side of its platinum band. He guessed it to be a sapphire of about twenty carats and he recalled who recently had been the big sapphire expert.

Sounds of amusement from outside got to him again.

He went back to Leslie's bedroom, to the window, looked out from that upper floor south. In the intermediate distance on the tennis court Hine and Sweet were bullying two older men at doubles. Beyond the court at the swimming pool a considerable amount of flesh was maintaining its sun tan. Gainer counted ten slathered bodies stretched out on loungers.

And then, there was the lovely incongruity.

Leslie's pale skin.

She had on a black maillot, simple and snug like a competitive swimmer's, and a wide-visored topless cap.

Gainer tried to will her to look up and notice him.

But at that moment she was preoccupied, kneeling beside a huge yellow towel that had someone on it.

Darrow.

He was lying face up, still as though dead.

Leslie bowed her head, clasped her hands beneath her chin, prayer-like.

She's going to try to cleanse his aura, Gainer thought, despising the idea. He felt like yelling out to her that it couldn't be done. Then he realized that cleansing wasn't what she was about.

She placed her forefinger on a spot about three inches center above Darrow's navel, held it there for a long moment, moved it up to the center of his chest, up to the start of his throat, to between his chin and lower lip, to between his upper lip and nose, to the center of his forehead and finally to the top of his head. Without pause she then ran her finger as though it were a blade and she was slicing him in two from his belly spot straight upward to his top spot. Ended with her hands cupped and placed parenthetically to the left and right of his head.

Darrow didn't budge. Eyes closed, he seemed to be soaking it up.

An involuntary sort of snarl from Gainer. He kept on trying to transmit his will, but after another minute of concentration so intense it made the back of his neck cramp, he quit it.

At the very instant he gave up, Leslie raised her head and aimed her point-of-view right at him. Despite her visor, she had to squint. She stood and stepped back into the shade of the cabana. What she saw through the diffusion of the window screen up there in the lesser light of her room could be nothing more than an astral projection, the spiritual replica of Gainer come to visit, was her thought. But then, did spirits usually wave like that?

In her hurry, she tripped over Darrow's legs and didn't even beg pardon, managed to contain herself to a fast walk until she was across the lawn. Ran up the steps and inside.

Gainer intended to nonchalant it, to be sitting slouched in a chair when she came in, but with the first sounds of her coming down the hall, he was up and moving to meet her.

They held, pressed so tightly it seemed they overlapped. Their mouths slicked together, being fed and feeding.

Gainer breathed her hair.

She breathed his neck.

The fabric of her maillot slipped against him. They were being pushed to the bed but decided it would be better saved and put half the room between them.

"You worried me," she said.

"Did Darrow let you know where I was?"

"Just said you were off somewhere doing a favor for him. I tried to pump him but that was all I could get. He didn't want to talk about you."

"What did he want?"

"Where the hell were you, anyway?"

Gainer told her, everything from the Concorde ride to Fraulein Foehr.

"For all I knew you were getting killed or something without me."

"I tried calling."

"I was just here."

"Where you shouldn't be."

"It was as near as I could get to whatever was happening to you."

Best of all possible explanations, Gainer thought. He went to the window, glanced down to the pool, saw a woman get up from a lounge and do a neat little dive. She climbed out almost as quickly to resume her sunning. "Who are the people?" Gainer asked.

"Darrow's wife showed up unexpectedly. I don't think he's very pleased about it. Her name's Barbara. From what I gather she's just touching home plate and while she's at it, taking a bit extra from it. She brought an entourage with her—a woman her age, apparently her long-time conspirator, and a young Spaniard who is doing his impression of a count or something. Please come over here." Leslie was on the fat arm of a summer-covered sofa, her legs straight out, parted and flexed.

"I love you," Gainer said without looking at her.

"I need another kiss."

"That piece of business I noticed you doing to Darrow down by the pool . . ."

"That?"

"That."

"I was raising his organs."

"Sure you were."

"He complained about his gall bladder and you know how I hate to see anyone suffer." She went over to the mirror above the dresser, examined her face briefly. "The insides of people get out of place," she explained, "from gravity and stress and a lot of things. So they have to be put back where they should be with white light. A healer taught me how."

"When?"

"Ages ago."

"You never did that to me."

"There are lots of things I've never done to you . . ."

"You expect me to—"

". . . but I intend to."

He went to her with a kiss. After it, he told her, "You worried me." And she told him, her eyes looking directly into his, "I've been good. I haven't even had the monies much. You know, I'm almost convinced I could live within your means."

Sapphires came to Gainer's mind. "Did you bring me a pair of swimming trunks?" he asked.

"Of course."

"I've already taken too much sun," she said, testing her shoulder skin with a finger.

"I want the edge of talking to Darrow while he's almost bareass."

Leslie got out of her swimsuit while Gainer put his trunks on. She was in the bathroom humming a fragment from a Karen Akers song:

> ". . . I've lost my taste for
> tears so many shoulders ago . . ."

was adding apple cider vinegar to the water in the tub, when Gainer left the room.

He went down and out. As he passed the tennis court, Hine was so taken aback at the sight of him that a serve that was hardly more than a lob went by him for an ace. Gainer acknowledged Hine with the flick of an upward first finger.

Darrow did not know until he opened one eye that it was Gainer who pulled a mat over and lay beside him.

"What are you doing back?" Darrow asked, calm but annoyed.

"Took the first flight I could get."

"Didn't Hine give you instructions?"

"Yeah."

"You were supposed to stay over there—no less than a week."

"He didn't mention that."

Typical of Hine, Darrow thought, the miserable son of a bitch. Purposely forgot. "Want a drink?" Darrow asked.

"I'll have a Savannah Sneak."

Darrow's gesture had a servant scurrying to them. "Bring Mr. Gainer a vodka and tonic."

"Stolichnaya," Gainer said.

Darrow settled again, eyes shut. He had some of that same sun-blocking white stuff on his nose. Big Chief Bird-Shit-on-the-Beak, Gainer thought. "Anyway," Darrow asked, "how did it go?"

"What?" Just to taunt, make *him* nervous for a change.

"The carry."

"No sweat."

"It got there?"

"Three plus one."

"It was supposed to be three even."

"I should have stashed the one."

"Seems someone can't count."

Bullshit, Gainer almost said. His drink was brought.

"Where did they put you up?"

"At the Dolder."

"First class, I presume."

"A nice room. Couldn't have been better."

Darrow's eyelids twitched twice. Gainer enjoyed the old liver spots on the back of Darrow's hands.

"How would you like to be put on as a regular?" Darrow asked.

"For a percentage?"

"And a draw, the same arrangement as Norma."

"Why?"

"It's the least we could do in return for her loyalty."

"I'll give it some thought."

"So will we." Darrow said with a double edge. He felt a flutter in his solar plexus. He liked dominating this unpleasant, brash young peasant. Couldn't remember when he'd gotten so much satisfaction from having his knee on someone's neck. And that would be the position for as long as he, Darrow, wanted it. He felt virtually smiled upon, the way things were turning out. How ironic that he should benefit from Hunsicker's man having missed. Not that he intended to let Hunsicker know that. Oh no, he'd put Hunsicker on the spit for it, for all the recent foul-ups, in fact. Only thing not so right, Darrow thought, was he could have made good use of more time with Mrs. Pickering. But even as it was, he believed he'd made quite a few points. "You're in my sun," he told Gainer.

Gainer pretended he hadn't heard.

Darrow repeated the same words in the same tone.

Gainer got up and walked around to a lounger on the other side of the pool. He removed the wedge of fresh lime from his drink with his tongue, sucked on it while he gulped. Evidently whoever had made the drink was a better strong-arm than bartender. It hadn't been stirred,

253

was topped by straight vodka that went down into Gainer like a molten wire. He just did manage not to make a face.

Off to his right, a dark-haired underfed young man stood halfway out on the diving board. Hands on hipbones, bars of his ribcage showing. The Spanish pretender, Gainer assumed. The young man was posed as though accommodating a photographer before at least a two and a half somersault with a twist. Maybe he was thinking what a long ways this was from a shoe factory in Barcelona.

Gainer blinked, imagined his eyes going *click*.

The young man sprang off the board and into the water feet first, unheroically holding his nose.

So much for him.

To Gainer's left, only one vacant lounger away, was a woman in a white two-piece sunsuit. Lying flat, face down. Her body appeared long, feet extended beyond the end of the lounger; no doubt she would be tall when upright. She turned her head and opened her eyes on Gainer. Wet her lips before asking: "Who are you?"

"I'm a Vanderbilt." For the hell of it.

"I thought so."

"Only a few of us left, you know."

"Pity, really."

"We don't issue too well."

"What do people call you, Vandy?"

"Archie." Silly enough name.

"You were probably named after the real Cary Grant. His first name was Archie, you know. I'm a Buckley myself," she said, rolling over and adjusting the back of the lounger to a sitting position. "You can call me Millicent, if you like."

"I don't usually like much," he said, laying on the world weary.

"Neither do I. I must have disliked practically everything at one time or another."

Gainer almost was enjoying the way she was going along with it. He noticed that any grays in her hair had been auburned. Indisputably a time fighter, he decided, one of those hoping for the title in her division. Sixty trying for forty, was his guess. Her face had been lifted and possibly relifted. Chin and neckline too tight not to have been tucked. Whoever had knifed had knifed her well, but no doubt there were scars left and right concealed by her hairline and those above and below her eyes were too fine to be discernible.

"What do you do, Archie?"

"I'm a handicapper." A shot of truth

"You cause people to become handicapped?"

"In a way. I tell them how to bet."

"Horses?"

"Mainly football."

"I only know horses." Her expression changed, especially her eyes, as though something forgotten took precedence over this banter. After a moment she came back to it. "You played football in school?"

"I would have been broke otherwise."

She laughed, and it wasn't good for her face. "What school?"

"Princeton. Cum laude."

"You majored in law, I suppose."

"Needlepoint."

She laughed.

"Tattoos," he said, remembering.

All the while, he'd been reducing his vodka and tonic, thinking with each gulp he'd reach the tonic level, but it was vodka straight to the bottom and already getting to him. He felt the base of his spine slacken. "Would you care for a drink?"

"A spritzer," Millicent said.

Gainer held his empty glass high and rattled it to get a white-jacketed man's attention. He also got the eyes of an aging blond in a minimal blue swimsuit who came coasting over in four inch espadrilles.

The blond mmm'd down and up scale in appreciation of Gainer, stood unnecessarily close. It was something she could have gotten away with, but probably wouldn't have resorted to, thirty years earlier, leading with her crotch like that. It was nearly level with Gainer's view.

"His name is Archie," Millicent told her. "Archie, this is Barbara Darrow."

Mrs. Darrow backed off a ways, either to accommodate her eyesight or the better to take in all of him.

Gainer saw that Darrow's wife was much overtanned, her skin blotched dry from too many seasons of Antibes and Deauville, Gstaad and Chamonix. She was sitting on sixty or more, another time fighter. However, she wasn't much of a contender, had only a few minor bouts left in her. The underflesh of her upper arms was hopelessly crepey.

Up to then, although Mrs. Darrow hadn't said a word, she'd said too much. She was either half-drunk or thoroughly bitter.

"Off with you," Millicent told her.

Mrs. Darrow smirked.

Gainer thought any second he'd go talk to the Spaniard.

"Not this time, Barbara. I'm warning you," Millicent said, almost letting her smile drop.

Mrs. Darrow sighed and made an unpleasant little pout that accentuated the vertical age lines above her upper lip. "You happen to know what a coward I am out of bed," she said, and walked away.

"She's actually quite good-hearted," Millicent said.

"Needs her organs raised," Gainer mumbled, considering Mrs. Darrow's pouched out belly.

"What was that?"

"Nothing."

Drinks came.

"Where were we?"

"Tattoos."

"I don't see any."

"I've got them," Gainer said.

Millicent's eyes said she understood. She looked as though she'd just smelled a pleasing fragrance.

Gainer noticed a gold link bracelet she was wearing, not quite large enough to fall off. It had the initial M inset with diamonds. She also had pampered feet, probably had hours spent every day on her feet. All toes straight, not even the sign of a callous on her little ones.

She reached over and clinked his glass. "Are you staying here?"

"Yeah."

"Which room is yours?"

Gainer stood, adjusted his trunks, glanced up at Leslie's windows.

Millicent reached with her foot, touched his calf. "Later on," she said, "as late as you wish, come find me and we'll make some old times out of some new times."

Gainer dove in.

AT five-thirty next morning Gainer came awake, suddenly, totally awake and sat up in bed as though something had yanked him.

The snuggling, bed-hogging Leslie was so used to him being up and around at all hours that she merely asked was anything wrong and went back to sleep before he could answer.

On the front of Gainer's mind, using, it seemed, the inside of his forehead for an illuminated billboard, was the so-called Millicent Buckley. At some time during his sleep she had assumed that foremost position and was still there. It occurred to Gainer, of course, that he might still be asleep and just dreaming that he was awake, but there on the bedside table was the green glow of the face and hands of Leslie's tiny Schlumberger travel clock, and when as a test he tugged sharply enough to hurt at a tuft of his hair, it really did hurt.

Millicent Buckley.

256

She kept on doing reruns of herself from the previous afternoon, her words and facial expressions, and Gainer also began to recall things about her that he hadn't realized he'd noticed. Her eyes, for instance, the color of them. Green with black circumferences. The handsome more than pretty mouth, resolute. Her hairline, shape of face and especially her voice. There was, in her voice, a quality, way back in under the broad A's and layers of other influences, that seemed as familiar as Norma's voice had been to him. Then, there had also been:

Millicent's inquisitiveness regarding him, an element of genuine interest to it now that he thought about it.

The oblique quickness of her humor, sort of her version of his own.

The possessive way she'd taken it on herself to protect him from the consuming cunt of Mrs. Darrow.

The gold link bracelet with the diamond M on it. Heavy enough to have been a man's bracelet cut down. The M for the long-ago Manny, whom Gainer had heard about. Could be.

Good God.

She was the right age and everything.

Gainer got out of bed, put on jeans, sweatshirt and canvas shoes. Did not need to splash cold water on his face. Hastily combed his hair with his fingers and went out. Drove recklessly to the city, to his apartment.

To the Cartier framed photograph.

Sat on the sofa with it in hand under a two hundred and fifty watt bulb. He mentally overlaid the face he remembered as Millicent's on the younger face in the photograph. Yesterday's face had not been very definable in the bright sun just as this one was washed out by retouching. It seemed the noses were close to a match, and the mouths too. The shape of the eyes were different but that could have been due to plastic surgery.

There was similarity enough, Gainer believed.

It was her, come back.

It was.

(Or was it that he wanted it to be?)

Anyway, she was with the Darrows, of all people. A hanger-on, so it appeared. Going along with what Mrs. Darrow did in order to be allowed to go along with her. How had she gotten in with that element? Wouldn't it be ironic if she'd once been a carrier, same as Norma?

Gainer believed he knew the exact moment yesterday afternoon when she'd recognized him. Had seen it register and go through her. Maternal instinct. She'd been short on that long ago, why long on it now? He hoped to hell she didn't son him and mother love him all over the place. That would be embarrassing. He wouldn't be able to recipro-

257

cate. She was just a woman he'd come out of, or so he told himself.

Chances were, she wouldn't let on. Women like her, no matter how they felt, avoided having their past spread out for one and all to poke around in as though it was a yard sale.

But if it happened that she did lose control, he knew how he'd handle it.

Just as she deserved.

At her expense.

He'd deny her, say she was nuts, gone off the end of her wishful thinking. Hell, he'd been born on the high sea somewhere between Cyprus and Madeira—and by Caesarean section at that. (Show your scar!) His parents were not divorced, but as separated as possible. Father a retired automobile dealer now doing quality bookbinding up in Nova Scotia. Mother a pediatrician in Moratuwa, Sri Lanka. She had contracted any number of tropical bugs over the last ten years but was still going strong.

And so on.

That's what he'd do.

He got a couple of the mother postcards from Norma's carton, took them and the framed photograph with him back to Number 19.

Just in case they were needed, he told himself.

Drove slower than the limit.

When he got there he saw that most of the high-priced cars were gone.

He went in, was headed up the stairs to Leslie when a hint of the odor of fried bacon turned him. He tracked it to the dining room.

Darrow was alone at the huge table.

"You were out early," Darrow commented.

"Business," Gainer said, remained standing, waiting to be invited.

"Sit," Darrow told him.

Gainer was tempted to bark. He took the chair to Darrow's right, told the servant no eggs, just bacon, toast and coffee.

"Mrs. Pickering prefers breakfast in bed," Darrow said, as though that was an inside observation.

"Dinner too most of the time," Gainer put in, and heard Darrow's knife cut hard across the Rosenthal plate.

"I understand you're a tout," Darrow said.

Gainer just took it with a nod.

"I wager now and then on football, mainly for the challenge of it, only four or five thousand a game," Darrow said.

It was hard for Gainer to imagine Darrow betting on anything other than a fix. Maybe, he thought, he should follow Darrow's action.

"Who do you like this season?" Darrow asked.

"I don't have an opinion yet."

"Only two weeks until the regular season opens."

"Time enough."

"Perhaps I should have you as my personal handicapper, Andrew. Does that appeal to you?"

No, Gainer thought, he wouldn't enjoy handicapping for anyone connected with Norma's killer. "I had close to a wipe-out last season, only three out of sixteen, one pick in the playoffs and I blew the Super Bowl."

"You're worse than Hine," Darrow said.

"How did he do?"

"I mean you insist on lying even when someone's looking down your throat."

Think, but don't say, Gainer advised himself.

"I played varsity football at Yale," Darrow said, "I was an end."

"You're built like an end."

Darrow accepted the compliment before it occurred to him that it might not have been one.

"Where's Mrs. Darrow this morning?" Gainer asked.

"Gone. She and all her chums."

"For the day?"

"To Beverly Hills. At least I believed she mentioned Beverly Hills. From there, who knows."

Gainer was both disappointed and relieved. "I met Mrs. Darrow just briefly yesterday," he said. "Also one of her friends. I don't remember her name. Good-looking, dark-haired woman . . ."

"Had on a white bathing suit?"

"That's her."

"Millicent Buckley."

"Is that really her name?"

"Why do you ask?"

"She reminded me of someone."

"Barbara and Millicent go way back."

"To where?"

"They won't say what year anymore, but they went to Smith together."

The nearest his mother had gotten to Smith was a cough drop, Gainer thought. "Are you sure?" he asked.

"Of course, I used to play squash with her brother."

Gainer overchewed a bit of toast and then gave up on breakfast, placed his knife and fork precisely across the edge of his plate, folded

259

his napkin just so and sat there stuck to his own foolishness. He'd never let anyone know, not even Leslie, especially Leslie, how he'd over-reacted to a mere resemblance. To get off it he told Darrow: "Cincinnati."

"You like the Bengals?"

"They should have a good year."

"Let me know whenever you think they'll win big or manage an upset. Will you do that?"

"Yeah."

"I enjoy an upset."

FOR the second time that morning Gainer got only a few steps up the main stairs on his way to Leslie. This time the bulk that was F. Hugh Sweet intentionally blocked him, looked down on him and said: "Hine wants to see you." Sweet took Gainer by the elbow, and although it appeared that was merely to guide him, it was such a grip it caused Gainer's hand to go numb.

Down the steps.

Out to Hine's car.

A two and a quarter hour drive, without conversation or radio, to Southampton, Long Island.

Hine's beach house was about two miles from the town proper, on the ocean side of Dune Road. It was on two point three acres bound precisely by a high white concrete wall. The house was constructed of the same white material, resembling, on its inland side, a coastal defense installation with ultra-contemporary blocky lines, no windows or other vulnerables. The interior was stark and soft. Hard, white surfaces contradicted by masses of colorful plush, as though saying, as long as you're here you might as well be comfortable.

The entire ocean front of the house was of glass, at least half of which could be opened, and was open now.

"Take off your clothes," Sweet said.

Gainer wanted to know why.

"Or I'll take them off for you," Sweet told him.

Gainer removed his shoes, sweatshirt and jeans. Sweet also stripped. His chest was twice as thick as Gainer's, had abundant hair on it and there was nearly as much on his shoulders and back. A powerful, straight up and down chunk with columns of muscle left and right of his spine down to his buttocks.

"Everything off," he said.

Gainer undid his wristwatch. Sweet took it, looked at it, placed it on

260

a low table on top of a deluxe edition of *Sappho,* by photographer J. Fred Smith.

Sweet steered Gainer outside. A deck area of natural bleached cedar ran across the front of the house, and a wide walkway of it ran down to the shoulder of the beach. The wood was hot and uncomfortably dry under Gainer's feet, felt as though it would cause splinters. After a short ways Sweet took him off the deck and onto the sand, up over the edge of a particular dune that was depressed, like a wide bowl decorated with tufts of beach grass.

In it, on the far side of it, lay Hine. He was nude, perspiring as though he'd just been doused.

"How are you today?" he asked amiably.

"The same," Gainer told him.

"Glad you made it out."

"Yeah."

Hine's gesture invited Gainer to share the dune with him.

Gainer took two steps down into it and squatted.

"Relax," Hine told him.

"This is good for the legs," Gainer said. He wondered why the change in Hine.

"Nice day," Hine said, "but it's going to cloud over. By four it'll be pouring. What time is it?" he asked Sweet, who sat with his ass burrowed into the lip of the dune and his legs extended down the inside of it.

"His watch said quarter to two. Nice watch."

Gainer thought that had the sound of Sweet putting his word in for the watch, come the time when they divied him up. Or tried to.

". . . Can I get anything?" Sweet asked.

"Don't interrupt," Hine snapped at him.

Sweet just took it, stuck his forefinger into his ear and rotated it to clean or scratch, scuffed at the sand with his heel. Sweet had been with Hine as far back as Hotchkiss, the prestigious preparatory school up in Lakeville, Connecticut, where Sweet was expelled in the third year for having killed a cow. He'd chosen that cow because it was the one with an udder most swollen with milk. Had sighted at that pinkish, somewhat transparent part and pulled both triggers of a ten-gauge shotgun. He claimed he was shooting at a rabbit. Hine corroborated that. Sweet's parents were indignant, came got him, placed him in another prep school on the circuit, one that was not so strict about pranks.

"This doesn't bother you, does it, being bareass?" Hine asked Gainer.

"Not me. I'm a natural-born flasher."

"You can understand why this is how it has to be."

"Sure." Gainer had at first thought it was to make sure he had no weapons, but now with all of them bare, he decided it was to eliminate the possibility of there being any concealed recording devices.

"If anything said this afternoon goes into anyone else's ear, I'll just deny it," Hine said.

"Whose ear for instance?"

"Let's say Darrow, for instance."

Gainer nodded. Play it street, he reminded himself. Whatever it is, string it out of him.

"You and I have something in common, we both dislike Darrow."

"I don't say I especially dislike him," Gainer said casually. "In fact as whiteshoes go, he's not so bad."

"You ought to hate him."

"Why?"

"That sharpshooter who almost blew you away last week was working on Darrow's order."

Gainer put together a dubious expression.

"I'm in close and I know. You see me there."

"Now that some time has passed, I'm seeing the incident more as Darrow does, that it was only a wild shot by some city crazy," Gainer baited.

"You were in France when two middlemen were killed."

"What's a middleman?"

"Ponsard, Becque."

"Mean nothing to me."

"Look, Gainer, I want to have this talk with you, and, believe me, it's in your best interest that we do, but if you—"

"Ponsard drowned."

A silent moment.

"It was also Darrow who initiated the order for Norma."

Gainer tried to stay unreadable.

Hine's eyes were on him, trying to see how he was taking it. "Want a drink?" Hine asked.

"No."

"Mind if I do?"

"The ice cube might be wired," Gainer said.

Hine had no sense of humor.

"You're cautious," he said. "Good. I need you to be cautious."

Hine arched his back, stretching. His ribs shed rivulets of perspiration. Beads of it hung shiny like decorations on his pubic hair. His cock lay doughy on his thigh.

"You don't seem to give a damn," he said.

"About what?"

"What Darrow did to Norma."

"I don't believe it. He liked her." Still baiting.

"As a matter of fact, he did in a way."

"So why would he want her killed?"

"She was skimming."

"That's more bullshit." Not baiting.

"She skimmed about twenty to thirty thousand from every carry she made over the last three years."

"She couldn't have."

"She did."

"No way."

"She found a way of sliding a hundred or two from a sheaf without disturbing the rest, she was very neat about it. She figured it was just a couple less pieces of paper to each sheaf. You met Fraulein Foehr?"

"Yeah."

"Her scales caught Norma."

"Why didn't they catch her the first time?"

"They did."

"And you let her go on with it?"

"Not me. Darrow. He kept using her, knowing at any time he could end it. Finally, he got fed up."

Gainer was stunned, felt as though he'd swallowed something so heavy it was impossible for him to move. It wasn't such a surprise to him that Darrow had, in some way, been behind Norma's death. What got him, dropped him, disappointed him, was the idea of Norma skimming, that she could have ever been that shifty. He pictured her going through it as Hine had described. Ever so carefully, slipping hundreds from each sheaf. Anyone might think of doing it but few actually would. Not his Norma, not her. He wouldn't believe it. Such scheming hadn't been in her. It was only Hine inventing, hoping to inflate his hate for Darrow for some reason, that was all there was to it.

No, that was *not* all there was to it.

Skimming fit, Gainer had to admit. Norma had been killed because she had skimmed. Well, so fucking *what?* The money was dirty, it was shit money, she'd stolen from the stealers, those who had put dishonesty in her hands in the first place. She hadn't deserved what she got. Maybe they thought so, but he still didn't, never would. The only thing Gainer blamed her for was underestimating Darrow and his people, which in itself only showed how naive, how innocent she actually was. Anyway, at least now he knew his man for sure. If what Hine

263

said was true the Mob was in it only to the extent that Darrow was Mob. But what gave Darrow the weight to instigate such hits? Something about that didn't lock. Keep leading Hine out, Gainer told himself.

Hine said: "You could kill Darrow, couldn't you? Especially now that you have access to him, just do it, point-blank?"

"Sure."

"Why don't you?"

"I'm not that stupid."

"But you are plenty pissed."

"That what you want, for me to kill Darrow for you?"

"You're dead anyway."

"Not yet."

"Darrow is just fucking with your head, keeping you around to sweat and kiss ass for a while. Not for long, though."

"He offered me a job." Baiting, drawing Hine out again.

"Carrying?"

"Yeah."

"You believe him?"

"No . . ."

"No matter, you're going to like my offer better."

"Not if it includes suicide. Why do you want Darrow dead?"

"I'm running up his back."

"Hire someone."

"I could, but it would be too obvious, risky. Besides, even if Darrow got hit by a car or someone this afternoon, chances are I might not be moved up into his spot. I'm in line to become Custodian, but they might put someone else in and I'd be no better off. Other measures are indicated."

Gainer wondered who "they" were. And what the "measures" were. "You've got a problem," he said.

"So have you."

"I'm working on mine."

"You'll work yourself to death," Hine told him.

Gainer's toes were sunk in and his squat had given way so that now the base of his spine took most of his weight. He brought himself up slowly, grateful that his legs were that strong. Standing, he saw over the lip of the dune, saw the drift fences awry and buried to various degrees across the beach. The wind had picked up, broken the ocean into uncountable repetitive scallops. Hine was right. There would be rain soon. Gainer saw a gull dive, dip into the calmer area between breakers, come up with a fish, only to have it beaked from him by another gull that swallowed it more quickly. Gainer sat down on the dune and after a moment went eyes to eyes with Hine, allowing Hine to read him.

Hine opened with: "The money our people carry, where do you think it's kept?"

"I don't know. Some bank, I suppose."

"What about right there at Number 19?"

Gainer thought of all those formidable servants. "Probably better than a bank, more convenient."

"How much would you say is there?"

Norma's carries had usually been three million, so maybe they kept ten around. That was his guess: "Ten million."

"Tell him how much Sweet."

"Today?"

"Today."

"Three billion, one hundred seventy-four million and change."

Gainer's mouth was open. "You're shitting me."

"It's there, I'll show it to you if I have to," Hine told him.

"Say that number again," Gainer said.

Sweet repeated it.

"That's the amount waiting to be washed," Hine said. "We call it The Balance. Last night you slept no more than a hundred feet from it."

"Where?"

"On that same upper floor but in the opposite wing."

Gainer recalled the windowless upper area he'd noticed a few days ago. Now he knew the reason for it. At various times over the years he'd heard there was a lot of dirty money, Mob money, stashed in a private house somewhere. But the rumors always had it in New Jersey. He'd never believed it. His mouth wasn't open now, however, he felt like snapping his head to get it to register. Three billion in that house?

The nearly paralytic way lower-class people were affected by huge sums always amused Hine. He had to suppress a grin. He waited for Gainer's mind to absorb the amount, then told him, "What I want you to do is steal it."

"Is that all?"

"The money is key. If anything happens to it, Darrow dies."

"He cries himself to death?"

"He dies as a matter of course."

"Who sees to that?"

"Don't ask," Hine advised him.

Gainer knew better than to want to know.

"You must understand, of course, I only want you steal the money temporarily," Hine said. "After Darrow is blamed and pays the price the money gets recovered."

"By you."

"Yes, and for that I am made Custodian and you're off the hook."

"The way I see it, I'm still on and wiggling."

"No."

"Why not?"

"The code is specific. When a Custodian dies or is replaced, his orders are automatically cancelled."

"Tell me about that."

Hine ran it down briefly for him. The procedure for orders, the unequivocal intolerance of mistakes, the extreme penalty. He used the case of Gridley as an example.

"Nice genteel folk, you whiteshoes," Gainer said.

Hine agreed with a shrug, not altogether without pride.

"So, I'd be stealing for my life."

"And to be a little richer. Let's say ten million."

"Cash."

"Cash."

"Ten million of the dirty—"

"Naturally."

"Make it twenty," Gainer said.

Hine was sure he had his man. "Tell you what, to show that my heart is in the right place, you can also keep the three million you got from Norma, with no further questions."

"What three million from Norma?"

"Her last carry, you know."

"I don't know."

"It never reached the bank. Darrow and everyone, including myself, have been convinced all along that you got it somehow."

"Is that why Darrow had me watched in Zurich?"

"Sharp boy."

"Just for that make my end thirty million," Gainer said.

"You're getting greedy."

"Thirty million is crumbs."

Hine, with a shrug, admitted that it was. "One thing more," he said. "You mustn't count on me. I'll pass on whatever helpful information I can whenever I can, but otherwise I won't have any part in it."

"Just me," Gainer said.

"Fuck up and I'll be facing the other way."

"Thanks."

"You'll be no worse off than you are now."

He had a point there, Gainer thought. "Tell me, Hine, if I take your proposition and Darrow's to die, how will he die? Can you guarantee some slow, excruciating, painful way?"

"I can't promise that."

"But he'll know he's dying?"

"From the moment the money is missing, he'll know that."

Gainer had to smile.

"Then we have a deal?" Hine asked.

"No."

"Why the hell not?"

"I want to give it some thought. I'll be back to you." Spoken like a true hot shit executive, he thought.

THAT night at a middling Szechuan restaurant on the Post Road, Gainer told Leslie all about his meeting with Hine. Going over with her the points of Hine's proposition helped make clearer his own thoughts on them.

Leslie set a new personal record for not interrupting. She took it rather like a wife whose husband had been offered a much better job. It was, she believed, a splendid opportunity. "Three billion dollars," she half-whispered, as though they were holy words. "I'll bet it would be the largest amount ever stolen."

"At least right up there."

"I think we could pull it off," she said.

Arguing with her now about the *we* would be wasted effort, Gainer realized, and told her: "We don't even have any idea what it involves yet."

"Doesn't matter, I *know* we could." She was so excited she gave up on her chopsticks, forked at the eggplant garlic dish she'd ordered triple hot. She'd already extended a sample of it across to Gainer and burned his taste buds so they didn't seem to trust anything else he offered them.

To divert and calm her, Gainer asked: "How did your day go?"

"I read, explored the garden and waited. You must have left very early. Your toothbrush was dry."

A cue for the Millicent foolishness. Gainer let it slip by. "You were bored, huh?"

"At least I didn't get the mopes or the monies," she said. "I usually do when I'm lonely and alone like that."

"But never when you're with me."

"Never," she fibbed. "You know, love, the Hine thing is an all-around answer if you want to see it like that."

267

"Yeah."

"We get to live and we get—"

"You get to live no matter what," he said.

"Don't be so sure of that."

"I have to be."

"You're my lifeline," she said.

"I thought Rodger was."

"He just gives transfusions."

"That you require."

"Less and less. But you, love, you're essential. Without you I'd be broke under any circumstances."

"Everything you say is true."

"I love you."

"Especially that."

She ate the eggplant as though it was as bland as a New England boiled vegetable dinner. Didn't even need to extinguish it with water. "You did say thirty million?" she asked.

"That would be my take-home pay."

"Nice, long figure, thirty million."

"Enough?"

"We could invest it," she said brightly.

"What in?"

"Us. We'll live on the interest and never touch the principal."

He loved that sweet play on words, so much that he allowed her to stroke another forkful of her hot stuff into his mouth.

"You know what's best about us?" she said.

"Yeah."

"Including that, naturally."

"What?"

"We get better," she said. "We keep getting better even when there doesn't seem to be any possibility for improvement."

"True."

"I want to admit something I've never admitted to any man—although, perhaps I've come close a couple of times. Anyway, when I'm not with you I'm terribly deficient, inside and out. I don't function well. My arms feel heavy, my head gets short-circuited and I'm awfully unfilled. I mean by that worse than ordinary empty."

"I think a lot about filling you."

"It's sexual. Oh God yes, it's sexual, but not only. My eyes need to be filled with you, and my ears and my lungs and hands. It's a dreadful admission, isn't it?"

"No, not at all."

"It imposes on you and reveals me. I'd keep it to myself if I could."

"What if I feel the same?"

"I believe I could handle it." She lowered her eyes, they clouded. "I was remembering something a man once said to me. I don't recall him particularly but what he said must have impressed me because it stuck. He was trying to seduce me in a cold roundabout way, wanting to use me like a whore and have me like a whore use him, hoping, you know, for that sort of mutual irresponsibility. Come to think of it, that approach was tried often in one form or another by several others. Have you ever come on like that with anyone?"

"No," Gainer fibbed.

"Anyway, this man said romantic love was never fair, not the equitable thing it was made out to be. Rather, it was like a surgical operation with one person making incisions while the other cried for anesthesia."

"Believe that?"

"It used to get proved to me a lot."

"Not this time. I need the hell out of you, Leslie."

"Dependency . . ."

"I honestly, straight out, lay it on the line need—"

". . . dependency takes courage."

"When I was on that carry for Darrow and out of touch, it wasn't just that I was concerned about you or that I missed you. For sure it wasn't ordinary missing. I felt that it was unfair that I should have to give any of my time to anyone other than you."

"How do you feel now?"

"Grateful."

He got up and went around to her, oblivious to the place, the other people there. He tilted her face up and brought his own down to kiss her. A long, light kiss. The Szechuan pepper on her lips made his own burn.

"Let's go find Hine and tell him he's on," she said.

"Too soon."

"What's soon have to do with it?"

"First we need some insurance."

JIMMY Chapin.

Gainer spent all the next morning and half the afternoon trying to locate him. Called the last number he had on him and even a back-up special number but got no answer. Went by Chapin's apartment on East Forty-ninth, buzzed for five minutes before giving that up.

There were other likely places.

The sublevel, swimming pool whorehouse on West Forty-second where Jimmy had a favorite working girl.

An early bar on Eighth Avenue. Six people there but only the bartender capable of rational speech.

"Jimmy Chapin been around?"

The usual reply to that would have been, "Who's Jimmy Chapin?" Gainer was known so he got a wary, "What's up?"

"Business, no beef," Gainer assured him.

"Haven't seen him in a week. Try his brother, Vinny, why don't you?"

"Where?"

"Down around Canal probably. Otherwise I don't know."

Gainer was sure his chances of running into Vinny on Canal Street were slim, but he went downtown and stood on one of the prime jewelry corners for an hour. Recognized several sleepless fences looping around, getting swag priced. But no Vinny.

By then it was noon. Gainer recalled that Jimmy often had lunch on Third Avenue, between Fifty-fourth and Fifty-fifth, a blue-fronted place called Elmer's. He went there, stood at the end of the bar with a draught Heineken. Down the way was Rocky Graziano, as good-natured as ever, knowing everyone. And, more restrained, Jake LaMotta. There were fight people and people who admired fight people. There were also racing people. No Phippses or Whitneys, but some takers and players and a few jockey-sized older guys who got information now and then.

Gainer helped himself to four toothpicked meatballs and three fried chicken wings from the free lunch hot trays. A waiter came with a fresh batch of meatballs. He was a waiter Gainer had overtipped at least three times in the past. A good one to ask.

"At the track, I think," the waiter said. "Last night when he was in I heard him mention something about going to the track."

Belmont racetrack was an hour's drive out, and a mention overheard by a waiter wasn't much to go on. Gainer almost decided to hang around places and let Chapin eventually come to him, if not today, tomorrow. He wished he had when he got into a traffic tie-up in the Midtown Tunnel behind a truck with a killer exhaust.

He arrived at Belmont and got parked just as the fifth race went off. Heard from outside the roar of the crowd, the loud urge of it abruptly changing into a sort of mumbling moan the moment the horses crossed the finish line and losers became the majority. Gainer bought his way into the clubhouse, let the escalator take him up to the unique atmosphere of tickets underfoot like worthless printed money, and greed and desperation almost deoxygenating the air.

He crossed over to the thick pipe railing that kept the common weekday player from the private boxes. The bright blue uniformed ushers stationed at entry points made sure.

Gainer scanned the boxes for Chapin. It was where he'd be if he was there. On his third scan Gainer caught on the back of a head that might be the man. A half-turn of that head revealed it was him. Six boxes down and off to the left, almost in line with the finish line.

Gainer borrowed a pen from a player to jot a note on the back of a discarded ticket. He put a ten dollar bill in an usher's hand and then the note, and moments later Chapin was standing, turning around, gesturing to him to come down to the box. The usher returned and stepped aside for him as though there had never been a doubt.

"Take any seat," Chapin told Gainer.

The box accommodated six on two tiers. It was the box of a well-known trainer kept for his new or faraway owners. Most weekdays it was unoccupied, as were many of the other boxes.

Chapin was with his brother, Vinny. They both had small, very expensive binoculars suspended from around their necks. From Vinny's sources, Gainer assumed.

"Got something going?" Chapin asked Gainer. He knew Gainer seldom, if ever, bet on a horse unless it was a special occasion, such as a ten-length lock.

"Something important," Gainer told him.

"What race?"

"Be a joke if it was the sixth," Vinny put in.

"It has nothing to do with a horse," Gainer said.

"Then keep it for later," Chapin said, a bit curt. "Right now I've got everything to do with a horse."

Chapin appeared relaxed enough unless one knew him as well as Gainer did. Gainer noticed the little giveaways. The tip on the cigarette Chapin was smoking was oval from extra lip pressure, and he didn't smoke it down short as usual, dropped it, overdid grinding it out. Normally he would have just made one stab at it with his heel. Also, his ears were florid.

Chapin was forty. He physically resembled the one-time, late mayor of New York, James Walker. Had that sort of small-boned build and Irish durability. He didn't look to be strong but it was said around that once at Jimmy Weston's he had, on a thousand dollar bet, lifted by its leg a chair containing a hundred and fifty pound hooker ten inches off the floor using only his left hand—and he was right-handed. Gainer hadn't seen it but he believed it. Actually, it was one of Chapin's lesser exploits. He enjoyed being talked about, doing the unexpected. "There are those who make news and those who merely read it," he'd said to Gainer one night when they were out running together.

Chapin was indeed a character.

By choice.

He'd earned a B.S.E.E. degree at Cal Tech and done graduate work at MIT. All the leading electronic firms had wanted him, recruited hard, and the two that he'd worked for had put him right in the middle of their most sophisticated projects. A lot of Chapin's subminiature circuitry creations had landed on the moon.

He could have stayed straight. He was offered everything this side of the chairman's virgin granddaughter to stay. But it was too narrow for him, too predictable. So he took his vacation with pay and never went back. On his own he found opportunities that were far more entertaining. When they weren't offered, he devised them.

Such as his scramble with the Federal First of Miami.

He opened an account under an assumed name at that bank, put in just two hundred dollars. Under another assumed name he got a job with an electronic servicing firm. Among its clients, he knew, was Federal First. For three months Chapin was a model employee, dependable, good at what he did and quiet. Before long, on a routine service call, he got his head and hands in the complicated electronic bowels of Federal First. He located the information chip that applied to his account, replaced it with another, identical except for one infinitesimal difference.

From that day on, each withdrawal Chapin made from his account registered as a deposit. In ten days he moved out two hundred thousand.

Federal First never knew who hit them.

It was doing such things as that that Chapin got the most kick out of. Devising ways of outsmarting the systems, especially the ones that were smug.

Ordinary electronic surveillance work was like child's play for Chapin. His reputation was that he could merely be in a room and sense whether or not it was bugged. The best wire man ever.

The Mob's wire man, it was said.

The Justice Department questioned him. Was it true he'd come up with a remote beaming device for listening in on a conversation? If so, it would make all bugs obsolete.

He told them he was working on it.

Then came their bottom line question. Would he come over, work for them?

He told them calmly, sincerely, just as if he had said, "Yes, I will," told them, "Go fuck yourselves."

Not long after that, Chapin did time.

Ten months of a three-year sentence in Danbury for an illegal wire tap.

No sooner had he gotten out on parole than he was picked up on another tap charge. However, this time he was innocent. Those involved were trying to give him up as part of their bargain. Their depositions hinged on one particular Wednesday night. It just so happened on that Wednesday night Chapin had been with Gainer. They had gone to the Garden to see the Knicks beat the spread but not, of course, the Celtics, and after the game up to Nanni's for fettuccine. Gainer enjoyed the evening. It was just after midnight when he dropped Chapin off at the East Seventy-fifth Street address where he had a sight-unseen prearrangement with a new young working girl.

As it turned out the girl was younger than just young and also had a couple of arrests for possessing controlled substances. A statement from her would only make matters worse for Chapin.

It was up to Gainer. Chapin's attorney took a walk with Gainer, told him what was needed. Gainer stretched his statement five hours. Swore that from Nanni's Restaurant he and Chapin had gone to his apartment, played backgammon until five or so. Yes, he'd been with Chapin for ten straight hours.

So Chapin owed Gainer at least three years of his life. A heavy debt but they both carried it lightly.

Now, there they were in a box at Belmont, watching the horses for the sixth race come out onto the track. Chapin handed his copy of the *Daily Racing Form* to Gainer. "What do you think of the number one horse?"

Gainer looked it over.

The number one horse's name was Snapshot. A four-year-old chestnut gelding with some Hail to Reason blood in him. According to his last twelve times out he was the sort of horse that some people thought ought to be good. Several of the better trainers had tried him. He could win at the thirty-five thousand claiming level but when stepped up into the allowance class Snapshot seemed to enjoy having the other horses in front of him. All the races his chart showed had been sprints of six and seven furlongs. Today he was in steep and long, going against better, pure allowance horses over a mile and a sixteenth. Evidently his current trainer was just trying something different, hoping for a positive response.

"Not much," Gainer said, folding the form and putting it into the rack in front of him. He saw that he wasn't alone with that opinion. At fourteen minutes to post time the Totalizator Board showed odds of twenty-five to one on Snapshot. And now flickering to thirty to one.

Chapin leaned to Gainer and said: "He'll win."

Gainer borrowed Vinny's binoculars. Saw that the horse was well-muscled through the thighs and quarters, broad enough in the chest. Nice conformation, a small refined head, neat ears. Snapshot certainly looked like a runner, even with all four legs wrapped. That was something Gainer always looked for, wrappings. As a rule he never bet a horse with four wrappings.

"Unless he falls down," Chapin added to his previous statement.

Gainer glanced at the racing form again, quickly handicapped his choice, the favorite. Then, thinking perhaps this was a joke at his expense, he looked at Chapin's eyes. All he could read there was straight stuff.

"Try some of it," Chapin advised. "But don't overload or give it to anyone, not even God."

"Chapin, for this horse to win God has to already know," Gainer said. He went up to a two dollar sellers window, asked for a hundred tickets on Snapshot. As an afterthought, because there was no wait, he had the seller punch out a hundred more of the same.

When he returned to the box it was five minutes to post time. The odds on Snapshot were forty-five to one. Chapin was getting edgier every second. Vinny was relaxed, like a guy who would survive and be well off no matter what. Vinny was the younger brother by three years but looked at least five older. He was heavier, wider faced, and, because his mouth had a slight, natural upward turn at the corners, gave the impression that he would be better-natured, which was not the case. Chapin had been carrying Vinny more or less for years—financed him and extricated him from various squeezes.

Vinny broke the tension of the moment by taking something from his jacket pocket that he slipped to Gainer. "Check that out," he said.

A diamond ring.

It needed cleaning.

"Two carats thirty points not counting the baguettes on the sides. Color's a little off to tell you true, but it's clean. You won't see anything in it," Vinny assured him.

"How much?" Gainer asked only to show some interest.

"Fifteen hundred a carat regular, a flat three geesuls to you."

"Ever get any sapphires?"

"I get what I get, you know."

"Or rubies?"

"That the only kind of material you're interested in?"

"Yeah."

"I've got a package coming tonight. If there's any of those in it, I'll put it aside for you."

Gainer dropped the ring into Vinny's jacket pocket.

Vinny felt to see if it was there.

The horses were at the gate, being put in. The jockey on Snapshot wore pale blue silks. The favorite was acting up, refusing to go in, as though indulging his temperament was an extra due him for the winning he was surely about to perform. There were nine horses in the race.

"The one horse never breaks well," Gainer said.

"Be no different this time," Chapin said.

Gainer offered Vinny his binoculars back, but Vinny pushed them away, told him, "Go ahead, you look."

The flag was up.

The gate doors sprang open and the horses lunged out. Snapshot was only a split second slow out of the gate but with his position in the number one slot that allowed all eight other horses to pull over ahead of him, squeezing him to dead last on the rail.

Going past the stands for the first time a pair of early speed horses had taken the lead. The favorite was fifth, well-placed, being rated, staying out of trouble and saving ground. Snapshot was twelve lengths off the pace and running as though he was merely trying to imitate the others. If form held up, the front speed would burn itself out, giving way to the second favorite, which would give way to the favorite, which would win by four or five, perhaps more.

That was exactly how the race was going when the horses were rounding the far turn.

Time for all bettors to stand.

Time for their urging and roaring.

The two leaders were falling back. The favorite was coming on.

Snapshot was still last on the rail.

Gainer glanced at Chapin. This was crazy, he thought. He'd just blown four hundred.

Chapin was intent on the race.

At that point the chestnut and pale blue that was Snapshot and rider made a sudden move. Passed the tiring horses, came around the stretch turn, went wide for room, all the way out to the middle of the track. Snapshot's front hooves grabbed, dug the dirt for speed. He closed easily on the favorite, went by him at the sixteenth pole and won going away by nine lengths. Snapshot's jockey had done nothing more than take the ride, never used the whip. The official time of the race was one minute, forty-one seconds, only three-fifths of a second off the track record. Snapshot came back to the winner's circle with his fine head up and his tail whipping, apparently enjoying the new experience.

Chapin sat, pinched his nostrils with first knuckle and thumb, grinned and double-winked at Gainer. "That animal really found itself," he said.

"What else might be found?" Gainer asked.

Chapin shook his head no, meaning not to worry. "I hope his owners have sense enough to enter him in a handicap."

The payoff evoked a mixture of gasps and growls and some glee from a group of fat ladies who were habitual long-shot show bettors.

Snapshot, it was flashed, paid one hundred eighty dollars to win.

Gainer cashed in. Ten tickets at a time at each of the long line of cashier's windows. Just being cautious. He knew someone had sure as hell put this horse over. Despite Chapin's reassurances to the contrary, whatever had been put into that horse might be determined. There could be an investigation.

What Gainer did not know was that no urine or blood sample could possibly show anything. To find out how the good-looking but lazy thoroughbred Snapshot had run a nearly record-breaking mile and a sixteenth at Belmont would have required vivisection. And even then, locating anything would have been a matter of extreme luck.

Three and a half years back Chapin had set it up, in collaboration with an old money-loving veterinarian in Lexington, Kentucky, a Dr. Healy. The doctor arranged with one of his horse-breeding clients to accept a foal instead of fees. For tax reasons. He registered the foal as Snapshot, made sure all papers were in keeping with the requirements of the Thoroughbred Racing Association.

When Snapshot was four months old Dr. Healy put him under anesthesia. Laid him out on the operating table and prepared him by shaving the hair from an eight-inch square area of his left loin. Chapin assisted.

Using fluoroscopy, the doctor determined Snapshot's left kidney and the suprarenal capsule situated directly anterior to it, the adrenal gland. It was not a simple matter. In a horse, as in a human, the kidney and even more particularly the adrenal, is tucked well up in under the last two ribs, making them not easily accessible.

Dr. Healy studied the field, marked a black cross on the pinkish flesh of Snapshot. The point of entry. He took up a 50cc syringe with a Number 10 hypodermic needle attached. The needle was about six inches long. He drew about 20cc's of glucose solution into the syringe.

The silicone microchips Chapin had prepared lay on a piece of gauze on an operating tray. They had been made sterile. Chapin had produced three chips, two as backups. Each was wafer thin and 3.2 millimeters or one-eighth inch square. Chapin took up one of the chips with sterile tweezers. Placed the chip at the opening of the hypodermic needle. The doctor drew back ever so slightly on the plunger of the syringe to suck the microchip an inch or so into the needle's shaft. Then, careful not to cause the chip to be drawn up into the syringe itself, he took an additional small amount of the glucose.

The angle of the needle was crucial to the procedure. The doctor pressed it into Snapshot's flesh, through the gelatinous tissue and cartilage between the second and third ribs and then slowly, deeper into the tissue, close as possible to the adrenal gland. Holding the needle at that depth, he pressed on the plunger of the syringe. The microchip was forced in, injected along with the glucose. It would remain lodged in the tissue while the glucose would be absorbed. Everything depended on whether or not the microchip was precisely implanted. A mere centimeter could mean failure.

Next morning, Snapshot was out in the pasture, acting as rompish as before.

His coat grew back.

Dr. Healy saw to it that he got the best of care. The following year, as a sleek two-year-old, Snapshot was put in the Keenland sales. A leading stable bought him for forty thousand and brought him along believing he could be more than a tax write-off. It took eight races for Snapshot to break his maiden.

Chapin followed Snapshot's whereabouts and performances closely. Several times circumstances seemed almost right and Dr. Healy expressed his impatience.

Chapin had waited until this perfectly suitable sixth race on this day at Belmont.

It all came down to the moment when Snapshot was rounding the far turn.

Chapin reached into his inside pocket of his jacket, flicked on the switch of a transistorized power transmitter designed by him to activate by remote control the microchip imbedded in Snapshot.

The microchip received Chapin's signal, triggered an electrical impulse to the sensitive conductors of its pure gold circuits. The amount of electricity discharged by it was, by no means, a jolt. Sixty-five millivolts. Hardly enough to power a lightning bug.

What Snapshot felt was merely a twinge as the electrical impulse arced into the greater splanchnic nerve. That nerve, in turn, sent it charging through the filaments of nerve routes serving the plexus of the adrenal gland—through the cortex, the outer shell of the adrenal and deeper to its inner part, the medulla. Responding in its natural intended manner, the medulla discharged adrenaline into Snapshot's bloodstream.

Snapshot had never felt so much power.

His heart seemed suddenly larger and in command. His lungs filled fuller than ever before. The very air that he was pushing around him was like a flow of fuel into his wider nostrils. His chest and shoulders and flanks felt immense to him, and lubricated, and his legs felt twice as long, capable of reaching far out in advance of him. He kept his eyes straight ahead but his vision was acutely peripheral now as well and he was aware of the other horses he went by, the white of the rail, the stippled texture of the crowd in the stands.

And then the bit was pressuring the corners of his mouth, a perverse counter to the call in him to continue at full speed. The bit insisted, slowed him, turned and controlled him. Brought him back.

A winner.

Chapin was.

Chapin was pleased with himself.

He had made no bet at the track, but he'd gotten down in Las Vegas for three thousand, in Reno for three more and had two spreads out among bookies he knew. Altogether his winnings would amount to four hundred thirty-two thousand. He wouldn't split evenly as he'd agreed with Dr. Healy. Not that the money was so important to Chapin. It was just that the doctor was bent over asking for it and Chapin couldn't resist sticking it to him. In fact, it would have been against a personal law not to. For one thing, the doctor had no way of knowing how much had been bet. Chapin would take a third off the top and then split with the doctor.

He waited for Gainer to cash in. They walked to the car park together. On the way Chapin put his hand on Gainer's shoulder, and as though one diversion had just concluded and another was needed in its place, told him: "All right, now . . . let's meet somewhere in town for a drink and you can tell me what's so important to you."

HINE peeked over the edge of the dune. Saw the two surf fishermen were still down on the beach. They had been there since early morning. He had noticed them first out his bathroom window while he was using the toilet, so he'd put on a pair of trunks and gone down to them, acting just casually curious.

Not many people fished the surf along that stretch but those two seemed to be doing well enough. They had a large orange plastic bucket for the fish they caught and the cheapest sort of white styrofoam cooler for their beer and sandwich makings. They'd already caught five ugly fair-sized fish. Their two poles were held upright by metal tubes in the sand so all they had to do was sit there and every once in a while feel the lines to determine if they had anything on.

Hine was satisfied that they were what they appeared to be. They were genuinely proud of those ugly fish the way they had lifted them up by the gills to show them to him, Hine decided.

He settled back into the depression of the dune. Squirmed his bare buttocks and back, causing the fine granules beneath him to give, as though creating a mold. He often thought of this sandy dip as his private baking container. He had done some of his best tanning and thinking here and believed it appropriate that here was where he should finalize his deal with Gainer. He'd been willing without a second thought when Gainer, through Sweet, had stipulated same place, same conditions.

Bareass in the dunes.

No possible tricks up the sleeves.

What a beautiful day to springboard himself up, right up over Darrow's head. A flawless sky, a timid breeze, the sun unchallenged. Hine was sure that Darrow would be out in it at Number 19, adding to his leisure color. Maybe the mortician would only have to shave him, Hine thought, and his laugh to himself was almost out loud.

He heard the sliding door open and close. That would be Sweet with Gainer.

Gainer, nude as required, squatted on his haunches on the inside of the dune as he had the time previous. Sweet remained standing on the edge.

Hine felt so confident that it was going to go as he wanted that he didn't get into it right away, small-talked a bit about some movie he'd seen and disliked recently and also inquired about the scars on Gainer's shins. When Gainer told him the scars were from playing soccer, Hine considered the pain, acted impressed and that was enough. To business.

"Well, what do you think?" he asked.

"I'm leaning."

"Which way?"

"Toward the deal."

"Good."

"But I need you to go over it again."

"It's simple enough, just what I said."

"I don't want any misunderstandings later. After all, it's not something we're going to have in writing. So give it to me again."

"From what point?"

"From the top."

Hine took in an impatient breath and outlined the proposal point for point. When he was vague or too brief, Gainer interrupted with questions. He got more from Hine this time regarding *orders,* how they worked, who could originate them and how they didn't get carried over from one Custodian to the next.

"Supposing everything goes as you say, except you don't get appointed Custodian, what then?" Gainer asked.

"Never happen."

"Are you really in that solid?"

"Yes . . ." Hine didn't believe he was stretching the truth. He was more than qualified for the spot with his Hotchkiss, Yale and Harvard Business School background. He had also attended the prestigious Advanced Management Program at the University of Southern California and he was married to a Whitcroft of the High Board Whitcrofts. ". . . I'm in."

There were other things Gainer wondered about and would have asked had he not felt better off not knowing. Such as where the money in The Balance came from and who it was Darrow and Hine answered to. It didn't quite sit that the Mob had Darrow and Hine types out front for them, but it made so much less sense the other way around that Gainer didn't even consider it.

"Is everything clear to you now?" Hine asked.

"Just about."

"Are we in business?"

Gainer nodded.

Hine smiled and, rather like he was celebrating the consummation of the deal, he sucked in his stomach, made his long waist so concave there seemed to be nothing in there between his navel and spine.

"I'll need something from you," Gainer said.

"I told you not to expect me to participate."

"I want a rundown on the security set-up at Number 19, as detailed as possible and don't worry about it being too technical."

"Sweet will see that you get that."

"Also, my end has to be forty million."

"That disturbs me."

"Why?"

"The way you keep nibbling."

"Nibbles to you, bites to me," Gainer told him.

"This better be the last of it."

"Yeah, it will, forty will do."

THREE hours later.

Gainer was at Chapin's apartment on East Forty-ninth. Leslie, Chapin and Vinny were there.

The apartment was a seven room duplex, the top two floors of a five floor brownstone. The lower floor was where Chapin did his living. It was a mess, the red long-fibered shag rug badly in need of vacuuming and looking as though it was hiding whatever had been dropped on it over the last six months. Nothing matched. A chair was a chair, a sofa a sofa, and that was all that mattered. There were lots of glasses with beer foam dried in them and ashtrays that were emptied but never washed so they were caked black. At least half the cigarettes stubbed out were lipsticked, various shades.

Vinny couldn't keep his eyes off Leslie's six carat D diamond ring.

The upper floor of Chapin's place was totally opposite to the lower. One long room immaculate and in perfect order. All surfaces were of white enamel or formica, the floor was seamed stainless steel. A large air exchange unit kept the atmosphere dust free. Banked along the walls and above work surfaces were electronic units for various purposes. Hundreds of switches, hundreds of indicators, black facades punctuated by tiny red power lights.

Apparently one item out of place was the fishing rod on the counter. Chapin had just detached the reel from it. His fingers had the delicacy and certitude of a surgeon. He spoke to Gainer as he worked. "Hope you sat as still as possible."

"I tried to."

"Any trouble getting it out?"

"No, except the leads broke."

"Expected as much."

Chapin was referring to a molded plastic capsule similar to the sort that contain small toys children get from quarter machines at supermarkets. This one, constructed by Chapin, encased a power source. It had been inserted into Gainer's rectum. From the power capsule a pair of wires, black and fine as thread, led out and ran left and right of Gainer's testicles and up into his pubic hair, where, entangled, they were lost from sight. At the top of each wire was a tiny module. One was a receiver, the other a transmitter.

As Vinny put it, Gainer really had a bug up his ass.

Vinny and Chapin had, of course, been the two fishing guys on the beach. Chapin's rod had served as an antenna, his reel and line a miniature tape recorder.

Now Chapin carefully wound the magnetic wire from the reel onto a proper spool.

"Maybe just a lot of hassle for nothing," Gainer remarked.

"Believe in me," Chapin said.

He put the spool on a playback unit, fed the wire through and fixed it to a take-up spool. Turned on the playback.

First heard was a range of scratchy sounds along with a mushy hiss.

"Hair and ocean," Chapin explained.

Then came Hine's voice, not perfect fidelity but understandable and, most important, unmistakably Hine.

They played the recording all the way through. It was all there, what Gainer could use as a backup to keep Hine straight. There would be no double cross. The moment Hine even seemed to be making such a move, one session with this tape would keep him in line. Forever.

Chapin filtered out most of the extraneous noises on the tape, refined it even more and transferred it to a regular cassette. He destroyed the original. "Where does this go?" he asked, handing the cassette to Gainer.

"In a deep, dark box."

"You could take it to this guy Darrow, use it to buy yourself an out."

"Could."

"Darrow ought to be eternally grateful."

"For a week or two," was Gainer's opinion.

"By that, you mean you're going to try to pull it off?"

"Somehow."

"You can't," Chapin told him.

"It's worth a shot."

"For one thing, do you know how much three billion weighs?"

Vinny winced at the amount.

"A billion in hundreds comes to twenty thousand pounds," Chapin said. "Three billion would be sixty. You can't handle it . . . not alone."

"I'll be helping," Leslie put in.

Chapin went across the room, snapped a few switches on and off to give his hands something to do. "Wouldn't it be great," he said, "to make a triple crown winner out of a cheap dog. A filly maybe to make up for Genuine Risk."

Gainer could sense Chapin's mental circuits working unrelated to the words coming from his mouth. Chapin glanced through a 30X magnifying glass to a microcircuit in progress. "It will take three guys, at least three," he said.

282

"Suggest something," Gainer said.

"I owe you."

"Not anymore."

"You didn't say that. What you just said was you feel I still owe you and you want me to even up by coming in on this thing with you. Isn't that what he said, Vinny?"

"That's what I heard, no question about it."

CHAPTER
SEVENTEEN

GAINER wondered if he really appeared to be appreciating the garden.

He was on one of its footpaths strolling leisurely while he took measure of the rear grounds of the house and the wall that ran uninterrupted along the perimeter. On the other side of that wall, Gainer knew, was Westchester County Airport property, a section of the outer reaches of the airport, actually a buffer area of woods and undergrowth. At no point did the wall come within fifty feet of the house; it came closest to a large shed connected to the back of the garage, but the garage was separated from the house by a good twenty feet.

Gainer picked a snapdragon. Squeezed the pink blossom to cause its mouth to open in beautiful ferocity. Meanwhile, he studied the objective, the solid back of that upper part of the north wing.

No easy way up to it. No way into it from the outside. He came to the conclusion that the only possibility would be from the inside. Hardly a prospect. What, he chided himself, had he expected, that stealing three billion weighing sixty thousand pounds would be a piece of cake?

He heard his name called out by Darrow, who was standing in the open french doorway of his study. Darrow beckoned once with a forefinger, and Gainer went up to him. "I'm sure you dislike hanging around here doing nothing," Darrow said.

"I don't mind."

"Where is Mrs. Pickering this morning?"

"She had an errand."

"Oh? So do you. I've decided to take you on as a regular carrier. How does that strike you?"

"Thanks."

"Perhaps you doubted my largesse?"

"Never."

"It's all arranged. You make your first regular carry tonight. That won't be an inconvenience, I hope." Implying it better not be.

"No."

"Did Mrs. Pickering by chance say when she would return?"

"She had a lot of business to take care of."

"Well, Hine has your carry all packed and ready."

"How much?"

"Three million. I suggest you get with Hine at once. And, by the way, Andrew . . . this time abide by the two-week stay rule." Darrow smiled with his lips and stepped back into the study, closed the french doors to be definitely done with Gainer.

Gainer entered the house by way of the rear hall, went up to his room. Hine was waiting for him there. A thirty inch suitcase with a red and white name tag stood near the door. Hine was strictly business. "Your passport is in order?" he asked.

"Yeah."

"Let me see it."

Gainer got it for him. Hine examined it.

"You're on the Concorde to Paris again," Hine said. "Leaving at two. Sweet will run you out."

Gainer packed. The bastards were hurrying him off same as before. He'd just gotten used to the idea of stealing for his life and fortune and now this lousy turn. He pushed his clothes into his suitcase.

Hine saw him down to the car. The final thing Hine said to him was: "You have two weeks."

Sweet didn't take the shorter route of the Bronx Whitestone to Kennedy. Instead he went down Route 95 and when they came to the Triboro Bridge he hung a right and went over into town. Gainer, only along for the ride, didn't ask about it.

At the Sovereign Apartments on East Fifty-eighth Sweet pulled the car over. A young man with a suitcase got in. He was about Gainer's age and build, had similar coloring.

Sweet demanded Gainer's passport.

285

Gainer handed it over and, in return, Sweet gave him a flat manila envelope and told him, "Get the fuck out. And stay out of sight for two weeks."

Gainer did. Stood on the curb and watched the car, containing the three million carry and his replacement, go down the street and turn out of sight. See, he told himself, how sometimes it's best to just go with the greedy flow of things. Obviously Hine had ordered the switch so Gainer could get on with his job. Better stay out of Darrow's sight for two weeks, though, like Sweet said.

He walked the seven blocks to the Forty-ninth Street garage and Norma's Fiat. Three-quarters of an hour later he was up in Westchester County pulling in at the drive to Rodger's house in Bedford. He'd never been there and his first impression was of all the places of Rodger's he knew, he liked this one most.

The house was set well back from the residential road beyond a well-chinked native rock wall and a grove of elms and oaks and dogwood. A New England Colonial of hospitable size, two and a half stories and twelve rooms with a separate servants' cottage and situated to best advantage on twenty acres. The exterior of the house was freshly painted white as white could be. Family white, Gainer thought. Each of its windows was eared by shutters enameled black, and hinged with gleaming brass. It occurred to Gainer that someone spent much of their life keeping all those hinges polished.

Leslie's Corniche was parked in the drive but she didn't seem to be anywhere about. Gainer finally found her down by the brook. Seated on a big, friendly flat rock with her white cotton dress hiked up and her feet in a slow-running pool. Apparently she was far away in thought, didn't seem to realize Gainer was there until he spoke up and asked what she was doing.

She hitched out of it. "When did you get here?"

"Just now."

"I was trying to get through to Lady Caroline or, anyway, allow her to get to me. The water usually helps."

"Maybe she's gone shopping or to the hairdresser's or something."

"Whatever."

"How does the water help?"

"It increases spiritual receptivity. I'm not sure of that but it makes sense. It's my own theory." Leslie took a deep breath. "Lady Caroline has been buzzing and hovering around but at the moment, I don't know, she's not being at all attentive. Have you heard from Norma lately?"

"Not for a while." He hadn't told Leslie about Norma's skimming

286

from her carries. Another important thing withheld. They were mounting. Such omissions might be best for his psychological comfort but they bothered him.

"Try your feet in the water," Leslie advised, taking hers out. Her feet appeared cold. She dried them on the bottom of her skirt. "Where were you?" she asked.

"At Number 19 and almost in Zurich."

"You can't go to Zurich, we've got money to steal."

Gainer agreed. He related how he'd gotten out of the carry.

"Bless Hine's heart," Leslie said.

They walked up through the cared-for woods to the house. The acorns, twigs and pebbles Leslie stepped barefoot on didn't bother her. Gainer recalled she'd once bought a pair of clogs that had inner soles of hundreds of hard rubber protrusions. He tried them and was unable to take more than four excruciating steps, but she wore them around for hours at a time, even while doing her windowing twenty blocks up Madison. Marvelous massage therapy for the internal organs, she'd claimed. Gainer hadn't commented, couldn't accept how painful pressure on, for example, the heel area might benefit one's prostate.

"Are you positive Rodger won't be coming here?" he asked as they reached the house.

"He won't."

"How can you be sure?"

"Rodger is always where he's supposed to be."

Gainer assumed by that she meant it was a clause in their arrangement, hers and Rodger's. To avoid embarrassing surprises. Rodger's Bedford house as a base of operations for the three billion robbery had been her idea. And a good one. It was private and only twenty minutes over back roads from Number 19. She had given the permanent servants and groundkeepers three weeks off. The only one who remained was an eighty-year-old foppy retainer who never went anywhere, kept to his quarters over the garage where he enjoyed issues of *After Dark,* drank banana daiquiris and watched late late Joan Crawford and Greta Garbo movies.

"I think," Leslie said, "first we ought to get a good look at that house."

"I did, this morning," Gainer told her.

"I mean a better look."

Leslie put on shoes and got behind the wheel of her Corniche. Drove to Harrison, the town proper, to the Town Hall on Hillside Avenue. The official building department was on the second floor. Across a hard, high counter, Leslie turned on her best model's smile for a middle-aged clerk and introduced herself as a writer doing research for a book on lovely older Westchester houses. She pretended not to know the precise address and the clerk had her point out the house on a plot map. The clerk looked up Number 19 in his files, found nothing, said he doubted he'd have anything on a house built that many years ago, at least nothing right there on hand. Next thing, against the clerk's built-in bureaucratic resistance, Leslie had him down in the basement storage area searching through files and cartons. She charmed and at the same time challenged him to perform his little heroic for her, and he was up to his crotch in blueprints when, finally, in a file behind a file, yellowed and blotched from age, he came across them.

A complete set of the original architectural plans for Number 19 Purchase Street.

Leslie was delighted, rewarded the clerk with a hug. That threw him way off. Telling her she'd have to sign out for the plans, have them copied and returned by the following day would have spoiled it for him. He just let her take them.

It was close to six o'clock when Gainer and Leslie arrived back at the house in Bedford. They agreed, before anything else, there would have to be dinner. Leslie would fix it.

Why didn't they just go out for a steak or even a pizza? Gainer said.

Leslie was already aproned and ready to get at it. She shooed him out of the kitchen, told him if he wanted to be helpful he could set the table out on the screened porch. The blue Spode china, she suggested.

Gainer's stomach told him to be irritated. He'd had nothing to eat since a light breakfast, was hungrier for more than a bunch of vegetables mushed up in the blender or some mysterious melange like ratatouille. Begrudgingly, almost to the point of grumbling aloud, he found the blue Spode and the silver and set two places. That done, he stole a quick peek into the kitchen, saw her at the huge Garland range, cooking mists seemingly rising from her hands. It was going to take hours, Gainer thought, and sure as hell it would be ratatouille. To divert his mood he went outside and picked some dahlias for the table. Also found some fancy little china placemarkers, used a felt-tipped pen to print WELSH RAREBUTT on hers and couldn't think of anything for his better than what she so often called him, which was LOVER. He printed that and wiped it off, replaced it with HANDYCAPTOR.

Dinner was ready.

Leslie tried to pretend it was an easy spur-of-the-moment thing, merely tossed together. However the curried cream of pea soup had obviously taken some doing in advance. For a main course there was Roquefort stuffed ground sirloin with mustard seed sauce encircled with heaps of pommes Lyonnaise. Warm brioche and chived butter. The wine she had decanted was a Brunello di Montalano 1945.

Gainer loved every mouthful. Who wouldn't?

The mustard seeds were tiny spicy explosions as he chewed, the potatoes crisp but not overdone, the wine like swallows of liquid silk with the flavor of currants and violets.

"Never met anyone else who could both cook and shave," he told her.

"Never will."

He complimented the wine, asking about it.

Because it was from Rodger's cellar she didn't tell him it cost a thousand a bottle. "Think I'd make someone a good wife?" she asked.

"By all means."

"Means aren't everything."

Gainer broke off a piece of a brioche, dipped it into his wine and took it to her mouth. "Communion," he said.

"We'll always have it. Don't you believe we'll always have it?"

"One way or another," Gainer replied.

Leslie reached over and stabbed up one of his potatoes. She still had some on her plate but wanted one of his. Offhand she asked, "Who is Millicent?"

"Who?"

"Millicent."

"Only Millicent I know is one of Mrs. Darrow's old friends."

"How old?"

"Sixty-some."

"Really?"

"Yeah, why?"

Leslie took a note-size envelope from her dress pocket. "This was slipped under your door at Number 19. I forgot to give it to you."

Gainer read the note that said: "Dear Andrew—Perhaps next time? Millicent."

Leslie knifed up a dab of butter for her tongue.

Gainer slipped the note into his shirt pocket, sipped wine and asked: "Been taking your Rescue? Seems to me you haven't. At least not that I've noticed."

Leslie allowed that to be absorbed by silence, then asked: "Perhaps what next time?"

"I about ten percent promised to teach her how to watch football."

"And she about ninety percent wanted to play."

"Don't be crazy."

"You really go for older women, don't you?"

Gainer reached over and with a finger gently widened the opening of Leslie's unbuttoned dress front. Appreciated matters in there a moment and then told her, "No."

After dinner they went upstairs with a tray containing desserts, the architectural plans for Number 19 and the manila envelope Sweet had given Gainer. Clothes off, propped up by many extra pillows on another of Leslie's luxurious beds, they kissed once good and long and went over the Sweet material together.

Sweet's handwriting was inconsistent, in places large and loopy, at other places smaller and crammed. It also changed within a syllable from slant to backhand. Nevertheless, Sweet had done a thorough job of it. There were thirty pages, including several ruler-drawn diagrams with some measurements indicated to the inch. An accurate detailed description of the security setup that guarded The Balance at Number 19, as well as a timetable of operation.

Now, Gainer and Lesie were brought to realize what they were up against.

The wall that bordered the grounds was at no point less than nine feet high. Along the top of the wall, running continuously from relay to relay was an arrangement of photovoltaic detectors. Unlike ordinary electronic eye alarm devices that throw a line of light, these were specially designed with stacks of multiple phototransistors so the beam created was a band of light an inch thick and twenty inches high. Any mass that penetrated the beam could be measured and evaluated. A bird or squirrel, for instance, would not activate the alarm.

The rear grounds, from the base of the outer wall to the terrace and from the far corner of the garage on the north to the fence of the tennis court on the south, was considered a crucial area. (Fifty-two feet, wall to terrace; two hundred feet, garage to court.) It was believed that if ever an attempt was made on The Balance it would come from that direction. Therefore an elaborate grid of undersurface pressure sensors had been incorporated throughout the garden in this section of the grounds. The pressure sensors were time-set, automatically put on alarm from dusk to dawn. Originally they had been hooked up with undersurface explosive devices, but those were removed when a forgetful gardener and a drunk security man had lost three legs between them. Now the pressure sensor alarm was connected to the water sprinkler system that serviced the rear lawns and gardens. Activated, these water sprinklers worked with a second system of sprinklers to give off an unavoidable mist of $H_2S_2O_7$ or fuming sulfuric acid. Anyone caught in the mist would probably be burned to death, or at the least, permanently blinded. The amount of weight necessary to set off the pressure system was fifty pounds. Which would exempt, say, most stray dogs and small children.

Sweet had parenthetically noted that the enclosed diagram of the pressure sensor grid beneath the rear grounds was only an estimate, could be as much as a foot or two off.

The roof of the house was sealed. The dormer windows not openable, their frames made of one-piece steel. The entire roof surface was equipped with a pressure alarm that would activate whenever anything in excess of ten pounds came down on it. That allowance to again avoid false alarms caused by birds or squirrels.

Inside the house.

The upper corridor of the north wing.

An ultrasonic vibration alarm unit was situated ten feet from the entrance to The Balance Rooms. It was inset in the opposing walls of the corridor and consisted of oscillators that generated compressional waves capable of picking up any vibration above the frequency of twenty thousand cycles per second. Thus, anything more than the slightest stirring in that atmosphere would cause the alarm to go off.

The door to The Balance Room was automatically opened or locked by an electronic tonal combination transmitted directly to the door-bolting mechanism from a touch-tone telephone located in Darrow's bedroom suite. Only Darrow, as Custodian, knew the combination.

The door itself was constructed of a steel alloy material, a space-age by-product, impervious to anything less than an 84mm recoilless anti-tank gun. The walls between The Balance Room and other rooms were internally reinforced with that same material, as were the floors of The Balance Room.

Within The Balance area itself was what everyone considered the ultimate feature of the security system. Heat sensor alarm units installed in the ceilings and walls. They were the refined application of the ordinary household thermostat. Far more sensitive, of course, they responded to the most infinitesimal change in the temperature of the atmosphere in the room. When The Balance area was bolted, the air in the room was quickly conditioned to sixty-eight degrees Fahrenheit by special air cooling units. That temperature was precisely maintained. If, for example, someone were able to merely expose their hand in the room, the heat sensors would react as though they had detected a four alarm fire. Furthermore, they were entirely remote, functioned without wiring. There were four such units in The Balance area, two fixed to the ceiling where the money was kept, two in the ceiling where it was processed. The heat sensor alarms were the reason why the men responsible for security at Number 19 relaxed at night—and why Darrow had one less, large worry.

The monitoring center for all alarms and prohibitive devices was located in the room above the garage. Indicators hooked up to the various phases were incorporated into an electronic console that was observed every second. A minimum of six security men were on duty at all times. There were eighteen altogether. They doubled as servants and answered only to the Custodian. Most of these men had come over to the private sector from government intelligence service, had that sort of training behind them. Such as the ability to kill swiftly with hands or with just about any object. An arsenal of conventional weapons, including automatic rifles and sidearms, was kept at the monitoring center above the garage.

The final page of Sweet's documentary was devoted to a map of Number 19 hand drawn by him out of scale but with dimensions noted. In the right hand bottom corner of the page was an unencouraging postscript.

Leave me your watch.

Gainer felt unable to move. His mouth must have been open because Leslie put a Teuscher champagne chocolate truffle in it. He thought maybe he should have carried to Zurich. Thought he ought to call Chapin and tell him to forget about it. He got up, went across the room and dropped Sweet's report in the bottom drawer of a Regence chest. Shoved the drawer shut, locked it with its silk tasseled key. Tossed the key under the bed. Leslie understood. She felt much the same about the report. No use having it around reminding them of how it had ruined everything.

Well, not really everything.

Leslie lay on her side. Gainer lay on his side. They pressed together. Face to face, their breaths seemed dependent, hers into his, his into hers, and every so often one tongue or the other moistening the other's lips. For as long as it took for the chrysalis of passion to enclose them. They parted, split like the matching halves of some elongated fruit. Two hands each were not enough for so much at once gentle avarice and generosity, but then no hand was needed for him to find her with himself, join himself straight to her.

The walls of her clamped but their own slip let him nearly escape. He kept coming back in to risk capture.

He was in and also into.

Filling and full.

Gone past the line of separateness so that each of her pleasant little swellings that increased and broke convulsively over her were as much his.

Blessed convolution of Gainer and Leslie. So many times let up and recommenced.

"Love me sore," she said.

And with that he lost hold and she knew, pulled the sweet string from him, one after one after one knots of excruciating, loving pleasure.

NEXT morning they didn't speak of robbery. Not a word. Around ten she remarked that she needed to buy some shoes, as though she was down to her last pair. They drove to the city to Maud Frizon. Leslie tried on while Gainer waited. Thirty pair that he thought all looked better on her than they ever would on anyone. She had it in mind to charge ten pair but cut that down to four when Gainer insisted on paying for them. At that, the bill came to twelve hundred and some. Snapshot winnings.

It lifted their spirits somewhat.

However, on the way back to the house in Bedford, Leslie didn't drive her usual fast and Gainer hardly said a word. Five minutes after they got home she took along a worn paperback edition of *Seth Speaks* and went down to the brook to stick her feet in.

Gainer roamed the house, not noisily, just restless. Ended up in what he presumed was Rodger's upstairs study. Gray flannel upholstered Louis XV furniture. Gray flannel on the walls. Touches of navy and white and leopard. A female decorator's impression of masculine without using leather. A nook of framed photographs. Rodger with a couple of presidents, Rodger with a couple of movie stars. The most prominently hung photo was a candid shot of Rodger with a white-haired man who looked like God in yachting clothes.

None of this helped alter Gainer's mood. If he'd been in the city he would have gone for a long walk, perhaps over on the West Side, up Columbus and down Amsterdam, but out here with just trees and bushes and blue and white *New York Times* delivery containers fixed to every mailbox post, a walk wouldn't have the same therapy, might subdue him all the more.

He glanced out and saw Leslie was still down by the brook, trying for Lady Caroline no doubt. He went out and drove away in the Fiat. Thought he was driving just anywhere down Route 22 through North Castle and Armonk to King Street. King ran parallel to Purchase and there, between them, was Westchester County Airport.

Not a vast commercial airport by any means, but a good deal more than an embellished landing strip. Westchester County Airport occupies seven hundred valuable acres and describes itself as the largest base for corporate aircraft in the United States. Mobil keeps its planes there. So does Union Carbide, American Can, Seagram, General Electric and Chase Manhattan. It is quite ordinary, for instance, to have one or the other of the Rockefellers taking off from there in one or the other of their Falcon 50s or Gulfstream III jets. The airport's main runway is north to south. Numerous taxiways network to it and further off along each side are ample aprons. There are two principal hangars. Hangar "D" on the east side of the field and Hangar "E" directly across the field about a half mile away. Next to Hangar "E" is the air traffic control tower and a large orange radar scanner. A short distance from the control tower begins the undeveloped wooded area that serves as a buffer zone between the airport and the private houses along Purchase Street.

Gainer left the Fiat in the airport's public parking lot while he wandered around. He noticed the closed main gate and the guard on duty, went down along the rear of Hangar "D" and used a door there. Assumed that old ambiance of belonging where he was as he entered a major hangar area.

The hangar's huge doors were open to the field, and the corporate jets stood in there like huge birds in sanctuary, as though any moment they might simply fly out. The gray-painted concrete hangar floor was cleared and clean, the planes white, shining and trimmed sky-blue. The white coveralls of the maintenance men were spotless, opened at the neck to show fresh white shirts.

Gainer did a friendly, authoritative nod at two of the men as he passed them on his way to the front of the hangar. Stood there in the opening, hands in back pockets, not apparently viewing the various aspects of this airport for the first time.

He watched a yellow Cherokee glide down and land and run its speed out. And only moments after it a Falcon 50 jet came in sleeker. Across the way in the distance, Hangar "D" and the traffic control tower were diffused by the hot day haze. Also, that wooded area. Gainer decided, as long as he was there, he might as well get a thorough look. He returned to the Fiat and drove around to Route 120 for the side road that led into that newer section of the airport. Parked the car outside the administration building in an empty spot with someone's name stenciled on it. Walked around the rear of the control tower and slipped unseen into the nearby brush.

Within twenty paces it seemed to Gainer that he was nowhere near an airport. The area was extremely overgrown, weeds and bushes up to seven feet tall. Thick twines and knots of wild grape and masses of nettle made the going difficult, and there was poison ivy everywhere.

A little further on were trees and undergrowth. Some oak and maple with trunks two to three feet thick. The ground was tricky, seldom level, outcropped with ledge and gullied.

Gainer did not see the fence until he was right up to it; it was that covered with vines. A steel mesh fence eight feet tall with three strands of barbed wire strung a foot and a half high along the top. He followed alongside the fence for quite a ways, then tore some of the vine from it for a look through.

There, six feet away, was the brick wall of Number 19. At that closer range he saw the relay points of its photovoltaic electronic beam. They were like oblong metal rods set every ten feet into the top of the wall. Beyond the wall Gainer could see only the upper reaches of the house, its aged blue slate roof silvery rich in the sun.

Impossible.

That was Gainer's conclusion.

He was only there because he hated giving up. In that short while he had grown used to the prospect of all those millions. The money and all it would bring had slipped in between him and his earlier motives. Of course, revenge for Norma and the saving of his own ass were still right there pushing at him, but the idea of taking care of everything in one fell swoop had been most attractive. As things were, he had no choice but to keep enduring Darrow and hope for another way at him, hope that Darrow didn't find out that he had not made the carry to Zurich. He would tell Hine it was off, and Chapin. He'd call Chapin that day.

Gainer drove back to the Bedford house.

Parked next to Leslie's Rolls was a new Cadillac Seville, obviously belonging to someone come to stay because there was luggage in the front hallway.

Leslie was out on the screened porch with Chapin and Vinny. Obviously she'd retrieved the tasseled key from beneath the bed to unlock the drawer because the pages of Sweet's report were scattered about. Chapin and Vinny had been there a while. Brie and crackers on a plate were almost gone and there were smudged wine glasses around.

"Hello handicapper," Chapin greeted him.

Vinny merely raised his hand for hello.

"I was just about to call you," Gainer told them.

"Thought we might not show?"

"We've been going over things," Leslie said brightly, her disposition up from where it had been. "They arrived right after you left."

"Caught her washing her feet in the brook." Chapin grinned.

Gainer filled a highball glass with wine, gulped some. "Any luck with Lady Caroline?" he asked Leslie, only because he thought she'd appreciate his interest.

"For a while," Leslie told him. "She's been in limbo."

"Great place for a vacation."

"Lady Caroline told me to tell you to go for it, steal the three billion—"

Chapin stopped her. "You didn't mention anyone else in on this."

"It's another thing altogether," Gainer assured him.

Leslie didn't like that.

Chapin didn't believe it. "There's another three billion I suppose."

"Lady Caroline is Leslie's spirit guide," Gainer explained with a self-conscious edge. "She gives advice from the other side. She's been dead since 1917."

"She's infallible," Leslie said.

"No shit?" Vinny said.

Chapin didn't laugh as Gainer had expected. "You talk aloud to her?" he asked Leslie.

"Not usually. Usually we talk inside me."

It was hard for Gainer to accept that Chapin might be a believer. Technical, calculating Chapin, who now extended his hand to Leslie's to demonstrate his understanding with a brief clasp. "The human level of observation is so limited it's pitiful," Chapin said. "We can't hear or see very much and what we know is probably a hell of a lot less than what we don't. We keep on amplifying and magnifying things and just when we think we've reached the bottom or the top of something all we find is another opening showing us we've still got a long ways to go."

Leslie agreed firmly.

"Most people don't want to think about it," Chapin went on. "Most people swear they believe in a god and yet they live by the rules of not accepting anything they can't see or hear."

Vinny got up and went inside to use the bathroom.

Evidently the topic had pulled one of Chapin's plugs, Gainer thought.

Chapin continued. "I remember once in a small town upstate, I had a tap going on a certain congressman. It was in October or November, just beginning to get cold. It was set up in an old farmhouse, a place that dated back almost three hundred years. One afternoon I went for a walk and was crossing an open field a short way from the house when suddenly I felt slowed down as if there was something in the air there that I had to use more effort to get through. After I'd gone about twenty feet it disappeared, like a release, making me stumble forward a little."

"A gust of wind maybe," Gainer said.

"It was so strange that I asked about the field and was told that part of it had been a family burying ground."

Leslie took in Chapin's every word as though they helped make up for a deficiency. "I had the same experience," she said, "at least a similar sensation. One afternoon in Altman's, of all places. There was hardly anyone in the store but it seemed difficult for me to go down the aisle, like I had to push my way along. Perhaps a lot of ladies from the other side who were once Altman customers had come back to look around."

"Was there a sale on?" Gainer asked.

Leslie shot him a look.

Vinny returned. "I've got a package coming tonight," he told Chapin.

"Forget it," Chapin told him.

"It's nice material," Vinny said, "clean, and I can get it for only twenty large. Probably there'll even be some sapphires," he added, hoping that might help his cause.

Gainer glanced down, realized he was standing on one of Sweet's pages. He picked it up and tried to straighten the crinkle in it. "What do you think?" he asked Chapin, expecting Chapin's opinion about the robbery of Number 19 was the same as his own. "Those alarms all over the place."

"The alarms don't bother me so much," Chapin said.

"No?"

"No, I think I can take care of the alarms. Getting in and out of there is the stumper. Have you given that any thought?"

"A lot," said Leslie.

"Some . . ." Gainer said.

"You concentrate on that," Chapin told them. "Let me worry about the alarms."

"The split," Vinny reminded Chapin.

"What do you think would be fair?" Chapin asked Gainer.

"You say."

"Okay, why don't we slice the forty down the middle. Twenty million each."

"That's still a nice long number," Leslie commented.

Gainer and Chapin shook on it.

During the next week Gainer and Leslie focused most of their energies on coming up with answers for their part of the robbery. They tossed suggestions back and forth rather competitively and whenever they hit on an idea that had a possibility they worked it out, checked it out, did a lot of phoning and running around to such places as Paramus, New Jersey, and Mineola, Long Island.

Also, Leslie found an old tailor's suit-form in the attic. The dimensions of Rodger twenty years ago. She set it up in front of a stone wall, pinned a hundred dollar bill where the heart would be so she and Gainer could practice with the ASPs. Gainer felt the same affinity for the weapon as he had in Paris. It went into his hand as though made for it, just waiting to be claimed by his grip. There were no ridiculous misses by him this time. His first shot from fifty feet put a hole through the edge of the hundred.

Every day Gainer and Leslie practiced for twenty-five rounds. From other ranges, angles and firing positions. Horsehair and cotton batting flew from the hole they blasted in the suit-form's chest. The hundred was shot to unspendable shreds.

Leslie invited Vinny to target practice with them but he said he didn't need it. Vinny did little at all that week other than eat very well, nap on the down-filled, silk-covered sofa in the drawing room and wander around the house in his stocking feet. At various times Gainer happened to notice Vinny taking close-up interest in an eighteenth-century, signed Piere Gillions silver tea caddy, paying a good deal of attention to a painting by Matisse and looking long into the hall cedar closet where Leslie kept a few furs. Either by habit or with intention of casing the place, was Gainer's impression. He decided not to mention it to Chapin.

Because Chapin was preoccupied with more important matters. Most of the while he kept to himself working with a note pad and a fine-tipped pen. His handwriting and the schemes he drew were so small it was a wonder he was able to make them out with bare eyes. When he was done with a problem he tore all the note pages into the smallest possible bits and flushed them down the toilet, keeping the solution in his head. Nearly every day he made a trip into town to his laboratory, where it was assumed he was preparing the devices he'd need. He also took those opportunities to get serviced by his working girls. He had to have his working girls.

On the seventh day Chapin announced that he had solved the photo-electric alarm system that ran along the top of the exterior wall of Number 19. Also the pressure alarms in the lawn and on the roof and the sonic alarm in the upper hallway.

"What about the heat sensor alarms?" Gainer asked. "The ones inside The Balance room?"

"Those have me stumped," Chapin hated to admit. "I thought all along they'd be a problem."

"Maybe Sweet didn't give us enough information."

"It's not that. I know what sort of units they are and how they work. Under ordinary circumstances they'd be the easiest to fool because they're remote. All I'd have to do is get a fix on their frequency and scramble the hell out of them, or jam them."

"So, why not do that?"

"We could, but I think the chances of getting away with it would be against us. The guys in that monitoring room aren't assholes. They're sure to have a way of detecting such a scramble or jam designed into that remote unit. I know I would. No, it seems to me the better try would be to somehow get me into the monitoring room. I'd need ten minutes, maybe only five to fool the alarm on that end."

"We'd need Hine's help."

"Tell him it's crucial."

"I'm sure he wouldn't go for it," Gainer said. "He was firm about not sticking his neck out any further than it is."

"Then I guess we're stuck," Chapin said.

"It's only a snag," Leslie encouraged.

The heat sensor alarm.

The heart of Number 19's security system.

To fool it they had to get to it. But how could they get to it when just being in the same room with it would cause it to go off.

They turned the problem over and over in their minds.

For help Leslie made up a special flower remedy that she called *Remedy R* (for Robbery). It had equal parts of madia and penstemon and Scotch broom in it. Madia to keep their thinking focused. Penstemon so they wouldn't be overwhelmed by the challenge. Scotch broom for perseverance and to offset feelings of what's-the-use. At least twenty times a day Leslie had Gainer, Chapin and Vinny tilt their heads back and open their mouths for her to squirt it into them. When the Remedy was used up, Leslie mixed another batch, doubled up on the Scotch broom.

It didn't matter.

The give-ups started setting in.

They weren't so smart after all.

Seemed as though it just wasn't meant to be.

Too bad they went to all the trouble for nothing.

Gainer took some of the time to catch up with business. He'd already missed the opening week of pro football. He'd been so wrapped up in this other thing. Now he got up to date on the injury reports, what players had been picked up or placed on waivers. He reached out for information from guys he knew in the cities of all the teams. When he phoned in to Pointwise, Inc., his people were about to make a pick of their own, they sounded neglected and relieved. He told them for Sunday to give out the Falcons over the Saints by ten and for Monday night, Denver plus four over Oakland.

Chapin, meanwhile, began doodling an idea to beat the telephone company. It would allow anyone, for only a hundred dollar investment in materials, to use satellite telephone transmission for nothing, forever.

Vinny went out and bought a package of swag with a lot of gawdy David Webb stuff in it.

Leslie baked some bread that came out well. She paged through several mail order brochures, including those from Neiman Marcus and Tiffany. She sent away for a lot of things.

She also washed her Corniche. Put on white short shorts and a T-shirt and red rubber boots, got a bucket, chamois and other things from the garage.

Gainer saw her from their bedroom window.

She was hard at it, sudsing the trunk and taillights with a big, sloppy terrycloth mitten.

He went down to her.

No, she told him, she didn't want any help. She stretched to reach across the hood causing her shorts to ride up.

Gainer sat on the nearby stone wall to enjoy her. As usual, her movements seemed choreographic to him. His love, washing her hundred and fifty thousand dollar car, he thought.

She sang to herself as she worked. "La dee da, see how they da. La dee da, see how they da. They all ran after ladadee da, she cut off their tails with a ladeeda, did you ever see such a sight in your life, la dee da . . ."

"Any loose change you find under the seat you can keep," Gainer said.

"Thank you, sir!" Leslie snapped brightly.

She went on washing and humming. Then she stopped as though paralyzed. Car washing suds ran down her forearms and dropped from her elbow. From the covered look of her eyes she seemed to be listening. Then, just as abruptly, she was animated. "Lady Caroline!" she exclaimed. "I knew she'd come through!"

CHAPTER
EIGHTEEN

USK.

Thursday, September 17.

The white truck was on Route 120 passing close by inlets of the Kensico Reservoir.

When it reached a point approximately two hundred feet from where the Westchester County Airport began, it pulled over and stopped on the wide, paved shoulder.

Vinny was at the wheel, Gainer beside him.

The truck was the sort of bucket-hoist vehicle used by tree service companies and New York Telephone and the State Highway Department. For reaching high places with a man. Behind its cab on a flatbed was housing for the motor that provided power for the hoist. The hoist could be rotated at its base. It consisted of two extensions or arms, each twenty feet long, connected in a hinging, adjustable manner, like an elbow. Fixed to the uppermost end of the second arm was a pair of plastic containers called buckets, waist-deep and large enough for a man to stand and move around in.

This particular bucket-hoist was painted white. The United States Government seal decaled on its doors was encircled with the words *Federal Aviation Administration*. Red, white and blue government license plates. None of that was fabricated. It was, indeed, an authentic official FAA truck. Stolen to order from Teeterborough, New Jersey Airport for a five thousand fee by a couple of Vinny's people.

Gainer climbed down from the cab. Both he and Vinny were wearing white, loose-fitting coveralls and had FAA photo identifications pinned above their left upper pockets.

Gainer studied the airport area ahead. None of the hangars or other buildings could be seen from there because of the terrain and high brush. However, the landing approach lights stood up in clear view on thirty foot stanchions evenly spaced in a straight line every fifty feet, a rack of five lights on each stanchion to help guide pilots straight to the runway.

Vinny handed the rifle and cartridges to Gainer. It was Rodger's rifle bought by him several years ago to take to Canada for bear. A premier grade Remington 760 Gamemaster carbine. Gainer was a little careless with it now as he crawled beneath the truck, scraped the butt of its stock on the pavement. He positioned himself close to the inside of the front wheel, where he was less likely to be noticed. The sparse traffic along that stretch of road at that hour also helped. Spread belly down, elbows supporting the rifle, Gainer looked through the 4-12 telescopic sight.

The sight brought the individual landing approach lights right to him. He cross-haired on one and squeezed the trigger. Saw the light and its reflector explode under the impact of the 30-06 bullet. The report of the rifle was loud but somewhat contained by the underside of the truck.

Rapidly, without a miss, Gainer shot out ten landing approach lights from four different racks. It sounded as though some old truck was backfiring badly or perhaps some kids were setting off leftover Fourth of July M-80 bombs. Before anyone could come to investigate the shots, Gainer and rifle were back in the truck and under way.

Vinny took a left for the road that ran along the eastern side of the airport. Past the Air National Guard hangars to the main access gate.

The steel-mesh gate was closed.

A guard on duty there came to the truck.

"About half your goddamn *Malsr* is out, maybe even the *Rail*," Gainer said brusquely, sounding technical and very much like an FAA maintenance man irritated by the inconvenience of so much work. *Malsr* was an acronym for Medium-Intensity Approach Light System Rail. *Rail* itself stood for Runway Alignment Indicator Lights, Gainer had learned.

"What do I know?" the guard said. He went into a cubicle and put in a call.

A Lear jet came sibilantly skimming in, blinking red.

The guard returned. "Control didn't know anything about it until just now when that Lear complained. What are you guys, psychic or something?"

"We got the call," Gainer said with annoyance.

The guard pressed a button and the electrically controlled gate rolled open.

Vinny drove through and in about a hundred feet. Stopped there. In their side mirrors Gainer and Vinny observed a gasoline tanker behind them stopped at the gate. An eighteen-wheeler. Orange and blue Gulf insignia and AVGAS 100LL painted on it. The guard waved it through. The tanker drove in all the way to the concrete apron, turned left and continued on—along the face of Hangar "D." Most of the doors to the various corporate sections were closed.

The tanker maneuvered and came to a stop on the apron, its front end facing the field. Idled there.

Vinny pulled the bucket-hoist truck up next to the tanker.

"How's your watch?" Gainer asked out his window.

"Six-forty-one," Chapin replied from the cab of the tanker. He was alone. The Gulf tanker was another acquisition by Vinny's people for another five thousand. Taken from an eating stop on Route 1 just outside Bridgeport. It was full when they took it so they'd made a little extra selling its eighty-six hundred gallons half price to an independent service station that was also a numbers office on Queens Boulevard.

"We'll wait until ten to seven," Gainer told Chapin.

Darkness had already come.

It was the best sort of night for a robbery. Clouds had formed a thick ceiling from horizon to horizon, were just hanging there a mile up. The three-quarters moon had no chance of getting through.

A twin-engine propeller job glided in three hundred from where the two trucks stood. It passed from right to left down the runway.

"I don't like this part," Vinny remarked.

Gainer didn't either.

Keeping headlights off, Vinny put the truck in gear and got it rolling. Chapin in the tanker was under way in the larger, longer tanker alongside. They went full-out through the pitch dark, across the apron and over a dry grassy strip onto the taxiing area, guessing where they were merely by the feel of the surface beneath the wheels. It was so dark Gainer had the sensation that they were about to go hurtling off an edge.

Within seconds they were passing over another area of grassy ground. This one wider and slightly depressed for drainage, and Gainer knew from his mental map of the airport that the next hard surface would be the main runway.

He looked off to his right.

Saw the landing lights of a jet on its approach to the runway. Large private jet coming in. Gainer was about to warn Vinny to brake but at that moment their wheels got hard runway and they were committed.

The landing lights of the jet grew wider apart as it came nearer. Like a pair of motorcycles forty feet off the ground. It did not see the two trucks until its beams caught them. It roared as though furious at having them in its way. Its undercarriage cleared the hoist-truck by three feet, the taller tanker by six inches.

"Vehicles on runway!" the jet's pilot radioed the control tower.

An official in a jeep went out on the runway to investigate, but by then the two trucks were on the fringe of the undeveloped area that buffered the airport from the residences on Purchase Street. Letting up on their speed but not stopping, the trucks, in tandem, plowed into the high grass and on through the brush that enveloped them.

Now they turned on their headlights, and Gainer got his bearings.

When he'd been in this area two weeks earlier he'd seen how dense it was, but he hadn't realized there were so many mature trees. The difference, of course, was being on foot and the reduced clearance that required. Now, with the trucks there were few spaces between trees that offered room enough, and several times it was necessary to cut back and go around in order to proceed. Also, the terrain had not seemed so uneven before. The huge trucks went bouncing, grinding, scraping along, few feet by few feet. At one point they came on an outcropping of granite ledge that was impassable, had to back off from it with great difficulty and find another direction. As it turned out that was fortunate, because it brought them to the easier going of a level clearing where they made better time, and then there was only wild sumac that their bumpers crushed down.

All the way to the steel mesh fence.

Gainer got out. He went along the fence. Every dozen or so steps he stopped, shined his flashlight through onto the brick wall of Number 19. When he found where the wall cornered, he used that as his reckoning and knew from the measurements Sweet had provided where it would be best to go over. He paced back along the fence to that point.

Vinny ran the hoist-truck up close parallel to the fence, cut its headlights. Chapin pulled the tanker up behind it.

They removed the white coveralls. Under them everything they had on was black: long-sleeved shirts, jeans, sneakers and a cloth pouch like a bib tied around the back of the neck and twice on each side. To serve as a deep carryall. Gainer had the ASP harnessed on. Chapin, a snub-nosed .38 Magnum. They took a moment to blacken their faces with greasepaint make-up and to pull on black stretch cotton gloves, snug.

Chapin put a tiny object into his right ear. Held it in place with strips of surgical tape. Gainer and Vinny did the same. Those were microcircuit receivers. They worked with separate remote transmitters about half the size of a pack of gum. Each of the transmitters was fixed on an identical frequency, thus anything one of them said would be heard by all. Chapin had designed these little "whisper-coms," as he called them, a couple of years ago as a Christmas gift to Vinny, whose people put them to good use during house break-ins. The receivers, supersensitive as they were and positioned within the ear, picked up the faintest whispers. A shout or scream would split the eardrum.

Chapin checked to see that he had everything he'd need. He lit a cigarette, took three overlapping drags and let it drop. He climbed up onto the bed of the truck and into the hoist's plastic bucket. Attached to the upper edge of the bucket was a control box and lever that allowed Chapin to maneuver the hoist, its rotating base and its arm. He'd had two days' practice with it at the Bedford house, felt he knew fairly well how to handle it.

He started the hoist engine.

Pressed the "rise" button on the control lever. The two sections of the hoist responded, worked like a flexing upper arm and forearm socketed by elbow the way they spread and elevated at the same time. In seconds Chapin was thirty-five feet up.

It seemed from that height that he was practically right above the wall of Number 19. He saw its photoelectric beam alarm running from relay to relay. Forty feet straight ahead was the groundkeeper's shed and the two story garage that it was attached to. Separate, larger, twenty feet off to the left of the garage was the main house, the rear of it, a number of rooms lighted at that moment. What lay between the wall and all else were the gardens and lawns. Veined with fuming sulfuric acid, the lovely blinding gardens and lawns, Chapin thought. It was too dark to make out any of the pathways or beds.

The lower section of the hoist was already angled sharply upward. Chapin reduced the angle somewhat, thus increasing the reach of that section. He used the control lever to rotate the entire hoist a full quarter-turn, brought it around so now he was truly above the wall, in fact, within its perimeter.

One final maneuver.

Most critical.

He lowered the upper arm, angled it downward, took the bucket and himself with it. How far down he could take it depended on clearance of the beam-alarm on the wall. It was difficult to tell the exact distance between the arm and the beam. Chapin pressed in and quickly let up on the lowering button several times, moving little by little. Until he felt he couldn't risk another inch.

He was still quite a ways from the ground and no telling precisely how far from the wall. He had studied Sweet's diagram of the pressure alarm grid. Located seven feet from the wall was a safe four foot wide strip and running off from that a mazelike series of safe lanes. But even Sweet had noted those measurements could be a foot or two incorrect in any direction.

Chapin looked to the ground. It was dark, nothing to go by. He looked to the wall. The black mass of it seemed less and then more than seven feet from him. Diagrams and measurements were useless now, he realized. He thought of using his whisper-com but, then, what good would it do to let Gainer know he was in trouble. It was his own decision. Go or no go.

He wanted a cigarette, a Dewars on the rocks, his cock in some part of a hooker.

He legged over the side of the bucket. Kept hold of the edge. Lowered himself. Hung on for a few seconds, because they might be his last.

Let go.

It was more of a drop than his knees expected. Needle pain shot from his heels to rump when he landed. He almost tumbled over, just did manage to remain upright. He waited, thought perhaps it might take a moment for the sprinklers to start spraying the fuming sulfuric acid.

Warm night bugs were sounding off.

A fragment of music came from a television set.

Chapin took a slow, deep-as-possible breath. By mere chance he was on some safe ground. Now, he had no choice but to find more of it.

The dark structure of the shed. Chapin guessed twenty feet to it. He had only what he remembered of Sweet's diagram to go by.

Four steps ahead. Each time he put his weight down on his forward foot he pictured the sod giving under him, pressing on the ungiving plate of the alarm.

Three steps to the left.

His shins met with low foliage of some sort. Flowers. He knelt, felt the petals. They were mums, a bed of mums. It was what he needed to determine the safeground pattern of the grid. Four cautious steps to the right, then turn right again for three, left for six.

The corner of the shed.

He'd made it.

He glanced up to that second floor above the garage. The alarm monitoring room and the quarters for the security men. Venetian blinds were drawn down on every window. If six men were on duty, as Sweet had said, six more were probably hanging around up there. Practically over his head.

His next step crunched gravel.

His next avoided that by keeping closer to the side of the shed. He made his way to the barnlike doors of it, oppositely hinged doors that could be swung open left and right. They were kept closed by a common hasp and a metal pin on a chain. After all, it was only a groundkeeper's shed. Chapin opened the door, slipped inside, pulled the door closed behind him.

Total darkness.

Chapin clicked on his flashlight that was not much larger than a roll of Life Savers but gave off a strong directional beam. A simple twist of its front collar changed its beam to a wide angle flood. He played the light around the shed.

One windowless room, twenty feet by twenty feet. Concrete floor. It smelled of fertilizers, insecticides and mildew. There was a large tractor mower and a couple of wheelbarrows. All sorts of gardening equipment hung neatly in place from the aged bare wood studs of the walls. Only the wall that adjoined the garage was Sheetrocked.

Along that wall was a workbench. Chapin went to it, cleared an area and climbed up, kneeled on it. He measured with the nine and a half inch spread of his hand, thumb to little finger, to determine where he should make the cut.

A thump from somewhere above made him pause. He heard heavy footsteps, the dribble of someone urinating, a toilet flush. That close.

The knife he used on the three-quarter inch thick Sheetrock was sharp enough to cut hair. He sliced out a foot square section, exposing pipes running vertically, two of copper, one of steel. The copper pipes were for water, Chapin knew. The other, the steel pipe, was the one he wanted. It was three inches in diameter.

He started on it. With a wire saw. A thirty inch length of steel wire coated with diamond particles and with a ring on each end. So sharp merely running one's fingers lightly along it would draw blood. He wound the wire once around the pipe, inserted his forefingers through the rings and kept tension on the wire. Pulled the wire saw one way then the other, just slightly. It made a faint gritting sound as it bit easily into the pipe.

Within five minutes Chapin had a section of the pipe cut away. It contained four sets of vinyl-covered electrical circuits. Red, green, blue, yellow. The circuits of the four alarms: the wall, the rear grounds, the roof of the main house and the upper hallway of the north wing. They connected individually into the console in the monitoring room above.

Chapin stripped the vinyl outer coating from the red circuit, exposing a black covered wire and a white covered wire. He separated the two, placed a device about the size and shape of a container of Four X condoms—Chapin smiled at the thought—between them. It had a clamp along one side that Chapin led the white wire through.

If successful, the device would neutralize the circuit by intercepting it, cause it to loop itself and function apparently as though it were connected all the way to the alarm.

Chapin abruptly squeezed the clamp shut. Its sharp metal teeth pierced and made contact with the enclosed live wire.

In the room above on the monitoring console the red light that corresponded with that circuit blinked once. The security man on duty at the console thought nothing of it. Birds and squirrels, a falling branch sometimes caused such brief blinks.

Chapin, working methodically, repeated the process with the blue circuit.

Crunch of gravel.

Someone just outside.

Chapin cut his light and let himself down from the workbench. Noiselessly he moved to the tractor mower, squatted behind it.

The security man on a routine round had noticed the metal pin removed from the hasp on the door to the shed. It was his acquired nature to be suspicious of even such a minor thing. He stepped inside the shed, shined his flashlight around. It cut through the dark above Chapin's head, ran along the assortment of gardening implements, across the wall above the workbench, passed over the hole in it that Chapin had cut. Came back to the hole. The security man walked over to examine it closer.

That put him on the other side of the tractor mower, six feet from Chapin. With the remnants of the stripped-off plastic and the section of cut away pipe and the exposed wires, the security man did not know exactly what he was looking at, obviously tampering of some sort. He had his back to Chapin.

Chapin stood.

The security man was about to turn and go to notify someone when Chapin took two swift, silent steps to him. In practically the same motion, Chapin looped the wire saw over the man's head and yanked at the loops on the ends of it.

The man's chin went up reflexively.

His back arched and he went up on his toes.

His arms tried to bring his hands up but before they could, the diamond-coated wire sliced into him. Cut easily through thyroid cartilage, severed the trachea, the esophagus and the common carotid artery.

The only sounds that came from the man were a sort of vacuum noise, like a croak from a frog followed by a slight plosive puff as his lungs let go air.

Chapin released the wire saw, eased the dead man down the front of him to the floor. He had been ready to kill tonight, but hadn't thought it would be necessary. It was the first time for him and it had been a gruesome way, although swift. A saving thing was how impersonal it had been because of the dark. At least he hadn't seen his victim's face.

Chapin decided it was best he settle for as much as he'd accomplished there, get out before someone else came looking. He found an aluminum stepladder, took it out with him. He closed the door, inserted the metal pin into the hasp, went around the shed to its more concealed side. Set up the ladder there and climbed it to gain the roof of the shed.

Now he used his whisper-com.

Reported that he had managed to neutralize the red and the blue circuits, the alarms on the perimeter wall and the roof of the main house. The other alarms were still hot.

Gainer heard.

Gainer was busy with the slides.

Six slides of twelve feet long by two feet wide, and two curved sections. They were molded identically so that they stacked compactly one in the other. They'd been easy to bring along, covered by a tarpaulin on the bed of the hoist truck.

Gainer had tried eight places before he located the slides in Brooklyn on Cleremont Avenue near the old navy yard. At a company called Elite Products. They were part of an order all packed and ready for shipment to a regular customer in Tucson. However, Gainer had gotten across how extremely important they were to him by coming up with five hundred extra around the deal, and Elite had broken them out.

They were swimming pool slides.

The ordinary backyard sort. Not the metal supports, just the plastic slide part. An eighth-inch of fiberglass laminated on both sides by a sixteenth of an inch of PVC, polyvinyl chloride. The slides had raised and rounded edges down each side, and their sliding surface was coated slick with polyurethane, which made them particularly slippery when wet.

Gainer unloaded the slides, laid three of them separately end to end where the ground was most level. He pried open the gallon can of PVC solvent cement he'd bought at the hardware store in Bedford. Using a wide paintbrush he slathered the viscous substance on the ends of two sections of slide. The underside of one, the upperside of the other. Immediately, the special chemical ingredients in the cement, the tetrahydrofuran and the cyclohexanone, caused the surfaces of the PVC to rise in temperature to the point where its chains of polymer molecules were moving about as a solution.

Gainer joined the cement-covered ends of the two sections, overlapped them six inches. Once the surfaces came into contact it was impossible to pull them apart; the adhesive power of the cement was that strong that quickly. Within minutes the solvent base of the cement was completely evaporated, the surfaces of the PVC coiled and hardened, leaving their molecular structure merged. It was as though they had been originally formed into a single piece. The shearing stress of the bonded joint was five thousand pounds per square inch. An elephant could walk on it.

Meanwhile, Vinny folded in the bucket and arms of the hoist-truck and moved the truck out of the way. Drove the gasoline tanker forward into position close alongside the steel mesh-wire fench. With a pair of leveraged two-handed cutters he snipped out a sizable opening in the fence.

Gainer had, by then, cemented three sections of slide, made them into a thirty-six foot length. That much of a length weighed only one hundred and sixty-three pounds but was unwieldy. He lifted one end, propped it up on the side of the tanker. Vinny went up to the top of the tanker and Gainer went through the hole in the fence, climbed to the top of Number 19's wall. He was standing right in the wide-eyeing beam of the photovoltaic alarm that Chapin had neutralized. He peered down from the wall to the darkness of the grounds, knew, according to what Chapin had said, that the subsurface pressure alarm grid was still on. He had to admire Chapin for having dared it. He looked toward the shed, thirty-some feet away where Chapin was supposed to be now. Couldn't make him out in the darkness.

After a moment the directional beam of Chapin's flashlight blinked twice, providing Gainer with a fix.

Vinny pulled the slide up to himself and fed it from the top of the tanker across to Gainer on the wall. Gainer in turn fed it hand-over-hand across the wider area to Chapin. He felt when Chapin took hold of it. Chapin laid it on the roof of the shed. Gainer used his whisper-com, told Chapin to take two more feet of it if he could. Chapin did, and now Gainer's end was resting precisely on the wall. Vinny handed another section of slide up to him. Gainer attached it to complete the span from shed to wall to tanker. Forty-eight feet overall.

Gainer went up the slide.

Carried along the two curved sections and cement. He didn't allow the idea of falling off to enter his mind, pretended he was just going up a ramp at Madison Square Garden. Step after step, his sneakers never entirely lost contract with the polyurethaned surface. When he reached the roof of the shed Chapin unloaded him.

No time to waste.

They each made several more trips down and back up the slide, bringing what they would need. Then they set to work on creating the final span. They joined two sections of slide. Lifted that twenty-four foot length and held it straight up. Moved it to the edge of the shed's roof, placed it down and wedged their feet against it to keep it from back-slipping. Aimed it, lowered it slowly and finally felt the end of it out there in the dark come down and settle upon the slant of the slate roof of the north wing of the main house. They tested it, gingerly at first, found that it wobbled. A slight shift to the right made it steady.

Footsteps below.

Leather heels on the concrete driveway.

A pair of security men making rounds, playing their flashlights here and there, sometimes upward. Gainer and Leslie had painted the underside of the slides black in case of such a situation, but there was still the chance that the security men might shine their lights upward and make out something that shouldn't be there.

They were directly below now, close by the entrance to the shed. Perhaps they'd miss their fellow guard, would enter the shed and find him. Chapin had briefly related the killing to Gainer while they were down in the tanker, explained why he'd been able to loop only two of the alarm circuits.

Both Gainer and Chapin breathed shallow and quietly as they stood on the edge of the shed roof above the two security men. Gainer had drawn his ASP with silencer on, would shoot the moment either man's fingers went for the door.

One of the men tucked his flashlight into his armpit, held it there while he fussed with something.

Gainer and Chapin heard the tear and crinkle of paper and noisy chewing.

The man, eating a candy bar, took his flashlight in hand again, proceeded with his partner to the steps of the rear terrace and disappeared.

Gainer and Chapin went back at it. They joined the two curved sections of slide and, after some adjustment, overlapped those in place. The angles and lengths Chapin and Gainer had calculated on paper seemed correct now that they'd been applied. A continuous slide with a ninety degree turn in it ran all the way from the tanker up to the north wing.

Gainer was first to try the twenty feet up to the higher main house roof. It was steeper going, and he had to climb in a crouch, thankful for the better grip of the better deck sneakers Leslie had bought to replace the Converse All-Stars he'd been ready to go with. Up he went to step off onto the slate roof and find it also steeper than he'd anticipated. He couldn't stand upright on it, got traction with the toes of his sneakers, squatted forward to the roof and made his way along it to the nearby chimney. Tall thick chimney.

Gainer used it to stand and lean against, pausing a moment to take stock. He wondered how far he was from those billions at that moment. No more than six feet was his guess. Merely a layer or two of roof and a couple of other obstacles between him and a long life, rich with Leslie. Don't count your chickens, he told himself, they're still only eggs.

Chapin came up.

Bringing ropes and pulleys. He left those with Gainer and made three more difficult trips for the two-by-fours.

Gainer measured from the base of the chimney and from the edge of the roof to determine the point of entry. Kneeling, he brought from his bib carryall a bar of steel like a strap-iron—only a sixteenth of an inch thick but unbendable. It was fourteen inches long and two inches wide. An inch of one end was turned up bluntly ninety degrees. The other end was tapered. About an inch from the tapered end were two deep V-shaped notches. One on each side. The edges of the notches were filed blade-sharp.

Gainer placed the tapered end of the steel bar in under one of the slate shingles, pried and jammed the bar in under. The shingle loosened. The V-shaped notch of the bar caught on one of the nails that held the shingle. Gainer tapped on the blunt end of the bar with a leather-covered hammer to sever the nail. The shingle was nailed in two places. He severed the second nail and then was able to wiggle the shingle, worked it free. He'd found out from an old roofer how to do that.

He removed twelve slate shingles in this manner, exposing an area about three and a half feet square.

Paused for a moment.

Heard television.

The unmistakable commentaries of Frank and Don and Howard doing a Thursday night special version of ABC Monday Night Football. The Steelers playing the Dolphins in Miami. It made Gainer consider where he was at that moment: on the high roof of a mansion in Westchester going for three billion. It made him feel strangely detached. He countered that to some degree with the reality that he had picked Miami to beat the spread of three and a half. The sound of the television, he noticed, was coming from an open window of the security staff's quarters. Good. Any noises he or the others made during the robbery were less likely to be heard.

He went back to it.

Ripped away the layer of tar paper to get at the subroofing. Planks three-quarter-inch-thick butted and nailed in place. Exactly what he'd expected from going over the architectural plans of Number 19. The planking was pine aged hard, but the wood chisel Gainer used was a good one, especially sharp, and it took deep bites from the wood. He chiseled away without letup, inspired all the more by the thought that when he'd cut through the planks what he might see was Leslie's face.

EARLIER that day Leslie had shown up at Number 19. Just drifted in on Darrow complaining that she was parched, would he please have mercy and mix something tall and original and not too weak for her?

Darrow was delighted, considered it a good omen that she should arrive at that exact moment when his mind was sorting through his various better prospects. He obliged by concocting what he called a Sacré-Coeur Swizzle, a combination of absinthe, Burgundy and lime juice.

They sat in the drawing room on cream silk damask in front of a dead cold fireplace.

Leslie said she hadn't been heard from for the last couple of weeks because she'd been away. With her husband.

Darrow responded as though that was the most forgivable of all possible excuses. "How is he?" he asked.

"Who?"

"Mr. Pickering."

"The same," Leslie replied.

That was the subject Darrow wanted to keep on, but Leslie casually inquired after Gainer.

"Andrew is out of town."

A little sigh of disappointment from Leslie.

"He's in Europe on the new job I arranged for him," Darrow told her.

"You put him to work?"

"Yes." Reluctantly.

"That was large of you."

"You mean that?"

"Certainly."

"Then you're not upset? I thought you might be."

"Quite the contrary. I'm pleased. It's high time Gainer found something other to do than me."

Darrow concealed his smirky feeling with motion, picked a speck of dust from his impeccable white antelope shoes.

"I hope the job pays well," Leslie said. "He's extravagant, you know, spends like a demon."

"I would have thought as much."

"Of course, that's not bad," Leslie said, "when one has it."

Truer words were never spoken, Darrow believed.

By six o'clock Leslie had him jumping through conversational hoops. She pitied the ferns and floral arrangements she emptied her Sacré-Coeur Swizzles into when Darrow wasn't looking.

She acted tipsy and tipsier.

Darrow moved from the matching *étage* across the way to the one Leslie was on, took her hand and called her a "beautiful friend," said how much he hoped he could count on her.

Oh, he could, she told him, he could count and count and count.

Well, then . . .

She developed a headache.

Was her room still hers?

Just as she'd left it.

She went up to it, on the way tossing over her shoulder to Darrow that she shouldn't be disturbed unless the house was in flames and then only if it was her part of the house.

A half hour later she was seated at the window of her room watching the day give way to night. She had changed into black: jeans, shirt, sneakers and carryall bib. Her hair was tightly contained by a black kerchief tied and pinned. Her face blackened. She had the receiver for her whisper-com in her ear. Her ASP harnessed on.

She waited ten minutes for a margin.

Used the time to check if she had everything. The squirmy sack, as she called it, in her carryall didn't bother her much, almost not at all. She felt it squirm just then against her stomach. Lots of the fears of women were merely traditional, she thought.

She cracked the door, glanced out.

To the left, to the right.

That wide upper hallway of the south wing was dim, lighted only by the special little bulbs directed on the paintings—the Winslow Homers and Gilbert Stuarts and James Whistlers—along the way.

She stepped out into the hall, hurried, kept the Persian runner under-foot. At the corner to the upper landing she paused for a peek around. The landing ran the entire length of the house, was better lighted. It was empty now but what would she say if she ran into Darrow or someone else—that she was on her way to a self-improvement class in mugging?

Her pace along the upper landing was close to a jog.

As she was nearing the corner of the north wing a voice stopped her. It took her a moment to realize she was hearing Chapin on the whisper-com, saying he'd been unable to neutralize the yellow circuit, the one that corresponded to the sonar alarm in the hallway leading to The Balance room. In another second she would have rounded the corner and walked right into it. All hell would have broken loose.

What to do now? Her end of the plan was vital. All of Gainer's, Chapin's and Vinny's efforts would be for nothing without what she had in her carryall. Perhaps, she thought, Gainer had decided to call off the robbery.

Better ask.

She brought out her whisper-com transmitter. "Is it still a go?"

No reply.

Was her transmitter on? Perhaps she wasn't holding it correctly. She whispered the same question into it. Again, no reply. Apparently something was wrong with the transmitter. She had accidentally dropped it on the marble floor in the bathroom while getting ready. That must have knocked it out. She'd have to rely on her intuition. Improvise. Try another way of beating the sonar alarm.

Vinny had told her how burglars often went one on one with such alarms. He'd told her about a guy he knew, an experienced wise-guy, who had succeeded in going up three flights of stairs and landings in a townhouse peppered with active sonars to get to a million dollars worth of jewelry. By simply doing what Vinny called The Sonar Shuffle.

Leslie took off her sneakers, shoved them in her carryall.

From Sweet's information she recalled that the first ten feet of that north wing hall were not covered by the alarm. She looked down the hall, saw the door to The Balance Room at the far end of it, forty feet away. She saw the alarm units, two subtle panels about eight inches square inset opposite to each other in the walls. Thirty feet from her. She hoped Sweet was right. She took two semi-giant steps.

Her destination was the second room on the left, well within the sonar's range. She'd have to go about three yards to it. The door to that room was closed. How would she handle that?

Get there first.

Doing The Sonar Shuffle.

It meant keeping her entire body rigid while using her lower legs to slip her feet along. Sort of like a mime doing a mechanical doll routine but without jerky movements. Slow motion, as slow as possible, so as not to disturb the air.

Her stockinged feet slid nicely on the surface of the Persian carpet runner. She kept her eyes on the alarm unit down the way. It had a tiny red light on its frame. As long as the light was out, she was doing okay. If it came on she had failed. One abrupt motion would spoil everything.

So far so good.

How far had she come?

She just did catch herself from turning her head to see, moved only her eyes.

Four feet so far, six to go.

It seemed she'd been shuffling for hours.

Her scalp was perspiring, so were her upper lip and underarms and everything. She felt wet all over, except her mouth was dry.

She hadn't traveled a straight line, rather a diagonal one, as though the wall was irresistible, its support a tempting relief from the strain. Her heels were only an inch or two from the edge of the runner. She kept shuffling and then felt the bare floor beneath her, the varnished and well-waxed oak floor.

Slicker, an advantage for her.

She remained in place for a long moment. Decided she would let her mind do more of the work. Instead of concentrating on the unpredictability of that little red light and thinking that it was so sensitive to the mere stir of the air, she would have her mind lock the rest of herself into the required posture, dictate to every part of her that it was impossible to move any faster than the alarm allowed. Meanwhile, on a more superficial level, she would think of other relative but not threatening things. Such as how everyone all their lives went scurrying about causing invisible collisions and never gave it a thought. For instance, when a person moved just one step the space he had just vacated had to refill with air. Air rushed in from all sides, dashed against itself and caused shock waves that on some infinite Richterlike scale never entirely diminished. Maybe that was the reason she liked to drive so fast, all the more to stir up more things. Hell, every move Joan of Arc or Madame DuBarry made was still vibrating around somewhere.

The entrance to the room.

She'd reached it.

She had an urge to jump on in.

She slow-motioned her hand to the doorknob, rotated the knob gradually, pushed the door open, degree-by-degree. It was tricky, seemed the most difficult part of all because she had to extend her arm completely to open the door enough.

Once again, then, The Sonar Shuffle. Over the slick threshold and into the room. In the same extremely slow, deliberate manner she closed the door.

She felt like collapsing in a heap with relief but she also felt like doing a fast run around the room. She stood there in the dark and shook herself vigorously from head to toe to fingertip, sort of the way a dog does to reorganize its coat. Gave her head a couple of extra shakes to snap back to normal speed. She was pleased with herself for what she'd just done, with her patience and nerve. She'd tell Gainer about it later, of course, but wished he'd been there to witness it.

The squirmy sack inside her carryall made its presence felt.

She clicked on her flashlight and went to the closet—a walk-in closet with some wire hangers lonely on the clothes rack, a three-step ladder for reaching the high shelves that were now bare except for a spare blanket that smelled of moth balls.

She shined the light on the ceiling. And there it was, exactly as the architectural plans had promised. A small, not obvious trap door. From the floor to the trap door was eight feet. The stepladder helped with two and a half feet of that. Standing on the top of the ladder Leslie pressed upward on the trap door. She'd expected it would just pop open, but evidently no one had used it in many years and coats of paint held it tight in place. She pushed more and then with all her might and with the top of her head as well. The trap door grudgingly gave way.

Holding the little flashlight between her teeth, she pulled herself up through the opening. Put the trap door back into place, shined her light around.

It wasn't an attic, rather a crawl space between the rooms of the north wing and the roof. Isolated from similar areas elsewhere in the house. There was about a four feet clearance at the highest point, tapering with the slant of the roof to no clearance along the exterior edge. Sturdy two-by-eight joists ran crosswise every two feet. The spaces between the joists were packed with fiberglass insulation. Overhead were the two-by-eight rafters that supported the roof. These also were set two feet apart. Leslie noticed the sharp ends of nails where they'd been hammered through the subroof planks about a half inch. The long-uncirculated air smelled of dust.

In a crouch, Leslie made her way from joist to joist to where she knew she was surely over The Balance Room. She determined an exact spot by measuring from the nearby chimney and from the outside edge of the crawl space. There, she used a well-honed pocketknife to cut away a large section of the fiberglass insulation, threw the yellow puffy mass and its brown paper wrapping aside.

Exposed now down between the joists was the smooth, gray surface of a Sheetrock panel.

Leslie was glad to see that. On the blueprints the architect had specified three coats of plaster over lathing and mesh. Apparently, when The Balance rooms had been renovated to suit their special purpose it had been necessary to tear down the original ceilings, and then it was decided its current-day counterpart would suffice.

That was luck.

Sheetrock was now going to make this part easier.

Leslie went to work at it.

Tested the thickness of the Sheetrock by pressing into it the point of a pin from her kerchief. Found it to be about three-quarters of an inch thick.

She was careful not to go quite that deep with her knife, scoring through the face paper and into the white, powdery core of the Sheetrock, creating a potential hole two feet by four feet. A short way from that she repeated the process for a second hole only an inch and a half in diameter.

That done, she switched off the flashlight and sat waiting. The two inch edge of a joist was hard on her bottom, cut off circulation, made her feet tingle. She refused to think she was waiting unnecessarily, that Gainer, Chapin and Vinny had retreated to the house in Bedford. Gainer wouldn't do that to her.

Ten interminable minutes.

She heard something hard and flat come down on the roof just above her. It scraped a little across the slate shingles. Then, footsteps on the roof that had to be his.

She stood on a joist, her head tilted up, only inches from the subroof, anticipating. Soon shreds of wood were falling on her face, and when there was hardly a large enough hole made she raised up on her toes, offered her mouth up. For the kiss that was taken. A long kiss, all things considered.

It was him all right.

Gainer and Chapin pried the planks away. The hole they made in the roof was above where Leslie had scored the Sheetrock. Above both holes Chapin had clamped together the various lengths of two-by-fours. He had braced them against the chimney in such a way that they formed a sturdy superstructure to which he attached a tackle arrangement of nylon lines and pulleys.

Gainer handed down to Leslie a shoebox containing dry ice. And a bundle of laundry bags, black nylon mesh bags each eighteen inches wide, thirty inches deep, with a nylon cord threaded through four grommets at the neck so it could be drawn closed and tied.

Gainer and Chapin lowered themselves down into the crawl space.

It started to rain. Not much, just a light sprinkle.

Gainer took a moment to check that they had everything they would need. They kneeled on the joists. Leslie brought out the squirmy sack. It was a flannel drawstring sack in Tiffany light blue with the Tiffany name discreetly on it. Originally, six years ago, a pair of engraved sterling shoetrees had come in it, a little nothing-something from Rodger.

Chapin finished cutting the small hole Leslie had started, the one and a half inch hole. He lifted away the little round cutout piece of Sheetrock. It was cut on the inward slant, so it fitted like a plug.

Leslie brought out a plastic baggy, unwound its twist tie and removed two Carr's water biscuit crackers and an inch square piece of aged ten-year-old Vermont cheddar cheese. She crushed one of the crackers into crumbs, broke off a few shreds of the cheese. Dropped some of each down through the ceiling hole.

Then the squirmy sack.

"Want me to do that?" Gainer asked.

Leslie didn't bother to answer, pulled the drawstring sack open, reached in and tenderly enclosed a live thing within her fingers.

A *Mus musculus.*

A house mouse.

It fit easily headfirst into the hole, and when Leslie let its sleek little shape slip from her hand she tried not to think that the creature was plunging an equivalent of fifty stories. It landed awkwardly, but without injury, on the floor of The Balance Room below. Any discomfort it suffered was offset by its immediate discovery of the superb cheese and crackers.

Chapin put the Sheetrock plug back into place.

In twenty seconds the heat sensor alarm unit reacted to the body temperature of the mouse. The alarm gave off an electrical squeal.

At that moment, in his second floor sitting room in the south wing, Darrow was in a Sulka robe and slippers watching the Steelers play the Dolphins in Miami. He had taken the three and a half points, bet the Steelers for a dime, in other words a thousand. Already he was a couple

319

of touchdowns behind and the Dolphins were on the twelve yard line going for more. Darrow felt he'd been sucked in, personally misled by Bradshaw and the whole old bunch from Pittsburgh. He had that enraged, futile, nearly bilious feeling of a bad loser. Andrew, he thought, would have probably told him to bet Miami.

The squeal of the heat sensor alarm jumped Darrow. He hurried into the adjoining room, got a .380 automatic from the top drawer of his nightstand. In the lower drawer was a telephone. He didn't have to lift the receiver, merely work the touch-tone dial. Dab out the tonal code that only he knew, the eight digits that would electronically, automatically release the elaborate bolting device of The Balance Room door at this hour. He rushed out and down the hall, coverged with five security men on the run up the main stairs. They had automatic rifles at the ready. They went ahead of Darrow along the hallway of the north wing to the closed door of the vault. Two security men flattened out against one wall, two against the other. Darrow ducked into one of the regular rooms for cover. The fifth security man warily approached The Balance Room door, shoved it open abruptly and in the same motion stepped aside, out of line of possible fire.

After a long moment, two of the security men charged into The Balance Room. Within seconds the lights were turned on in there and the two men appeared in the doorway with their automatic weapons relaxed, gesturing that all was safe. They shut off the squeal of the alarm and went back to their regular duties.

Hine and Sweet appeared on the scene. They followed Darrow down the hall and into The Balance Room. Darrow now had the superior air of an inspector.

The mouse had scurried beneath a lower shelf when he heard all that rushing about. However, he wasn't about to be denied the first delicacy he'd had in days. He came back out and hoped he'd be overlooked there on his haunches in the middle of The Balance Room floor, nibbling on cheese and crackers as fast as his jaws would allow.

Darrow was actually relieved when he saw the creature, but he didn't let it show, decided it was an opportunity to piss on certain people. He turned on Hine and Sweet.

"I've had it with you," he told Hine.

"What the hell did I do now?"

"Both of you," Darrow said, including Sweet with a glance.

"We were down in the library going over next week's carries—"

"I've told you time and time again there was to be no eating up here," Darrow said, gritting. "Now we've got mice, look at the goddamn mouse!"

The mouse had one eye on them. Only his mouth was moving.

"I can't depend on *anyone.*" Darrow even raised his voice. He brought his right hand from the pocket of his robe, pretended to forget that he had the .380 automatic pistol in it. He gestured wildly, underscoring the words. "I especially can't depend on you, Hine. You're obviously intent on fucking things up. I don't care how many degrees you've got, you're only smart where the skin's off. I swear I'm going to have you replaced," Darrow said, and then added just ominously enough ". . . or something."

Hine and Sweet couldn't help but duck away from Darrow's jerks and waves of the automatic. What made it so bad was if it went off and blew one of them away, Darrow wouldn't even be punished.

"I'm to blame," Hine said.

"Then catch the fucking mouse," Darrow told him.

Hine got a carton from the collating area.

The mouse, with a jawful of cheddar, almost evaded the inverted carton that was dropped over him.

Hine slipped a piece of cardboard under the carton and handed the whole thing to Sweet, who promised to do away with the creature.

"I ought to make you eat it," Darrow said.

Sweet shrugged, as though that might not be worse than a lot of other things.

They left the north wing. Darrow returned to his bedroom, put the .380 automatic back into the drawer and performed the tonal sequence code that rebolted The Balance Room door. Went into his sitting room, heard the lopsided score in favor of Miami. Thought he might go pay a bedroom visit to Mrs. Pickering. The young Andrew came to mind. A comparison by Mrs. Pickering would be unavoidable. Darrow decided he wasn't up to it tonight. He clicked on the Betamax to watch a Vittorio Gassman film. He'd seen it several times. He had about every film that Italian actor ever appeared in. Someone had once told Darrow he resembled Gassman.

In the crawl space, Gainer, Leslie and Chapin had overheard every move and word that they and the mouse had caused. As soon as Darrow closed the door to The Balance Room a faint whirring sound began. It was the air cooling system down there. Gainer had timed it, until it shut off, found that it took two minutes and forty-eight seconds for it to lower the temperature of the air in the rooms to sixty-eight degrees—the point at which the heat sensor alarms automatically reset.

Chapin removed the Sheetrock plug.

Leslie dropped more cheese and cracker crumbs down through it.

And three more mice.

Again, after mere seconds, the alarm began its squeal.

Again, the five security men came on the run with their automatic rifles. Darrow, only momentarily startled by the sound, didn't bother with his automatic pistol this time, merely touched off the tonal combination to release the locking mechanism of The Balance Rooms and went down the hall in a quick but unhurried pace.

By the time he arrived on the scene the security men were already inside The Balance Rooms. Their report to Darrow was more mice.

Darrow was no longer in the mood for histrionics. He merely let Hine know with his clipped, harsh tone that this compounded his feelings. He instructed Hine to arrange for an exterminator in the morning and meanwhile to somehow get rid of those three mice that were sitting there on the floor enjoying a late snack. Notify him when they had, so he could lock up the damned place.

Darrow returned to his rooms and the Gassman film.

The mice, with no holes to retreat into, just scurried about and hid behind the legs of things. It took Hine and Sweet ten minutes on their hands and knees to capture them. They left The Balance Rooms, closed the door behind them.

The air cooler went on again.

At once Chapin and Gainer began cutting all the way through the Sheetrock where Leslie had scored the two-foot-by-four-foot hole. It went fast, easy, they simply broke most of it away with their hands.

They had a length of half-inch rope attached to one of the roof rafters. Dropped that ten feet down into the room.

Gainer slipped down the rope.

Then Chapin.

Leslie tossed down the shoebox of dry ice.

The half-inch-by-five-inch squares of dry ice were individually contained in heavy clear plastic bags.

The heat sensor alarm units were where Sweet had said they'd be, two pair of them on the ceiling and the wall above the door in each area —storage and collating. The units were disc-shaped, four inches in diameter, raised in concentric layers around a half-inch opening in the center.

Hurry.

Racing against the cooling system.

The air in the rooms was already chilling down.

Gainer kicked away some money and stepped up onto a shelf to reach the heat sensors in the money room. Chapin climbed up on the counter in the collating area to get at the units there. The dry ice within the heavy plastic bags was difficult to handle, so cold it stuck to their fingers, burned. They used staple guns from their carryalls to attach the bags to the ceiling and walls around each of the heat sensor units, shot in staple after staple until the units were entirely covered by several layers of the dry ice. Just did get done when the air cooler went off and the alarm reset.

With one hundred and sixty degrees below zero to contend with the heat sensor alarms would not be picking up any body temperatures this night.

Leslie dropped down the bundle of laundry bags and the tackle line with a good-sized blunt hook on the end of it.

Gainer and Chapin took a moment to get the feel of where they were. Their awe silently rotated them in place. The sheaf upon sheaf of stack after stack on shelf after shelf.

Of money.

Floor to ceiling, wall to wall money.

Three billion dollars of it.

How's this for stealing, Norma?

"Get *packing*," Leslie whispered from above to break the spell.

It was ten-three when Gainer spread open the mouth of the first laundry bag and tossed in the first half million. He did not overload the bag, only put about three million in it so that at sixty pounds it would be easy to handle. He drew its nylon cord closed, knotted the cord and slipped it onto the hook.

Leslie was up on the roof. The rain was a bit more than a sprinkle now. She drew on the tackle line, brought it up hand over hand to herself. The pulley made it practically effortless for her. Like drawing a drapery.

The sixty pound bag came up through the roof and out. When it neared the top of the pulley, Leslie needed only to give it a slight push with her foot to swing it over and transfer it to the slide.

Quickly she undid the hook.

The first three million went zooming down.

The rain on the slide's polyurethane surface increased slickness. The bag was probably doing thirty miles an hour when it took the ninety degree banked curve at the roof of the shed and continued on down the longer, less steep portion of the slide to Vinny.

Vinny had moved the truck so it was in perfect position with the slide. He was up on the flat ramp that ran the entire length of the tanker's compartments. Gasoline fumes were rising thick from them, making Vinny feel a bit heady.

The first bag flew off the slide.

Vinny stopped its momentum and let it drop through the open hatch, heard the slight percussive thump as it hit bottom inside the empty metal tanker. It was difficult for Vinny to accept that what had just passed through his hands was three million. He didn't have much time to think about it because here came another.

By midnight two hundred and forty million dollars had been packed, pulleyed up, slid down and dropped into the belly of the tanker.

Vinny moved the tanker so the slide fed to the next compartment.

Leslie and Chapin traded responsibilities, just so she could be down there with Gainer for a while. She gave Gainer a swig of Tupelo honey, a half teaspoon of cayenne and a couple of squirts of Rescue before they got going again.

Gainer had the packing of the laundry bags down to a system that wasted no motion. He swept the sheaves of money off the shelves with his forearm, and if some happened to miss the mouth of the bag, he didn't bother with it. The only trouble was that by now a layer of money was underfoot, most of it torn from its bindings and scattered around. To make matters worse, the rain that fell through the hole in the roof and ceiling was causing a lot of the loose hundreds to become soggy, mushy as *papier-mâché*.

By two A.M. most of the shelves were still stacked neatly, untouched. They had managed to get only five hundred million or so into the tanker.

Leslie was working like a woman possessed.

During a pause Gainer observed her hard at it and wondered if being surrounded by such an enormous amount of cash had caused her to have an acute, intense attack of the *monies*. She must have felt his eyes on her because she glanced his way and blew him three rapid kisses, one with the tip of her tongue out. However, her hands never let up on the money.

Gainer knew, of course, he was required to steal a lot of The Balance, not necessarily all of it. What they had already would be enough.

Chapin suggested that when he came down to switch responsibilities with Leslie again.

Gainer was tired, sweating, had worked harder than any of them, but he wanted to keep at it, was determined to get away with as many millions as possible. He had his mind set on no less than a billion.

At six A.M. they had to stop.

Chapin climbed up the rope.

Gainer took a final look around at the empty shelves and those still neatly stacked, untouched. He estimated they'd gotten about a third of what had been there. He climbed the rope and joined Chapin and Leslie on the roof.

Chapin was the first to take the slide down. He just got up into it and let go. Next thing he knew he was on the tanker ramp with Vinny.

Leslie was next. She kept hold of the edges of the slide, spread her legs and angled them over the edges left and right to brake herself. It took some doing, but she slid down the slick steep a foot or two at a time to the curved section. Rolled off the slide onto the roof of the shed.

Gainer got onto the slide and let himself go deadweight, swooshed full-out all the way to the tanker.

Its hatches were closed, ready to go.

Vinny, behind the steering wheel, had the engine idling. Chapin was next to him. Gainer swung down to the cab and climbed in.

The tanker started mowing down saplings and undergrowth.

Leslie remained on the roof of the shed until she felt sure the tanker was under way. She could see only the upward flare of its headlights moving beyond the high wall. The sound of its engine, baffled by the wall, seemed a long way off.

Dawn was coming on.

Everything turning gray, becoming defined.

Leslie noticed some black, humpy shapes in a flowerbed beneath the span of the slide, halfway to the wall. Laundry bags of money, several that had apparently taken the curve too fast and been flung off by momentum. If even one of the bags had landed in a sensitive area of the pressure alarm grid . . .

Leslie climbed down the stepladder to the ground, hesitated there to remove a small black bundle the size of her fist from her carryall. She unsnapped it, shook it and helped it blossom out into yards and yards of a full-cut, practically weightless rain cape. She inserted her head through its opening, and the fabric fell around her, enveloping her.

Removed her gloves.

Used those to quickly wipe the black make-up from her face.

Then she stepped out from behind the shed and walked around to the front of the house to her Corniche. Got in, started it up, took an appraising look at herself in the mirror on the sun visor. She'd missed some black around her nose and neck. Wiped it away with a tissue. Yanked the kerchief from her head, shook her hair loose and combed it with the fingers of one hand while her other hand steered the winding drive down to the gatehouse.

The security man on duty there saw her coming, recognized her, her car. Nevertheless he glanced at the current "Allowed and Expected" list and found she was on it. He did not think it unusual that she would be leaving that early. "Allowed and Expected" people came and went at all hours at Number 19, didn't they?

CHAPTER
NINETEEN

DARROW stood in The Balance Room, soggy money squishing beneath the soles of his white buck shoes. "Sweet Jesus," he murmured.

Hine had discovered the robbery when he'd routinely let the collators in at eight. He immediately summoned Darrow, not telling him what was wrong because he wanted the pleasure of Darrow's reaction.

Darrow put his hand on Hine's arm to steady himself.

Hine drew his arm away.

"Get security up here," Darrow said to everyone. His voice had more *please* than authority in it. His eyes traveled up the knotted rope to the opening in the ceiling, the opening in the roof, the sky.

The clouds that had been solid for the last twenty-four hours chose that moment to break and display some blue high above them. Darrow did not like the looks of it.

"How much do you think is missing?" he asked Hine.

Hine did a little shrug with his hand. "It'll have to be counted."

"Will you do that for me?"

"Glad to," Hine said.

"Better not touch anything until security's had a look."

Darrow closed his eyes, turned, slipped a bit in the greenish-gray mush and left The Balance Room. He walked slowly down the hall, as though his feet were lead, unaware of the smile from Hine that was hitting him in the back. He trudged down the main stairs and into the dining room. Sat for breakfast across from Lois Hine.

"Someone got into The Balance," he told her, subdued.

She was having something to eat before she went up to bed. She yawned and then crunched a corner from a piece of crustless toast with her perfect front teeth.

"It appears they took a lot of it."

"*Tant pis,*" she said. So much the worse for dear Darrow. She removed the top from a sterling jam server, ate a straight spoonful of conserved strawberries that had once grown wild in a field in Scotland, got up, took her coffee with her. Not the saucer, just the cup that dripped from its bottom onto the Kirman carpet as she left Darrow sitting there.

He sat slouched, brought himself up but only to slouch again. Couldn't keep his legs still under the table. The sunny-side up eggs that were placed before him were an inappropriately light-hearted color. He unfolded the *Wall Street Journal* as he usually did. His hands seemed detached, two separate performers. The couple of headlines he read got only as far as his eyes.

Steve Poole appeared in the doorway, waited for Darrow's permission to enter. A nod brought him to the table. He assumed a parade rest stance, hands clenched together behind him as though hiding something. Poole was supervisor of security at Number 19. He had once been Secret Service assigned to the White House and before that with Defense Intelligence. This Number 19 job was softer, paid more. Darrow himself had taken him on nine years ago.

"What have you found?" Darrow asked.

"We're still looking, sir."

"So far."

They had found the dry ice, the pulley, the slide, the hoist-truck on the airport side of the wall. They had found the security man in the shed with his head nearly cut off, the looped alarm circuits, four laundry bags of money among the roses in the rear garden. "There's a lot to go on," Poole said.

A drop of encouragement in Darrow's bucket of despair.

"Right off, sir, I would say those who did it were extremely experienced professionals."

Darrow tried to imagine what such professionals would look like. Ugly, sneaky types.

"And," Poole added, "they must have had some inside knowledge of the place, first-hand or otherwise . . . the way they avoided our alarm systems."

"Someone now working here?"

327

"Possibly . . ."

The faces passed through Darrow's mind like a rogue's gallery, including Hine and Sweet.

". . . but more likely someone who used to work here," Poole said.

Darrow had dismissed only three security men since he had been at Number 19, and a couple of collators. Three or four others had quit. They all seemed prime suspects now that he remembered them. He told Poole that.

"We've kept track of them," Poole said. "All we have to do is reach out."

Darrow felt a sudden rise of rage, like severe actute indigestion. He wanted to tell Poole it was security's fault, that security had been incompetent, probably asleep all night or watching television or jerking off one another. He wanted to say that he blamed Poole, personally, for misleading him into believing the alarm systems were impenetrable. However, his anger would have to wait. He needed Poole and the security people now more than ever, their expertise. His only hope was that the money, at least most of it, might be recovered and back in The Balance Room before anyone between himself and the High Board got wind of it.

"We'll keep this to ourselves, won't we, Poole?"

"Yes, sir."

"Do whatever you must, spend whatever is necessary."

"I understand."

"When will you get back to me?"

"By the end of the day."

Poole hurried out.

Darrow flexed his legs beneath the table and complained that his eggs were cold.

What else could he do?

THE Gulfstream II jet that touched down at Westchester Airport at three that Friday afternoon seemed too imposing to be carrying only one passenger. However, only one man stepped out down out of it and transferred to the Lincoln stretch limousine waiting on the apron.

Five minutes later the Lincoln passed through the gates of Number 19, made the climb and stopped at the front entrance. The man got out, went up to the door and walked right in. His two pieces of luggage followed.

He paused in the reception hall to survey the place. He'd never been to Number 19 before, but it was close to what he had expected.

His name was Horridge, Leland Porter Horridge.

A man in his early fifties. Slight but with a paunch. Business length gray hair beneath a gray homburg that matched his gray vested suit. His chrome wire-framed glasses were bifocaled. His plain eighteen karat cufflinks had belonged to his grandfather. His briefcase was the old-fashioned expandable sort but relatively new, made of fine black calf.

Horridge removed his homburg, placed it and his case respectfully on the hall console. He did not look at himself in the mirror above the console, merely stretched his neck to ease down a bit the starched collar of his shirt.

He went looking for Darrow.

Found him in his downstairs study, at his desk reading the New York *Post*, trying to get his worry off the robbery by going over the football opinions of the sportswriters and some of the more seamier items. Only the black cook knew he read that paper, brought it secretly to him each morning and disposed of it for him before she left each night. This was the first time he'd ever been caught with it. A social felony.

Horridge reintroduced himself.

Darrow recognized Horridge before hearing his name. They had met several years ago in Newport during America's Cup Week.

Handshake.

Chair offered.

Horridge conveyed with a brief downcast of his eyes that nothing would follow until that New York *Post* was out of sight. He looked aside long enough for Darrow to drop it into a wastebasket.

"I understand you had somewhat of a calamity," Horridge began.

"Can I get you a drink?"

Horridge declined but then on second thought decided he'd have some port. "Any kind not Spanish," he said.

Darrow called for it.

"Is that correct?" Horridge asked.

"I beg your pardon."

"You've had a calamity."

"Nothing that can't be dealt with."

"A robbery, I believe."

"A robbery."

"How much was taken?"

Darrow had received the figures from Hine just a half hour ago. It had been painful enough reading them, now he had to say them aloud, "One billion, eighty-two million."

329

"That's distressing," Horridge said with about as much emotion as someone observing a dented fender.

The port was brought.

Sips.

That bastard Hine, Darrow thought. Couldn't wait to pick at his bones, had to call Boston. Well, on the reverse side of every problem was an opportunity. He'd always gone by that, at least said it. Perhaps this would turn out to be a chance for him. To demonstrate his efficiency at dealing with crisis. If . . . no, *when* security recovered the stolen money. "We're rectifying the situation," he told Horridge stiffly. "In fact, only minutes ago I received a report from my security people telling me they were onto something that looked very promising." That was a lie. When Horridge arrived Darrow was anxiously awaiting word from Poole.

"How long is it now that you've been with us, Edwin?" Horridge asked.

"Twenty-two, going on twenty-three, years." Horridge knew damn well, Darrow told himself. He would have been briefed.

"How many years here at this installation?"

"Since 1970."

"And before that?"

"With Coville, Blankhard and Biggar." The Boston law firm.

"Then surely you're aware of how we prefer to handle such nasty matters as this."

"Yes."

"It's just not prudent to go chasing after people, stirring a private mess into a potentially public one."

"I hope to have it tidied up in a day or two."

"But the question and the point is how tidy?"

Darrow knew how precarious the line was under him. The most he could do was buy time from Horridge. Horridge had the authority to grant that. He wasn't High Board, never would be, but he was its direct emissary, its secretary of state, so to speak. "I've kept that in mind, of course," Darrow said.

"Have you now?"

"I've always carefully abided by our procedures. There can't possibly be any marks against me, certainly no major ones—"

"Until now, no."

"That ought to count for something—"

"There you go, thinking like an outsider. That's exactly what I'm apprehensive about."

"I didn't mean that the way it sounded."

Horridge tilted his head back and looked down his nose at Darrow. His eyes became magnified by the bifocal-lensed lower portion of his glasses. "It's most distressing," he said. "How much did you say was taken?"

"One billion, eighty million."

"Eighty-two million," Horridge corrected. He cleared his throat, his fingers were precisely laced in his lap. "The loss itself, even though it is a sizable amount in this case, does not concern us that much. In fact, we'd prefer to just forget the money part entirely."

Darrow wished it could be as easy as that for him.

"Money," Horridge continued, "has a way of replenishing itself, particularly money of this sort. A cash loss is only a temporary wound that more cash quickly heals. Do you understand our thinking, Edwin?"

"I believe so."

Silence hung between the two men.

Darrow couldn't read which way Horridge was leaning. If his way, it was only very slightly.

"I did not come expecting to settle this in an hour," Horridge said. "I'll be staying on a day or two. If in that time you happen to recoup the stolen amount, then we'll take a look and see how trimly you've managed to do it. Yes, we'll see . . ."

That was Friday.

On Monday, Poole made his summary report.

The hoist-truck was traced back to Teeterborough Airport in New Jersey. No one had witnessed it being stolen. It had just been there one night and not there the following morning. Number 19's security men had gone over every inch of the truck inside and out. There were palm and fingerprints all over it, some old, others recent. The problem was too many prints. It would take months to lift them all and run them through for identification. Security had, at random, lifted eight recent prints. All eight, as it turned out, belonged to Federal Aviation Administration maintenance personnel. Poole had connections inside who verified that.

A second truck had been used in the robbery. Evidently a heavy transport van of some sort, an eighteen-wheeler. Tread marks identified its tires as Michelin 11-245's. There were no usable footprints either on the airport side or the garden side of the wall, on account of the rain.

The guards at the airport gate were questioned on the pretense that there had been a theft of some radar equipment from one of the corporate hangars. One guard recalled admitting the hoist-truck, had it entered in his log, but could not give a helpful description of the men in it. The log showed no entry for the transport van, only normal airport vehicles. Poole had thought it best not to go nosing too deep around the airport.

However, he had taken the swimming pool slides all the way. Traced them to Elite Products, a plastic manufacturing firm in Brooklyn. The owner of Elite had excellent recall of the sale of the slides. They were bought with cash by a man named James Bishop. Forty-five to fifty years old, gray hair, gray bushy mustache, a bit on the plump side, stoop-shouldered, sloppy dresser, dirty-collared shirt, ketchup stains on his tie. Bishop had taken the slides away in a station wagon bearing North Carolina license plates.

The electronic looping devices used to neutralize the alarms were especially designed for that purpose. Poole considered himself highly knowledgeable in the area of surveillance and alarm systems, but he had never seen anything like these loops.

Poole himself had put the word out discreetly to key informants in New York, Connecticut and New Jersey. A hundred thousand dollars was promised for a substantial lead, proportionately as much for any lesser information. This, in Poole's opinion, was where their best chance lay. Predictably, criminals let money burn holes in their underwear. They would be spreading it around, making impressions. Someone would take notice and capitalize on it sooner or later. One might be able to physically hide a billion eighty-two, but to psychologically keep it from surfacing was impossible, Poole said.

Nothing.

Darrow sat there feeling hope abandoning him.

"You don't intend to pursue this any further do you?" Horridge asked.

"Whatever you advise," Darrow replied.

"I believe it best to drop the matter. We certainly don't want a network of dubious types chattering about us, no matter how subterranean they happen to be." Horridge addressed Darrow as though Poole wasn't in the room.

Darrow nodded submissively, told Poole to resume his regular duties, get security back on normal schedule.

"There was no robbery," Horridge put in.

Poole said two "yes sirs" and left.

OVER the next two days Darrow did everything possible to charm Horridge. They had lengthy conversations that Darrow subtly steered to topics Horridge knew most about. Dogs, for example. Horridge owned and bred water spaniels, proudly recited the geneaology of his champions. Horridge also recited Emerson, whom he referred to as Ralph Waldo. He'd read Emerson entirely, many works over and over. Some of the essays were canon to him. His favorite was "Conduct of Life."

Darrow was not normally a good listener, but as Horridge went on and on about water spaniels and Ralph Waldo, he remained apparently interested, his eyes directly on Horridge's, and managed not to fidget. After all, he was listening for his life.

Monday came.

Horridge had said he'd be leaving on Monday. Darrow expected that at any moment Horridge would just pick up and go, with a handshake and a thank you like any other guest. Probably no mention of Darrow's fate. Darrow wondered exactly how it had been handled with his predecessor, Gridley.

They were in the library. A smaller room than the others on the ground floor, seldom used. Wall to wall, floor to ceiling leather bound books, a fireplace of Antique Verde marble, leather upholstered chairs. At the moment Horridge had his collar unbuttoned, tie knot slipped loose two inches. Darrow believed that a good sign. He thought if only he had time he'd go into the city for a goddamn first-edition Emerson, possibly one that was autographed.

A bird flew onto the window screen, clung to the wire mesh with its talons. Common sparrow, white underside exposed.

"Well . . ." Horridge said within a sigh.

Silence.

"Edwin?"

"Yes?"

"Leave the room."

"Certainly."

Darrow went out, closed the door behind him. He walked down the hall to his study, through and out to the south terrace, down the wide stone steps and across the lawn to a huge copper beech. Paused beneath it, touched the bark of it, gray and textured like elephant hide. It had been thirty years since he'd touched any part of a tree, Darrow realized.

He returned to the house.

The library door was open.

Horridge was seated in a different leather chair now, nearer to a window. He had a book resting open on the thigh of his crossed-over leg.

Darrow noticed the telephone, a change in its position on the side table.

Without looking up, Horridge told him: "Don't get your hopes too high, but I've arranged for an appeal. We leave for Florida in the morning."

CHAPTER
TWENTY

THE U.S. Department of Commerce's national oceanic map number 12327 is like a look at New York Harbor from ten miles up.

Viewing that map with a somewhat bizarre imagination one is brought to realize the remarkable similarity between the harbor and a cross-section of the female genitalia.

The Upper Bay, as it is designated, is the vaginal cavity. The only way in or out of it is below, where the pelvic structure of Staten Island and Brooklyn squeeze nearly together to form what is appropriately known as The Narrows. Manhattan, the way it extends downward into the Upper Bay, is of course the uterus and ascending right and left from that are the fallopian tubes—the East River and the Hudson River.

There are three islands in the vaginal Upper Bay. Of the three, Governor's Island most suggests a plump spermatozoon headed upstream. The other two, Liberty and Ellis, appear to be the same but, by comparison, seem frail, weak, lagging. Particularly Ellis Island, which favors the New Jersey waterfront and appears close to splitting in two.

Ellis, like everything else, once belonged to the Indians. The Mohegan tribe called it Kioshk or Gull Island. It was only about three acres then, but when the trading ships came they dumped their ballast close to Ellis and that about doubled its size. There were many oyster beds around Ellis, really fine oysters, so during the late seventeenth and eighteenth centuries the British would boat out to the island and rake

335

about. In fact, it became such a favorite spot for such activity that for a time it became known as Bucking Island. It is not difficult to picture certain lords and ladies chasing through thickets with paste-studded buckles flashing and garlands flying, finally getting down to a state of complete *dishabillé* on some sufficiently soft spot where they would open and slurp oysters, and conceivably one another. More likely, though, there wasn't all *that* much wasted frolic in it. There was also a pesthouse on the island where numerous pirates literally had the floor knocked out from under them.

In 1890 the federal bureau of immigration became interested in Ellis, took it over from New York and spent five hundred thousand dollars to build on its facilities to process immigrants. The project was completed on June 13, 1897. It burned down the following day. The architectural firm of Boring and Tilton redesigned the place on a larger scale. Featured was the main building three hundred and eighty feet by one hundred and twenty feet constructed of red brick and with a broad ashlar of gray limestone and four identical towers each one hundred and twenty feet high. Together with the expansive roof of the main building and its towers of green-and-gilt copper, its style was French Renaissance, adulterated slightly by Greek Byzantine. Quite imposing, considering its purpose.

From the year it opened to its official closing in 1954 Ellis Island grew to thirty-five similarly styled buildings on twenty-seven and one-half flat, filled acres. Over those years it processed fourteen million immigrants. Not all immigrants, however, passed through Ellis. Those steamship passengers who arrived in first class and those in second class who shook hands with a twenty in their palm were never so inconvenienced. They were given perfunctory medical examinations and had their entrance papers approved while their ship was in the Lower Bay. Stick out your tongue. Ink pad, rubber stamp, swak swak was, for them, the most there ever was to it. First classers and others of means never set foot on Ellis. They went straight down the gangplank ahead of their trunks to the Astor or the Ansonia, where suites awaited.

The rest came knotted and dazed out of steerage with everything they owned on their shoulders and in their hands. Frightened to the point of paralysis as they were barged from a West Side pier to the island they had heard about, where they might fail examination by merely displeasing an official's eyes. Be turned away, shipped back for smiling at the wrong time or for not answering a question asked in a language they did not understand or for being pretty and refusing to open mouth or legs behind some locked door.

The United States stopped taking people in on a mass basis in 1924.

From then on, Ellis stood out there looking to be used. During World War II it served well as a detention center for enemy aliens and saboteurs. That was its last function of any importance. There were proposals to convert it to a middle-income apartment house, a school for retarded children (back to the pesthouse?), a narcotic and addiction treatment center, a liberal arts college, a museum. Groups lobbied. Congressmen and senators used the place for years and years of patriotic debate. Ellis Island deteriorated. Ran down so much the cost of renovating it exceeded its value.

The bureau of prisons and the army and the navy raped the place, removed from it whatever equipment they thought usable. Then came the petty scavengers. Came by boat by night to pull out all the copper wire and switches and sold them by the pound. They also took anything of brass and porcelain and every piece of furniture that was still sturdy. As the months went by they repeatedly pilfered the place of increasingly less valuable things.

Then there also were the vandals that came for the excitement of smashing, practiced their pitching arms with rocks on glass panes, thrived on the sound of shattering, demonstrated their strength and let out their hostilities by demolishing already crippled chairs and disabled desks and file cabinets.

Until Ellis Island was there, but nothing was there.

Until Ellis Island was an ideal place to hide a billion eighty-two million.

One of Rodger's yachts was used for transport. A one hundred and eight foot power cruiser designed by Bennetti that Rodger kept berthed at the Indian Fields Yacht Club in Greenwich. Leslie didn't need permission to use it. She had operated the yacht a number of times and despite its good size she found it only a bit more complicated than a Rolls. Standing at the control console up in its wheelhouse, she merely had to turn a key and press a button to start the vessel's GM-V-16 engines. Her left hand minded the wheel and made turns while her right tended to the throttle lever. It was a kind of coordination that involved both hands but nothing of her feet. No brake for fast stopping. Better she should remember that than run this two million dollar beauty up the stern of a scow or something.

Chapin was with her. He freed the mooring lines and took in the bumpers. Leslie maneuvered the yacht into the channel, minded the buoys, proceeded at a restrained speed to the open water of Long Island Sound. She executed a sweeping quarter-turn starboard and shoved the throttle full forward to have the sleek, slicey yacht doing twenty-five nautical miles per hour.

At that rate and with an easterly wind, it took less than two hours to be in The Narrows, passing beneath the Verrazano Bridge and headed on a course due north.

Gainer had stayed with the money.

He and Vinny in the gasoline tanker truck crossed over the George Washington Bridge and picked up the New Jersey Turnpike southbound. He kept to the far right lane and exactly on the speed limit all the way to where the silver underbellies of 707s and 747s coming into Newark were intimidating, the way they roared not very high above them, reminding them of the close call they'd had at Westchester Airport the night before. They turned off onto an extension of the thruway that served the harbor area.

Along there were the enormous spheres and stumpy cylinders of oil storage tanks, and the ugly sulfur odor. Off to the right beyond a flat of spiky marsh grass were ships tied up in the Port Newark Marine Terminal and along the Pierhead Channel. Cranes at work on freighters, emptying one hold while filling another, clearing deckspace only to restack it neatly with identical containers nearly the size of boxcars. White, silver and for some reason, a few bright yellow.

Gainer and Vinny continued on the turnpike extension as it cut back and ran north around Bayonne. Off to their right was the Upper Bay of New York Harbor, a khaki color, patched near shore with the black mud of tidal flats. After a couple of miles they came to Interchange 14B where they paid what toll they owed and took a sharp left. A minute later they were well within the digestive tract of the old waterfront; were the only moving thing along those cobbled ways. Every warehouse was as closed as a fortress, rust on rust on everything of metal, including the miles of railroad tracks that ran down to the docks. The Central Railroad of New Jersey, the Lehigh Valley, others.

A sewage disposal plant was a landmark for them.

They found it, turned right and rumbled over sixteen sets of tracks to get onto a dirt road. Nearly a mile of deep, rutted, bumpy road that ended when it turned and came parallel with a cement seawall. Jutting out from the wall every two hundred feet were old wooden piers, collapsed in several places.

Vinny backed the tanker in under a railroad shed, cut its engine.

Their view directly ahead was Ellis Island. The backside of it only five hundred feet from the tip of the old New Jersey piers.

They had hours to wait.

They napped, got out, stretched and walked a bit. Gainer was grateful for the cheese and sprouts on seven-grain-bread sandwiches Leslie had packed for them. And the big thermos of honey and vinegar drink.

He even voluntarily took a hefty pinch of cayenne because if she'd been there she would have wanted him to. Vinny had a sandwich but wouldn't even try the honey and vinegar although Gainer assured him it was a lot like lemonade.

They passed some of the time talking sapphires. Vinny was never without his loupe and had brought along sapphires that had been part of his most recent package. The stones, "popped" from their settings so they could not be identified, were contained within the folds of a piece of waxy tissue that was contained within the folds of a heavier white paper about two inches square.

Vinny explained that these were blue stones, although sapphires came in all different colors. The cheapest was the white or clear, the most precious an orange-red called a *padparadschah*. There were two main varieties of blue, the lighter blue Ceylon and the darker Burmese. The latter, when it was bright like a cornflower, was the most desirable. Most sapphires, Vinny said, had tiny white fiberlike flaws in them that were referred to in the trade as "silk."

Gainer used the loupe on one of the stones, saw for himself. For a few moments he was in a sterile blue atmosphere. Vinny said he wouldn't trust a stone unless it had at least a little "silk" in it. Fifty, sixty years ago a lot of very believable synthetic sapphires were made and sold and many were still around passing for genuine. The thing was, they made those synthetics too perfect. Whenever he was buying a package from a thief that included sapphires he was always glad to find some "silk," Vinny said.

Gainer recalled that twelve carat Ceylon sapphire Darrow had wanted to buy at Parke-Bernet's auction in October. A Tiffany stone, Darrow had said. Gainer imagined it, saw himself standing in the back of that place where he had once worked, casually, subtly gesturing another thousand with his rolled up catalogue to outbid everyone for that special chunk of blue. He would give it to Leslie, of course, not for Christmas or her birthday but as a little everyday gift to show that his heart and head and balls were in the right place.

At five-twenty, when the sun looked as though it was only two inches from touching the horizon, the sharp pristine prow of Rodger's yacht appeared beyond the end of the pier, cruising at only a couple of knots. It almost ran past, shuddered and made the water rile as its engines reversed. Leslie backed it slowly into the slip between the piers all the way to the seawall.

Vinny started the tanker truck, maneuvered it so it stood parallel with the pier, only inches from the edge. Meanwhile Gainer was up on the ramp that ran along the top of the tanker. He opened all three of its hatches, and the gasoline fumes that rose from them made the air look watery. He held his breath as he reached in, grabbed up one of the black laundry sacks of money and heaved it down onto the aft deck of the yacht.

For two hours it was quick, hard work, lifting and heaving. The black bags piled up on the deck. While Gainer and Chapin threw them down, Vinny and Leslie tried to keep them organized. Three bags went overboard, Leslie managed to recover them with a gaff. She was tempted to allow one to get out of reach and out into the current so some poor old guy fishing from a pier in lower Brooklyn might snag the catch of his life. However, more likely, she thought, a Wall Street type coming in on his eighty foot flush deck Trumpy would scoop it up.

It had been dark for an hour by the time all three hundred and fifty-seven bags of money were aboard. Vinny backed the truck into the railroad shed and they leaned up some old boards to conceal it.

Leslie started the yacht, snapped on its running lights and gave it a little forward. There was no reason to take in the bumpers. The yacht moved slowly from the old slip. When it was surely clear Leslie made it do a ninety degree turn to the starboard and a minute or two later repeated the turn to port.

She hadn't missed it by much, they saw. The beams of the yacht's spotlights hit on the texture and hue of granite about a hundred feet away—the seawall that ran straight along the entire south side of Ellis Island.

Leslie maneuvered the yacht to the seawall, brought it in closer and closer. She was not sure there was enough depth along there. It certainly looked as though it would be shallow. Any moment she expected to hear the keel of the yacht scraping bottom. Finally, the bumpers collided with the wall. She steadied the wheel and worked the throttle alternately forward and reverse to keep the vessel in place while Gainer and Chapin jumped over onto the seawall to secure the stern mooring line to a maple tree and the bow line to the building situated on the island's southeast point—ran the line in through the space where a window had once been and out where there had been a door.

Leslie switched off all lights.

No point in inviting a harbor police patrol.

At once they set about transferring the money, bag by bag, into that building on the point. They stacked it up in the corner of one of the first floor rooms, found some old mattresses that they layered on top so the heap looked like it was all mattresses.

By then it was eleven-thirty.

Chapin wanted a drink, and although tired, a working girl.

Vinny wanted home and bed.

Gainer would stay with the money.

Leslie got the yacht under way. Did not exceed the night-limit harbor speed as she went up the Hudson to the Seventy-ninth Street Basin. Moored the yacht neatly and exchanged it for a Riva 2000 speedboat that Rodger always kept there.

Feeling more in control and closer to the swiftness she could cause, she put the Riva in gear and growled it loudly out of the Basin and down river.

To Ellis Island.

That same seawall.

But to a spot along it where wild sumac grew out over the water. She steered the Riva in under the leafy branches, where it could not be seen.

Gainer was right there, waiting.

Leslie had packed the Riva two days earlier with things they would need and a few extras. It took them three round trips to carry everything to the location they had chosen for their post, which was not in the building with the money but in the building adjacent, once the residence of the commissioner of immigration and his family.

Gainer and Leslie climbed the three flights of stairs to its attic—a forty-by-forty space with high, raw rafters. It was cleaner than elsewhere because it was free of plaster dust, and ordinary dust as well. The windows of its large, arched dormers were gone, frames and all, and the wind often swept fiercely through. The attic also offered an excellent vantage point from which to keep watch over the money. From the southeast dormer one could easily see into the building next door, in fact right down into the room where the money was heaped.

Leslie inflated the double air mattress. Exhaled into it so rapidly she got light-headed, had to stop four times, refused to let Gainer contribute. Finally it was firm enough. She positioned it on the floor near a window, covered it with a sheet that she tucked tight. Pulled the cases onto two down-filled pillows, plumped the pillows and spread a light mohair throw.

The ASPs.

She placed his on one side at the head of the mattress, hers on the other side.

"Hungry?" she asked.

"Tired." His shoulders and arms especially. They were burning with fatigue from having hefted all those bags of money.

"Undress."

"I'd better not."

"Don't worry lover, we're safe as a couple of birds here," she said.

341

He glanced at the ASPs, but then thought she was right and that he was just overedgy because he was tired. Where, he wondered aloud, was she getting all her energy.

"I didn't do nearly as much as you," she told him.

He took off his clothes and so did she. He sat on the mattress and she knelt behind him, kissed him lightly on the neck and behind the ear and hugged her breasts against the muscular flat of him for a long moment before beginning. Massaged his shoulders, used her fingers to knead the tension from him, seemed to know where he had knots of it and firmly, lovingly untied them. Squeezed his trapezoidal muscles left and right and held pressure on them. When she let go the tightness also let go and his shoulders dropped a couple of inches, relaxed.

She guided his head down to his pillow, made sure his position was comfortable, then covered him with the mohair throw. Kissed him on the cheekbone, the sort of brief but assuring good night kiss a boy would get.

"You need a shave," she said.

The mohair lay lightly, slick and luxurious on him. The down pillow seemed a bottomless sinking place for his head. He reached out and touched the cool steel of the ASP. That he was literally floating on the breath of his love was his last thought before going under.

AT dawn there were doves in the rafters.

Leslie had her pillow over her head trying to escape their cooing.

Gainer threw one of his sneakers at them and they flew. He got up and went to one of the dormers, took himself in hand, aimed and urinated out. The city was only a mile away but seemed closer, almost looming. The harbor made it look as though the city was presenting itself on a silver tray. The variation of spires appeared lifeless, no movement discernible. The money buildings, the twin towers of the Trade Center and those mainly black ones of the financial district were most prominent.

Gainer bent his knees slightly to arch higher his liquid ribbon. Piss on them.

He went over to the southeast dormer, glanced down and saw the old mattresses that covered the billion were in place. A billion was heavyweight, he thought. If ever again he had a chance to steal that much, no matter how easy or sure, he wouldn't do it. He got back under the mohair and snuggled Leslie, who made a little animal sound of pleasure.

It was Leslie's opinion that they should consider the money safe where it was, and while away the interim more at ease at her place on East Seventy-fifth. They could buzz over in the Riva every once in a while to check on the billion.

Gainer would not have it. He insisted on remaining close to the money, although he wondered what he would do if someone innocently happened upon it. Would he kill that person? He didn't know.

Gainer and Leslie spent most of that day, Saturday, exploring the island. The one time they were previously there to determine a suitable spot for the money, they'd seen only a fraction of the place. Now they realized the extent that it was given to decay. It was oppressive but at the same time intriguing. Powdery plaster from ceilings and walls lay thick on everything and filled every angle. In places it was mixed with the dust of brick into a pink coating. Painted surfaces were crackled like maps with no captions, enamel curls waited to fall at the slightest touch.

There were numerous animal tracks in the plaster dust, the marks of claws. Leslie asked what kind of tracks they were. Gainer diverted her attention.

Among a disarray of papers Leslie came across a well-drawn scheme of Ellis. And hundreds of reproductions of it. Evidently they had been handed out to immigrants to find their way around. The overhead-view outline showed that Ellis was almost divided equally in two by a ferry slip two hundred feet wide. Every part of every building was numbered and named according to purpose.

The room Gainer and Leslie were in at the moment had once been a medical examining room. In fact nearly all the structures on the southern part of Ellis had served as hospital facilities and wards. A corridor connected them, a seven-foot-wide corridor with casement windows along both sides. It ran almost the entire width of the island, eight hundred feet, straight as a shot. Gainer's perspective from the east end of the corridor gave him the impression that it was a sort of trap, the way it seemed gradually to diminish. Its long receding lines were interrupted only by vines that had grown in through broken panes.

At one time the corridor had probably been a pleasant place to walk, Gainer thought, as he and Leslie proceeded down it. A door on the right bore a small baked-enamel plate that said *Ward 26* in white on dark blue. There were hospital wards all along there, large, high-ceilinged rooms set at right angles to the corridor. Outside, the ground space between the double-storied ward buildings was thick with growth—tall locust trees, varieties of weeds such as pokewood and mullet, burdock and briars.

At the west end of the corridor, according to the scheme, was the morgue and the crematorium. The morgue was a twenty-by-twenty room with a concrete floor. A light and reflector hung from the ceiling to eye level, and there was an eight inch drain, just a hole in the floor directly below the light. A free-standing sink was near the drain. Those were overlooked by ascending levels of concrete tiers. At the facing end of the room were eight wooden doors like those found on old iceboxes. The doors were identical, two feet wide by a foot and a half high. They were arranged in two vertical rows of four so that the top doors were up seven feet. Each door had the kind of spring release handle and prominent triangular-shaped hinges old iceboxes had and, indeed, screwed to the exterior frame was a metal nameplate bearing the logo, *Frigidaire*. Here, of course, was where the dead were kept on ice. The concrete tiers had accommodated chairs so that in amphitheater fashion the sectioning of cadavers could be observed.

Gainer opened a couple of the morgue boxes, glanced in, saw they weren't individual enclosed spaces but one large space sectioned off by slatted platforms on rollers. The crematorium was adjacent. The door to the crematorium furnace was open and a shovel was sticking out of it. Alongside the furnace was a strange-looking metal contraption, a boxlike table three feet high by two feet square with a six inch square hole in its top surface. A turning handle like that of an old-fashioned meatgrinder, only sturdier, was attached to one side; it was locked with rust. Gainer looked down into the hole and found no clue to the function of this piece of equipment, which was a device to pulverize bones. Better not to have known *that*.

He and Leslie continued on. They were more acclimated to the deterioration now. They turned right into another passageway, this one of brick with fewer windows, twice as wide as the other and just as straight though not quite as long. This brick passageway was partitioned off on one side so that in effect it was two passageways—parallel, a narrow one and a wide one with ten foot openings between them at regular intervals, an arrangement something like the barriers bullfighters scurry behind. (Actually the narrower corridor was a storage area for stretcher-carts, wheelchairs and other such equipment.)

There were no wards off this brick corridor, only one huge hall that had obviously been used for entertainments. It had a stage and slots high up through one wall for motion picture projection and spotlighting. An upright piano stood in the center of the hall. Lonely, abused piano, looking as though half the world had plinked or pounded on it. A gilt decal on its face said it was a "James and Halstrom Transposing Keyboard" and that it was the kind that had been awarded a "First Premium, New Orleans Exposition."

Gainer tapped several dead keys.

Leslie hit on a live one right off.

Elsewhere in other buildings they read faded graffiti on the walls of cubicles where immigrants had been detained. Some they were easily able to translate, such as *prendre la lune avec les dents* (to seize the moon with the teeth) and *la bonne blague!* (what a joke!), but they weren't sure of the meanings of *besser ein halb ei als eitel Schale* (better half an egg than empty shells) and *tutto di novello par bello* (everything new seems beautiful). They more or less figured out that *il danaro è fratello del danaro* meant money is the brother of money, and of course there were many *quelle affaire!* and *Eireann go Brat!* printed around in various sizes by different hands. A tiny inscription written vertically up the side of a bedpost said in plain English, "Fuck this place forever."

They saw a pair of old black leather hightop shoes hung by their laces from an overhead pipe six feet out of reach. They came across a tipped-over wooden file cabinet, a large one with many drawers. The drawers were packed with five-by-five index cards and each drawer had an elaborate label on its brass-plated pull, designating Italian, Dutch, German, Irish, Polish and so forth. A number of drawers had the word "Denied" on them. Leslie pulled out one entire drawer of "Denied" and carried it back to the commissioner's house.

Before going to the attic, Gainer checked on the billion, was relieved to find it untouched.

"See what a lot of money will give you," Leslie said.

"Give me?"

"The worries."

"And first class everything," Gainer said. "Anyway, I was checking mainly because *our* millions are in there."

Leslie liked the *our*. "I'll bet being rich will change you," she said.

"I'm counting on it," he told her.

Gainer found a rattan porch chair in one of the second floor rooms of the commissioner's house. Its seat was broken through and it was dusty down into the crevices of its weave. He tied a rope to it and threw it into the harbor, washed it by yanking it around, put a board in its seat, and his pillow. Sat with feet up on the edge of a dormer, looking out.

Leslie screwed open a bottle of that thousand dollar Brunello di Montalano 1945. She moved the air mattress close to Gainer's chair. They passed the bottle, swigged from it. Leslie sat with her legs crossed tight to her, the file drawer of "Denied" in front of her. She pulled cards randomly from it. They had last names, first name, age, sex and nationality on them, and various notations. Such as: Ruzkowski, Matthew, twenty-nine, male, Polish, escaped convict.

345

"Take a card, any card." Leslie held several out to Gainer.

He chose one and read it aloud. "O'Toole, Mary, twenty-three, female, Irish. Infected with moral turpitude."

"Wonder who she caught it from."

"Her resistance was low."

"Probably a pretty lass who didn't believe she was." Leslie read another card aloud. This one was a thirty-five-year-old Bulgarian polygamist, said to have eight, perhaps twelve wives. "Poor fellow," Leslie sympathized.

Gainer agreed.

There were designated prostitutes, pederasts, scabs, anarchists, and all manner and variety of criminals in the file, but by far the most common reason for being denied entry was lack of money. Card after card had the word "Pauper" scrawled across it.

Leslie put the file aside, took two swigs of wine, stretched her back and said, as though she was talking to the atmosphere: "I'm pregnant, you know."

"What?"

"Pregnant, me."

"You're kidding."

"That's another way of putting it."

"I know you're not."

"How do you know?"

"Hell, I can count. Only in the movies guys can't count when it comes to that."

"Anyway," Leslie said, "suppose I was?"

Gainer allowed his attention to be distracted by the Staten Island Ferry, yellow-orange, headed for Battery Park Terminal at the tip of Manhattan. He hadn't been on it since the great escape from Mount Loretto. Norma, as she'd been that day, came clearly to him, even the gray cotton dress she'd worn.

"Don't be evasive," Leslie said.

"I'm not."

"So, answer."

"If you were pregnant, Rodger would be upset."

It wasn't the answer Leslie wanted. She got up quickly, walked to the opposite side of the attic. Gazed out the dormer there at the roofs of the other buildings and skylights. On the ridge of an eave, a female pigeon was submitting to being hopped on. "This place is thick with spirits," Leslie said. "Didn't you feel that today?"

"Sort of."

"What were all those tracks?" she asked.

346

"Rats."

"Maybe they were rabbits."

"Only rats leave tail tracks like that. Probably brown rats, the *Rattus norvegicus,* or sewer rat."

"I didn't know you were such a rat expert."

"One whole week when I worked at the library I made rats my subject for research. New York is full of rats."

A knowing scoff from Leslie.

"What it amounts to is two and a half rats to every person. Fortunately rats only have a three or four year life span. A four-year-old is older than a man at ninety. No animal wiser than a four-year-old rat. He can steal the bait out of any trap and seems to know exactly when to expect an exterminator. Old buildings like these are great places for them."

Leslie hugged herself, but she was interested. "How big do they get?"

"Ten inches, not counting tail. But that size would weigh in at a pound and a half, maybe two pounds. That's a lot of rat."

"I still think the money is safe without our staying here."

"You go, I'll stay."

"Rodger's rifle is in the Riva. Should I get it?"

Gainer didn't see any reason to.

That night Leslie moved the tin of Carr's water biscuit crackers, the oranges, especially the round of Edam and all the other eatables, to the furthest corner of the attic. She got under the mohair throw and pressed tight against Gainer while they watched the four inch portable Sony television. Cute little mice were one thing, big snarly rats quite another.

Several times she sat up and shined her little flashlight around the attic.

"I love you," Gainer told her every half hour.

That helped

About three o'clock the following afternoon Chapin and Vinny showed up in a motored skiff they had rented from a place in Sheepshead Bay. They brought along an eight pack of cold Heineken, five pounds of barbecued ribs and some french fries. Chapin looked rested, relaxed and Vinny was in high spirits.

Vinny expressed his appreciation for the view out of the dormer on the harbor side. "Hey, you can see all the way to Wallabout Bay," he said. (Wallabout is a spot in upper Brooklyn where the East River makes such a sharp bend it forms an elbowlike backwater. The ebb tide deposits all sorts of things in that backwater and anything loose that comes down river also gets carried into it—a lot of driftwood, lobster traps, fuel drums and particularly corpses. The bodies of bridge jump-

347

ers, unwanted newborns, out-of-favor wise-guys and what have you. Corpses tend to pop up in the spring when the water warms. Wallabout is the first place Harbor police look for anyone missing and believed to be dead. They pull out twenty-five to thirty bodies a year there.)

"We thought we'd take over for a couple of days," Chapin said. "You must be getting tired."

"That's okay, we're fine," Gainer told them.

Leslie disagreed, made a face.

Chapin and Gainer watched the Dallas-Giant game. The tiny screen miniaturized the players, seemed to lessen the importance of their feats. Gainer and Chapin bet on completions and first downs at a hundred dollars a whack and on total yards gained, ten a yard. The field was hot and Dallas didn't strain, just kept ahead. The Giants believed they were good because they tried all out and were beaten by only eight points. Gainer came out eighteen hundred ahead. Chapin paid from a wad.

"New York should have a winning football team," Chapin commented. "Could if they'd let the Mob own it."

"At least then it would lose only when it was told," Gainer said.

Vinny laughed. "We've been watching the obituaries," he said.

"Too early for that," Gainer said.

"How about putting a call into Hine," Chapin said.

Gainer wasn't for it.

"Pretend you're calling from Zurich, just checking in or something."

Gainer did wish he knew what was going on at Number 19, what Darrow's reaction had been when he saw that much of The Balance gone. Like Orpheus, looking at his own death.

"Anyway, when do you think we'll be able to unload the money and take our cut?" Chapin asked.

"No more than a week, Hine said."

"You plan to stay over here for the entire week?"

"Long as I have to," Gainer said.

"Doesn't seem fair. This is a rat hole."

"It's not bad."

"It's not exactly Caneel Bay," Leslie put in.

Gainer told her: "No reason for both of us to be here. Why don't you go get a good night's rest?"

"Maybe I will," she said.

Gainer didn't think he should leave the money, didn't think he could. He'd been with it all the way and something kept telling him to stick with it. However, he thought, possibly he just wasn't listening to another side of him that complained he was being too cautious, stubbornly tough on himself.

Chapin took him aside, told him: "Listen handicapper, really, Vinny and I don't mind hanging out here, keeping watch over the stash for a couple of days or so."

"Thanks but—"

"What is it . . . you don't trust me, or what?"

"It's not that, it's—"

"Do you good to take a break. I know Leslie could sure use one."

Gainer glanced past Chapin to Leslie. She really wouldn't leave without him, he thought. He ought to consider her, what she was having to go through because of her caring about him. The least he could do was make it a little easier. Loud enough for her to hear he asked Chapin: "Can you take it here for a couple of days?"

"No problem."

"Okay, say until Tuesday morning."

Leslie had already gathered up their ASPs and was headed for the stairs.

An hour later she was at her place on East Seventy-fifth taking the longest bath of her life. As the suds of a huge bar of Penhaligon soap fluffed like worked-up cream on her, she thought that her allotment of two and a half rats definitely weren't here. Did that mean someone had five?

Gainer showered. He had noticed the glow of a tiny red light on the wall next to the dimmer in the foyer, had never noticed it before. When he was drying off he asked Leslie about it.

"That's Rodger," she said casually.

"How is it him?"

"When the light's on it means he's home next door in case I want to see him for some reason. You know, if I feel like talking or have a problem or whatever."

Gainer thought of Rodger only a wall away, a man he'd never met but had come to think of as someone he knew well.

"Don't let it bother you, lover," Leslie said.

"It doesn't," Gainer lied.

When Leslie was out of the tub and dried, she put on a white floor-length cotton robe, so fine a cotton it was nearly transparent. She had Gainer sit before her dressing table and be shaved. He let her but didn't completely relax, pressed her breasts with the round of his shoulder, kneed her mound as though not knowing he was doing it while she stroked away his three-day bristles. She was astraddle his thigh when she finished beneath his chin.

He was hard.

As though she hadn't noticed until that moment, she did a little

349

"Oh!" A mixture of surprise, delight and mock fright. She kneeled, kissed his cock as she would his mouth.

He noticed she still had the open straight razor in her hand.

"It's been days," she said.

"Has it?"

"Only in the movies women don't keep count when it comes to that." They laughed.

"But before anything," she told him, "I need to have my aura cleansed. Will you do it for me, lover?"

"Sure thing."

She removed her robe and lay front down on the bed. Gainer started at her feet and performed his version of her air-scouring motions with his hands. He felt foolish at first but then he got into it, scoured vigorously and as close as possible to her skin without touching her.

"Don't forget to discard the negativity," she said.

Gainer imitated what he'd seen her do, snapped his hands as though flinging a filthy substance from them. He cleansed the length of her the required three times back, three times front.

"That's better," she murmured.

He was still hard.

MONDAY brought rain.

Not on and off sprinkles but a steady drizzle with umbrella destroying gusts.

Gainer had to put out of mind going up to the Bronx for an afternoon of soccer. That prospect was an additional reason persuading him to leave the money and Ellis. Damn rain. He didn't mope about it but mentioned it to Leslie a couple of times while they stayed in, read and nibbled and napped feet to feet and sometimes toes to crotch at opposite ends of a down-filled *lit de repos.*

They were like that when he jumped up and started to dress.

"Where are you going, lover?" Leslie asked.

"Just thought I'd take a run out to Ellis to make sure everything's all right." A twinge of distrust had gotten to him, shot through him like an all-over gas pain. That money out there was his life.

"Stop worrying."

"I can't."

"Chapin and Vinny won't let anything happen to the money."

Gainer got as far as the door, slowly turned and came back to her. Still feeling uneasy.

They went out early for some honest pasta at Il Monello and then

350

used the intermission at the Winter Garden to sneak into the second part of the Twyla Tharp Dancers.

Got to bed and to sleep before midnight.

Again, around four, the security of the money out on Ellis was so heavy on Gainer that he had to get up and decide whether or not to go check on it. He got as far as one shoe on.

He slept badly until seven.

It was an ideal morning, the rain having washed the air. Not a cloud, the sun had the sky all to itself. Today's weather should have been yesterday's, Gainer thought.

He and Leslie returned to Ellis. The money was exactly as they'd left it.

But not the attic.

There were soft drink and beer cans, pizza crusts and a couple of battered pie tins full of stubbed out cigarettes. Half-finished sandwiches, Hostess Twinkie wrappers, at least a dozen porno magazines. Evidently Chapin had made himself right at home.

Chapin and Vinny were glad to leave the place. Stayed only long enough to ask if Gainer had heard anything from Hine and to say that a Harbor Police Patrol launch had cruised close by along the east seawall that dawn but hadn't appeared to be suspicious. Probably a once-a-week routine patrol.

As soon as Chapin and Vinny were gone, Leslie set about cleaning the attic. Inspired by the possibility of having to endure every rat in the place. Gainer helped, hauled the trash and leftovers down and out to the incinerator building that was located on the extreme opposite corner of the island, as far away as possible.

When he returned from doing that he tried to just sit and watch the comings and goings in the harbor, but he was fidgety.

Leslie was relaxed, content reading *The Seth Material* by Jane Roberts.

Every time Gainer shifted his position the rattan chair complained with creaks.

Without taking her eyes from the page, Leslie told him: "Tell you what. You go play soccer and I'll keep watch over the loot."

"No."

"You'd really like to play, wouldn't you?"

"It's not that important."

"Okay."

Then, after a silent while, she asked, "Where would you play today if you were going to?"

"Up in the Bronx."

"Same place where I went with you to watch that time?"

"Crotona Park."

"You ought to go play."

"Think so?"

"Definitely."

"I wouldn't feel right about it."

"You don't feel right now."

"You'd be stranded out here."

"So, I'll run you over to the Seventy-ninth Street Basin and pick you up there later in the afternoon. Say, five-thirty. Wouldn't that give you time enough?" She seemed to be asking herself as much as him.

"You wouldn't mind being alone?"

"Not at all."

"Sure?"

"I'll just read."

That he'd needlessly worried about the money the day and the night before helped convince Gainer that he ought to be at least a little less paranoid about it. Soccer was tempting.

"You deserve it," Leslie said.

An hour later, shortly before noon, Gainer was in the Bronx, crossing over from One hundred and seventy-third Street into Crotona Park. The loose-fitting shorts he had on were old and unevenly faded, his T-shirt had holes in it and the sweatshirt tied by its sleeves around his neck was a gray five-dollar second from a street vendor. His soccer shoes, connected by their laces, were slung over his shoulder. He had better gear, a couple of expensive warm-up suits, but never wore them up here.

As soon as grass was beneath his feet Gainer picked up his pace, from a stride to a lope to an easy jog. Across Crotona Parkway to the playing field. He hadn't been there for several weeks and some of the guys let him know he was welcome by acknowledging that he hadn't been around, asking if he'd been sick or away or in the can. Santiago and Tricky Rodriguez had arrived about half an hour earlier and were just completing their warmups. They came over to Gainer and did a few more while he did his.

"We got shirts today," Santiago told Gainer. "They dropped out of a window."

Tricky Rodriguez held one up, a green, long-sleeved mostly acrylic shirt with two white bars around the chest and two around the upper arms.

"Sharp," Gainer said.

"I saved you one," Santiago said, tossed it to Gainer, who tried it on. The shirt was extra, extra large.

"Wrong one, that's mine," Santiago said, exchanging it. Not that he was large enough for that shirt; he preferred whatever he wore to be loose. He was a rangy two-hundred-pounder, had long legs and arms. His coloring was medium to very black, his teeth somewhat tobacco-stained. The red irritation in the corners of his eyes and around his lids was also from a kind of smoking. It was Gainer's guess that Santiago was thirty. He was sure Santiago had served time because he often referred to one guy or another as someone he'd been "inside" with. Tricky Rodriguez was only about five-seven and a hundred forty. He was a freckled Puerto Rican with a slight speech impediment, a lisp that gave his Spanish a Castillian flavor. He could not have been more than twenty-three or -four. One reason he was called Tricky was he was good at magic, especially sleight of hand. Saturdays he dealt a three card Monte game on the bottom of a cardboard carton downtown on Fifth Avenue and around Rockefeller Center and along Fifty-seventh. He could handle the cards as well as anyone, but someone else had to do the spiel for him and that cut down on his take.

"We' ain't playing just pick up today," Tricky said.

"The guys from Sound View Park are coming up," Santiago explained.

"Trying to tell me you already have a full side?"

"We ain't got but eleven shirts and I just gave you yours, didn't I?"

"You sure?"

"Hell, yeah, we need you." For emphasis, Santiago gave Gainer a playful but sharp shot to the stomach that Gainer toughened up for just in time.

Gainer continued with his warmups. Did thirty toe-touchers and twenty side-stretches. Some backbends that made him feel the knots come undone along his spine. After that he did some deep breathing, taking air in slowly, holding it in for a long moment to get all the goodness from it before letting it out. He deep breathed for each part of himself: head, shoulders, thighs, calves, deep breathed as though all his skin were capable of inhaling, ventilating, nourishing. He got up, stood with feet apart, felt solidly related to the earth but at the same time light on it, balanced and capable of making swift shifts of movement. The state of mind and body soccer players call being "grounded."

Gainer would need to be very grounded, considering the condition of the field. It was a bare, overplayed place at its best. Now, from Monday's rain, its dirt was mud and and the critical areas in front of each goal were puddled. The dimensions had been paced off, one hundred and thirty yards by seventy-five yards, and marked with flour, a twenty pound bag of Pillsbury someone somehow didn't pay for.

The match began at one-thirty only because that happened to be the time when the ball was put into play. It would last as long as anyone felt the need to score. There would be a half time or time out when the majority of both sides decided they wanted it.

Green shirts and white shirts went at it. A swarming kind of game resembling the so-called Total Soccer that the Holland and West German teams had improvised in 1974, but lacking its strategy. All ten players on either side played both attack and defense as the opportunities and spirits dictated. There were no absolute territorial positions, no assigned zones of responsibility as in classical soccer. The result was often a melee with twenty players crowded into a section of the field trying for the ball. And, as a further result, there were many breakaways, some going almost the entire length of the field.

The outstanding player for the Sound View team was a mestizo from Santa Marta, Colombia, by the name of Jeanaro Lopez. He had had two tryouts with the Tampa Bay Rowdies of the North American Soccer League. Ten minutes into play Jeanaro took a long, leading cross pass and had only Gainer to beat. Jeanaro came right at him, controlling the ball effortlessly in stride as though it were attached to his feet. He misled Gainer with his eyes and shoulders, skipped on one foot, did a couple of little stutter steps and was that quickly by and on his way to the goal. The goalkeeper had even less of a chance. Santiago's shrug at Gainer said he himself couldn't have done any better.

Gainer recovered some face five minutes later when he worked a perfect give-and-go with Tricky Rodriguez just inside the penalty area, evaded a sliding tackle that caught his right ankle, dribbled left, changed pace by stopping the ball. The ball was his. No one could get it from him. He owned it. He suddenly feinted right and cut left for the shot. Whipped his foot and caught the ball with his instep.

The ball hit the goal post.

Ricocheted right back to Gainer.

The goalkeeper was yards out of position.

Gainer easily booted the ball through. He would have felt better about it had it gone in the first time.

After about an hour of play the score was six to six. Gainer had scored twice and Jeanaro had five goals to his credit. It wasn't unusual in matches of this sort for scores to end up fourteen to twelve, or eighteen to eighteen.

Along the sidelines were thirty and sometimes as many as fifty spectators to give the players more of a sense of performance. They were hecklers and advisors, loyalist girlfriends and scampering children. People using the park for a shortcut paused to watch for a while. Older persons, envious of the energy they observed, enjoyed believing they would not waste it in such a way.

Gainer was entirely caught up in the action. For the moment, there was no Number 19, no Darrow or Hine, or billions. He was in another world that centered on a twenty-eight-inch-around, sixteen ounce inflated black and white ball. He was, he felt, running well, able to reach into himself when needed for acceleration beyond his normal limit. The ground beneath his feet seemed to be his ally, helping to push him along. No matter that he had a stitch in his side, that exhaustion was blurring his vision, that his right cheek was badly bruised from having taken an elbow from someone when he went up for a header and both his shins were kicked sore from instep to knee. He was being washed by the strain, his reservoir of anger opened, and being depleted by exertion and punishment given and received.

A pass from Tricky down the right sideline sailed above Gainer's head. The ball had spin on it, landed softly with hardly any bounce so that Gainer's foot could come beneath it and carry it along in stride. Gainer saw, peripherally, no green-shirted teammates coming from mid-field for a centering pass. He took it himself, changed direction nicely and kept going full out to be in front of the goal.

He heard screams, shouts. Cheers for him, he believed.

He pivoted. Went easily around one of the Sound View defenders. Had only the goalkeeper to beat.

The goalkeeper came out, apparently to challenge.

Gainer was about to take the shot when the goalkeeper ran past him, leaving the goal empty.

Gainer stopped so abruptly he slid in the mud, went down in the goop. He kneeled up, snapped his hands to rid them of the filthy-feeling stuff. Looked to the far end of the field and saw the gray Datsun.

A five-year-old hatchback without license plates.

The car had come up over the curb of Claremont Parkway and across the open area of the park, steering clear of baby carriages and wheelchairs, guys with bottles in paper bags and lovers oblivious in the grass. For a car to be where it should not be was far from the most flagrant thing ever seen around here. It was just another way of someone's going against instead of with.

Hardly any reaction to it.

Until it reached the field where the soccer match was going on.

It came onto the north end of the field at one of the corner kick quadrants. The driver had a black nylon stocking over his head to disguise his features and hide his hair. He stuck his arm out the car's window and let go of something.

355

Whatever it was flew up into separate pieces.

Scattered in the wake of wind created by the speed of the car.

It was a joke.

They were counterfeit.

Pieces of paper with a dead President's picture on them.

Hundreds.

They looked real.

The beneficent gray Datsun circled around elusively. Repeatedly, the arm of the driver emerged to make more money fly.

Players and spectators alike gathered it up. Word traveled fast. Everyone in the vicinity ran to the soccer field for all they were worth. Even the elderly and feeble were able to get a share. Children shoved bill after bill inside their shirts and blouses. Girlfriends stuffed their panties. People were on their hands and knees in the mud.

Real hundred dollar bills.

A middle-aged woman out of breath in the thick of it paused only long enough to make the sign of the cross on herself while glancing gratefully heavenward.

In ten minutes Santiago managed to grab up almost ninety-five thousand for himself.

The gray Datsun departed as anonymously as it had arrived, sped across the open area between benches and trees and off the curb to Crotona Parkway, where it became just another car in the impatient traffic.

Gainer had hardly moved, stood there in front of the goal with the ball under his arm.

AT five-thirty, the appointed time, he was at the Seventy-ninth Street Basin. Leslie was ten minutes late. She brought the Riva in fast, bow up. Slowed but didn't stop as she skimmed along the dock. Gainer had to jump for it. At once she demanded the boat's top speed, executed a turn so tight it almost sent Gainer overboard.

She headed the Riva downriver in the direction of Ellis. She was enjoying the speedboat now, its unique sort of maneuverability, the spaciousness of the surface that was offered her, so much more than a mere highway. If only the boat could do better than forty-five.

She zigzagged sharply, playfully.

Her nutmeg-colored hair whipped.

She was in an up-mood, singing something Gainer could not make out because of the wind and the engine.

He reached over and turned off the ignition key.

The bow of the Riva settled down.

"Why?" Gainer asked.

"What why?" Leslie worked her eyelashes some.

"No use, I know it was you."

"Did you make any goals today, lover?"

"Where did you get the gray Datsun?"

"You have a terrible bruise."

"Where?"

"On your cheek." She tried to get to it with a kiss but he pulled away.

A tug came by, tooted.

"Borrowed it," she said, "from a cheap parking lot on Webster Avenue. They should be more conscientious about looking after the cars."

"Stole it?"

"Only for twenty minutes. I put it back exactly where it was. Why are you so bothered about the car?"

"It might be traced to you."

"Never. It wasn't even missed."

"You were supposed to stay on Ellis with the money."

"I didn't absolutely, positively promise that. Anyway, I just looked at it a moment ago. The money is all there."

"Except what you threw away."

She smiled her *forgive me* smile.

"How much?" he asked.

"Just one bagful."

Three to four million.

"Why?"

"Lady Caroline told me to."

Same old excuse, Gainer thought.

"Lady Caroline had a dreadful time getting through to me. Almost didn't . . . because of all those heavy spirits hanging around Ellis looking for someone to complain to. They kept scrambling her."

Head back, deep shoulder-heaving sigh from Gainer. "Why don't you admit it . . . just this once, to me and yourself. It wasn't some sort of instruction that came to you out of thin air. You had an irresistible fit of the monies, that's all it was, the monies."

"You're really pissed aren't you?"

"Damn right!"

"All the way down to making your toenails red pissed?"

Gainer felt like an actor being audienced by himself. He thought of

357

Santiago and Tricky, imagined the times they would have with their windfalls. He started laughing inside.

Then outside.

He laughed all the way to the attic.

CHAPTER
TWENTY-ONE

I N the early morning of the Wednesday of that week.
Darrow and Horridge were on the ninth fairway at the Jupiter
Island Club.

Both their drives had been off to the left and hadn't carried well in
the humid air, nor had they gotten much roll with the dew not yet
burned from the grass. Horridge was a good if inconsistent golfer. He
would double-bogey one hole and birdie the next. Darrow only appeared to be the better at it with his leanness and style. He was wearing
light-gray English flannel slacks, deeply pleated, and a pale blue lisle
shirt that matched his strapped-around sun visor.

The day was so ideal, the place so exclusive that Darrow was almost
able to put his predicament out of mind. Here was where he fitted,
where he should have been all along, Darrow felt. Rubbing social
shoulders where the blood was blue and the money old. Even the sun
seemed to strike richer on everything here at Hobe Sound.

Horridge had been straightforward with him about what to expect
if the appeal was not decided in his favor. They had spoken briefly about
it during the flight down on the Gulfstream. Darrow would be given
two choices. He could, commencing next week, make frequent visits to
a certain doctor at Sloan-Kettering in New York City—ostensibly for
a series of vitamin B_{12} injections. The solution injected intravenously
would indeed be vitamin B_{12}, but it would also contain certain live
cancer cells.

That would be the prolonged way.

Darrow's other choice was swifter and required nothing of a change by him. Sometime soon in the normal course of his way of life, he would unknowingly ingest, in his food or drink, a concentrated amount of thromboxane, a potent clotting agent normally found in the body. Such a large dose of thromboxane would induce platelets to stick together and form clots in the bloodstream. An embolism, a stroke, a heart attack would be the result.

Either way, Darrow's demise would appear to be due to a natural cause.

It was High Board policy, not to be questioned.

It had proven to be more decorous and orderly than other ways, Horridge said.

Darrow assumed by that that many others had gone before him, perhaps not all so voluntarily. Not just Gridley, but others who had died suddenly or been taken by cancer. To mind came certain politicians, criminals, journalists, even heads of countries. It had occurred previously to Darrow how strangely coincidental and convenient it was when a person who had become a crucial witness or a political embarrassment, a Wall Street troublemaker or whatever, solved and calmed things by dying. Darrow had never connected it up before.

Anyway, it would not happen to him. He would succeed with his appeal. In fact, he would come out of it better off. He'd always felt he needed only exposure to the upper echelon to be realized. This, of course, was not the most desirable way of getting it, but he would turn it around.

Did Horridge have any instructions for him about the appeal, perhaps a hint or two that might be to his advantage? What should he expect? Who would he be seeing?

Horridge had answered by cleaning his glasses with a tissue and his breath, and by removing from his case a small leather-bound volume of Ralph Waldo's poems.

Now, Horridge lined up his second shot, smacked it toward the green. Darrow hit his ball into one of the bunkers to the right of the green.

As they walked together Darrow told Horridge: "I'll forfeit three strokes rather than play the bunker."

"What, and just toss your ball to the pin, I suppose."

"I'll drop at the edge of the green. It's just that I'm terrible in a trap. I might be in there all day hacking away."

Horridge agreed.

Darrow's real reason for avoiding the bunker was he didn't want to risk messing his flannels.

They arrived at the green, three-putted it and headed for the tee of the tenth hole.

"What's your opinion of Hine?" Horridge asked out of the blue.

"Bright young fellow," Darrow said.

"Splendid background."

"If anything, too ambitious."

"Can't hold that against him. Often it's good to have that sort inside. Tell me, how is his marriage to that Whitcroft girl getting along?"

"They're close, exceptionally close."

"Good, Boston has had an eye on him."

"Really?"

"Not a microscope, just an eye."

Was it possible, Darrow wondered, that Horridge was grinding him a little to see how he'd take it? No matter, he couldn't chance saying what an insufferable young shit he believed Hine really was. To speak negatively would only reflect the same upon himself at this time. When this was done with, he'd pull every goddamn thing out from under Hine.

Horridge was about to place his tee when an electric golf cart approached.

Two men in it.

The man in the pale yellow shirt was the younger, although he was in his seventies. He had a tan speckled pate and pronounced jowls.

The other man was wearing a lightweight cotton knit sweater of a pale green shade, his white chest hairs exposed by the V-neck of it. His hair was white, not silvery white, but as white as hair ever gets. He had it combed straight back. His face seemed to be trying to hide his eyes, looked as though it had a mild case of elephantiasis or some sort of pituitary problem. His cheeks were built up with coarse flesh, as was his chin and forehead. His nose was bulbous, textured with large pores. From the set of his jaw, one would have thought he had something between his teeth that he refused to let go.

The two men got out of the golf cart.

"Do you mind if we play through?" Green Sweater asked.

"Not at all," Horridge told him.

Darrow did not say anything but his annoyance was readable. Why should he and Horridge make way for these two undoubtedly slower old farts? Where the hell had they come from? They hadn't been following on the ninth or any of the preceding holes. Perhaps they were playing the last nine because that was all they could manage.

Yellow Shirt teed his ball. Took a couple of practice swings, choppy, not enough back swing or follow through.

Darrow rolled his eyes up intolerantly.

Horridge remained expressionless.

Yellow Shirt stood to his ball, measured it, sighted down the fairway, measured his ball again and was about to drive it when he motioned for Darrow to move away from his field of concentration.

Darrow stepped back without looking.

The heel cleats of his right shoe came down on the toe of the other, older man, the white-haired one in the green sweater.

The cleats left an ugly, muddy imprint on the man's immaculate white shoes.

Green Sweater said nothing.

Darrow was disgruntled over having been made to appear clumsy. "Go ahead and hit, for God's sake," he told Yellow Shirt.

Yellow Shirt decided he didn't like the ball he was about to drive. He went to the pocket of his golf bag, took his time choosing another.

They seemed to be deliberately stalling, Darrow thought, as Yellow Shirt was now undecided on where to plant his tee.

Meanwhile Green Sweater had stepped aside and off a ways with Horridge. He and Horridge were faced away, exchanging quiet, covered words.

Darrow thought Green Sweater was probably apologizing.

Finally, Yellow Shirt and Green Sweater played their tee shots. They thanked for the courtesy, got into the golf cart and proceeded down the fairway.

Horridge shoved his driver back into his golf bag, slipped the protective leather cap over its head. Looked at his watch.

"It wasn't just that you dirtied his shoe," Horridge said.

Darrow was perplexed.

"Nearly every morning he pays some attention to the television news on Bill Paley's network. This morning CBS made quite a show of a pack of rabble scrambling and clawing for money that someone literally threw away yesterday—several million in cash. Most unfortunate for you that he saw it, and drew his own natural conclusions about where it came from."

"Who?"

There was disdain for Darrow's lack of knowing. "In the green sweater, Gordon Winship."

CHAPTER
TWENTY-TWO

THE funeral of Edwin Lawrence Darrow.

On Sunday, September 27, at Saint James Episcopal Church in Harrison, New York.

Forty-seven persons attended. More than half were security men and other employees of Number 19, required to be there. Hine and wife Lois sat in the front section reserved for family, along with Mrs. Barbara Darrow, who showed up an hour before the ceremony with an entourage of six, including her companion Millicent Buckley and a muscular Mexican cliff diver.

Horridge sat in the rear row apart from everyone. He had returned to stay on at Number 19 and oversee the return to normal functioning. His first recommendation influenced the appointment of Hine as Temporary Custodian.

Gainer and Leslie were there, for no reason other than Gainer wanted to see first-hand that Darrow was truly dead and gone. They had what were comparable to excellent orchestra seats: tenth pew, center. Leslie chose to wear a bright red Cardin suit, claimed she had nothing else more appropriate.

Darrow, the centerpiece, was surrounded by tall creamy tapers and such an abundance of white trumpet lilies that he appeared to be afloat in a marsh. His gray-bronze casket was half open and tilted for a better view of him. Its white satin acetate lining would have played up Darrow's tanned complexion if the blue cast of death had not set in, and if the mortician had not tried to compensate for that with a thick application of pinkish based pancake make-up. As a result Darrow would be last seen looking rather mauve. The mortician evidently hadn't had one of his better embalmings. While shaving Darrow he'd nicked him badly above the lip and the collodion he used to glue the wound built up visibly, giving Darrow a scar he had never had.

Another thing.

Darrow was positioned with his arms at his sides, extended beneath the lower closed section of the casket lid.

That hid his hands.

If Darrow had not already been dead, he would have died.

A flutist and an organist played almost continually, a sort of funeral version of Muzak, and one of Darrow's old Yale Law School chums delivered the eulogy, saying sad, complimentary abstractions about Darrow and pausing after only a few sentences to blow his nose to demonstrate sincerity. He knew less of Darrow than anyone there, outside of the Mexican cliff diver. Hadn't seen Darrow in nearly forty years.

It was during the eulogy that Gainer's glance locked momentarily with the glance of Millicent Buckley.

"Who's that?" Leslie wanted to know.

"What's-her-name."

"Millicent?"

"Yeah, that's it."

"Cradle robber."

Gainer no longer saw any resemblance at all between Millicent and the mother photograph. It was ridiculous that he ever could have. Not even the vaguest resemblance. He ignored her.

Final respects.

Barbara Darrow at the casket plucked a two carat diamond stickpin from her husband's silk tie, said a ten-second prayer and told the funeral director, "Close the damn thing."

The pallbearers, six security men, carried the casket with irreverent haste out to the waiting hearse, rolled it in and tossed a lot of lilies in with it.

Black Cadillac limousines waited.

The Episcopal minister consolingly tried to capture Hine's hand. Hine shoved his hands into the safety of his pockets, backed off when the minister stepped within reach.

Hine beckoned to Gainer.

They walked around the side of the church and into an old grave-yard.

"Nice going," Hine said. It was their first contact since.

"Thanks."

"Any regrets?"

"None."

"Where's the money?"

"In a room somewhere."

"Why don't you just say where and I'll have my people pick it up."

"I haven't sliced off my end yet."

"I thought you would have by now."

Gainer and Chapin had enjoyed figuring ways to wash their money. Chapin knew a lot about it. Offshore would be easiest, best. And not all in one place. Liechtenstein, Andorra, the Channel Islands, even Hong Kong.

"Anyway," Hine continued, "just as well, I've decided to increase your take."

"To how much?"

"An extra ten, fifty million altogether. How does that appeal to you, Andrew?"

"Make it sixty."

"No."

"Fifty's fine." Another ten million just like that, Gainer thought. It caused him to distrust Hine that much more. No matter, he had to take his chances with Hine, and there was the Southampton tape for protection, the tape with Hine on it making the proposition. For safety's sake he should make Hine aware of that tape now.

Lois Hine came over to them. The spike heels of her black sandals in the grass made the going difficult for her. One sandal came off. She swore, retrieved it, used a weatherworn gravemarker to steady herself while she slipped the sandal on, hiked her knee way up to do it.

No rule about having to wear underthings to a funeral, Gainer thought.

"I just snapped your picture," Lois told Gainer.

"What do you want?" Hine asked her brusquely.

"You're holding up the whole sorry convoy," Lois said.

"I'll be a minute more," Hine said.

Her smile was crooked. "I like you at a funeral," she told Hine. "We ought to have one more often," and then returned to one of the limousines.

"No reason why we shouldn't settle our deal today, is there?" Hine asked Gainer.

"What would be a reason?"

"I mean, the money's there, isn't it?"

365

"It's there."

"Sweet will take you, or follow along if you prefer. I'll send some help with him to handle the billion."

"You'll also need a boat."

"No problem. Just tell Sweet. By the way, here, I almost forgot this." Something from his jacket pocket.

Gainer's passport.

"The guy who substituted for you on that carry was hit by a wine truck in Zurich."

"Hit?"

"He was you."

Gainer pictured it.

"At four in the morning on Birmansdorferstrasse. He'd been drinking. Do you know Birmansdorferstrasse?"

"No."

"Dead, practically no traffic at that hour. It was as though someone stood him up in the middle of the street, held him there until the last second."

As good a way not to go as any, Gainer thought. Well, with Darrow in the ground, he'd no longer have to be bothered about that. Nor would there be trouble of that sort with Hine. "Before we go any further, Hine, there's something you should know."

"Just see that I get the money—"

"That day when we were out in Southampton, the second time, I got it all on tape."

Hine did not believe it.

"Every word," Gainer said.

Hine thought for a long moment, then smiled. "Great!" he said. "Play it for me sometime." Before another word he turned, hurried to the limo and was gone.

CHAPTER
TWENTY-THREE

LATE afternoon of that funeral day Gainer and Leslie were at the rendezvous point: out in the harbor, midway between the tip of Manhattan and Governor's Island.

Sweet and his detachment were just now coming into view. Gainer had expected them down the East River, but they came the opposite way, up through the Buttermilk Channel off the waterfront of Brooklyn.

A fifty foot red tugboat, wide beamed and pugnacious looking. Escorted by four *Cigarettes,* those incredibly fast speedboats built in Florida by Halter Marine. The *Cigarettes* were thirty-five-foot "Awesome" models, each worth two hundred thousand dollars. Powered by dual four hundred horsepower engines, they could do eighty-five miles per hour. All four were painted black, no contrast striping or trim, entirely matte-black. There were two security men in each of the Awesomes. Four others were aboard the tug with Sweet.

Gainer was taken aback by the sight of such an ominous flotilla. He had anticipated one fair-sized boat, Sweet and a couple of men. He had Leslie pull the Riva alongside the tug so he could talk to Sweet. "No go," Gainer told him over the idling sputters of the engines.

"Why not?" Sweet asked.

"The odds are out of line."

"I brought some help—to get this over with soon as possible, that's all."

"Too many."

"You tell me, then."

"Three counting yourself, no more."

Sweet agreed. Two of his four men on the tug were transferred to Awesomes. The Riva and the tug remained where they were while the Awesomes headed in the direction from which they had come. Gainer watched them until they were specks lost among the textures of the Brooklyn waterfront. Gainer waited ten minutes longer before instructing Leslie to throttle the Riva and lead the way across the upper harbor to Ellis.

As they approached the seawall on the south side, Gainer saw no sign of the outboard skiff Chapin and Vinny had been using. He had left them with the money around nine that morning. Probably, he thought, they'd been gone only minutes, had noticed the Riva and the other boats headed that way and took off in order to keep their involvement unknown. Chapin had said that was how he wanted it.

"I'll leave it up to you to collect the forty million," Chapin had told Gainer.

"Whatever's best for you."

"We'll split later at my place, how's that?"

"You trust me that much?"

"What the hell, we haven't got anything if we haven't got trust."

The Riva came in alongside the seawall and tied up. From shore Gainer shouted to Sweet aboard the tug, had him maneuver it close to the corner, most convenient to the building where the money was. Sweet jumped ashore. He was very much in charge. He told the two security men to stand by while he went into the building.

Gainer and Leslie went ahead of him up the steps to the porch and on in. Sweet was a bit startled by how run-down the interior was, glanced leerily around. The place certainly didn't look like a billion, he thought. Smart of them to stash it here. He followed to the doorway of one of the side rooms.

Gainer and Leslie were already in that room, standing amidst a bunch of old, mildew-stained mattresses.

Gainer shook his head sharply as though they might correct what his eyes were registering. The mattresses weren't piled as before. Where the billion had been was now . . . nothing.

"It's not here," Gainer murmured incredibly.

"What the fuck do you mean it's not here?" growled Sweet.

Gainer had never found it so difficult to think fast. "Wrong room," he said, "these rooms all look alike."

"They always mix me up," Leslie added.

Sweet stepped aside for their exit. "You don't remember where the fuck you put a billion dollars?"

"Sure, I mean, I thought I did." Gainer tried to act only slightly peeved with himself. He indicated several rooms across the way. "You look into those and we'll try these."

Sweet kicked aside a large round lightbulb reflector that went skittering over the plaster-dusted surface and clanged against a wall. The first room he looked into had only one old cast-iron radiator sitting in the middle of it. The door to the next room was stuck shut. He put his weight to it, crushed it open.

Meanwhile, on the opposite side of the building, Gainer and Leslie crawled out a window, hurried through the high weeds to the commissioner's house next door. They ran up the four flights to the attic.

Leslie practically tore off her red Cardin suit. A target she might soon be, but at least she wouldn't be one so obvious. She legged into jeans and a chambray shirt and sneakers. When Gainer had last worn his sneakers, he had, as always, pulled them off without untying and now he was desperately picking at a knot. He wouldn't survive if he had to slide around in the dressy leather soles and heels he'd worn to the funeral. Leslie grabbed the sneakers from him, coaxed the knot with her fingernails.

It came undone.

The growl of speedboats. The four Awesomes were approaching Ellis. From across the bay they had kept track of the tug and the Riva with powerful binoculars. The Awesomes tied up along the seawall, the other ten men jumped ashore.

Gainer and Leslie harnessed on their shoulder holsters, checked their ASPs, threaded silencers on and put in pocket extra clips. They could hear Sweet directly below outside the commissioner's house. Issuing orders.

"We'll do like Mr. Hine said," Sweet told the men. "Get the money and whack out the man and the woman. There's a bonus in it for the guy who makes the kill. A ten thousand bonus. Let me know as soon as you come across the money. Don't start counting it or stuffing your shorts, let me know right away."

Gainer peered down, saw the men had automatic rifles. He didn't know exactly what kind, didn't know they were Colt Commandos, compact versions of the AR-15 with a telescoping butt and shortened barrel, capable of firing at a rate of eight hundred rounds per minute. Same as those used by the U.S. Army Special Forces Unit. Gainer guessed that the cylindrical mechanism at the end of each barrel was a sound compressor, a larger cousin of the silencers he and Leslie had on their ASPs.

Which seemed puny by comparison. No matter, they had to go with what they had. One advantage: they knew the place.

They climbed out a dormer on the west side of the attic, sidled along a limestone ledge slippery with pigeon droppings to where they could hang from a gutter drain and land almost noiselessly on the roof of the adjoining building. Only a slight pitch to that roof. They crossed over it, lowered themselves to another level. Now they were on the second story roof of that long straight corridor, the one with all the windows. In a winglike arrangement, that roof gave access to the roofs of all the wards and other buildings. For the time being, no place was safer.

They paused behind a raised skylight. Their only chance was to get to the Riva and the mainland. Gainer motioned Leslie to remain there. He moved quickly in a crouch further down the length of roof to a spot overlooking where the Riva and the Awesomes were tied up at the seawall. Through the lacy leaves of a tall locust tree he made out the figures of two armed men stationed at the boats. He observed them for several minutes and decided they were alert. Too alert.

He returned to Leslie, put his mouth to her ear and told her in a whisper hardly louder than his normal breathing the Riva situation as he'd seen it. Best to wait. They'd stay where they were concealed by the skylight. When dark came, maybe make a try for the boat. They sat, back pressed to back, so no one could steal up on them. Every so often they tilted their heads back and caressed with their cheeks.

Time to think about Chapin and Vinny now.

Little good it did for Gainer to label them with every obscenity the streets and salons of New York had ever taught him. Nor was there any psychological comfort in hoping Chapin and Vinny would somehow pay for their betrayal. They'd get theirs? Shit, they already had theirs. A billion plus. Gainer had never put any stock in the inevitability of retribution. That was something for the marks, the victims, to hang onto, to keep them from feeling all was lost. But fate was not an avenger.

In fact, Chapin and Vinny now stood a better chance than ever of avoiding knocks and living to be a hundred. They were up to their hard hearts in fuck-you money. Cashmere all the way. And when they did happen to be in the proximity of one of life's falling trees, they now had the *push* to make it more likely it would not go down in their direction.

Chapin.

The prick etcetera.

He'd planned it, and Vinny, as usual, had followed him. Chapin with his circuitous, intricate mentality had had it in his head from the start, no doubt. That meant everything from him had been bullshit and selfishness, and the mutual trust and regard Gainer had felt had actually been one-sided. Shouldn't have fallen for it, Gainer thought. Hindsight was having an eye for an asshole. He should have stayed with the money every minute, like his instinct had told him.

Except, ironically, if the money *had* been in that room down there, he and Leslie would be down there now—dead from holes. That they were saved, momentarily at least, by its not being there was because Chapin had taken it. Well, he got no gold stars for good intentions, the son of a bitch.

Hine, he'd never, of course, trusted. Strange, Hine's indifferent reaction to the Southampton tape. The tape was supposed to be the saver, the equalizer. It still might be, Gainer thought. Hine just hadn't believed such a tape existed—otherwise he wouldn't have dared throw all this shit at them. Gainer blamed himself for not taking the time and care to convince Hine, to send him a duplicate of the incriminating tape. *He* knew he had it, but Hine didn't—and that was what counted.

Well, Norma?

Leslie tilted her head back far enough to kiss him behind the ear, one of her special kisses that felt as though all of her was turned inside out and concentrated wet and warm on that spot. "I love you, lover," she whispered.

"We don't have much of a chance," he said.

"How much?"

"Ninety-ten, maybe less."

She didn't agree. "I'd say eighty-twenty, maybe even fifty-fifty."

"I'm sorry," he said, again feeling responsible.

She turned so he couldn't miss her look. "If I hear one more apology, I'm going to get up and walk right off the roof."

A long silent moment.

Gainer looked over to Manhattan. The city looked motionless, apathetic. He had the illusion that he could reach out and rearrange it, pick up the Woolworth building by its spire and place it wherever he pleased. Topple one of the Trade Towers with the tip of his finger. His city.

"Tell you what," Leslie whispered. "Let's make a pact."

"Sure."

"Next lifetime, you come back as me and I'll come back as you."

"You said we had fifty-fifty."

"I'm sticking to that. This is just in case. You be me and I'll be you, next time around, okay?"

"Why?"

"I want you to feel all the marvelous things you've made me feel."

"Maybe that's what we're doing this time," he said.

"Possibly." She smiled and he saw the pink pillow of her tongue. "God I wish I had some Rescue," she said.

So did he. Any kind would be welcome.

AT that moment inside the building a security man came on the stairway-up that the skylight served. He was, at that point, only twenty feet below Gainer and Leslie. His stalker's instinct, working like a sensitive instrument, told him they were not far away. He'd been moving quietly and swiftly from room to room, not darting or otherwise making himself less of a target, because from what Sweet had said and he himself had seen, the man and the woman were not armed.

Now, he stood at the bottom of the stairs with his automatic rifle just a bit readier. Stopped breathing so he could hear anything. Heard the crunch of plaster dust beneath his shoes as he shifted his position, but nothing more. This place, he thought. He wouldn't want to go up against anyone weapon-to-weapon here. Too many blind spaces and traps in all these rooms, and unpredictable debris.

As things were the plaster dust helped, the shoeprints in it. No one could move about without leaving a trail. He examined the stairway, found only rat tracks in the inch-thick dust on the treads. The man and the woman had not gone up there. He turned his head abruptly, hoping to catch sight of someone in the hall area to his left. All was still. No matter, something continued to tell him he was close.

The skylight above the stairway landing. He raised his eyes to it. Three panes missing, numerous others partially broken out. The density of light coming through some of the panes along the near edge suddenly altered, he noticed. A subtle but discernible change. He watched for it again. This time it seemed more pronounced and also cast a dull, soft-edged shadow on the wall below the skylight.

It went away.

In seconds reappeared.

There were ten steps up to the landing. He took them as separate obstacles. Not placing weight on a foot until he was certain there was nothing beneath it to crunch and give him away. He even squatted and swept the dust from some steps with his hands to reveal and then avoid pieces of plaster. He'd taken greater pains at other times for less than ten thousand, he thought.

When he reached the landing he was ten feet nearer his objective.

That indistinct shadow was still on the wall. His eyes traveled from it up to where its source should be.

The panes of the skylight were coated with dust that was caked on by rain and dampness from the harbor. The security man gauged how opaque they were by comparing where a pane was missing. No shadow was possible through those dirty panes, he decided. He felt he'd gotten too carried away, gave the blame to the afternoon sun rather than his eyes—

But then . . . in the corner of one of the opaque panes, where a triangular piece no larger than an inch was broken away . . .

The color of nutmeg, for a moment.

The security man recognized it, brought his automatic rifle up, didn't need to sight at that range. Firmed the butt of the rifle against the muscles forward of his right hip, leaned back and pulled off a burst.

And another burst.

The glass of the skylight shattered upward like a fountain of shards. Its frames split and flew in all directions.

SEVERAL of the .223 inch caliber bullets came so close to Leslie they singed her hair.

At once she and Gainer rolled away, got up and were on the run along the corridor roof for about fifty strides and then onto the roof of one of the medical ward buildings. The surface of that roof was interrupted by a slightly raised structure about three feet square. Apparently the lid of a trap door. Gainer and Leslie tried with all their strength to lift it off, but it was either solidly stuck or bolted shut from the inside. They gave up on it, went to the edge of the ward roof. Found an exterior metal ladder fixed vertically to the side of the building.

Leslie was first to start down. The ladder hadn't been used in fifty years. Rust on its rungs came off in flakes as Leslie gripped them. She climbed down swiftly, watching the placement of her feet, believing that Gainer was no more than a rung above her and in his hurry might accidentally step on her fingers. When she reached the ground and looked up she saw he was still at the top of the ladder.

He was standing on it with his arms through the top two rungs. His forearms rested on the edge of the roof, one hand steadying the other that gripped his ASP.

He figured they would come up, was hoping they would choose that way. He concentrated on the trap door, and after a couple of minutes saw the lid of it shift a little and then suddenly hinge open.

Gainer had expected they would be more cautious than that, thought he'd have trouble holding back long enough to take full advantage. But one, two of them came up and out of the opening with little more care than if they'd been city roofing inspectors. They stood there looking around, shielding their eyes from the sun.

They were only twenty feet away.

One of Gainer's first shots hit within an inch of where he aimed. The .380 hollow point slug went into the man just a fraction above where his collarbones came together. It tore through his windpipe and esophagus and partly severed his common carotid artery. The slug was nowhere near spent when it struck and shattered the first dorsal vertebra at the top of the man's spine. The man stiffened as the upper third of him was driven back by force of the slug. The rest of him crumpled, and he went down in a sort of extreme back bend.

Gainer's next shot was nearly as sure, and required only a slight adjustment of aim. The second man had just time enough to get both hands on his automatic rifle before being hit. The bullet entered a couple of inches to the right of his sternum, smashed against the upper portion of his fourth rib. The impact divided the slug into several chunks that glanced off into different directions, ripping cartilages and the tissues of his organs, shredding through veins and arteries in his chest and abdomen. His automatic rifle went flying. For a moment he was balanced on one leg, like a discus thrower in bad form, arms flailing. And then he collapsed.

Gainer waited a few seconds, but no one else came up onto the roof. He holstered his ASP and practically slid the two stories down the ladder to the ground.

Leslie had taken cover, was kneeling among some tall weeds. She stuck her head up briefly for Gainer to find her. He hurried to her, kneeled beside her. Why was it such a relief to be off his feet? He hadn't exerted himself enough to be breathing so hard or for his heart to be going at this rate. He worked up some saliva and moved it around the inside of his mouth but his mouth went quickly dry again. Told himself he shouldn't react badly to having killed those two, especially not the deliberate way he'd killed them, without giving them a chance. That was street, that was smart. He had better learn to think even more like that. Take the sucker shots when he could, pick up the regrets and other pieces later.

Full deep breath.

Go away hollow.

Come back legs.

He was a quick, cold-headed killer, he was. At least he would be with some cooperation from his heart that was still zapping.

He looked to Leslie, believed what he saw in her eyes was both praise and fright.

She believed his wink. He hoped.

The weed patch, Gainer decided, was not a substantial enough cover. They moved in a crouch through it, beneath where some wild grapes had a many-season stranglehold on a dogwood tree. Fifteen feet further on was the rear of one of the buildings. Three concrete steps up to a concrete platform and a partially open door.

They made a dash for it.

The door was metal and its hinges had rusted in place. Maybe it could be pulled open more, but not quietly.

Leslie was able to squeeze sideways through and in. It was tighter for Gainer, and at once point it seemed the door and its sharp-edged jamb had him unable to move at all. Leslie pulled on him. He gritted and scraped painfully in.

What they'd gotten into, they discovered, was a large old toilet area. Evidently for men. Situated along the length of one wall were ten toilet bowls, and along the wall opposite were as many urinals. The floor where it was still intact was made up of white octagonal ceramic tiles. Years of grime on everything. The ceiling had surrendered long ago, dropped its plaster in uncountable chips and some huge chunks. Almost in the middle of the room stood four displaced sinks, two-legged porcelain sinks meant to have a wall to lean against that now depended haphazardly on one another. Other sinks of the same sort were thrown in a six foot high pile in one of the deepest corners. Directly above them was a leaky ventilating shaft, so those sinks were layered with wet mold, like someone had poured a scummy green topping on them.

An unlikely, and safer, place, they decided. They sat in the corner behind the pile of sinks.

Gainer's watch told him five after five. Another hour and a half or so before sundown and even then there would be leftover light for quite a while. He watched the sweep hand of the watch complete the circle and he drew encouragement from thinking only ninety more of those, which then didn't seem so terribly long. He recalled how Sweet had coveted that watch. An Audemar Piquet from Norma two years ago. Gainer could practically measure his life by the various watches Norma had bought him in Zurich. From the first Phillip Patek to the Baume Mercier that had been his favorite next to this one.

He pictured Sweet rolling him over dead and unbuckling the watch from his wrist. He hated the thought of Sweet telling the times of *his* life from this watch. Sweet would never get it, Gainer vowed. He'd smash it first, would smash it now if he didn't have the need for it.

Ten minutes went by.

Leslie snuggled in the cave of Gainer's right arm. Part of her was remembering little luxuries, giving them their due and including them in things she'd miss. At the same time, most of her was listening. Even the most innocent sounds made her start.

She elbowed Gainer. Walked fingers on her thigh to convey that she thought she heard footsteps.

Gainer couldn't hear them.

And then he did. The pulverizing of chunks of fallen plaster under someone's weight. Not stalking steps, not someone trying to be stealthy, but a regular stride at an easy pace, like that of someone who knew where he was headed.

Closer footsteps, louder.

Bound knowingly for Gainer and Leslie, it seemed. Bringing a certain confrontation.

Gainer drew his ASP.

So did Leslie.

Their view of the entrance of the other end of the room was blocked by a three-quarter partition, making it impossible for them to see who it was that passed by the entrance and continued on.

The footstep sounds receded.

They stopped.

They returned to the toilet area.

The man appeared from behind the partition like a performer making an entrance from the wings. He stood there in the low light facing only as much as he could see, an audience of toilet bowls and urinals. One hand held the automatic rifle by its grip, as though its seven and a half pounds were next to nothing. The rifle seemed undersize compared to him. There were white smudges of plaster dust on his black trousers and jacket. He glanced right at the pile of old sinks in the far corner and then let the muzzle of his rifle relax.

Gainer wanted to shoot him. So did Leslie. However neither had a positively sure heart or head shot. The four sinks that were propped up in the middle of the room were in the way. A miss or mere wound would trigger an answer from that automatic rifle. Better not to risk it.

The sinks would save the man.

He was about to turn and leave when he noticed a door. Only four steps and a reach away.

He opened it.

They were too quick for the rifle to do him any good, although in reaction he did squeeze off one wild burst. He had no chance to run.

They had known he was there, and in their chronically nervous manner had anticipated the intrusion. The single hole in the rear of the large old mop-and-pail closet could not accommodate a swift enough retreat for so many. They had to accept that they were hemmed in, and when the opening came they attacked. Some were old four-year-olds, most were at least full grown. They could leap four feet ahead and two feet straight up.

They were afraid of humans.

They hated humans.

This was human.

They went for his legs, his calves and thighs. Got onto them, clawed in, sunk their teeth as they climbed around and up him. He tried to beat them off with the butt of the rifle, tried to knock them off with his hands. Their bites clamped them to his hands.

When they reached his shoulders he hunched his head to protect his neck, and he did not scream until they got to it. He threw his weight against the wall, hoping to crush them with himself. Some were stunned and fell off him. He scraped his body along the wall. But as many as brushed off, twice as many leaped onto him.

The man knew if he went down they would finish him. He stayed upright, used the walls, reeled from one wall to another. Fell over one of the urinals, managed to regain his feet only to go off balance again against the sinks in the middle of the room. The sinks would not save him. They fell over. The man collapsed awkwardly among them, and was reduced to kicking and flailing.

Gainer stood up. He squeezed off two shots that thudded into the rats. Two more shots caused a squeal rather than a snarl, and as though that was a signal the pack scattered, scurried back into the closet and out the entrance, except a few that slunk along the edge of the room behind the toilet bowls, peering, quivering.

Gainer approached the man.

His clothes were shredded. He was bitten a thousand times. Both his ears had been chewed off. His eyes were open, apparently dead eyes.

Gainer avoided those eyes. He retrieved the automatic rifle and found a spare magazine in the man's jacket pocket. Took the time to put a full clip in the ASP.

Leslie could not get out of there quickly enough.

Gainer glanced back. The rats were already returning, snarling and snapping at the air.

That toilet area, as it turned out, was located off a main passageway, the one with walls of bare brick and storage spaces built parallel. Gainer and Leslie recognized it and were at once reoriented. When they were previously there they hadn't noticed how dim the passageway was, the only light coming from the few doors of the rooms connected to it.

Which way now? In one direction the passageway would take them to the north part of Ellis, where they'd seen those old shoes slung over a high pipe and the dormitory with the graffiti. They could go that way and, later on, work back around to the Riva. But wouldn't it be expected of them, as amateurs, to run as far as possible from where the danger had first shown itself? It would be less predictable for them to remain around here in the thick of it, Gainer decided.

They headed south along the passageway, single file and close to the wall. On the lookout for a good hiding place. They had not gone twenty paces when they heard voices ahead. They stepped into the deeper shadow of one of the storage spaces just in time. Two of their adversaries entered the passageway.

The men's voices were resonant in the tunnellike atmosphere.

"Me, I'd swim for it."

"You'd wash up tomorrow down around Sandy Hook or someplace. The channel might look easy but it's full of rips."

"We're going to be here all goddamn night."

"Could be worth it."

"Screw the bonus."

"Okay. Seeing that's how you feel, if you make the kill, say I made it so I can collect. I can use ten large. You think Sweet meant ten for wasting both or ten for each?"

"You're a money hungry bastard."

"Who isn't?"

"Some shylock must be into you. Either that or you've got yourself a spinner with a tight ass and a cold nose."

"I need, that's all."

"Christ, I hate the white powder shit that's all over this place. Probably asbestos. Asbestos will give you cancer, you know. I can already feel it getting to my sinuses."

"So, don't breathe."

The man sneezed twice and blessed himself.

By then the two were well down the dark passageway, having passed within a few feet of Gainer and Leslie. It hadn't occurred to them to search the storage spaces along there, apparently presuming someone else already had.

But the next who came along might be more conscientious, Gainer thought. He and Leslie checked both ways before slipping out into the passageway again. They tried to keep their steps light but could not help making crunches and cracklings. Any moment now, Gainer expected one or more of them would jump out and fire from point-blank range.

378

He himself had an automatic rifle now but it was the first time he'd ever even held one and its unfamiliarity made it seem less dependable than his ASP.

Thirty more paces brought them to an opening of double doors, one door being held awry by a single screw of its lower hinge. Inside was a moderate-sized room with ceiling and walls blistered to the third degree by moisture. Gainer and Leslie realized it was a room they hadn't been in. Nor had anyone else for a long while. No human tracks in the plaster dust that lay like flour sifted onto every surface. It was not a possible hiding place, their footprints would give them away.

Across the room on the outer wall were three sash-type windows that presented a view of the New Jersey docks on the other side of the channel. Sumac and locust branches reached in through broken panes. Gainer's mental map of the island told him he was near the southwest corner. An outside hiding place in that general area would be advantageous when the time came for them to try for the Riva.

The lower section of one of the windows was open about ten inches.

They walked quickly back and forth several times from the window to the entrance, so that from their tracks no one would be able to tell whether they'd come or gone. Gainer tried raising the window further. All three windows were metal-covered and rusted stuck. It would be a squeeze. Leslie went head and shoulders first out the window, just did manage to wiggle her way out. She dropped hard to the ground five feet below, landed in a sprawl.

Gainer wanted so much to make it through the opening he believed he could. But this was inches worse than the door he'd scraped through earlier. He got his head out by turning it sideways, but his shoulders and surely his chest would not go.

"*Try,* lover," Leslie urged. She reached to pull on him.

The last thing Gainer wanted was to get helplessly stuck in a window and be blown away from the rear.

"I'll find another way out," he told her. He retracted his head and stood upright. Glanced down and out to her and knew from her expression she was feeling what he was—the wrench of this sudden separation. Both realized now how much they had been drawing on one another.

For Gainer, a new urgency was now added to the danger. Perhaps that was why on his way from the room he brushed against the precariously hung door, caused its last holding screw to tear loose.

The door fell flat with a clap as loud as a shot.

That was sure to bring them.

Gainer rushed down the corridor to his right, searching for a way out. He came on several doors and tried them. Some gave to closets, dead ends. They would be literally that for him. Others were either locked or stuck shut. The place was a maze of small windowless rooms and sidehalls. Gainer took so many rapid lefts and rights he worried that he'd turned himself around, might be headed back instead of away. If so, he'd run right into them. That small table crushed almost out of sight behind a disconnected radiator—wasn't that the same he'd passed along the opposite way just moments ago?

Don't panic.

Don't feel cornered.

He continued on and, finally, there was an area he recognized from his explorings with Leslie. The crematorium. Only one room away from the extreme southwest corner now, he realized. Running out of options. He stood stock-still, hoping he wouldn't hear them, hoping they had taken the fall of that door as something accidentally caused by one of their own.

No such luck.

He heard them coming from all directions, even from overhead, converging on this part of Ellis. They weren't at all careful about their noise. It sounded as though some were running full out, rushing to be first to get off the ten-thousand-dollar shot.

Gainer hurried into the next room.

The morgue.

It had a line of windows on its outer wall. They were high up, out of reach by four feet. Metal casement-type windows. A couple were even slightly open. Gainer looked around, but there was nothing for him to stand on. Killed by four fucking feet, he thought.

Should he stand there and let them come to him or charge them like a kamikaze idiot? One thing for sure, he'd take as many as he could with him.

Appropriate place to die, huh Norma?

He didn't want to die for at least a million reasons, all Leslie. He tried to picture her and it was difficult because it seemed all the many lovely parts of her he'd come to know so well wanted to be last remembered. He couldn't even settle on her mouth, although her smile was very persistent and her hands, her hands that had conformed to the various shapes of him so many times.

Not enough.

God no, he hadn't kissed her enough or touched or held or done anything enough with her. And again, as it had been with Norma, he felt the futility of all the things left unsaid. Fuck the bullets, *this* was the suffering of it. Never again anything Leslie.

380

He hoped she was safe. He shouldn't have allowed her to get into this mess with him, her and her nicely laid out, long, soft life. She was resourceful, somehow she'd survive, Gainer wanted to believe. And if there was another side, as she claimed, he would perch himself up there on the edge of a cloud or whatever and do nothing but wait.

Arrange that, Lady Caroline, wherever you are. Please?

By then four security men and Sweet had already reached the point where the door had fallen. They had correctly read all the footprints as a deliberate attempt to confuse and therefore thought the noise of the door had probably also been meant to throw them off. Still, while they were in this area they might as well give it a thorough going over, Sweet told them.

They spread out and moved down the hallways of that southwest corner, methodically searching all possible places, closing in gradually on the morgue. Within five minutes they had eliminated every other room.

Two of the men now came into the morgue with their rifles at the ready.

Sweet took one step in and quickly scanned the room. It was where, in the old days, meat had been butchered and kept, Sweet guessed. The concrete floor and especially the big old wooden icebox with its eight green painted doors made him think that. From the size of the doors, only two feet by one and a half feet, it certainly appeared they gave access to individual compartments that weren't very deep.

Gainer was in the third one up on the left. Trying to be as still as death. He knew they were out there. Surely they would open the door, grab his feet and yank him out. Not that it mattered, but it was going to be embarrassing, being found cowering, especially inside such a thing. Maybe they wouldn't bother to pull him out, just find him, kill him in there, close the door on him. In that way make it into a funny old anecdote they could remember and retell for years:

"*. . . there he was in the morgue cooler all laid out ready to die, so, of course, we accommodated him!*"

They'd get a lot of mileage out of it.

Gainer tried to get his mind off them by concentrating on the rack-like platform directly above him. It was identical to the one he was on. Constructed of evenly spaced hardwood slats, no doubt to allow the cold air to get in to the underside of a corpse. A far cry from that modern morgue in Zurich, Gainer thought. Attached to each of the slatted racks were wheels that fitted down into the grooves of steel tracks so that the racks could be rolled out or in with little effort. When Gainer had climbed up to where he now was he'd had trouble keeping the rack from rolling forward. It was that movable. Once he got stretched out on it, the rack stayed in place, but the slightest shift on his part could start it rolling. The rear wall of the cooler was only a couple of inches from the top of his head. It was metal-lined, as were all the other interior surfaces, and there was a metal container at the base of the rear wall for big hunks of ice.

A coldness passed through Gainer from toe to chin. It was beyond a chill, more like an animated gust that could have its own way with anything. As though not yet done with Gainer, it wound under, over and around him. The back of his neck shivered from ear to ear.

A draft, he thought. Probably made by his own fear. However, if as Leslie had said, there were lots of spirits hanging around Ellis, this old icebox for the dead must have a gang of them.

Sweet's voice.

Gainer couldn't make out what was being said.

Sweet was impatient, extremely upset. What was supposed to have been an easy pick-up of cash and a couple of quick killings had turned into a shitty problem. This fucking island, Sweet thought, this fucking island had complicated things and before long, night would add its disadvantage. Well, no matter. He couldn't go back to Hine with nothing but excuses. He'd been right about that falling door being a diversion. He shouldn't have wasted time on it or any of these rooms.

Sweet turned abruptly, shoved two of the men aside and strode down the hall away from the morgue. He was bound for the buildings on the north section of Ellis, where he believed Gainer and Leslie would more likely be. And the money. He didn't order the men to follow, just assumed they would.

All but one did.

He hung back from the others, and when they were far enough ahead and out of sight around a corner he went back to the morgue. He was the man Gainer and Leslie had overheard in the brick passageway, the money-hungry one who was supporting either the habit of a spinner or a shylock. He'd known the morgue was a morgue the moment he'd seen it, and if his need hadn't bit his tongue he would have said so. He'd suspected those little icebox doors that appeared so incapable of hiding anyone, hadn't shared this suspicion because it would have meant also sharing the ten or twenty large bonus. Now, he'd have it all.

He remained quiet. Just outside the entrance to the morgue. Listened, heard nothing. By moving his head gradually to the right, the vertical edge of the entranceway revealed more and more of the room to him, and eventually his view included the green, wooden, floor-to-ceiling icebox. All eight of its doors. He'd thought he might catch the man and the woman in the act of climbing out, but now that he saw the doors were unchanged, he doubted his theory. No reason for them to stay in there when they believed they were in the clear.

Less cautious but with automatic rifle at the ready, he entered the room, approached the morgue cooler, jerked open one of its lower doors. Saw the slats of the empty rack. Crouched and took a closer look. Saw all the way in.

He pulled open one of the doors second from the bottom.

Nothing in there.

And then, third door up on the left.

Gainer had to time it perfectly. He used the rear wall to push off with his hands and send the rack rolling suddenly forward. It flew out the open door, and the man caught only a glimpse of the soles of Gainer's sneakers before the end edge of the hardwood rack smashed across the bridge of his nose.

Knocked the man staggering back.

His finger on the trigger of his rifle was included in his involuntary clutching at the pain. He pulled off a burst of shots that were wild and pocked across the ceiling.

He lurched sideways, grabbed at the air as though it might support him, tripped himself, went down hard with his rifle clattering under him on the cement floor. He at once sat up because he knew staying down would be death. He lifted his head as though it weighed more than all the rest of him, shook his head from side to side, and the blood that was streaming from both his nostrils splattered left and right.

By then Gainer was standing nearby with his ASP in hand. It appeared the man would give in to unconsciousness. Which would be better for them both, Gainer thought. The man rolled over onto his side, braced himself and managed to slowly rise up onto one knee. He tried to recover the rifle, groped around for it, finally got it. He was bringing his eyes and the muzzle of the rifle up to Gainer when Gainer killed him.

The racks of the morgue cooler were seven feet long. Gainer pulled out one all the way. He propped it against the wall and with its slats it became a ladder, providing easy access to those high casement windows. Gainer climbed up, pushed one of the windows open. He dropped the automatic rifle out to the ground and then himself.

He immediately looked for Leslie. There, in the weed growth by the west seawall, was where he'd last seen her, but apparently she wasn't there now. He went around the corner to the south side, moved in spurts, kept low and close to the foundation of the buildings, and when he'd gone about halfway along the south side—there she was. Using a contest of tangles between wild rose and greenbriar for cover. The relief Gainer felt at the sight of her told him how worried he'd been. He crawled into the thicket to her. They hugged. A short one and then a longer, tighter one.

"What took so long?" she whispered.

"I almost got lost."

She was grateful for the ambiguity.

Gainer got to his knees and parted the leaves to look out in the direction of the seawall. He was surprised to find the Riva and the Awesomes tied up only about forty feet away. No sign of the men who'd been guarding them before. That was strange. He'd expected to have to kill those two to get to the boat. Maybe they were hidden somewhere close by. He asked Leslie.

"They're not here anymore," she said matter of factly with a slightly perplexed shrug.

They decided not to wait for dark. They came out from the brambles. Gainer crouched along through waist-high goldenrod and Queen Anne's lace. Leslie rushed ahead and was behind the wheel of the Riva by the time he reached the seawall.

There were the two guards.

Gainer nearly stumbled over them.

One had a hole in his head, the other in his heart.

Not here anymore? For damn sure.

Gainer unhitched the mooring lines and tossed the fenders aboard. He shoved off from the wall to set the Riva drifting, hoping to catch a current that would take it noiselessly out for a fair distance. At a point twenty feet from the seawall the Riva became caught in a conflict of currents, was held right there.

Leslie started the engine.

It gave off a loud initial growl, then settled into a gurgle as Leslie kept it going as slowly and quietly as possible. Now they made distance, put one, two, three hundred feet between themselves and Ellis.

But that growl carried. It was a sound Sweet and his men were on the alert for. The moment they heard it they recognized it and ran full out for the seawall, where they'd left the boats. They looked out toward the Statue of Liberty, spotted the Riva. Climbed into their Awesomes.

The engines of the four Awesomes roared.

Leslie asked the Riva for all it had, and suddenly it surged forward. She made a tight turn to head for any part of Manhattan. It seemed to Gainer from the way they were cutting the water and the way the wind was buffeting that no one could catch them. He wasn't accustomed to going that fast on water. He looked back toward Ellis, saw the four

Awesomes rounding the southeast corner. Their hulls raised up by their speed, they formed black triangles with the horizontal line of the water. He kept his eyes on them, saw how quickly they were growing larger and knew they were overtaking.

Leslie glanced back at them. She beat on the teakwood wheel of the Riva with the heel of her hand, as though to make it realize it had to go faster, but the speedometer needle was laying on forty-five and there was no more throttle to give it.

The Awesomes came up behind them, four across in a line like a squadron on the attack. Doing ninety. They could run rings around the Riva. As they drew closer, slapping against the wake of the Riva, the men not behind the steering wheel of each Awesome leaned up and out, aimed their automatic rifles ahead and opened fire. Bullets sang against the wind a foot or two above Gainer and Leslie. Bullets hit the water, causing lines of splats along both sides. Impatient shots. In another few seconds the Awesomes would be alongside at point-blank range.

Gainer couldn't just not fight back. He took up the automatic rifle. It felt heavy but not solid. He turned and kneeled on the seat, hunched down, used the top of the seat cushion to support his aim. Aimed at the men in the nearest Awesome.

The trigger would not squeeze. Where the hell was the safety release? Gainer felt along the rifle's housing, found a couple of protrusions and finally one that moved a notch.

The Awesomes were on them now.

Leslie threw the Riva into reverse. Cut down so suddenly on its speed that the Awesomes swooshed past without getting off a shot, outmaneuvered by their own swiftness.

Gainer tracked them with the sights of the rifle, squeezed the trigger, was surprised by the rapid fire burst and the upward bucking, as though something was trying to yank the rifle from his grasp. Before he could let go of the trigger the rifle fired another burst at the sky. The goddamn thing. Gainer didn't know it and it didn't seem willing to let him.

Leslie turned the Riva hard to the left and gave it full power. The hull of the boat nosed up abruptly, loomed like a mere surfboard, all its underside showing. For Gainer, the Trade Towers and other buildings of the city skyline were nearly on their side, the line of the water almost vertical. The Riva came within inches of flipping over. Its hull finally smacked down on the water.

Leslie stayed with it, put it on course, made a run for the New Jersey shore a quarter mile away.

The Awesomes turned and continued the chase. They were coming on so fast now that only their propellers were in the water. Leslie gained some distance by cutting around the front of a string of garbage barges that a tug was pushing down the Hudson—six laborious barges, each sixty feet long and setting too high in the water to see beyond. They got in the way. The Awesomes had to check speed, go upstream a ways to get around them. By the time the Awesomes were in the clear and able to go full ahead again, the Riva was approaching the New Jersey side.

A graveyard of barges.

Hundreds of old wooden ones, of all sizes.

Silt bound, stuck in the umberish shallows that were as much mud as water. All but the thickest wood of their bones rotted from them, they lay as though haphazardly dropped dead there from some great height. The way they were situated, their relative angles and overlaps either formed channels or blocked them.

Leslie randomly took one of the offered openings. Between two long railroad barges. She slowed the Riva to twenty-five, which was still too fast considering all the pilings and hulls that barely showed above the water line. Hunks of wood large as telephone poles and waterlogged not quite to the sinking point had to be watched for.

Leslie steered the Riva right and right again, left and left again, going by instinct, hoping not to choose a blind alley.

The Awesomes followed into the labyrinth. Each took a different way in, cruising, stalking the Riva. One caught sight of it for an instant through the ribs of a huge hulk, but there was no access to it and by the time a wide enough way was found the Riva was gone from there.

Leslie's idea was for the Awesomes to be distracted by searching in among those abandoned barges while she slipped the Riva out and across the river to safety. However, she herself had lost direction. The sun-setting sky told her which way was east, but the channels were circuitous and they more or less determined which ways she could go, and she always seemed to end up headed wrong.

Trying to correct course at one point, she steered round the stern frame of what had once been a coal barge, committed the Riva to a long narrow channel between that barge and another similar one. No sooner had she completed the turn when she saw an Awesome come into that same channel two hundred feet ahead.

Leslie shoved the Riva in reverse, hoping to back out from the channel and get away.

The driver of the Awesome put his boat into full forward speed. He was too intent on the Riva to notice the piling that had rotted off its base and floated free. Two feet in diameter, it was half submerged, caught in place in such a way that it extended across the channel.

The Awesome was up to fifty when it hit the piling. For a moment it was out of the water by eight feet, propellers whining as though they resented the air. The sharp bow of the Awesome stabbed into the rot of the barge on the left. The stern snapped forward, and the whole boat flipped. It struck the barge on the other side and flipped again, plowed through feeble timbers and ended upside down with air bubbles boiling around it.

Leslie tried another narrow channel. It turned out to be a dead end, blocked by an old white painted barge half-sunk and jammed in place. It was Gainer's guess that the white barge was all that lay between them and the open river. Again, the channel was not wide enough to turn the Riva around. Leslie was about to start backing out when Gainer had her hold it right there. He climbed over the windshield to the bow. The hull plankings of the barge ran vertically, were about fourteen inches wide. Gainer tested some of those with the flat of his foot. Even that slight pressure caused them to give a bit. As one plank fell off completely Gainer saw how it was wet-rotted away just below the water line. He motioned for Leslie to go ahead slowly.

The Riva pressed at the old hull planks with its bow. That the planks might resist was an illusion. They swung up and inward as though hinged from above. The rusted nails that held them creaked as they were twisted out.

Gainer and Leslie ducked down in the cockpit to avoid the planks that dropped. The windshield passed beneath a huge horizontal beam, cleared it by mere inches.

Now the Riva was in the open belly of the barge. Its propeller clanked against hard underwater debris, perhaps there would not be depth enough. The Riva pitched once to the right as it collided with some mass below the surface but at such low speed it recovered quickly, apparently undamaged.

To the opposite hull of the barge was thirty-five feet. Gainer and Leslie hoped the planks there would be just as cooperative, but when the bow of the Riva was butted into them, they didn't budge. Leslie tried planks to the left of that spot and found those to be equally solid. Perhaps only the hull on the shoreward, muddier side was rotted away. If so, they would have to retreat if they could.

The sun had gone. Only leftover light now. They would be lost for sure among the barges.

Leslie tried some of the planks to the right. They also held fast. Then, persistently, others in that direction. She rammed harder with the bow of the Riva and finally a plank gave, was knocked completely away.

Through the opening of it, they saw the lighted city skyline across the river.

Encouraged by the one plank that had come loose, Leslie butted the Riva against the plank adjacent.

It did not give.

Leslie was through being cautious. She backed the Riva as far off as she could, gave it half throttle, sent it bulling into the planks. The sleek speedboat was not made for or accustomed to such abuse. The planks were tough old workers. It seemed a standoff, but then, the old planks buckled with impact, they split in two. Their sharp, splintery ends scraped resentful scars along the varnished forward deck of the Riva, bit hard enough against the windshield to cause that to crack. Gainer and Leslie just did get down out of the way.

The Riva emerged from the old barge, enjoyed deeper water with a kind of victorious surge. Leslie headed it upriver in the direction of the Seventy-ninth Street Basin. She switched on the running lights, feeling that confident that they had gotten away. Actually, night had not brought much of a change. The moon was close to full and visibility almost as good as it had been an hour earlier, especially out here on the water.

Two hundred feet ahead on the left.

Suddenly appeared an elongated black shape that had to be an Awesome. It came roaring out from the dead barges, having finally found a way.

Leslie swung the Riva sharply around. Cut the running lights and ran full speed.

The Awesome happened to be the one with Sweet aboard. Sweet spotted the Riva, directed the driver's attention to it. There would be no getting away this time. Sweet had an automatic rifle with a full magazine and a couple of spares. He would wait until he was close alongside the Riva. He had revised his thinking somewhat. More convenient for him now if he wasted only one of the two. Either the man or the woman, it didn't matter which. Save the trouble of having to search all over that fucking island for the money. Then, of course, he'd put the finishing touch on the whole matter by finishing off that one. The most difficult thing under these circumstances was how to be careful enough to waste only the first one. That problem made Sweet lean back toward his original intention—just spray a couple of magazine loads into the cockpit of the Riva, really put a lot of holes into both the fuckers.

The Riva had a head start of about two hundred yards, but it would not take long for the Awesome to close that gap. Leslie knew once they

388

were in the open bay there would be no hope. She put the Riva on a diagonal course off the tip of Manhattan.

One short blast from a nautical horn.

There, ahead, were three horizontal rows of lights, one above the other. Long symmetrical rows moving on the water. As the Riva proceeded in that direction the lights transformed into identical windows and the yellow-orange mass they were a part of could be made out.

The Staten Island Ferry.

Three decks high above the water line, three hundred feet long.

On its way to the ferry terminal at the Battery.

Leslie kept the Riva headed straight for it. It seemed she meant to ram it but she timed the speed of the ferry precisely with her own, cut across its wake and under its stern. She executed a fairly wide turn to the left and, at full speed, ran for the ferry's bow to cut back in front of it.

The Awesome was only seventy yards behind. Its driver was not fooled by Leslie's evasive tactics. He followed her around the ferry.

By then the ferry was approaching its slip at the terminal. It grumbled and shuddered as though slowing was a strain. The outer reaches of its slip were no more than two hundred feet ahead—huge pilings driven deep into the river bottom so they could stand firm fifteen feet above the water line; hundreds of them bunched to form extensions like a pair of spread legs, a wide but narrowing opening that the ferry could easily find and be fitted into.

Another blast from the ferry's bow, so brief it seemed either bored or timid.

Twice more the Awesome chased the Riva completely around the ferry, following without difficulty but not making up much distance because of all the turning. Sweet's impatience was edging him. All this going round and round was a waste of everyone's time. It was also making his stomach queasy.

On the third time around Leslie cut even closer to the stern of the ferry, and as soon as she'd cleared it she asked the Riva for its sharpest, shortest turn to the left. Again the Riva's bow went nearly straight up, twisted like it was undecided about whether or not to flip over. Only its propeller was in the water for a moment, and then it smacked down on the water so violently Gainer and Leslie were almost thrown overboard. Leslie slowed and ran the Riva close alongside the ferry, so close the Riva's gunwale scraped along the ferry's metal hull. At midship she brought the Riva to match the slowness of the ferry, held it there in touch.

Gainer glanced up ten feet above to the lower deck within the lighted ferry, saw a man reading the *Daily News* and a woman wearing a white nurse's cap. The light they were in prevented them from seeing out into the darkness.

The Awesome came chasing around the stern of the ferry. It swung as wide as before, spotted the Riva but too late, due to its own speed and the degree of the turn. It went by. No matter, it would simply go around again. Sweet believed the Riva had given up, was pressing up to the larger vessel out of desperation, anything for protection.

The ferry reached the outermost pilings of its slip, played its powerful spotlights on them. More often than not it did not come in straight and neat but rather approximately, using the pilings and the way they narrowed the slip right and left to finally have the lip of its landing ramp align with the ramp of the terminal.

This time the ferry came in at an angle to the right. Its bow collided with pilings on that side.

The pilings creaked and gave way some under the tremendous pressure.

Still Leslie kept the Riva midship of the ferry, close as possible to its hull.

It seemed to Gainer that they were headed into a lethal wedge, that there was no way they could avoid being crushed between the ferry and the pilings. And now the Awesome was coming up on them, nearly rammed their stern with its pointed bow.

The forward part of the ferry caromed off the pilings on the right and went for those on the left, all the while moving slowly but steadily deeper into the slip.

Leslie gave a sudden throttle to the Riva. It surged forward through the opening now between the ferry and the pilings on the right.

The Awesome followed.

Leslie swung the Riva sharply around the bow of the ferry. There was barely room to maneuver.

The ferry pounded against the pilings on its left. The pilings absorbed the stress and slung the huge vessel in the other direction. Creating an opening on the left.

But not much of an opening. It looked no more than six or seven feet wide.

Go for it! Gainer believed he actually shouted that because it was so loud in his mind. It was their only choice. In another moment the huge mass of the ferry would crush them.

Leslie asked the Riva for all it had.

The Riva answered as though it too knew it was going for its life. The squeeze couldn't have been tighter. The Riva scraped against the ferry on one side, against the pilings on the other. Scraped through. Ran clear and swiftly from the slip.

The Awesome was wider-beamed. Sweet yelled at the driver to follow the Riva through that opening but the driver saw he couldn't possibly make it. He reversed the Awesome, managed to get it turned around. Only to find that on the opposite side the space between the ferry and the pilings was even narrower.

The Awesome was trapped in the slit.

Sweet only had time to think about jumping overboard because, next moment, there was no longer any water to jump into. The ferry splintered the Awesome, crushed it, the driver and Sweet, like they were in a trash compactor.

RATHER than go to the Seventy-ninth Street Basin and risk running into another of the Awesomes, Gainer and Leslie went up the East River to the Bristol Pier.

Before mooring the Riva there, Gainer flung the automatic rifle overboard, gave it a hateful heave for all the good it hadn't done him. The plunking splash the rifle made as it hit the water seemed appropriately to punctuate the end of their New York Harbor miseries.

They walked beneath FDR Drive to First Avenue, caught a taxi up to Forty-seventh Street.

Chapin's apartment.

Gainer buzzed, kept the buzzer pressed in. When there was no response he tried the street-level door. It was open. So was the entrance door to Chapin's living quarters.

Chapin wasn't there but he wasn't long gone. Gainer tested some of the stubs in the piled ashtrays. Most were stale and stiff, perhaps weeks old, a few were still pliable, had been mashed out that day. Two glasses on the side table, among a lot of dry smudged others, had wet rings under them from recent condensation. Three or four hours ago at the most, Gainer estimated.

He looked around, inside dresser drawers and closets for any sign that Chapin had gone for good or might possibly be returning. It appeared as though everything had just been left there, including a Smith and Wesson 0.357 magnum revolver in the cabinet of the nightstand, loaded, and a well-worn red leather personal telephone-number book among the tortured bed linens. The book had the numbers of at least a hundred working girls in it. No second names, all first. Many scratched out, many with numbers changed six or seven times. Despite appearances, Gainer didn't believe Chapin would be back. Presumably money could replace anything—with something better.

They went upstairs to Chapin's workroom.

As soon as they opened the door they heard Chapin:

"Gainer, my boy, you didn't ask me."

It was only Chapin's voice coming from four perfectly positioned speakers. The opening of the door had activated a tape. There was such fidelity to it and it was set at such a normal conversational level that it seemed Chapin was there, in person.

"You assumed when you should have asked," the tape went on. "I would have told you how I'd be, maybe. But probably not. Anyway, I've never yet been able to resist a fucking when it was bent over for me. That's my bedrock nature."

Gainer was making fists in his jacket pockets.

Chapin's voice went on: "Usually I don't have compunctions about it. Usually I slip it to someone and if it hurts it hurts. But I like you about a million times more than anyone around and I've got considerations. I don't mean by that I've got a bothering conscience, just considerations."

Gainer went over to one of the speakers, jabbed his elbow into it and tore its cone. No matter, the other three speakers continued right on.

"Gainer, believe me, all that money would have made you dead. No one can fuck with so much and be out front with those he's dealing with. The way things were for you, of course, you didn't have much choice. The way I saw it you were going to get whacked out no matter what. With me it's different. I'm the invisible man, old pal no name, who nobody knows had anything to do with it. Only you can connect me and you don't have the legs for that, the way you stand."

A long pause but the tape was not over.

"I've really thought this one out, Gainer, believe me. Now, all it has to do is come off the way I see it. Incidentally, this tape, as it's being played is also being erased. Kiss Leslie for me and try to thank me for the fucking."

"Thank you," Gainer muttered bitterly.

They left Chapin's apartment, and when they were out on the street it occurred to Gainer that they had no safe place to go. Surely not his apartment, and no, not Leslie's either.

Leslie waved down a taxi, told the driver to take them to the Mayfair Regent on Sixty-fifth Street west of Park.

Gainer didn't ask why there, just went along with it. On the way

Leslie explained that Rodger kept a suite at the Mayfair Regent for whenever he had an unexpected onset of lavender friends on hand and felt they were worthy of such a place. Also, at Rodger's favor, some deeply closeted senators and such had trysted there. Leslie herself had been in the suite only once and no, certainly not for that. It had been an afternoon three or four years ago when she was having high tea in the hotel's lounge and spilled some on a St. Laurent white linen suit that was one of her favorites at the time. She'd gone up to the suite to try and save it.

Gainer hadn't been in that hotel since he was nine. It was, for a while, like the Pierre and the Sherry Netherland, one of those where he'd sit in the lobby to watch and listen. As he recalled, the Mayfair Regent, or the Mayfair House as it had been known then, was the smallest and uppitiest of all his sitting places. He seldom went there that the bell captain or the manager or someone hadn't asked whose young man he was. No hotel in the city gave off more of an air of insular self-sufficiency. People needed it instead of the other way around. Especially widows who preferred it over their Westbury estates because it was one of the only places left where they could confidently wear large diamonds at any hour and meet whomever they wanted in privacy.

High in Gainer's memories of the Mayfair Regent was the bony old lady with blue hair who had taken him into the lounge to sit with her on a banquette and have hot chocolate from a silver server. Such thick chocolate, it was like drinking a melted Hershey bar. The old lady didn't say more than a dozen words to him. She stared at him with her eyes that looked coated with yellow plastic and she grunted when he, trying to please, told her he liked the way her powder smelled. Before she signed the check and left him sitting there, he got the feeling that she didn't really like him, that she regarded him as a competitor for some unknown reason.

Now here he was returning to the Mayfair Regent, aware of the censuring glance from the doorman and the way others of the white-gloved staff in the lobby stationed themselves around in case they were required to jump him. He and Leslie were quite a couple, of course, caked as they were with plaster dust and whatever else they'd picked up in their escape. Numerous proper people in proper dress were passing through the lobby at that moment on their way to dinner, probably at Le Cirque or La Grenouille or some such.

Leslie ignored everyone, raised her chin and tone to an imperious level. "Keys to the Pickering suite, please."

The accommodations clerk with impeccable sideburns and cuticles raised his chin and tone right back at her.

393

"I am Mrs. Pickering," Leslie informed, her eyes daring the clerk to disbelieve her.

Moments later, on the way up in the elevator, Leslie sneaked her hand around and gave the right cheek of Gainer's rump a squeeze. "Don't fret, lover," she told him.

"I'm not."

She wished he'd take a squeeze of hers.

CHAPTER
TWENTY-FOUR

INE'S rage was catatonic.

If he said anything he would scream. If he moved he would go for their throats.

The security men who had returned to Number 19 empty-handed had just made their report and stood there awaiting the consequences. They had, of course, put the blame on Sweet.

It took some five minutes for Hine to be able to speak. Calmly then, in a normal tone, he told the security men to go back to Ellis Island and clean up the mess, sack up and do away with the dead and when that was done to search the place thoroughly for the money. They were not to discuss what had occurred with anyone, not even talk about it among themselves. Just do as told.

The security men left, not really understanding why there had been no reprimand.

Hine closed and bolted the doors to his study.

He took three deep breaths, reminded himself that the matter was by no means closed. Not that he believed the money would be turned up out on Ellis. That was merely a loose end, meant more than anything as something to put those security incompetents through. No, Gainer and the Pickering woman had the money. At that moment they were somewhere sitting on the billion—laughing their asses off. But they'd be found, and the money with them.

Quick and quiet was how it would have to be. Any day now he

expected someone selected by Boston to arrive and relieve him of his status as Temporary Custodian. He'd have to step back and be no better off than he was with Darrow, an underling. That Horridge was still in the house was encouraging, though. As long as Horridge remained at Number 19 the situation was not resolved.

But heaven help him if Horridge got wind of any brash effort to recover the money. Such as yesterday's fiasco. Horridge had told Hine in no uncertain terms that he was there to see things were normalized rather than more stirred up. He had also said how pleased he was that Hine too was concentrating his efforts toward that objective.

Horridge would never know.

Although Sweet had almost fucked up everything.

No more F. Hugh Sweet.

Hine felt little sorrow, considerable relief.

He glanced out a window. Saw Horridge was where he would have predicted Horridge would be. Quite a ways from the house out on the lawn beneath a huge copper beech. Horridge had had a pair of wicker chairs and an ottoman and table taken out to that spot, and it was where, with a decanter of port and several volumes of Emerson, he spent most of every afternoon.

Hine thought it would be in his own best interest if he went out to him. Truth was, he found Horridge almost unendurably boring. The man acted as though he was Jesus Christ in a vest.

Horridge removed his legs from the ottoman when he saw Hine approaching, and when Hine was close enough he gave him his only smile, which was mostly with his lower lip and jaw. He offered Hine a port, put aside his Emerson and poured precisely.

"Sorry to hear about your friend," Horridge said.

It took Hine an instant to realize he meant Sweet. Hine nodded and revised his eyes to communicate grief.

"I heard it on this morning's radio news."

"I didn't want to concern you with it."

"Nonsense. What was his name?"

"Sweet."

"It really hurts when one loses an old school chum like that."

Hine was sure he had never told Horridge how far back he went with Sweet. It might be a good sign that someone on Horridge's level had been interested enough to look into him that closely.

"Why on earth was he speedboating at night?" Horridge asked.

"As I understand it he developed engine trouble earlier on and when it got dark the boat washed into the ferry slip."

"I suppose that would explain it. Does he have family?"

396

"I spoke with them this morning," Hine lied.

Silence apparently closed that subject.

Hine almost placed his glass on a yellow pad on the table, realized just in time Horridge had been using it to jot down some Emerson quotes.

"How is The Balance Room coming?" Horridge asked.

"The roof is completely repaired now, of course, and so is the ceiling."

"What about that new back-up alarm you were telling me about?"

"It was installed the day before yesterday."

"Working dependably?"

"It certainly seems to be."

"Would you stake yourself on it?"

"I most certainly would."

The back-up alarm was one that detected any change in the volume of solid substances within the room.

Horridge looked off down the slope, as though seeing ahead. When he brought his attention around to Hine again, he said, "You know, Hine, I'm impressed with the way you've taken charge."

"Thank you."

"Despite Darrow's catastrophe it's been business as usual—because of you."

Hine managed a modest shrug.

"With any kind of boost from the right direction, I believe you could take over here as permanent Custodian."

"Boost?"

"It wouldn't take much really. A little something more in your favor to put it over."

Hine's eyes asked Horridge for it.

Horridge read them, told him: "I've already leaned in your direction as far as I can. I'm not High Board, you know."

Hine thanked him again.

"Lois," Horridge said.

"What about Lois?"

"She wouldn't happen to be pregnant, would she?"

"Why do you ask?"

"That might be just about boost enough."

"Well, she's not."

"You are trying, I assume."

Nosy old fuck, Hine thought, but said brightly: "Doing my best."

The impregnating of Lois was important to Hine's future. Unlike most High Board families the Whitcrofts were a sparse line, and a child

397

from their Lois would be especially valued. It would irrevocably hyphenate Hine to them. Recently, at various times, he had come within a word of suggesting to Lois that they physically cooperate. He was afraid, however, that once she had been in such intimacy she would make more of it than he was willing to bear. Out of spite, she would do it. It was impossible for him not to associate in his imagination what might happen with Lois with what had happened with the whore in New Haven. When he was eighteen. When the expanding erotic sensations he felt from being bare against the whore and having his private self in the grip of her hole were overcome by nausea and he had shriveled inside her and thought she'd laugh and he'd paid her fifty dollars extra for having thrown up in her hair.

His reaction then was not an isolated one but rather the emergence of a deep-grained phobia. He gave in to it. Shaped his sexual and social requirements to accommodate it, accepted it as a part of him like a graft. He did not want to touch anyone. Female or male. He did not want *anyone* touching him. A kiss on the mouth was enough to turn his stomach.

Only his ambition married Lois Whitcroft.

Her Whitcroft pride kept them married. Besides, as it turned out, and as she said, she enjoyed all the different ceilings she was seeing while lying on her back.

Early on he approached her with the suggestion of artificial insemination. It was, he reasoned, not really that much removed from the natural way. Lois wouldn't have it. She told him if he wanted so much to get her with child he'd have to get it up and in.

That left Hine with the hope that she'd make a slip with someone else. What luck for him if in the heat of one of her many promiscuities she forgot to take her pill or do whatever she did to prevent. He kept track of Lois's periods on a calendar, and each month when she was due he investigated the contents of her bathroom wastebasket. So far she'd been as regular as the moon, but if it did happen that she became pregnant Hine was prepared to put her in shackles to keep her from running to an abortionist. The only thing about it that concerned Hine was the chance of his taking credit for Lois's big-bellied condition and then having the child pop out half-black or -Oriental or who knew what.

"Another spot of port?" Horridge offered.

"No thanks. I have to see to tomorrow's carries. It was one of Sweet's responsibilities."

"We'll get you a new assistant," Horridge promised with a note of sympathy. He swung his legs up onto the hassock. The laces of his white casual shoes were undone. He returned to Emerson.

Hine went back into the house and up to The Balance Room. He saw that twelve million was correctly distributed and packed into five well-traveled pieces of luggage. The word *boost* remained foremost in his mind. How right he'd been, he thought. So right it hurt. If his scheme with Gainer had gone as planned, the money recovered with no apparent hassle, he'd already have the boost Horridge said he needed. Christ, how he despised Gainer and the Pickering woman.

The Pickering woman . . .

Hine changed his shirt and tie, put on a fresh pair of woolen socks and a different pair of shoes. He always felt better in fresh socks. He considered wearing a hat, a dark brown fedora, tried it on with a jaunty tilt but decided against it and had to rebrush his hair into place.

He went down and out to his Porsche 928. Drove north on nonstop Route 684 for eight miles and got off on the local road that was Route 172. From there he needed a Westchester County road atlas. He knew the address he wanted, had looked into that quite a while ago merely as a matter of having it in case it was needed. He located it on map 8, marked it with a red-felt-tipped pen and then determined and marked the most direct way to it.

The roads turned out to be more winding and narrow than the map showed, but it took him only ten minutes of slow driving to get there. He pulled the car over next to the rock wall of the place, let it idle while he decided whether or not this really was what he should do.

Ambition and expediency could not be talked out of it.

He turned the car into the drive, followed the drive through the grove of old, well-cared-for trees. Up to the house. A Rolls-Royce Silver Spirit was parked in the turn-around. Hine parked his Porsche next to it. From the look of it the Rolls could have been bought that very day. Hine ran his hand along its side and did not pick up any dust. On his way to the entrance of the house he took the time to take in the perfect placements of the flat granite stones that made up the walk, the ivy sheared so evenly along the sides and so gleaming-green in its bed it looked as though every leaf had been separately polished. Not a finger smudge on the large brass Colonial door handle.

A fastidious man, Hine concluded. That was good. No doubt he would not want any dirt in his private life either. This had been an excellent idea. He should have thought of it sooner. Why, he wondered, hadn't it occurred to Darrow?

Hine pressed the doorbell.

No one came.

He pressed it again more insistently, and after a wait decided to go around the side of the house to the rear grounds. There was a man about a hundred feet from the house on a level spot between two large oaks.

The man noticed Hine but went on with what he was doing, which at that moment was stacking firewood, picking up splits of logs from a pile and placing them onto a stack. The logs were all the same length, so that in a stack their raw sawn edges formed a neat pattern.

The man was sweating. Despite a nip in the early autumn air he was stripped to the waist, had on a pair of heavy work shoes and cowhide work gloves. A chunky man in his sixties. Solid chest, thick upper arms and neck, the sort of overdevelopment that usually came from a life of hard labor.

Hine went halfway up to him. "Where might I find Mr. Pickering?"

The man's glance took in Hine. He picked up four logs and found snug places for them on the stack.

Hine was about to repeat his question when the man asked: "What do you want?"

"Mr. Pickering."

"He's gone to hell."

"What?" Hine thought he hadn't heard right, but if he had this was an insubordinate son of a bitch. He'd kick his old ass and fire him if he was Pickering.

"I'm Rodger Pickering," the man said, taking off his gloves and slapping them down on the stack to demonstrate his annoyance at the intrusion. "Who are you?"

Hine was so put off balance that he extended his hand, something he had not done in seventeen years. "I'm Arnold Hine."

Pickering took one step forward for the shake that was brief and crushing on his part.

"I happened to be nearby and thought I'd drop in and introduce myself," Hine explained. "I'm related to the Whitcrofts."

"You don't look like a Whitcroft."

"By marriage. I'm married to George Whitcroft's daughter."

"I've met George on occasion but I'm closer to Phillip."

He would be, Hine thought. Lois's uncle Phillip was the High Board Whitcroft.

"Can I offer you a drink or anything," Pickering asked.

"No thank you, sir."

"Phillip and I do business now and then. Had dinner with him recently in Washington. I presume you know he donated his old master collection to the National Gallery."

"He's always been generous." Hine was feeling more on top of this now. However, he reminded himself not to get smug, to remember who and what Pickering was. For the past few years, Pickering had been on the brink of becoming nearly High Board, as close to High Board as anyone not entirely qualified could ever get, way above Horridge, for example. First opening that occurred on that level Pickering was slated to drop right into it. It wasn't just a rumor. Hine had heard it mentioned by his father-in-law. Yes, he thought, Pickering was perfectly positioned to give a boost.

"Is Mrs. Pickering about?" Hine asked.

"Mind if I work while we talk? I'm cooling off and I want to get this done."

"Not at all."

Pickering put his gloves back on. He slapped his grip onto a whole thick log that had to weigh a hundred pounds, rolled it aside and stood it on end for a seat for Hine. There was a motorized log-splitter nearby, a long low machine with a pair of wheels. Pickering stepped over it to get at some split logs.

Hine brushed off the face of the log and sat down. He offered to help but it hardly came off as wholehearted.

Pickering did not want help.

Hine decided a little bridge was called for. He gazed around and complimented Pickering on the appearance of the grounds, how natural looking they were and yet not overgrown.

"You enjoy the outdoors?" Pickering asked.

"Not particularly."

"Thought not."

Enough. Hine again inquired after Mrs. Pickering.

"She's around."

"I've met her."

"I'm not surprised."

"Exceptional woman," Hine said, testing.

"The great beauty of my time."

Hine agreed.

Pickering believed he knew now why this fellow Hine had come calling. Happened to be nearby? Bullshit. Twice in the space of only a couple of minutes he'd asked after Leslie. That was what he was there for, something to do with Leslie and very likely one of her affairs, her latest with that young man, Gainer, no doubt. Hine had come to inform on her, trade some information, maybe even photographs, for whatever he wanted, a favor of some sort, or money. Over his years with Leslie others like this Hine, unaware of the Pickerings' marital arrangement, had made similar approaches. Usually money was expected. This fellow Hine, however, did at least have a sort of calling card. He *was* married to a Whitcroft, or at least so he claimed. Didn't matter, Hine still had that snitcher's look and nervousness about him. Maybe he'd been turned down by Leslie and his balls couldn't handle that and so he was here to recoup. Well, not at my expense, Pickering decided. With unmistakable point he told Hine: "Leslie can do no wrong so far as I am concerned."

Hine was amazed at the sensitivity of Pickering's antenna. He had planned to ease into the topic of Leslie Pickering and gradually reveal her involvement with Gainer and the robbery at Number 19. He had thought that surely Pickering would see how such a thing might jeopardize his imminent appointment to a post that was so close to High Board and would be glad to settle on a trade: not having that known in exchange for a boost.

Hine had not, however, expected Pickering to be as much man as he was. Now, Hine's instinct told him it would be at least professionally unwise to cast even one pale beam of bad light in Mrs. Pickering's direction.

Hine took the conversation to business, and as modestly as he could got the point across that he was not naive about what the air was like in the upper stratospheres. Such as Boston. He also got on to a couple of his theories about how investment could be put to use in Africa to gain ultimate control. If from this he at least made a positive impression, it was worth something, Hine figured.

The split wood was stacked.

Pickering started the pneumatic splitter. Its engine was too noisy for talk.

Hine watched Pickering lift a whole heavy log in place on the splitter. The blade of its sledge drove into the end of the log, crackled and splintered it in two. Hine was glad that log wasn't his head. He got up and signaled that he was leaving. Pickering didn't pause from his labor, merely acknowledged by raising his hand. As he went up the path, Hine believed he could feel Pickering's smile on his back, a smile directly related to what had *not* been said.

A few words held back. The whole thing had come that close to coming apart. If Rodger Pickering had learned what his Leslie was into, the robbery at Number 19 and the rest of it, he would have had no choice but to act on it, use all possible means to straighten it out. It would have meant cutting Leslie from his life at once and he would have done it or, at least, had it done as swiftly and cleanly and thoroughly as possible. To avoid contamination of his proximity to the High Board. Leslie's death would have been hard on Pickering, but despite his genuine fondness for her, actually a kind of love for her, one had to accept things in the order of their importance. He would have done it, and then he would have done in Arnold Hine.

TWENTY minutes later Hine was driving south on Purchase Street. Up ahead he saw a Harrison Township police patrol car, its light rack strobing. The police car was stopped near the entrance to Number 19. Officer McCatty appeared from around it. He recognized Hine's blue Porsche, gestured that Hine should pull over.

Now Hine saw the problem.

It was the last thing he needed.

He got out and strode angrily in the direction of the gate. McCatty fell in beside. "I just got here myself," McCatty explained. "All I know is it wasn't here when I went by ten minutes ago."

The way the tanker truck was parked lengthwise close up to the gate it prevented all traffic to and from Number 19. It was a huge eighteen-wheeler with the blue, orange and white *Gulf* logo on its long cylindrical body along with the words AVGAS 100LL and flammable.

Officer McCatty pointed out the tire tracks of the tanker where it had been steered onto the shoulder of the road and over some rough going so that it could be positioned as it was. "Looks deliberate to me," McCatty said.

Three security men were going over the tanker.

Hine stood clear. The thing might be set to explode. It appeared dangerous. In fact it had the word *Danger* painted permanently on it in several places. Hine imagined how much of an explosion such a mass might make. He backed off another twenty feet, to the opposite side of the street where there was a rock wall he could get behind.

"The keys are in it," a security man called down from the cab of the tanker.

"Don't touch the ignition," McCatty advised him.

The other two security men opened the panel of the housing along the left side of the tanker, where its five pumping connections and valves were located. They examined the capacity indicators attached to each valve. "It's empty," one of the security men reported.

Or, more likely, made to appear that way, Hine thought. Any moment he expected someone to touch whatever it was that would set the tanker off. What would Horridge think? Such an explosion was sure to draw attention. Horridge would hate that, and he, Hine, would have to take all the blame. This certainly had not been one of his better days, Hine thought.

A security man was now up on the ramp that ran along the top of the tanker. He undid the hatch to one of the compartments. Gasoline fumes hit him. He peered down into the tanker. "Someone get me a flashlight," he said.

McCatty got one from the patrol car.

The security man beamed the flashlight down inside.

His first impression was that he was looking at enough *plastique* explosive to blow away Number 19 and all its neighbors. Bags and bags of it. Black mesh laundry-type nylon bags.

He lowered himself down into the compartment. Moments later his head and shoulders emerged. He motioned to Hine.

Reluctantly, Hine went to him, climbed up on the tanker.

The security man spoke to him in a low tone.

"Don't bother with it," McCatty was saying to Hine, "I'll call in and have someone come take it away—"

"No you won't." Hine was actually grinning.

McCatty directed traffic on Purchase Street, even stopped it and had it backed up quite a ways while the tanker was maneuvered forward and back time after time, its air brakes hissing. It took some doing and once it seemed impossibly jackknifed, but finally it was straightened out and headed in the right direction. The gates to Number 19 were opened. The tanker was driven in and up the winding drive, parked at the north end of the house. Except for the AVGAS 100LL designation the tanker displayed, it was not out of place, could well have been there for a regular delivery of heating fuel oil.

The security men and the collators were put to work. Hurrying, but with care, to cause as little fuss as possible, the bags containing the cash were hefted out of the compartments of the tanker and carried up the backstairs to the second floor north wing and on into The Balance Room. Most of the money was still in its original bound sheaves. Hine examined it as it was weighed on the electronic scale. He kept an exact record of the pounds and ounces that registered. Soon the last million was neatly back in place on a Balance Room shelf. They had done it without disturbing Horridge, which was what Hine wanted. He would break the news to Horridge in his own way.

In the confined atmosphere of The Balance Room all that money together gave off an even stronger odor of gasoline. It would gradually disappear, Hine thought, but to help, Hine instructed that the heat sensor alarm system be turned off so the air conditioning could be set high for ventilation. He also had the new mass-measuring alarm adjusted before he closed and bolted The Balance Room door.

By then it was nine o'clock.

Hine sent word down to cook that he would take dinner in his quarters. He ordered poached scrod and some boiled vegetables, bread pudding with hard sauce for dessert, and tea.

While waiting for the food to arrive he sat in the leather chair Darrow had so often previously sat in, kicked off his shoes and crossed his legs on the matching hassock. Using an electronic calculator capable of performing to fifteen digits, he converted the weight of the money that had been recovered.

The figure he came up with was 1,038,000,000.

One billion, thirty-eight million.

Gainer, the stupid fucker, had even shorted himself. Withheld only forty-four million instead of the fifty million they had agreed on. Hine thought Gainer must have miscounted because he was scared. That wild business yesterday on and then around Ellis Island must have shook him. Why else, except to try to buy his good will, would Gainer have put the money right there on Number 19's doorstep? No matter, Andrew Gainer still had the big one coming.

Hine checked his figures again. They still came out one billion, thirty-eight million.

He sat back, stretched.

He felt absolutely blessed.

It was almost as though he'd been favored by an omnipotent force. The way he had gotten the idea in the first place and the way Gainer came to fit so perfectly into it. The way Gainer and the Pickering woman hadn't been killed yesterday. Killing the Pickering woman would have been a terrible error, he now realized. And trying to leverage her husband would have been just as bad. Now the money, at least the bulk of it, was back in The Balance and he would be the new Custodian for sure.

He was, indeed, blessed.

Should celebrate himself.

Decided he would.

He waited until dinner was brought, placed on the table near his window. He was hungry, but when the servant was gone he did not touch the food. Turned the night lock on the door.

Assured of privacy, he undressed. He pulled a silk-covered comforter from the bed. So light and plumped it practically floated to the floor. He spread it, neatened its corners almost ritualistically before sitting on it. Its texture seemed to appreciate his ass.

He had no fantasies, required none. Any image outside himself, just as any other hands, would have spoiled it. For a long while he teased and hardened his cock, all the more by not touching it.

THE following morning when Hine went down to breakfast he was disappointed to learn that Horridge had departed for Boston at about seven-thirty. On the Gulfstream III from Westchester Airport. Word was that he would return by midafternoon.

Hine and his surprise would have to wait.

To counter his impatience, Hine attended to his normal daily responsibilities. He would never be the lax and too easily distracted Custodian that Darrow had been, he told himself. Darrow's downfall was his, Hine's lesson. Nor would he allow himself to get stuck in this dangerous notch the way Darrow had. After four, perhaps only three, years of his efficiency Boston would be putting the next safer rung under his foot. There was a limit to his ambition, of course. It wasn't realistic to hope for High Board, but no reason why he couldn't reach the echelon close up next to it. The Pickering level would satisfy him, Hine thought.

He went up to The Balance Room, saw that the collators were hard at it, perched on their high stools, their counting fingers a blur. Hine had a cordial good morning for them while thinking he would somehow put a stop to each of them getting away with a hundred dollar bill every day.

He noticed two green trashbags off to the side. Those would be the brings of the groundkeepers and the garbagemen. The loose-money bin was full. It would be a busy day. He stepped into the inventory area. The gasoline fumes from the recovered money seemed only slightly less. He called security control to make sure the ventilating system was circulating outside air. It was. Was it on full force? It was. Oh well, they'd just have to live with it for a while.

The head collator handed him a piece of notepaper. Hine took it with him down to the study and placed it on the desk beside a ledger sheet. He would be the absolutely best Custodian they ever had, he thought, as he pulled up the leather chair with the seat cushion conformed to ten years of Darrow's sitting.

He went over the flow.

How much had been brought yesterday.

How much had been carried yesterday.

Six million, eight hundred thousand brought.

Twelve million carried.

Good, Hine thought, he'd keep ahead of them. He'd improve every phase of this operation, increase the number of carriers, interview and cull the prospects himself. Keep them scared and in line. Gainer was an example of how remarkably effective fear could be.

The ledgers on the desk were Hine's personal accounting of The Balance.

It was a pleasure for him to make the entry of 1,038,000,000 and then add it. Making the bottom line total 3,105,000,000.

Three billion, one hundred five million.

The Balance.

Horridge returned at three o'clock. He had scarcely put down his attaché case before Hine was leading him to The Balance Room.

"What is that ungodly odor?" Horridge wanted to know.

"Gasoline."

"Is something wrong up here?"

"Quite the contrary, the—"

"What is it I'm here to see?"

"The Balance."

"I don't enjoy looking at money."

"The Balance is now three billion, one hundred five million," Hine said with understated pride.

"Really?" Horridge said, as though informed that he had three apples rather than two.

"Yesterday we managed to recover almost all of what was stolen. One billion, thirty-eight million of it, to be exact."

"How much of a ruckus did you cause doing that?" Horridge inquired casually.

"None."

"Are you positive?"

"Not a stir."

They went downstairs. Horridge told Hine to wait outside the closed door of the study while he made a call. It took only a few minutes.

Horridge invited Hine in and told him: "It has been decided that you should be assigned as permanent Custodian."

Hine managed to keep his face as straight as Horridge's.

"However, you are to understand and to accept the responsibilities that traditionally go with the job."

"I understand."

"I'm sure you are aware of the advantages, but what of the penalty that will be imposed for any consequential blunder?"

"I am aware of the penalty."

"And you accept?"

"I accept."

"The Balance is in your hands."

Horridge went upstairs for a warm bath and a nap.

Hine remained in the study. Within a minute or two after he had been made Custodian he put to use the prerogative of the position. He called Intelco's New York office, asked to speak to Donald Hunsicker.

The Distributor.

Hunsicker's secretary said he was out of town, would not be back until the next day, Wednesday.

Was he reachable?

Hunsicker was in California staying at the Bel Air.

Hine direct-dialed the hotel. Hunsicker had to be paged. When he came on, Hine told him he had an important order.

Hunsicker said he was not aware Hine was qualified to issue orders. Hine assured him that he was now.

In that case, Hunsicker said, he would meet with Hine at Number 19 on Monday morning next.

Not good enough, Hine told him. Tomorrow, when Hunsicker got in he should come directly from Kennedy.

That urgent an order?

Yes.

Hine clicked off and thought what a pleasure it was going to be for him to put Gainer's name in Hunsicker's ears.

CHAPTER
TWENTY-FIVE

"REMEMBER the movie, *The Champ?*" Leslie asked.

"Yeah."

"The part where the champ, at the sacrifice of his own feelings, tells the kid he doesn't want him around?"

"That's not how this is," Gainer said.

"You didn't really mean it just now when you said I was too old for you."

"I meant it."

"Like hell. Say you didn't."

"You were only a phase, Leslie. What I've got eyes for now is inexperience."

"Stop breaking your own heart."

They were in Leslie's Rolls Corniche, parked on Barnes Lane just off Purchase Street. Leslie had turned and stopped there because they were approaching Number 19 and the matter wasn't settled.

Gainer suggested: "Why not wait in the car and have a chat with Lady Caroline?"

"Are you ridiculing me?"

"Yes."

"Any other time I'd punch you out for that."

"You're unreasonable."

"Uh huh."

"You're selfish and reckless."

"Right."

"You're a lousy lay."

"Whatever you say, champ."

"Leslie, for the last time, here's what's going to happen: I'm going to get out and walk up to Number 19. You're going to stay here and wait. If I don't come back in an hour, you go home."

"No deal. Here, take some Rescue." She fumbled around in her handbag and came out with the little brown bottle, undid the cap and squeezed some up into the dropper. Gainer wouldn't cooperate, kept his head turned away so she couldn't get to his mouth.

She squirted it in his ear.

He whirled around angry, knocked the dropper cap from her hand. It flew into the back seat.

"I couldn't resist," she said. "You were being so obvious." She got to her knees and felt around in the back for the dropper cap.

Gainer let go, let his cheek press her hip. "Oh, Leslie," he murmured. He hugged her left thigh.

She had found the dropper cap but remained as she was, allowing Gainer to work it out.

"It's just that I love you so much," he said.

"I know, lover, I know," she said. On the glint of the rear window everything they'd had together reflected in an instant for her. That might not be a positive omen, she thought. She turned and sat. They kissed. Not as well as either wanted, an awkward front-seat kiss. Then Leslie snapped on the car's lights, raced the motor because she couldn't remember if it was on, put the car in gear and went left on Purchase Street. Every commonplace action seemed significant.

After a short ways she turned in at Number 19 and drove the vertical chrome-slatted grill of the Corniche up to within inches of the outer gate. She gave the headlights several impatient blinks.

A security man came from the gatehouse. Rather than have him shine a light in on them, Leslie clicked on the interior light. The security man was one of those who had survived the battle of Ellis Island. His expression almost betrayed his surprise. He asked their names as a matter of course. Were they expected? When told they were not, he excused himself and went back inside the gatehouse. He checked the allowed list, saw neither of their names on it.

Gainer saw the security man inside the gatehouse on the telephone. Day before yesterday, there they were being chased all over Ellis Island and New York Harbor with intent to kill, and now, Gainer thought, here they were driving in like a couple of friends come unexpectedly to call. Well, not exactly.

The gates swung open.

The security man hunched down to the car window and smiled. "Mr. Hine said to say he's glad you dropped by."

Leslie proceeded slowly up the drive. When she parked near the front of the house the main entrance door was already open and two security men were waiting. There was nothing subtle about their frisks this time. One of the security men thoroughly patted Gainer from shoes to collar. The other ran his hands over Leslie in an efficient manner. A .25 caliber automatic was found in the zipper pocket of Leslie's handbag. It was a Baby Browning identical to the one Ponsard had in Monet's garden.

"Oh damn," she said working her eyelashes, "I forgot that was there. This must have been the handbag I carried last time I was out at night with some of my jewels on."

A reproachful glance from Gainer.

Contrite eyebrows from her.

He had told her absolutely no weapons.

The tiny automatic was confiscated.

"I want that back later," Leslie said.

One of the security men led the way, the other followed, with Gainer and Leslie between. Down the hall, past the portraits of Bostonian saints, pink-fleshed and stern. When they came to the little library, Leslie was told to wait there. She complied, had no other choice, actually, as one of the security men used his bulk to press her into that room.

Gainer was taken further down the hall to the study. He was left there with Hine. Just he and Hine and the door closed. Gainer had expected at least one security man would be within grabbing distance of him at all times. Maybe, he thought, the boisserie paneling on the walls had a hole through which a gun was kept on him. One wrong move by him or a certain signal from Hine and *phutt.*

Hine was reading *Barrons,* the financial weekly. He had his jacket, vest and tie off. The cuffs of his white silk shirt were rolled twice up and the front of it was unbuttoned four down. He closed the paper, folded it once and tossed it into the brass wastebasket beside the desk. "Sit if you like," he said instead of hello.

Gainer sat.

"The money . . ." Hine began.

Gainer wanted to play his number and leave, not have to listen to a lot of whiteshoe wailing. But he listened.

". . . was a sight for my skeptical eyes."

Gainer's chin and attention went abruptly up.

"For a while there I thought you might be letting down on your end," Hine told him.

Gainer, trying to recover, said "never" with a shake of his head.

"You came through. That's all that matters."

What the hell was Hine talking about, "came through"? "Where's the money now?" Gainer asked, offhand.

"Upstairs, all put away." Hine seemed to enjoy saying it.

"Don't I get a receipt?"

Hine only smiled.

"But the money was all there?"

"Except that you held back for yourself."

"Fifty million."

"Is that how much you kept?"

"That was our deal."

"You counted the fifty, I presume."

"Twice."

Hine's eyes clouded. "The amount that was thrown away in the park was from your end."

"No. I considered it an expense." Gainer was improvising, doing his best to keep it going to learn as much as he could . . . Evidently the money was back and he was getting credit for it. Translated, that meant Chapin had somehow managed to return it without giving himself away. The scheming little bastard no doubt figured it was how he could turn off the heat and have the fifty.

Wait a second . . . It occurred to Gainer that he hadn't told Chapin about the extra ten million Hine had volunteered in the graveyard after Darrow's funeral. In fact he hadn't seen Chapin since then. Which meant Chapin had sliced out only forty million and that was what Hine was now hitting on. Hine had gotten back more than expected. Gainer thought: If only he hadn't said he'd counted it *twice*. What he should have said was a silly little oversight had caused ten million to be returned with the bulk. Then when this meeting was over, maybe Hine would have gone upstairs and bundled up that ten for him, But now Hine must be upset. He, Gainer, had just said that without question he'd held back the fifty million, he hadn't made a mistake in his count as Hine must have assumed. Which to Hine meant *his* calculation of the total Balance was incorrect.

Gainer was right. Hine had always prided himself with knowing within a hundred thousand or so how much The Balance was. Unlike his predecessor Darrow, who had pretended to know while really having only a vague idea, a hundred *million* one way or the other. Hine hated the thought that his own sure figures were obviously off. The only remedy for that was to do a total count. What a chore that would be. It would take days, disrupt the routine and, if he was to believe the count, it would require his constant presence. Hell, Hine thought, he just wasn't in the mood for a total count. Such a damned mundane task. He was in too good a mood, except for the discrepancy in the count. He'd let it slide for the time being, do it soon. The big issue was settled, he'd pulled it off, gotten the appointment he wanted.

The only item on the well-cared-for surface of the desk was a gold Mont Blanc pen. Hine spun the pen as though it was an indicator. It came to a stop pointing at Gainer. "Is that the only reason you're here tonight," Hine asked, "to make sure the money was received?"

"No."

"I must say I wish you'd chosen some way of hauling it other than a gasoline truck. The Balance Room smells like an Exxon station."

Give it a try, Gainer told himself. Right across to Hine he said: "There was a mix-up regarding my part of the money. Ten million of mine was inadvertently put in with what you got back."

"But you said—"

"It was included by mistake *after* I counted it twice."

Hine concealed his relief. As usual he was right. "Are you certain?"

"Yeah. It's easy to be certain about ten million."

"According to our count you got what was due you."

Lying prick, Gainer thought. "There's a ten million fuckup in your favor," Gainer insisted.

"I think not." Hine capitalized each word.

Gainer had the urge to go over the desk for Hine. He remembered the boiserrie. "The other matter I want to take up with you is what happened last Sunday when we went for the money."

"I heard."

"Your Mr. Sweet and company almost whacked us out."

"I had nothing to do with that."

"It was all Sweet's idea?"

"He wasn't very bright . . . or nice, as you know. Somehow, he got it all mixed up, thought that that was the way to please me, poor fellow—"

"You're slime."

Hine was unfazed.

"You're what people on the street call a scumbag," Gainer said.

Hine spun the pen again.

"You got Darrow's job, didn't you?"

Hine's silence said yes.

"So now you figure you can have me whacked out any old time."

"As a matter of fact, I can."

"Kill me, you kill yourself," Gainer told him.

"Your opinion."

"I brought along something you better hear."

Hine stood abruptly. "I don't have time for any more of this. You came here attempting to cheat me out of ten million. When you didn't succeed you resorted to insults—"

"Got a cassette player?"

"You're low, Gainer. You're not merely below the salt, you aren't even on the table."

"Piss on your white shoes," Gainer told him. "Get me a cassette player." He took a cassette cartridge from his breast pocket, placed it on the desk.

Hine considered the cassette for a moment, and then Gainer, who had the look of a bettor with a sure thing. "That, I suppose, is your alleged Southampton tape." He got a portable cassette player from a nearby cabinet. Loaded the cassette and pressed the play-switch, smiling like a man sure he was calling another man's bluff. But not so sure. Not anymore.

When Hine heard his own voice he raised the volume, leaned forward in his chair. As he listened he matched the words with visual recall— Gainer and himself bareass that day in that dip of sand. Not a sandal or a stitch on, yet somehow Gainer had recorded everything they'd said. Every syllable was clear with only the sound of the ocean faint in the background.

"How did you manage that?" Hine asked, trying to sound more curious than disconcerted.

"It's all on there," Gainer told him. "The entire proposition just as you made it."

"I can't say I like my voice—"

"I do."

"The quality is sort of reedy. Do I really sound like that?"

Gainer told him: "If anything happens to myself or Leslie, a copy of this tape will be heard. Believe me."

Hine sat back, arms crossed. "Heard by whom?"

"I know some connected people, including a certain made guy who's close to the top. The way I've arranged things, he'll see that the tape reaches the right ears."

"Mafia? Organized crime people? Unpronounceable names and garlic breath? Or perhaps shiny-suited Jews with ugly complexions or liver-lipped niggers. Are they the sort you're threatening me with?"

Bluffing, Gainer thought.

Hine laughed around his words as he said, "God, you're naive."

Gainer decided Hine wasn't bluffing. But Hine had gone to a lot of trouble to make sure he wasn't wired when they'd met in Southampton. Why all that unless there was someone Hine wouldn't want to hear what was on the tape?

"You're pathetic," Hine said. He stopped the tape, popped out the cartridge and tossed it to Gainer. "Here, go play it for the boss of the bosses."

Gainer didn't catch the tape, let it fall to the floor. If not the Mob, *who*, he was wondering. *Who?*

AT that moment upstairs in The Balance Room.

Halfway up a stack of three million dollars on a shelf containing many other such stacks. Among all those millions upon millions.

A microchip.

It was one-tenth the size of Hine's little fingernail and not nearly as thick. A sliver of a square stuck to one of the bills, covering Benjamin Franklin's right eye like a patch. A simple device, as microchips go. Not nearly as complex as, for example, the 256K RAM Random Access Memory chip used in some computers capable of handling 262,144 pieces of information. This chip sandwiched by money in The Balance Room was designed with only one circuit, intended to accomplish only a single purpose in response to a remotely transmitted impulse.

There it was now, the impulse.

The microscopically arranged wires of the circuit reacted, sent an electronic charge to the point where all the wires converged. The body of the chip itself was impregnated with sulfur, making it very flammable. The charge ignited the chip, exploded it into a blue flame.

Seven identical incendiary devices elsewhere among the money were also set off. At once the small but intense flames found the gasoline fumes that still permeated the money. Fire ran from shelf to shelf, around the room.

The outside air flowing in through the ventilating system acted like a bellows. The heat sensor alarm could not alert anyone because it was turned off.

Hundred dollar bills, layer after layer of sheaf after sheaf of them caught and curled into pieces of black paper ashes.

The steel alloy panels inside the walls and floor of The Balance Room prevented the fire from spreading. They also kept it from being discovered ten or fifteen minutes earlier. The Balance Room was like a covered incinerator receptacle until the flames ate around the roof of the north wing.

A security man on his regular rounds looked up to the roof and saw the smoke, the unmistakable licks and colors of the flames. He ran into the main house shouting fire.

When Hine heard it he rushed from the study, left Gainer there.

Gainer's instinctive reaction was to hurry out, but by the time he'd reached the door he realized there was no close danger. He didn't care if the place burned down to its wine cellars. He went at a leisurely pace down the hall to the little library. To Leslie.

Apparently she also couldn't have been less concerned. She was sort of straddling the end of a fat arm of a black leather Chesterfield sofa. She had been fussing with her hair, with the couple of wisps that lay like gathers of fine letter Cs above her right eye.

"You started it," she said.

"I thought you might have."

"Maybe lightning struck the place."

"No. It's nice out tonight, not a cloud."

"A bolt still could have struck."

They went out the french doors to the terrace and around, in the dark, to the front of the house. They found Horridge's wicker furniture beneath the big copper beech. The crystal decanter of port and some used glasses were on the table, as was an ivory and appliqued silk fan Horridge had been using to shoo insects. A good spot for Gainer and Leslie. From there they would have a splendid view and yet be removed from the scurry of emergency activity.

It was evident to them now, of course, what part of the house had caught fire. The flames were reaching high above the roof, appeared to be slapping against the night sky.

Gainer poured two ports, didn't mind that he swallowed a couple of dead-drunk gnats with his first gulp.

As for Leslie, someone would have thought her a pyromaniac the energetic way she was using Horridge's fan to encourage the blaze.

The roof fell in, causing a fusillade of sparks to fly up, rather festively. The air all around was filled with the charred fragments of money that would disintegrate at the slightest touch.

All the fire trucks of the Town of Harrison growled up the drive. Their huge tires sank in and slashed across the lawns, crushed the tended hedges and bordering flowerbeds to get at the north wing. The firemen braced with their hoses, arched in tons of water. They extinguished the glow. They made The Balance Room hiss.

But they were three billion, one hundred five million dollars too late.

CHAPTER
TWENTY-SIX

HINE was frightened to his marrow about how Boston would view it.

All he could do was bide time there at Number 19, await word or some indication. He'd gotten nothing one way or the other from Horridge, although Horridge had not *seemed* upset by the fire or the loss. "How distressing," was the extent of Horridge's reaction. Horridge had flown out at dawn, while The Balance Room was still smoldering. Bound for Boston to present the facts and exonerate him, Hine hoped. After all, he had been recommended by Horridge. And he had been Custodian only a few hours when the catastrophe occurred, could hardly be held accountable.

Boston would see that side of it, he thought but didn't really believe.

For nearly a week there had been no flow.

No money brought, none to be carried.

And it was not a good sign that Hunsicker had not shown up to hear his order to eliminate Gainer. Hunsicker hadn't even bothered to phone with an excuse. If anyone knew the temperature of the undercurrents on the inside, it was Hunsicker and his people.

Hine called his uncle-in-law, Phillip Whitcroft. Asked with a please for a meeting, stressed how important it was.

Phillip Whitcroft sounded most receptive. Certainly he would make time to see Hine, and Hine was not to worry meanwhile. Whatever the problem he would direct his efforts to solving it. Just come ahead.

The call loosened Hine.

Next morning he dressed in his best Boston conservative suit and had a large breakfast to hold him. Made off in his Porsche. Took the Merritt Parkway North.

As he passed exit 53N at Shelton he felt a slight discomfort.

As he came down the long grade and onto the Housatonic Bridge it hit him in the chest. Like a stomp of some giant beast, crushing all the breath from him and replacing it with pain. His arms from shoulder to tips of fingers, coursed with electrical sensations. Lost all their strength. His hands dropped from the steering wheel.

The Porsche, on its own, picked up speed. It drifted toward the metal divider of the bridge, scraped along that for quite a ways, then swerved abruptly. Crashed into the guard rail with such impact most of its front end was shoved back into the driver's seat.

The accident did not kill Hine.

He died of natural causes . . .

. . . from breakfast.

CHAPTER
TWENTY-SEVEN

G AINER was in Zurich.

Tending to loose ends.

Alma, for one. Gainer had lunch with her at the Dolder Grand Hotel, where he was staying. She was still employed there, still keeping books.

Alma was not drawn with grief as she had been the last time she and Gainer had met. Nor did she have to smoke to keep her angry hands occupied. Evident to Gainer now were some of the qualities in Alma that must have attracted Norma. The emotional honesty of her, her neat, pretty, comforting way.

They had a long lunch.

At the start Gainer gave Alma a framed, enlarged copy of the snapshot he had found in Norma's wallet, the one he particularly liked of them. Alma was delighted and grateful. Her eyes went watery when she looked at the photograph, and when Gainer told her he had had a duplicate enlargement made and framed for himself and that he enjoyed seeing it every day, Alma extended her hand to his.

Gainer also gave her the love letters. All tied with sweet ribbon. Alma was especially grateful for these. She put them in her lap beneath her napkin. After a short while, on second thought, she brought the letters up and held them out to Gainer. She offered him any one he might want. He declined but she insisted, and he pulled one at random from the others. Slipped it into his inside pocket.

Time passed quickly because they wanted to know so much about one another. They exchanged answer for answer until Gainer glanced at his watch. He had to get to a bank before it closed.

Alma kissed him on the cheek, called him Drew.

Gainer watched her go, still carrying her love with her.

THE bank he needed to get to was one where Norma had kept her numbered and coded account.

PRIVATE BANK WALDHAUSER
BAHNHOFSTRASSE 12–24

Gainer believed most of what Norma had earned from carrying would be there. Her deal had been one and a half percent commission. From what Gainer knew, her carries had averaged three million and she made about six carries each year.

Which came to two hundred seventy thousand a year for her.

More than two and a half million over ten years.

Up that to three million when the amount she had skimmed was included.

He was going to have it transferred to a bank in the Caymans. Had it all arranged on the Caymans end. Gainer had thought at first he would invest that money in something sure and reasonably high-interest bearing. It could bring three to four hundred thousand a year tax free and he could still keep the three million intact. However, now his plans for that money had changed.

He would spend it.

On Leslie and himself. On them.

As fast as their impetuosity and tastes required.

No prices asked. Not ever.

Maybe they'd run through the three million in a year, or maybe, especially with Leslie's help and considering how far money didn't go these days, it would be gone in just six months. Didn't matter. For once Gainer was going to enjoy that limitless feeling. The Rodger feeling, as he thought of it. And when the three million dwindled he wasn't going to regret a dollar, just take it all the way down to zero and be better off for the experience.

In other words, fuck Benjamin Franklin and his frugality.

Private bank Waldhauser.

It looked like a diehard town house being squeezed by larger commerce on either side. Only four stories and no brass nameplate on its exterior, just its address numbers in a discreet size and conscientiously polished.

Gainer went to a reception area. Black and white marble floor arranged in a diamond pattern. A graceful ascending stairway with an intricate wood bannister, and a runner of leaf green disciplined by brass carpet rods. Nobody here, nor any sounds of banking. Gainer was about to go outside and check the address when a man came down the stairs. His black suit was the sort of wool that would outlast him, and his tie was supposed to, and did, look expensive. He was in his early forties, appeared older because he was so dour.

He introduced himself as Herr Bremlich, an account manager.

Gainer thought it would be wrong if he said his name. He had come prepared, handed Herr Bremlich a card with account number SF-1259, code word *Necco* printed on it and said, "I want to make a transfer."

Herr Bremlich went upstairs for ten minutes. When he returned he handed the card back to Gainer. "We have no such account," he said.

Gainer was positive he had printed the correct number, and certainly he couldn't be wrong about the code word *Necco*. He told Herr Bremlich, "You'd better go check again."

Up and down again for the account manager. "There is no account with either that number or code at this bank," he informed Gainer.

"This *is* the Private bank Waldhauser, isn't it?"

"Yes."

"Was there ever an account here with this number?"

"I cannot say. Most likely not."

Gainer read the lie in the man's eyes. Other than wrecking Herr Bremlich and this nice neat place—what could he do? He made fists in his pockets and walked out.

The bastards. The cheap, greedy bastards. Darrow or Hine or whoever had gotten to Norma's money. No wonder they didn't mind for such a long time that she was skimming.

Gainer used the Rathaus Bridge to cross over the River Limmat and set out for the hotel. The forty-some block walk of long strides did not help dispel the cloud around his head much as his street sense did. People who had the reach to confiscate three million as cleanly as that had the power to do damn near anything. They were no longer in his life, and the sooner he got them out of his mind the better. And safer. Forget them and the three million. Besides, the three was a paltry sum compared to what his old buddy Chapin had done him out of.

Chapin.

There was more to him than the double-cross, Gainer had decided. He wished he had Chapin's farewell tape to play over. He remembered the essence of it but would have liked to listen to it carefully, evaluate the inflections. "... *all that money would have made you dead,*" Chapin had said, and been right. "*I've really thought this one out . . . now all it has to do is come off the way I see it.*" Those Chapin words were not as cryptic to Gainer now—not since the return of the money in the gasoline tanker and the well-timed three billion dollar fire that had doomed Hine and saved him. Gainer wasn't sure that was how it had gone but it was how it felt to him, and the way he wanted to think.

When he got to his room at the Dolder he had the urge to phone Leslie. She had not wanted to come along on this trip, had some things to tidy up she had said. Gainer decided no, he wouldn't call her. Instead, he'd get back to her as soon as possible. Next flight was out at nine.

It was now five.

He booked an economy class seat and started packing so as to have that done. Scattered on the floor around a chair were some of Norma's papers. He had brought those along in a manila envelope, all documents of hers that had anything to do with Switzerland. Just in case. That morning he had gone through them again and found nothing that looked important.

He kneeled, started gathering the papers, shoving them back into the envelope. His eye caught on something that he must have passed over before. It appeared so insignificant. Merely a slip of paper, but with the Dolder Grand insignia on it. (The insignia had been covered up by another piece of paper the last time he'd looked.) Along with a scribbled number and initials and date. Gainer only vaguely recalled having taken it from Norma's wallet. He recalled more clearly now that he, himself, had had in hand another similar slip the last time he was in Zurich.

He hurried down to the lobby, asked for the porter.

The porter came with his chrome ring of keys. He led the way to a far end of the lobby, used one of the keys to open the door of the room there.

Gainer presented the slip.

The porter examined it.

Probably come up empty again, Gainer thought.

The porter went deep into the room, returned with a Mark Cross bag, a thirty-incher.

Gainer recognized it, its red and white leather name tag.

Norma's last carry.

She had checked it into the porter's luggage room when she arrived

too late for the bank that day. She had thought it would be safer there
—and it had been.

Now Gainer had the bag by its handle.

Three million in cash on the end of his arm.

Now he would call Leslie.

CHAPTER
TWENTY-EIGHT

THERE was nothing worse for the nervous system than being jarred awake, Leslie believed.

Usually, on a day when she had to be somewhere, her miniature bedside clock struck gold for her—a single resonant *ding* that not only said good morning in a nice and rather apologetic way but also told her there was still time to lie there a while and gradually emerge, give her eyes a chance to become accustomed to being open again. And to stretch. Especially stretch, like a sensible animal.

However, this morning when her clock went off she was already awake and its *ding* seemed only to rub in the fact.

No doubt about it.

Today, of all days, she had the *monies.*

Perhaps, she thought, they were only psychological resistance to what she had in mind to do. Once she was up and around they might subside—although they never had before that she could recall.

She was too buzzed up for breakfast, left the *Times* folded up, hurried through her shower and took twice as long as usual for her make-up. Last night, last thing, she had assured herself that tomorrow would not be crucial, that she would scoot right through it. What between then and now had caused such a turn on her? All she'd done was sleep.

In her dressing room she chose and hung out what she would wear —a black Armani suit that she adored but had never worn, had been sort of *saving.* Its shorter jacket had one black bone button at its collarless high neck. Underneath it and for just enough of a contribution to the neckline and cuffs, she wore a plain white silk St. Laurent blouse. Also her best low-heeled shoes, a pair of black antelope with a touch of fancy stitching in the same black; the only pair like it in New York, she had been told by both Susan Dennis and Warren Edwards.

She dressed and appraised herself in one of the full-length mirrors and thought she looked terribly serious, as though she were about to make an appearance in court somewhere or at someone's new graveside.

She took that outfit off. She opened another section of her dressing room wall, where some of her more casual things were organized. Quickly, barely making a decision, she brought out a flecky, oatmeal-colored light wool dress by Perry Ellis. Two years old, worn twice. It had always struck her as having a lot of independence to it. More her mood, Leslie decided, certainly more suitable. She put it on and a pair of tassled brown snakeskin loafers. Loaded up a brown Fendi shoulder bag and then again asked the mirror.

She was not going to stay there dressing and undressing until the last minute, she told herself.

She went out.

She considered being driven but it would take at least ten minutes for the driver to get into his jacket and cap and bring the car around. She went to the corner of Seventy-fifth and Madison, glanced once for a taxi before starting downtown on the west side of the avenue.

At Sixty-fourth Street she crossed over to see what Fred Leighton thought enough of to put on display. Just curious, she told herself, but needed grit not to go in.

Her trouble, she thought as she continued on, was that she appreciated extravagance. She had never, however, wanted anything out of greed, although she had known quite a few people who were like that. Greed was so ugly. You could read it in people's hands as well as their faces, and it was the most obvious whenever they were buying anything —the way they sort of gobbled things up. She hoped she bought with at least a touch of grace, a kind of near-reverence for the moment, even when she knew she was being impulsive. Perhaps especially then.

Doors were opened for her at the Morgan Guaranty Trust and "Good mornings" were accómpanied by her married name.

She went downstairs to the safe deposit boxes, signed in and produced her key. Hers was not the largest sort of box but the second largest. Within minutes she was alone with it in one of the private rooms. She made herself comfortable. It was going to take a while.

She removed everything from the deposit box, including all the square and shallow and oblong little boxes of Winston and Bulgari, Cartier and others. Placed them to one side. Had a pen and pad ready. Systematically she opened the little boxes and noted down their contents: a fourteen carat emerald ring, a diamond bangle of thirty-seven carats, a cushion-shaped twelve carat ruby ring surrounded by tapered baguettes, a *soirée*-length strand of twelve millimeter natural pearls, a pair of unmounted pear-shaped diamonds weighing eight carats each, a strand of forty-three imperial jade beads graduating from eleven millimeters to eight millimeters with diamond rondels, a ten carat canary diamond penant, a six carat pink diamond solitaire, a diamond necklace of one hundred and forty-six carats, including twenty-seven pear-shaped diamonds of two carats each.

And so it went.

Clasp after ring, bracelet after pendant.

Some she had bought herself at various times in Paris shops. Or had outbid the competition at Parke-Bernet and Christie's. Or even bought from women acquaintances who said they were selling a certain ring or whatever because they had become bored with it. That's what they said, and Leslie never dreamed of questioning them. Others, the more important pieces such as the one hundred and forty-six carat necklace, were gifts from Rodger over the years, accumulations from birthdays, Christmases and anniversaries. It was not unusual, even lacking an occasion, for her to arrive home and find on her hall console a Winston box containing a treat. No card ever. The sentiment went without saying. Even since she had been only with Gainer, that had happened numerous times.

She listed everything and made extra notations when they were pertinent. For example, the twelve carat ruby ring as well as several other items were Jean Schlumberger; this was from Winston, and that from Bulgari. She tried to approximate the years when they had been acquired. Most important was how much were they now worth? Diamonds were not priced as high as they had been two years ago; down as much as twenty-five percent, she'd been told. Would she be better off if she dumped the entire lot in someone's hands, someone like Winston perhaps, or might it be to her advantage to spread them around, a few at Cartier's, a few at Van Cleef's and so on? There was also the option of putting everything up for auction at Parke-Bernet and/or Christie's, though she didn't believe the commissions they charged were fair when off the top there would also be taxes.

Her fast, optimistic total came to somewhere between seven and eight million.

Enough if she sort of skimped.

426

That didn't exactly mean thrift shops and cheaper butchers, but she had to consider that one of her sables and her Corniche together cost nearly a third of a million dollars. And those were only things to wear around and get around in.

Your values are out of shape, part of her said.

She's sensible, part of her said.

Hell, who knew where the dollar was going the way it was going? It would be awful to be beyond middle age and dowdy because a truckful of dollars were required to buy one or two nice things. It already seemed there was hardly anything that didn't cost five hundred dollars. Her bikini panties were fifty dollars a pair at Montenapoleone.

Leslie abruptly shut the lid on her glittering cache, disillusioned with it, relegating it to its enemy darkness. She and one of the vault attendants locked the safe deposit box into place, and moments later she was outside. She stood there on Madison in the October sun, undecided about whether or not she should have lunch and give the whole thing some more thought.

There was a phone booth on the corner. She would call Gainer in Zurich, use Rodger's satellite line. Hearing Gainer might help clarify things one way or the other.

No.

This was her own battle.

The damn *monies*.

She was a victim of advantageous circumstances.

Otherwise there'd be none of this ambivalence. She'd just do what she felt she really wanted and there was no doubt what that was.

Think about down the road, some of her said.

Yeah, garden clubs and charities, some of her said. All the way to having her make-up overdone by Frank E. Campbell.

She remembered something said once by someone she didn't remember. An axiom that seemed to apply now: *One never does anything one doesn't want to do.* That was true, Leslie thought. Also consequences determined everything.

Well?

What she ought to do was take a taxi to La Grenouille, sit in the front room, order Scotch salmon and eat it slowly, little pieces. Have fresh raspberries for dessert with *crème fraise*. Afterward, maybe she would go to the woman on Sixty-ninth she'd heard about, the one who gave spiritual alignments. Three hour vigorous massages accompanied by penetratingly loud quadrophonic music that unknotted the kinks left over from past lives.

Leslie started for the curb to wave down a taxi. After only three steps

427

she turned around and went into the General Motors Building.

Her legs were not minding her, it seemed.

Next thing she knew she was in an elevator to the forty-sixth floor, one of the floors of Bidwell, Reese, Minton and Dernby.

I love you, Leslie, she told herself as she told the receptionist her married name and that she wanted to see Mr. Bidwell.

"May I ask which Mr. Bidwell?"

"The old one."

"Is he expecting you?"

"God, no." Bidwell, never in the short time that was left of his life, expected her to come there to sign the divorce papers. Those perpetually maintained divorce papers that were part of her deal with Rodger. Bidwell, like everyone else, believed she would stay on that sweet ride. No doubt he'd clear his throat a half dozen times and ask was she *sure* she wasn't being rash?

No matter, there was no stopping her now.

A secretary came to accompany her down a walnut-paneled hallway, punctuated, of course, with hunting scenes, to Bidwell's corner office.

He was instantly up with his hand out and offering her a chair. He looked forlorn, but then, that was his normal expression.

Leslie was about to blurt out her reason for being there when Bidwell started clearing his throat. "Terrible about Rodger," he said, "terrible."

Don't say anything, Leslie was told by the voice in her that she attributed to Lady Caroline.

"We were just this moment trying to reach you," Bidwell said. He plopped down in his leather chair. "You don't have to concern yourself with anything. We've already seen to the difficult arrangements."

Say thank you. "Thank you."

"Rodger, Rodger, Rodger," Bidwell said with a tinge of reprimand, and then to Leslie. "You don't want a large funeral, do you?"

Say no. "No."

"Good. Better all around. He was killed instantly when a huge earthmover toppled over on him while he was inspecting that project of his in Táchira."

"Where's Táchira?"

"Venezuela."

Leslie felt as though she also had to clear her throat. A lump was in it, deep sorrow gathering. There was too much feeling and water in her head, and the water was coming from her eyes. In her own way she really had loved him.

"That's the story the *Times* and everyone else will get," Bidwell went on. "The truth is, Rodger was killed by a sailor in Caracas. We don't

428

know the identity of the sailor nor will there be much of an effort to find out. You understand."

At least Rodger went out swinging, Leslie thought.

"For the past forty-five minutes or so I've been going over Rodger's estate, but I doubt you feel like getting into that now?"

Leslie tried to swallow the lump. "Go ahead," she said.

"I'm named executor, of course," Bidwell said, "so there won't be any surprises. I've always made it my business to know Rodger's financial picture."

Leslie's gaze fixed on the tower of the Sherry Netherland hotel across the way, pigeons perched on it like they owned it. "What is it?" she asked.

"What?"

"Rodger's financial picture."

"Assets and holdings come to . . ." he opened a portfolio on his desk, flipped past a couple of pages ". . . five and a half billion dollars."

"That much?"

"Not all his, of course. There are a number of limited partners and individual shareholders, considerable corporate intricacies, both here and overseas. I should think the last thing you'd want was to get involved with that mishmash."

Smile, Leslie. A faint, grateful smile.

"Your concern should be with his personal estate," Bidwell told her. "Naturally, we have always tried to keep that as minimal as possible."

"Naturally."

"Let's see . . ." Bidwell did some figuring on the back of one of the pages in the portfolio.

"A few million?" Leslie said.

Lady Caroline told her to keep still.

Bidwell glanced up at Leslie, thought this woman wasn't going to be a problem, not at all. He could assure Boston of that. "After all the necessary reductions," he told her, "what you should end up with—and mind you, this is only a rough figure—is about four hundred million."

Rich me.

She stood a bit wobbly. "I don't have my car," she said.

"I'll have my driver take you. Will you be home if I need to reach you?"

"I don't know."

"But you will be in New York."

"Yes."

She arrived home at twenty to three. She immediately tried to phone Gainer, and while she had the Dolder Grand on one line a call from him came in on her other line. He was at a pay phone at Flughafen Floten about to board a flight to Paris, where he'd connect with a Concorde flight home. He'd be landing at Kennedy around eight o'clock. He had a great surprise for her.

She didn't press him to tell her what the surprise was but he couldn't keep it to himself.

The three million he was bringing home.

To her.

He was so enthusiastic about it, so happy. He told her his prodigal attitude toward it and some of the extravagant things they would do. She hardly had a chance to get a word in, and then he would miss his flight unless all they said was I-love-you.

LESLIE was at Kennedy at a quarter to eight, had the driver take her in one of the Rolls. She waited in the International Arrivals building and right up to the moment when she saw Gainer coming through— him with a here-I-am, isn't-it-great-to-to-see-me spirit to his step, she hadn't yet decided how she was going to break it to him about the four hundred million. That news was right there in her mouth practically crying to be said.

But she didn't want it to dampen his enthusiasm, diminish his high. She didn't want it to make him feel inadequate, not ever. Didn't want it to make him feel, well, self-conscious that he hadn't earned their money or stolen or inherited it. Didn't want it to make him have the slightest qualm whenever she was being extravagant with him in Rome or somewhere. Or when they were at Tiffany's or having their fifteen room Trump Tower apartment done over or when he had it in his heart to buy a new Rolls Corniche for her. Should she keep her mouth shut? She didn't want all that money to come between them and their happiness for a second.

It didn't.

EPILOGUE

I n November of that year the oldest, most established realtor in Greenwich pulled one off. The largest residential transaction in a decade.

He sold the Rakestraw estate on Round Hill Road.

Forty-seven acres with a thirty-six room main house. A ten foot spike-topped wall around it all.

The man who bought the Rakestraw place was R. Hamilton Ward. Like Edwin Darrow had when he bought 19 Purchase Street, Ward paid cash, rumored to be in the neighborhood of twelve million. Ward was a graduate of Princeton Law and qualified to practice in New York, Connecticut and Massachusetts. Retired now, however. Originally, he was from Maryland, a shore family.

The Rakestraw estate had not been occupied for several years. It would take a great deal of renovating to get it to where it suited its new owner's tastes and purpose. And even then, it would require a lot of upkeep. Coming and going.

Gordon Winship is still alive.